Aunt Edie was on the doorstep. As usual, she looked a treat. For a start she had an hour-glass figure like an Edwardian woman. And she favoured large hats, like the one she had on now, with wax flowers decorating it. Her peach-coloured dress showed her calves. Jimmy had the idea she found the shorter fashion a bit of a lark – well, being a pearly queen she would do, especially when she did a cockney knees-up at the charity concerts put on by the Camberwell pearlies, which meant showing her legs.

From the door step she smiled at Jimmy, a chip off the old block with his grey eyes and a bit of his dad's twinkle.

'Well, young man?' she said.

'You're a nice surprise, Aunt Edie,' said Jimmy. 'Come in.' She stepped in and he ducked under the brim of her hat and kissed her.

'I'm going to do what I shouldn't,' said Aunt Edie. 'I'm going to interfere.'

Jimmy sighed with relief. At last things were going to improve in the Andrews household.

THE PEARLY QUEEN

Mary Jane Staples

CORGI BOOKS

PEARLY QUEEN
A CORGI BOOK 0 552 13856 8

First publication in Great Britain

PRINTING HISTORY
Corgi edition published 1992

This book is set in 10/11 Plantin by
County Typesetters, Margate, Kent

Corgi Books are published by Transworld Publishers Ltd,
61–63 Uxbridge Road, Ealing, London W5 5SA, in Australia
by Transworld Publishers (Australia) Pty. Ltd, 15–23 Helles
Avenue, Moorebank, NSW 2170, and in New Zealand by
Transworld Publishers (N.Z.) Ltd, Cnr. Moselle and
Waipareira Avenues, Henderson, Auckland.

Printed and bound by CPI Cox & Wyman, Reading

To Joanna and Niall

CHAPTER ONE

When Dad Andrews came home from his work on Friday, the eve of the August bank holiday, he knew something was up. His son and two daughters were waiting in the kitchen for him and couldn't find a single smile. Nine-year-old Betsy, usually ready for a kiss and a tickle, looked unhappy. Thirteen-year-old Patsy, who could always give a good account of herself, looked upset. And sixteen-year-old Jimmy, who could be comical while looking as serious as an owl, seemed as if he'd lost a quid and not found even a farthing as consolation.

'What's up?' asked Dad. 'Where's your mum?'

'She's gone and joined something called the League of Repenters,' said Patsy, coming straight out with it.

'What?' asked Dad, a lanky and sinewy man of thirty-nine.

''Fraid so, Dad,' said Jimmy, who had recently lost his job as an apprentice with a builder. The firm had closed down for lack of orders, and Jimmy was finding a new job hard to come by. 1923 hadn't been a good year for new jobs. Nor had any year since the war. Jimmy was gritting his teeth about his prospects. 'She said she's got to do the Lord's work now.'

'That's a fact, is it,' said Dad, upset for his kids. His own feelings were of a kind to keep to himself. He was fed up with his wife Maud and her religious crankiness. Religion was all right, it was good for most people as long as it only meant paying your respects to the Lord in church and doing right by your neighbours. But if you kept bringing it home with you, week after week, year after year, like Maud did, it was bound to make a man fed up, and his kids as well. However, Dad had no intention of making it worse for them by rampaging about and swearing his head off. He could go after Maud, he supposed, and drag her back home. No, let her stew. His job at the moment was to cheer his kids up. So he said in a good-humoured way, 'I knew she'd get religion for keeps one day. Well, don't you worry, we'll manage.'

'She went and poured your beer down the sink,' said young Betsy dolefully.

'The whole bottle?' asked Dad.

'All of it,' said Patsy. 'Jimmy could've stopped 'er, only he was out lookin' for a job most of the mornin'.'

'That's done it,' said Dad with a wry kind of smile.

Jimmy grimaced. A glass of Watney's brown ale now and again was Dad's one treat, and there was usually a bottle standing on the stone floor of the larder.

'She said drink's sinful,' said Betsy, mouth drooping.

'No Watney's left, then?' said Dad. 'I suppose there's no supper, either.'

'Oh, us is doin' it together,' said Betsy. 'I done the greens, Patsy done the potatoes, an' Jimmy's doin' the chops. You best look at them now, Jimmy.'

'They're all right for a bit,' said Jimmy. He felt sorry for Dad, who was only thirty-nine. He'd married their mum in 1906, when he was twenty-two and she was nineteen. Jimmy felt thirty-nine was young for a man to find his trouble-and-strife had turned religious for good. He and his sisters thought him a good old dad, and he'd done his bit in the war against Kaiser Bill.

Dad's name was Jack William Andrews, he'd been born

in Camberwell and had set up home with his wife, Maud Ellen, in a terraced house in Manor Place, Walworth, close to the public baths. The rent was only ten bob a week, and there were three bedrooms upstairs, and a parlour, bedroom, kitchen and scullery downstairs. Dad managed the rent comfortably out of his wages as a delivery van driver for a firm of grocery wholesalers operating on the south side of London Bridge. The van was drawn by two horses, which he called Patty and Cake.

'Fancy calling them that,' said Mum Andrews. Dad said it was from an old nursery rhyme. 'But calling a horse Cake,' said Mum, 'when it's one of Joshua's proud creatures.'

'Who's Joshua?'

'He was anointed of God,' said Mum, 'and threw down the walls of Jericho.'

'Must have been before my time,' said Dad.

Jimmy, their first child, had escaped being called Joshua only because Dad put his foot down. 'Well, Elijah, then,' said Mum, devoted to the Old Testament and its prophets and heroes. Dad nearly had a fit. He wanted their first born to be called Alfred, after his own dad, Alfred Edward. Mum suggested Isaiah Luke. Dad said he'd shoot himself. Mum didn't want that to happen. Committing suicide was a mortal sin. All right, but not Alfred, she said. Edward Alfred, said Dad. James Alfred, said Mum. Mum won.

Aunt Edie, her cousin, told Dad that no Walworth boy should have to go through life being called James. She was going to call him Jimmy, she said, which she did, right from the start, and so did everyone else in the end, including Mum.

Dad being a Territorial soldier, he was called up immediately war broke out in 1914. It put Mum in a bit of a paddy, and she went about saying it was criminal and ungodly for a man to go off to war when he was a husband and father, and Betsy only a baby at the time. But on the day he departed to do his bit, she gave him a large square biscuit tin with a big round fruit cake in it. It was a sign she'd prayed to the Lord to forgive him, and that the Lord had answered and said, yes, all right and bake him a cake.

She'd started getting irritatingly religious well before the war, and it was at the beginning of 1914 when she took to praying. She said the Lord nearly always answered her when she prayed hard enough. She prayed once for something to be done about Mr Maggs, a neighbour who was always accosting women's bosoms whenever he'd had one over the eight. The very next day, when he was lurching up to Mrs Shaw's bosom in the Walworth Road, he fell over and broke his leg. On top of that, the day the plaster was removed, Mrs Maggs reminded him about his accosting ways by hitting him over the head with an egg saucepan. Mum Andrews said it was the Lord's hand at work. Jimmy, eight at the time, asked if she meant the Lord's egg saucepan. Mum Andrews said, 'I'll give you something, my lad, if you take the Lord's name in vain like that.'

'I was only asking,' said Jimmy. Only asking was a standard riposte from most Walworth kids.

When Mum Andrews gave Dad Andrews the cake to go off to the war with, she told him to make sure he went on all Army church parades, then the Lord would take care of him. Dad said he'd like it if the Lord would just take care of the cake tin, as he already had his rifle and kitbag to carry. Mum told him not to talk unholy. He managed to cart the tin off with him. But how he managed to go all through the war, mostly out in Mesopotamia against the Turks, was a bit of a miracle. Four times he was wounded, and in 1917 the Army sent him back to Blighty in a hospital ship to recuperate from shrapnel wounds in his chest. It had been touch and go for him in the Army hospital out there in the heat of Mesopotamia, but he was tough and gutsy, and wasn't going to give in to any Turkish shrapnel. Mum took the children to visit him in a hospital in Middlesex, where he was making a recovery and tried to read bits from the Old Testament to him, the fire and brimstone bits. Dad nearly had her chucked out.

Aunt Edie also went to see him, taking ten-year-old Jimmy with her. She was a single woman, the same age as Mum Andrews, but much livelier and much more fun. She was also a pearly queen. Her mum and dad had been pearlies, and she followed in their footsteps. Pearly kings and queens were plentiful all over cockney South London. It was an easy-going fellowship devoted to upholding family togetherness, to bringing good cheer to life, and to giving kids a good time. Extrovert Aunt Edie was a natural bringer of good cheer and accordingly a natural pearly queen. She had suffered one sad happening, however. When she was twenty, her fiancé was drowned following a boating accident on the Thames. Dad was a caring and stalwart friend to her during the subsequent months, helping her to get over the tragedy, and Aunt Edie never forgot just what his friendship and help had meant to her.

So, of course, when she went to see him in hospital, she bucked him up in a brisk and scolding way that hid her emotions. She told him that after three whole years of getting himself wounded, she hoped he wasn't going to be silly enough to get his head knocked off when he went back to the war. That could be fatal, she said, and would upset a lot of people. Dad answered her back, of course, and Aunt Edie gave him some more talking to, and Jimmy thought it all bucked his dad up no end, he had grins all over his face. Aunt Edie said she didn't know what he was grinning at, he could still do something daft.

'Have a cup of tea,' said Dad, 'I'll get the nurse to bring you one, and Jimmy as well.'

Aunt Edie said, 'Bless you, you silly old soldier, Jimmy and me could do with a nice cup.' Jimmy thought her eyes were a little bit misty. But when they left the hospital she looked a little bit angry.

'What's up, Aunt Edie?' he asked.

'It's just not right,' she said, 'your dad's a fine man, a fine soldier, and deserves better—' But she broke off and didn't say any more, not for a few minutes, anyway. Then she said, 'Don't worry, Jimmy, your dad'll pull through. Your dad's a man, Jimmy.'

Dad did pull through, his toughness saw to that. Mum Andrews said the Lord had done it, the Lord knew Dad had repented. Patsy, seven at the time but already owning a tongue, asked what Dad had repented of. 'Of his sins,' said Mum.

Patsy, fond of her dad, asked, 'What sins?'

'We're all sinners,' said Mum, 'we're all weak creatures.'

'Not my dad,' said Patsy with spirit. 'My dad's a soldier.'

'Don't answer me back,' said Mum. 'Answering back's a sin.'

Dad was nearly as good as new when he came home for a fortnight's leave from a military convalescent home. He was given a rousing welcome by his children, and Mum Andrews proceeded to do her Christian duty by taking him out and about for walks and exercise. She cleared a path for him with her umbrella if people got in his way. Mum Andrews was rarely without her umbrella. Dad, fighting irritation, said, 'Turn it up, Maudie, I'm not a cripple.'

'Never mind that,' said Mum. 'The Lord didn't help you get better so that you could gallivant about and fall over people and injure yourself.' Having no sense of humour, she couldn't think why Jimmy grinned and the girls giggled. Jimmy said he'd heard gallivanting about was supposed to be good for soldiers on leave, it was what they came home on leave for, to do a bit of gallivanting about. Well, that was what he'd heard, he said.

'Well, I don't know who you've been listening to,' said Mum, and gave her son a tap with her brolly to let him know she expected him to be more careful about who he listened to in future. During these outings, she made her children walk behind whenever they were part of such excursions. She said it would be the work of Satan himself if Dad got injured by falling over his own flesh and blood.

She was very 'churchified' by then, she'd got religion on the brain. In one way, it had its funny side, but there was too much of it, it went on all the time. To avoid upsetting the kids, Dad spoke to Mum more than once in private, telling her to put a sock in it. It made no difference. She responded with some of her fire and brimstone stuff. By this time Dad, whose loyalties were pretty constant, was beginning to lose what affection he still had left for Mum. But he put up with her because she was the mother of his kids, and he thought the world of them. And he was not a man who'd make them unhappy by having stand-up slanging matches with their mother.

Towards the end of the war, when Dad was back in Mesopotamia, she became chronically religious. She took to carrying her umbrella as if it were the sword of Joshua. Woe betide any drunk who got in her way. She'd land the point of her brolly right in his overloaded paunch, and order him to go home and repent. When Dad was home for good and with his old job back, she managed to calm down a bit during the first year of peace, which allowed the reunited family to settle down to post-war life without having to listen to too many biblical quotations.

Then the call of the Lord hit her again in extreme fashion. By 1922, she was set on getting everyone to repent. Patsy asked what for? 'Be sure your sins will find you out,' said Mum. That always foxed Patsy, and Betsy too: they couldn't think that sins had anything to do with them. True, they had occasionally nicked apples down the market, but only specked ones, and only from under a stall. Jimmy had pinched lots when he was younger. All Walworth kids did.

Patsy asked if Jimmy was a sinner. Mum said her son must ask his conscience. Jimmy spent half a minute asking it, then said he didn't think he was a sinner yet, but he might soon be because he was tempted to run off to Gretna Green with Susie Brown down in Brandon Street, whom he saw nearly every Sunday in church. 'But she's seventeen and goes to work,' said Patsy, 'and you're only fifteen and only an apprentice.'

'I know that,' said Jimmy, 'but I still feel sinful about her.'

Mum nearly collapsed with the shame of his confession, delivered with a straight face, and by the time she'd recovered, Jimmy was well out of the range of her punitive umbrella. Still, she was able to berate Patsy and Betsy for giggling.

She was thinner than she used to be. Her wedding photograph showed her with a prettily plump figure. Her roundness had gone, although some of her attractiveness remained. But she was prim. She let Dad know that marriage was for having children, and that as they had children, desire was now a sin. Dad's natural good humour, which had been taking a beating for too long, deserted him at this point. 'Don't make me laugh,' he said. 'In fact,' he said, 'it's me duty to inform you, Maudie, that you're about as exciting as a wet weekend under Southend Pier.' Well, she never had been much good in bed, except at the beginning. It was no hardship for him to give up what she called sinning.

She took umbrage at his remarks, but made no attempt to get her figure back. She didn't believe in vanity or in women being plump. She said plumpness was a sign of gluttony in most cases, and that the Lord frowned on it.

'What about plump men?' asked Jimmy in the spring of 1923.

'Disgustin',' she said. 'I 'specially don't like gluttony in men and no repentin' of it. You're not gettin' plump, are you?'

'Not yet,' said Jimmy, who was lean like his dad.

'I don't want to have to put you on bread and water,' said Mum.

'Couldn't it be toast and marmalade?' asked Jimmy.

'Don't give me no cheek now, and don't let me see you growin' up fat,' said Mum. 'I won't 'ave no gluttony in this fam'ly.'

However much Jimmy tried not to take her seriously, the fact was plain to him and Dad and Patsy: Mum was a sore trial to her family. Her talk about gluttony was barmy. Jimmy knew there wasn't much of it among the London cockneys. Gluttony was the last thing they could afford. Not that he and his family suffered an empty larder. In the spring of 1923, he and his dad were both working, although his wage was only that of a builder's apprentice. Still, the family could afford decent food and for Mum to do regular baking, except that lately she'd done very little. She had decided things like treacle tarts, fruit cakes and fruit pies encouraged sinful eating. On top of that, she was making Patsy do some cooking. Patsy actually didn't mind, and when Dad bribed her by giving her a shining new sixpence she promised to learn how to bake cakes and tarts.

In July, Mum gave very serious thought to doing far more work for the Lord and a lot less for her family. Dad, in private, told her she was doing a lot less, anyway.

'Don't you talk to me like that, Jack Andrews,' she said.

'Listen, my girl,' said Dad, 'you go off too often on account of the Lord, and you might come home one day and find the family's shut the door on you.' In response to that, Mum told him to remember Joshua, and how he took up the sword and slew the enemies of Israel.

'Maud, you're bleeding barmy,' said Dad. It was water off a duck's back.

Mum thought about joining the Salvation Army or an organization called Sanctuary for the Fallen. It didn't take her long to decide the Salvation Army was actually a bit heathen: all that shaking and rattling of tambourines by women in queer bonnets with red ribbons didn't seem very reverent to her. And all their smiling, too, as if they didn't take the Lord seriously. As for the Sanctuary for the Fallen, she discovered it was near to disgraceful. What it did was to take in drunks and sinful women, and not do anything about making them repent. When they came out of the Sanctuary, the drunks made straight for the nearest pub and the sinful women went and did more sinning. Mum declared to her husband and son that she didn't think the Lord would approve of any sanctuary that didn't make people see the error of their ways.

Dad said, 'Well, Maudie, you've taken on ways I don't approve of myself.' Jimmy asked if the Lord had ever actually had a word with her about it.

'You're both impertinent,' said Mum, 'go an' repent.'

As this order was given after dinner one Sunday, Dad took his son and daughters to Ruskin Park, and they all repented together by walking the paths in silent and solemn fashion, although Betsy had to struggle to keep her giggles at bay. She gave up eventually, and her giggles burst forth.

'That sounds like someone's sinning,' said Jimmy.

'Yes, who is it?' asked Dad.

'Me,' confessed Betsy.

'Well, we'd better do some more repentin', then,' said Dad, 'we needn't get back till teatime.' It was his way of cheering his kids up, particularly Betsy who was unhappy about her mum. He made a game of the outing, and it hid the fact that he was swearing to himself most of the time.

It was the following week that Jimmy lost his job. His sisters were upset for him, and Dad knew it was a real blow to his son. Mum said it might not have happened if Jimmy had been more religious. But it didn't greatly concern her, not at this moment, for a new organization called the League of Repenters had come to her attention. She homed in on it like an eager bee catching a whiff of the first rich blooms of summer. She was immediately impressed by its leader, a man of majestic appearance and dignity, one Montgomery Wilberforce, known to his followers as Father Peter. In his wide-shouldered tallness, he looked to Mum as if he had been cast in the same mould as Joshua himself. To Mum, Joshua was a most awesome servant of the Lord.

She noted that Father Peter's followers, mostly women, were serious and devout, dressing with quiet soberness. They were dedicated to the task of bringing redemption and salvation to sinners before the Day of Judgement arrived. Some were like herself, some were from the suburbs and some sounded quite posh. She felt she could do very good work with the League. It might mean her family having to do a lot more for themselves, but no-one could say she hadn't already given them the best years of her life, and the Lord ought to have His turn at commanding her services. So she applied to join the Repenters and went daily to their headquarters in Bloomsbury for instruction from Father Peter on the principles of dedication. She believed, as he did, that the hope of the world was repentance, and she promised to commit herself to the task of helping to redeem sinners. Father Peter received her into the League and was most kind to her.

She told her son and daughters of her new life on the morning of the Friday before the August Bank Holiday, after their dad had departed for his work. Jimmy had no job at the moment, and his sisters were on school holiday, so they were left to tell Dad when he came home.

'Where's your mum now?' he asked.

'Whitechapel,' said Jimmy.

'Eh?' said Dad.

'Yes, rotten 'ard luck, Dad,' said Jimmy, 'but she dressed herself up in black—'

'The black she wore to Grandpa's funeral last year,' said Patsy.

'Wiv a new black 'at,' said Betsy, looking unhappy again.

'And off she went to Whitechapel after givin' us bread and cheese at midday,' said Jimmy.

Dad, for the sake of his kids, hid his more extreme reactions. An old soldier, he had a few choice words at his command. He used none of them. Jimmy popped into the scullery then to turn the mutton chops in the pan in the gas oven. He also took a look at the cabbage and potatoes in their saucepans. He came back into the kitchen and broke the suffering silence.

'She took a banner with her.'

'I don't suppose it'll do me much good to ask,' said Dad, 'but go on, let's 'ave it, what was on the banner?'

'REPENT YE SINNERS,' quoted Jimmy.

'I might've known,' said Dad. 'Is she comin' back?'

'She said she was,' replied Patsy, not bothering to hide exactly how she felt, cross and disgusted. 'She's been given a new Bible by this League, and she's goin' to read it to us this evenin'.'

'All of it?' said Dad. 'All of it at once?'

'She'd better not,' said Patsy.

'I don't fink Mum likes us any more,' said Betsy worriedly.

Dad, hating the thought of young Betsy being unhappy, made an effort and said brightly, 'Cheer up, Betsy me pickle, there's worse things at sea, as me old sergeant-major would say. Your mum can't help bein' fond of the Bible, but that don't mean she's not fond of you any more. And I'm not against the Bible meself, I'm just sayin' we don't want all of it at once, do we? Bless yer, Betsy, your mum's got her funny ways, and we'll just 'ave to go along with them.' He ruffled Betsy's hair. 'Mind you, with any luck, we won't get any Bible at all this evenin', not if she's been to Whitechapel. Whitechapel people don't go much of a bundle on preachers and the like, they chuck rotten cabbages at them.' Do Maud a power of good, that would, he thought. 'It wouldn't surprise me if your mum comes 'ome lookin' like she's been in a greengrocery war. She might need some sympathy and a mite of cheerin' up, she might even 'ave a bit of a headache.'

'So might we,' said Jimmy, 'she talked about puttin' all of us on bread and water for a while.'

Dad, having taken things manfully so far, greeted this

new piece of information in prickly fashion. 'There's not goin' to be none of that rubbish,' he said.

Jimmy mentioned that Mum had said they all ate too much. Betsy protested she hadn't ever eaten too much, that she just ate till she was full up. Patsy said that Mum had said that Joshua and the Israelites had to put up with a lot of bread and water.

'Well, we ain't Joshua and the Israelites,' said Dad, dark brown hair thick, with a widow's peak, and grey eyes that often showed a twinkle.

'Jimmy told 'er that,' said Patsy.

'And Mum landed 'im one wiv 'er brolly,' said Betsy.

'Hard luck, Jimmy,' said Dad. 'Anything else?'

'Yes,' said Jimmy, 'it's about callin' her Mum. She said Mum doesn't befit her any more, that she'd been anointed by a bloke called Father Peter and he'd named 'er Mother Mary.'

'I'm hearin' things,' said Dad. 'Still, wait till the cabbages start flyin'. All the same, when she gets 'ome, we'd better humour her, we'd better call 'er Mother and let 'er do a bit of Bible readin'. Best to humour her, and while she's like this we've got to rally round the old fam'ly flag, eh?'

'You could tell 'er she ought to repent for muckin' the fam'ly about, Dad,' said Patsy.

'Well, good on yer, Patsy,' said Dad, 'we can think about that, we'll work up to it gradual, same as me and the old battalion worked up to givin' Johnny Turk one in 'is mince pie.'

'Did he repent, Dad?' asked Patsy.

'Come again?' said Dad, wondering just how to go to work on his wife.

'When you give Johnny Turk one in the eye, did he repent?' asked Patsy.

'He didn't say so, Patsy. He said, "Oh, Ali Baba, me flamin' eye," and fell over. Well, I'll treat meself to a bit of a wash now after me day's labours, then we'll 'ave supper. You sure it's cookin' all right, or d'you want me to take a look at it?'

'Oh, the spuds!' gasped Patsy, and rushed into the scullery.

'And what about the chops, Jimmy?' asked Dad.

'I've got confidence in me chops,' said Jimmy.

'Well, good,' said Dad. 'We'll manage, Jimmy, don't you worry, and you'll get another job soon.'

'Dad, d'you fink our mum's gone a bit barmy?' asked Betsy worriedly.

'No, she's just got religion, Betsy love,' said Dad.

'Point is, can she be cured?' asked Jimmy.

'Well,' said Dad, 'she might be cured already, they might've chucked a whole barrow-load of cabbages at 'er in Whitechapel.'

'I don't fink that's very funny,' sighed Betsy.

They were at supper a little later, around the kitchen table, which was always covered by a green and white check oil cloth. It was very practical and only needed a wipe with a damp cloth to look clean and shiny. As in all cockney homes, the kitchen was the hub of family life. It was where setbacks, triumphs, giggles, laughs, arguments and mother's laying down of the law were all part of the way the character and spirit of the family were shaped and nurtured. There were signs, however, that Mum's priorities had changed. The kitchen range and the iron fender that guarded the hearth hadn't been blackleaded for ages. In the scullery, dirty washing had been piling up in a large tin bath on top of the copper.

Dad ignored all that for the moment. He knew his girls

were upset about their mum. Jimmy was old enough to take it in his stride. Dad commented on the supper, saying he'd never had greens more green, mashed potatoes more tasty and a mutton chop better done. Betsy asked if she was going to have to do the greens every day.

'Only till cauliflowers come in,' said Jimmy.

'Crikey,' said Betsy, 'I hate cauliflowers.'

'Well, you need only hate them till runner beans come in,' said Jimmy.

Betsy said, 'What, me slice runner beans every day?'

'Only till sprouts come in,' said Jimmy.

'Ugh, I hate sprouts worse than cauliflowers,' said Betsy.

'Oh, well, greens come in again after sprouts,' said Jimmy.

Betsy, thinking about the washing, said, 'Dad, I only got one clean pair of fings left.'

'Well, dear oh lor',' said Dad, taking off Mrs Shaw, a gossipy neighbour. 'We can't 'ave that, lovey.' He regarded his girls. Betsy at nine had a cheeky-looking face and was full of tricks. She had her mum's light brown hair and brown eyes. She was a giggly pickle. Well, normally she was. Patsy at thirteen was active and lively, with fair hair and hazel eyes that could look blue when the sun caught them. She liked her hair left long, tying it with a ribbon at the nape of her neck. Her mum had been very pretty as a girl, and Patsy had a lot of that prettiness. And she always had a tidy look, whereas Betsy always had a rumpled look, as if she'd just had a pillow fight. Pillow fights made her yell with excitement. They made her mum call up and threaten to give her something.

As for Jimmy, he was a good-looking boy with a lot of sense. He could be very funny. It had been a blow to him to lose his job, but his sense of humour was keeping him going. During the war, when he was only eight, he wrote to the prime minister about the air raids, asking if the government couldn't train pigeons to go up and do a puncturing job with their beaks on German zeppelins. Although the prime minister must have been very busy, he'd actually sent a reply saying he'd talk to some pigeon fanciers about it. Mum showed the reply to neighbours, some of whom said it sounded dangerous, they didn't want punctured zeppelins falling on top of them.

'I got to 'ave more clean pairs of fings,' said Betsy.

'So 'ave I,' said Patsy, who liked everything she was wearing to feel clean. She was sorry for girls who came to school looking as if their frocks hadn't been in a copper for ages.

'Well, I tell you what,' said Dad, 'how about cartin' everything off to the Bagwash laundry in the mornin' while I'm at work? Say the bedsheets and pillow cases as well. Could you three manage that?'

'Then bring it all back later and 'ang it on the line?' said Patsy.

'Just in case your mum's not goin' to do anything about it,' said Dad.

'What about the ironing?' asked Patsy.

'Well, if your mum's not in the mood,' said Dad, 'I'll try me hand at it.'

'Dad, men don't do ironing, they do their own work,' said Patsy, who wasn't going to have her mum's mood make things that awkward for her dad.

'Most men don't do ironing, I grant yer,' said Dad. 'But a lot of old soldiers could, and I've done some darnin' in me time, too.'

'I'll do the ironing,' said Patsy.

'We'll see, me love, we'll see,' said Dad. 'Now it's me pleasure to tell you the supper was a treat—'

'Oh, me rice puddin'!' exclaimed Patsy, and rushed out to the oven.

'Who said rice puddin'?' asked Dad.

'Patsy,' said Jimmy.

'She done it with milk,' said Betsy, 'it's been cookin' hours and hours.'

'Bless the girl,' said Dad.

Patsy reappeared and placed the hot dish down on the bread board in the centre of the table. The skin was brown with grated nutmeg. 'Patsy, I'm proud of you,' said Dad. 'Did I ever mention we used to 'ave rice puddin' in the Army? Well, boiled rice mostly, with jam. A bit like sticky glue, but nourishin', of course. We had a roll call just after dinner once, and the sergeant-major got to a bloke whose monicker was Rafferty. Rafferty didn't answer. "Rafferty!" hollered the sergeant-major. There still wasn't any answer, but Rafferty was present all right. "Rafferty!" bawled the sergeant-major. So I spoke up, bein' Rafferty's platoon corporal, and I said he couldn't answer because he'd 'ad two helpings of boiled rice with jam, and that his Irish north-and-south was all stuck up in consequence. You should've seen the sergeant-major havin' fifty fits all at once. Well now, look at that, Patsy's rice puddin'. You're a treasure, Patsy.'

'Good as the Queen of Sheba, that's me,' said Patsy.

'I've never 'eard the Queen of Sheba did rice puddings,' said Jimmy. 'I thought she just went in for puttin' rubies in her belly button.'

'That's rude, sayin' belly button, ain't it, Dad?' said Betsy.

'Dimple, I call it,' said Dad.

Patsy served out rice pudding to all, and everyone began to enjoy it.

'Someone's comin' in,' said Patsy, lifting her head. Footsteps sounded in the passage.

'It's Mum,' said Betsy, looking nervous.

'Mother,' said Jimmy, looking solemn.

'Just act natural,' said Dad, 'and as if we're all doin' some repentin'.'

CHAPTER TWO

Mother entered the kitchen: a slender woman of thirty six, she still owned a measure of attractiveness, despite her lack of make-up and despite the disordered look of her clothes. The long jacket of her black costume had lost all its buttons, and the skirt seemed very sorry for itself. Her black velvet hat was slightly askew, held in that position by her hatpin. Her umbrella was in one hand, handbag in the other. Crikey, her clothes, thought Betsy. She's been in the wars, thought Patsy. Good old Mum, she's at least come out alive, thought Jimmy.

'So you're back,' said Dad, then adjusted his welcome. 'Glad to see you, Mother.'

Mother gazed in shock at the rice pudding. 'You're all eatin' rice puddin',' she said accusingly.

'Well, we couldn't just sit and look at it,' said Jimmy, 'we thought we might as well eat it, 'specially seein' Patsy made it.'

'And Jimmy cooked the mutton chops,' said Patsy.

'What?' said Mother in new shock. 'You've all 'ad mutton chops as well as rice puddin'?'

'And greens,' said Jimmy.

'And mashed potatoes,' said Patsy.

'I don't know how I can 'old my head up,' said Mother, 'knowin' you've all been gourmandisin'. I was goin' to give them mutton chops to the poor.'

'What a shame,' said Jimmy, 'they've all gone now.'

'It's just been supper, Maudie,' said Dad easily, 'just a bit of custom'ry eatin'.'

'I left a loaf of bread in the larder,' said Mother sternly, 'and a jug of water on the table. To think you've all been 'aving mutton chops and rice puddin'. I can't turn my back a minute without you doin' some sin or other.'

'Never mind, Mother,' said Jimmy, 'we've been doin' some repentin' as well. And you can see how Patsy's repentin' for makin' the rice puddin'.'

'Yes, I don't 'ardly know where to put my face, Mum – I mean Mother,' said Patsy.

'Still, it would've been more of a sin not to eat it,' said Dad, 'you can't let good food go to waste. Like a cup of tea, Mother?'

'Well, I could do with a cup,' said Mother, 'I've 'ad a tryin' day on behalf of the Lord. But don't put any milk or sugar in.'

'That's not tea, Mum, that's ugh,' said Betsy.

'Don't call me Mum,' said Mother, 'it don't befit me.'

'I forgot,' said Betsy, feeling and looking very upset.

'Be your age, Maudie,' said Dad.

'Sit up,' said Mother, walking around the table to give each member of her family a critical look. She addressed Jimmy. 'What d'you think you're doin'?' she asked.

'Finishin' my rice pudding,' said Jimmy.

'What impudence,' said Mother. 'And where are you goin'?' she asked Dad as he came to his feet.

'To put the kettle on, seein' you're so busy doin' nothing,' said Dad. 'Try sittin' down instead of standin' in me way.'

'Yes, I can do with a sit down,' said Mother. She put her handbag and umbrella on the dresser and sat down. 'I've been among sinners nearly all afternoon, and it's been a sore trial.'

'We're sufferin' a sore trial ourselves,' said Dad from the scullery.

'That's what comes from gourmandisin',' said Mother.

'You been an' lost all yer buttons,' said Betsy.

'Gave 'em to some poor woman who hadn't got any, I suppose,' said Jimmy.

'Yes, you've always been a givin' woman, Mother,' said Patsy. *I'll give you something*, that had been her mum's favourite expression for years.

'To the poor, I expect,' said Jimmy.

'We're poor,' said Betsy. Mother frowned at her. Nervously, Betsy added, 'I mean we ain't rich, are we, Dad?'

'Not yet, Betsy,' said Dad, doing his best not to let his kids down by rowing with his wife. What was plain, of course, was the fact that Maud had not only gone religious for good, but she'd gone completely barmy as well. Not much anyone could do with a barmy woman except give her her head. 'Still, as me old sergeant-major used to say, if you keep your buttons shinin', your boots polished and your expectations modest, you've got as good a chance of fallin' down a goldmine as anyone else.'

'Behold, the Day of Judgement is nigh,' said Mother.

'Might be the day when I get a job,' said Jimmy, and got up to fetch cups and saucers from the dresser.

''Eathens, that's what those people in Whitechapel are,' said Mother.

'Crikey, did they chuck—' Betsy checked herself. 'Did they treat yer a bit rough, Mum?'

'Don't call me Mum.'

'I keep forgettin',' said Betsy.

'I'll forget something meself in a minute,' said Dad darkly.

'I want proper respect,' said Mother. 'As for them

'eathen sinners, the Lord 'as commanded me to go among them again, which I'm goin' to do tomorrow, with some of my sister Repenters.'

Dad, waiting for the kettle to boil, muttered.

Jimmy said, 'What about the fam'ly washin'?'

'I 'aven't got time for that sort of thing now I'm workin' on behalf of the Lord,' said Mother. 'I'll be away a lot, so don't forget about 'aving bread and water for some of your meals, I don't want to find you've had mutton chops again and more rice puddin'. Young man, what's that you're doin'?'

'I'm havin' seconds of Patsy's rice puddin',' said Jimmy.

'It don't befit you to 'ave seconds,' said Mother. 'There's people starvin' in some places.'

'Jimmy knows that,' said Dad, 'so do the rest of us, and so do most people round 'ere. About time you cooked some rice puddings yourself, Mother, an' gave them to the starvin' poor instead of pokin' them with your fiery sword.'

'Oh, 'elp,' breathed Betsy.

'Sticks an' stones may break my bones, but words won't never 'urt me,' said Mother.

Dad made the tea and brought the pot to the table. 'Anyway, what 'appened in Whitechapel?' he asked.

'It wasn't nice, I can tell you that,' said Mother, vexed. 'I went among them with Mother Verity to offer them salvation and repentance.'

'Mother Verity?' said Patsy.

'She was Miss Celia Stokes till she was anointed,' said Mother.

'I hear you've been anointed Mother Mary,' said Dad.

'I was done that religious honour by our minister, Father Peter,' said Mother. She frowned at what was left

29

of the rice pudding. 'Perhaps I'll 'ave a little of that,' she said. Betsy fetched a spoon and plate, and she helped herself from the dish. 'I've been very sore tried this afternoon,' she said. 'I can do with a bit of eatin'.'

She ate the lot and scraped the dish. Dad poured the tea, Patsy milking the cups. She looked at him. He winked and nodded. She put milk into all five cups. Mother took her cup without commenting.

'Sugar, Mum – sugar, Mother?' invited Betsy, pushing the bowl forward. Mother absently sugared her tea.

'Father Peter and 'is assistant, Father Luke, are both comin' with us to Whitechapel tomorrow,' she said.

'Sounds Roman Cath'lic to me,' said Dad.

'Excuse me, but we don't 'old with no Pope,' said Mother. 'Father Peter says the Vatican's full of cardinal gluttony. And our League's not Protestant or Cath'lic, it's just to bring the word of the Lord to the land, like the Israelites did when Moses led them out of Egypt and Joshua went among the sinners of the land for their own good.'

'Barmy,' said Dad under his breath.

'What's that?' demanded Mother.

'Tea all right?' asked Dad.

'Who put milk and sugar in it? You know I've given up that sort of thing.' Mother looked put upon as she sipped her tea.

'We're takin' the washin' to the Bagwash laundry tomorrow,' said Patsy, 'and after it's been out on the line, Dad says 'e's goin' to 'ave a go at doin' the ironing.'

'What?' asked Mother.

'Yes, fancy Dad 'aving to do the ironing,' said Patsy in disgust.

Mother gave her a puzzled look. 'What's that girl's name?' she asked.

'Patsy,' said Jimmy.

'Well, Patsy, if that's who you are,' said Mother, 'mind what you say about Mr Andrews. I 'appen to be in holy wedlock with him.'

'I thought you'd forgot that,' said Patsy pointedly.

'What! Where's my umbrella?' asked Mother.

'You can forget that,' said Dad.

'By our sins we shall be punished accordin',' said Mother. She put her empty cup down. 'I'm goin' out now.'

'You've only been in ten minutes,' said Dad.

'I'm goin' to the public baths for a bath,' said Mother. 'I'll see to some bread and water for all of you when I get back.' She rose from the table, picked up her brolly and handbag and went to the downstairs bedroom she shared with Dad to collect a change of clothes. Then she took herself off to the public baths, open on Friday evenings. She left the members of her family looking at each other.

'What a palaver,' said Dad, trying to sound cheerful. 'Still, she'll get over it in time. Just for the present, though, I don't think we'd better tell the neighbours she's started to call 'erself Mother Mary.'

'Dad, I don't want no bread and water,' said Betsy. 'I just 'ad me supper and a cup of tea.'

'Let's clear up,' said Dad in hearty fashion.

They cleared up, washed up and tidied up, then Jimmy went out for a walk. No-one asked where he was going. They knew he was going to walk around and talk to himself. He'd been doing that a bit in the evenings since he'd lost his job.

This is a fine time for Mum to go off her chump, he said to himself as he began his walk. Dad's handling her fairly well, but Betsy can't think what's happening, and Patsy's going to lose patience quick. And I've got to get . . .

''Ello, Jimmy, fancy seein' you,' said neighbour Mrs Shaw from her open door.

'Yes, I only just got back from the North Pole,' said Jimmy.

'Beg yer pardon?' said Mrs Shaw.

'Just a joke, Mrs Shaw.'

'I saw yer mum a bit ago,' said Mrs Shaw. 'She went in the public baths. Is she all right? Only I 'eard she's been goin' out a lot, every day I 'eard. 'As she got a job doin' daily cleanin' or something now you lost yer own job? Me old man says that's terrible 'ard luck on a young bloke like you, 'specially now yer old enough to start takin' girls out. Not that we've 'eard if you've got a girl or not, only Mrs Carey was only sayin' to me last week she expects a 'andsome boy like you is bound to 'ave a girl somewhere. You're not sayin' much, I notice.'

'Well, you're doin' fine by yourself, Mrs Shaw,' said Jimmy. 'I don't feel you need a lot from me. You carry on.'

'Well, I do 'ope you get another job soon, Jimmy, and that yer mum's all right,' said Mrs Shaw, deaf to little digs from anybody. 'Only I said 'ello to 'er the other day when she was on 'er way somewhere, and she just walked by me as if I wasn't there, like, and today I saw 'er goin' up to the Walworth Road with a banner. Mind, it was folded and under 'er arm, so I couldn't see what was on it – 'ere, where's 'e gone?' She addressed the startled question to empty air. Jimmy had resumed his walk. 'Well, what a funny fam'ly they're gettin' to be.'

Poor old Ma Shaw, said Jimmy to himself. When they get like that they finish up talking to lampposts. I reckon lampposts have a lot to put up with, what with dogs weeing over them and kids shinning up them. What does she mean, do I have a girl? Fat lot of use I'd be to any girl while I don't have a job. I know what I have got, a gorblimey headache on account of no work. I don't like being unemployed, I'll have to buy some daily papers that advertise situations vacant. I think I fancy a well-paid job with a firm that won't go bust. Suppose I got fixed up with a decent boss whose daughter fell for me? Crikey, I like the sound of that, no good being too proud. Watcher, lamppost, fancy being on the wrong end of a chat? I'll send Ma Shaw along, you're bound to get to know her sometime. He walked around in this fashion for a while, it helped to ease his frustrations. He didn't like the thought of Dad being the sole provider for the family again, especially now Mum was being a barmy worry.

He was back home a few minutes before Mother returned wearing a fresh blouse and skirt and carrying her discarded costume. She said nothing about doling out bread and water, she said she'd met a nice religious woman while they were both waiting for baths to become available. The woman had a husband who was a shocking sinner, he went in for drink something chronic. So Mother said she and her friend Mother Verity would try to give him something more to think about than drink.

'Well, best of luck, Maudie,' said Dad, 'do a good job on 'im. We had a Private Ashby who liked a few. One time we laid claim to some crates of Palestine beer that 'ad fallen off an overloaded camel. Private Ashby drank four pints too many, and it turned 'im funny and made 'im fall about. Up came the sergeant-major. "On yer feet, that man!" he hollered. Well, Private Ashby managed to stand up. He looked at the sergeant-major and said, "Gawd 'elp us, that camel's come back for the empties".'

Betsy giggled, Patsy laughed and Jimmy grinned.

'Have you finished, Jack Andrews?' asked Mother.

'Yes, that's all, Maudie,' said Dad.

'Well, I'll make us all some cocoa now, then read me new Bible to you.'

'From the beginning?' asked Jimmy.

'I'll go deaf,' said young Betsy. Mother gave her a look. Betsy gulped. 'I mean . . . oh, 'elp, I don't fink I know what I mean.'

Someone knocked on the front door, and Betsy escaped more looks by running to answer the summons. On the doorstep was harum-scarum Lily Shaw, from several doors down. She was thirteen and one of Patsy's street friends.

''Ello, Betsy, can Patsy come out?' she asked.

'I'll ask me dad,' said Betsy, and called from the door. 'Can Patsy go out with Lily, Dad?'

Mother appeared, the new Bible clasped to her slender bosom. 'Into the parlour with you, my girl,' she said to Betsy. 'You as well,' she said to Lily.

'Me, Mrs Andrews?' said Lily. 'In yer parlour?'

'At once,' said Mother.

'But it ain't Sunday, Mrs Andrews,' said Lily.

'Never mind that, the Lord is present every day,' said Mother, and shooed both girls into the parlour. Patsy, Jimmy and Dad joined them, Dad having said everyone had best humour Mother. Jimmy thought Dad was right, humouring her was the best thing to do at the moment.

'You can all sit down,' she said graciously. She herself remained standing beside the old upright piano, which she only allowed to be used religiously these days, and only on Sundays.

'Patsy, we goin' to play parlour guessin' games?' asked Lily, who was a plump tomboy.

'No talkin', if you don't mind,' said Mother, and gave Lily's plumpness a disapproving look. 'Someone else 'as been sinfully over-eatin', I see,' she said.

'Who d'yer mean, Mrs Andrews?' asked Lily in all innocence. No-one did any over-eating in her family, she was naturally plump. 'What yer lookin' at me for, Mrs Andrews?'

'Who is that girl?' asked Mother. 'What's she doin' here?'

'It's only Lily, Patsy's friend,' said Dad.

'She should 'ave said. Now everyone listen, if you don't mind, and be humble before God.' Mother opened her Bible, removed a bookmark, and read from the third chapter of St Matthew. '"In those days came John the Baptist, preachin' in the wilderness of Judea and sayin' repent ye, for the kingdom of 'eaven is at hand."' Mother looked up, a triumphant expression on her face. 'There, you all 'eard that, you all 'eard that John the Baptist said it himself. So what 'ave you all got to say for yourselves?'

Lily looked puzzled. Patsy rolled her eyes at Jimmy. Betsy looked uncomfortable. At nine she couldn't make her mum out. Jimmy spoke up.

'Well, Mother,' he said, 'if you don't mind me sayin' so, you forgot the cocoa.'

'Yes, you said cocoa first and this after,' remarked Patsy.

'I don't mind some cocoa,' said Lily, 'but I—'

'Stop talkin',' said Mother, and read some more. '"And they were baptized of him in Jordan, confessin' their sins." There, you all 'eard that too, didn't you? It was the people repentin'.'

'Please, Mrs Andrews, I best go,' said Lily. 'Me dad'll wallop me if 'e finds out I been listenin' to the Bible. Dad don't believe in God an' the Bible, Mrs Andrews, 'e says 'e wouldn't 'ave come out of the Boer War with chronic rheumatics from a wound if God 'ad been in 'eaven lookin' down on 'im.'

'Well, I never 'eard anything more blasphemous,' said Mother, closing the Bible and putting it on the piano. 'I'd better come 'ome with you and bring my umbrella, your father's got to be spoken to. We'll go straightaway.'

'Oh, me gawd,' gasped Lily, 'I wouldn't do that if I was you, Mrs Andrews, me dad's—'

'Come along,' said Mother.

Dad let her go with Lily. He felt the best way to cure her was to keep giving her her head. She came back ten minutes later, and at an undignified run. Lily's dad was roaring after her, despite his stiff leg. Mother rushed into the house. Behind her, Lily's dad reached the open front door. From there he bawled at her as she ran through the passage to the sanctuary of the family kitchen.

'Yer daft loony!' Lily's dad let himself go. 'What d'yer think you're playin' at, comin' round my 'ouse and pokin' me with that bleedin' umbrella? You there, Jack Andrews, are yer? Well, keep yer daft missus to yerself, or she'll send us all barmy.'

Dad went to the door. 'No 'ard feelings, Gus,' he said. 'Maudie's got ideas lately about doin' good works.'

'Well, don't think I don't sympathize with yer,' said Lily's mottled dad, 'only I don't want 'er doin' any good work on me, it'll aggravate me rheumatics. I dunno, I can 'ardly walk back 'ome as it is. Come right in with Lily, she did, talkin' about blasphemous sinners and pokin' me with that umbrella of 'ers. I asks yer, Jack, is that neighbourly, is it friendly?'

'Just a notion she's got about makin' us all good Christians,' said Dad.

'That's 'er game, is it? Well, ask 'er to leave me out, I ain't partial to bein' a good Christian, I just want to mind me own business an' give me rheumatics a rest, I don't want umbrellas pokin' it about.'

'I'll tell her,' said Dad. By the time he got rid of his aggrieved neighbour, Mother had decided she wouldn't make cocoa, after all, that it was too rich. She wanted to empty the contents of the tin into the sink and flush it away. Jimmy was thwarting her, saying it would do more good to give it all to the poor.

'Oh, yes,' she said, 'and while you're about it, give everything else away too, except the bread.'

Dad said he'd brought home some free packets of tea and a tin of mixed biscuits from the firm. He couldn't give those away to the poor, the firm's rule was that such things were only for employees and their families, and he'd get the sack if he broke the rule. Mother said that didn't sound like a Christian rule, and Dad said it had to be because the manager was a churchwarden in Streatham. Mother asked why everyone was arguing with her.

'I ain't,' said Patsy.

'Nor me, am I, Dad?' said Betsy.

'Stop bein' contradict'ry, or I'll make you say the Ten Commandments twice over in a minute,' said Mother.

Later, when she and Dad were in bed, Dad said, 'If you've got to be religious, I suppose you've got to be, but take it easy with Betsy and Patsy.'

'I don't know what I'm doin', bein' in bed with you while I'm sayin' my prayers,' said Mother, 'it's just not decent.'

Dad sighed.

CHAPTER THREE

Saturday morning and Dad was up first, as usual. As he didn't have to get to the London Bridge depot until nine o'clock on Saturdays, he was making the breakfast porridge. Although Mother was up and dressed too, she was still in their bedroom doing some religious contemplation. She had refused to say exactly what happened in Whitechapel the afternoon before, but he could guess. The East End cockneys didn't mind the Salvation Army, but they had no time for people who came and preached at them.

Mother appeared when Patsy, Jimmy and Betsy were down, and Dad began to dole out the porridge from the saucepan.

'What's that?' asked Mother.

'The usual porridge,' said Dad.

'I don't like all this rich livin',' said Mother.

'It's only porridge,' said Patsy.

'With syrup,' said Dad, 'as it's Bank Holiday weekend.' He put a tin of Tate and Lyle's golden syrup on the table. That was another gratuity from his firm.

'Crikey,' said Betsy in bliss. 'I didn't know we 'ad that in the larder, Dad.'

'Brought it home last night,' said Dad.

'God bless golden syrup,' said Patsy. Porridge with golden syrup was a real treat in Walworth. Patsy thought there ought to be a large tin in every home. Some families didn't even have porridge, or decent boots or shoes for everyone. While Patsy was proud of her dad for what he provided, she was sad that not every dad had a job, and that some didn't earn very good wages. When Jimmy had been working, the family had been almost well off. She knew her brother hated losing his job. He didn't show it, but she knew.

Syrup was spooned on to porridge. Mother frowned at her breakfast. 'I don't know I can eat this,' she said.

'All right, Maudie, take it to Whitechapel with you,' said Dad.

'Perhaps I'll eat just a little,' said Mother, 'then I've got to sew some buttons on my costume jacket.'

'Syrup, Mother?' said Jimmy, pushing the tin across. From the window, Walworth's morning light fell across the table and made the surface of the syrup gleam with translucent gold.

'No, I couldn't eat no syrup with it,' said Mother.

'All right,' said Dad, and Mother absently helped herself to a spoonful. Coming to, she shuddered at her indulgence. It caused her to eat the sweetened porridge in a suffering way.

'I'll be gone for a week,' she said.

'You won't,' said Dad.

'I'll do some packin' this mornin',' she said.

'Talk sense,' said Dad, ready to go over the top.

'I'm bein' called to higher duties,' said Mother. 'I'll be in Whitechapel with the League this afternoon, then I'll be stayin' at our 'eadquarters in Bloomsbury. I don't want no-one to worry about me.'

Dad breathed hard. 'You're a worry to all of us,' he said, 'and a—' He meant to say and a bloody headache to him, but Betsy was already upset enough, and Patsy was biting her lip. 'There's other things beside this cock-eyed League, Maudie, there's your fam'ly.'

'And the cookin' and washin' and housework,' said Jimmy from the scullery. Having finished his porridge, he was toasting slices of bread under the gas grill.

'I 'appen to 'ave taught you all not to be 'elpless,' said Mother, 'and your dad's been a soldier.'

'I don't 'appen to have been a bleedin' housewife as well,' said Dad, and Betsy looked near to crying then. But spirited Patsy flashed a look of encouragement at him. It urged him to let himself go, but he didn't want Betsy in tears. 'I've got my job, Maudie,' he said, 'an' you've got yours.'

'I'm being called to higher duties,' said Mother again.

Jimmy brought in four slices of toast and handed them out. Mother began to eat hers as it was, dry. Dad and the girls put marge and marmalade on theirs, with Betsy glancing unhappily from one parent to the other. Jimmy put other slices of bread under the grill. Patsy, seeing it was no use relying on her mum to preside, poured the tea.

'Maudie,' said Dad, 'let's get this straight before I go to work. You're goin' away for a week?'

'I've got the Lord's work to do, me and the Repenters,' said Mother. 'We're goin' to march on the city of Satan, which is London, and bring the 'eathens to redemption.'

'You won't like what 'appens,' said Dad.

'Sticks and stones may break my bones, but words won't never 'urt me,' declared Mother.

'What about rotten cabbages?' asked Jimmy from the scullery.

'That boy, what's 'e talkin' about?' asked Mother.

Bringing more toast in and sitting down, Jimmy said, 'Listen, Mother, I suppose you realize Patsy and Betsy are short of clean knickers?'

'That's it, tell everybody, you cheeky beast,' said Patsy.

'What disgustin' language,' said Mother, looking at Jimmy in shock. 'Who is this young man, might I ask?'

''E's our Jimmy,' blurted Betsy, then gulped and hid her face.

'Well, I still don't want 'im usin' language like that,' said Mother.

'I'm just tellin' you, that's all,' said Jimmy, not liking the atmosphere of edginess and its uncomfortable aspects.

'Do a bit of listening for a change, Maudie,' said Dad. 'Listening to us, I mean.'

''Aven't I spent the best years of me life listening to all me fam'ly?' said Mother. 'Now it's me duty to listen to the Lord and all 'Is commands.'

'Oh, it's the Lord, is it, who's told you to push off for a week?' said Dad.

'I don't know about a week,' said Mother. 'Father Peter says our work among the sinful multitudes might be lastin'.'

'What's lastin'?' whispered Betsy to Patsy.

'A lot more than a week,' said Patsy.

'Oh, 'elp,' breathed Betsy, and gulped again.

'I don't like the sound of lastin',' said Dad, 'you'd better shake yerself up a mite, Maudie, you'd better start doin' some sensible thinkin' about what you're gettin' up to. It don't make any kind of sense to me, nor your fam'ly.'

'The Lord 'as called me to 'elp carry 'Is fiery sword,' said Mother.

'I bet He's not goin' to bless you for pushin' off for a week,' said Jimmy.

'Where's my umbrella?' asked Mother, giving her son a sharp look.

'Never mind your daft umbrella,' said Dad, getting up. 'I've got to push off meself now, to me job. Listen, Maudie, don't make it so that I'll 'ave to come after you,

41

which I will if I've got to. I might not be as close to the Lord as you are, but no-one's goin' to make me believe 'E's in favour of wives an' mothers carryin' 'Is fiery sword.'

'Now then, Jack Andrews, don't you—'

'I don't 'ave time to do more arguin' at the moment,' said Dad. 'So long, loveys, see you later.' He kissed his girls. 'Look after things, Jimmy,' he said, and departed like a man who knew he'd got problems.

'Dad's right,' said Patsy, 'you just can't go off as if you're the lodger, Mum, it ain't fair on Dad, nor on us.'

'And it's not befittin', either,' said Jimmy, getting that one in with relish.

'I don't want any sauce,' said Mother, 'you've all got to understand about me religious callin'. While I'm away it won't do your Dad any harm to be a help to 'imself and 'is children.'

'We're your children, too,' said Patsy crossly.

'You can all 'elp each other,' said Mother. 'Well, I've got things to do now, includin' sewing some buttons on.'

'We've got more things to do than you 'ave,' said Patsy heatedly. Jimmy put a hand on his sister's arm, knowing she was near to shouting at Mother.

'Not worth it, sis,' he said.

'Don't commit no sins while I'm not 'ere,' said Mother, 'and don't forget to 'elp the poor.' Up on her feet, she left the kitchen. Patsy sat fuming. Betsy's face crumpled a bit, and Jimmy put an arm around her shoulders and gave her a squeeze. Betsy gulped.

Dad only worked a half-day on Saturdays. The main delivery journeys to the retail shops had all been done by Fridays. On Saturdays, he usually arrived home about one o'clock. Today, having got on the right side of the manager, he was back home by half-past eleven. The family was in crisis, and he'd got to put his foot down. That would amount to tying Maud up, as good as, and that in turn would really upset Betsy. He felt the best bet was to let Maud get repentance and redemption out of her system, to let her chuck herself in head first.

She'd always been religious, of course. He'd first found out how pretty she was as a girl of eighteen, how nice she was to kiss and cuddle when they were courting, and nor did she mind kissing and cuddling, except she'd sometimes say 'Now then, Jack Andrews, don't take liberties.' He found out she was religious when she began to make him go to church with her on Sunday mornings. She even carried her own prayer book. But she made a pretty and willing bride, and a conscientious wife, although after a few years she began to act at times as if going to bed with him was a bit improper. He thought that funny at first. Then he thought it bloody ridiculous. And then religion really did begin to get a hold on her, and among other things she insisted on having a family Bible and reading out loud from it on Sunday evenings. He'd fallen in love with a pretty girl who had nice ways and was sweet to kiss and cuddle. He slowly fell out of love with the kind of woman she became. He still retained some affection for her, and always had the right amount of loyalty to her as the mother of his children. But things now were really getting on his nerves. And what was worse, the kids were suffering. Patsy was getting ratty, Betsy was getting distressed, and Jimmy was losing all respect for his mum.

Arriving home, Dad found that Mother had finished her sewing and packing, and intended to depart in ten minutes or so. The girls had taken the laundry to the Bagwash early, and Jimmy had collected it an hour later. Now it was all hanging on the line in the yard, and the August

43

sun, strong enough today to pulverize the Walworth haze, was at its drying work. Dad felt he had treasures in his kids, and he had to give Maud some credit for that. For four years, while he'd been in Mesopotamia, she'd had to manage them by herself. But, frankly, she wasn't a woman any more, not a proper woman. There was no warmth there.

Mother was in the bedroom. He cornered her there, and spoke his piece as firmly as he could without raising his voice. He reminded her again that she was a wife and mother, and if she couldn't see what that meant, then her kind of religiousness wasn't the kind he'd recommend. 'Ruddy hell, you're a disgrace the way you keep going off and leaving the kids to look after themselves until I get home,' he went on in angry vein. It made no difference. Mother was adamant that she had to go. She said if it meant she'd be away from home for a while, it couldn't be helped. Dad didn't think much of that, it was too indefinite, too vague. And she was getting vague too about the family, so much so that he had a feeling she was likely to forget she had a family at all. He wanted to shake her hard.

Someone knocked on the front door. Jimmy answered it, passing his parents' bedroom on the way. Aunt Edie was on the doorstep. As usual, she looked a treat. For a start, she had an hour-glass figure and wore tight-waisted clothes like an Edwardian woman. And she favoured large hats, like the one she had on now, with wax flowers decorating it. Her peach-coloured dress showed her calves. At thirty-six she was the same age as Mother, her cousin, but she was a different kind of woman. Jimmy had an idea she found the shorter fashions a bit of a lark. Well, being a pearly queen, she would do, especially as she appeared in charity concerts put on by Camberwell pearlies. She probably finished her turns by doing a cockney knees-up on the stage, which meant showing her legs. And good legs were best for a knees-up.

One of a large family, Aunt Edie had come up the hard way, for her dad had had a very poorly paid job as a metal worker with a firm that always laid men off when orders were a bit low. She'd known years of patched clothes, leaky boots and not too many good meals. But from the moment she was lucky enough to secure a factory job when she left school at fourteen, she was determined to make a decent life for herself. She applied that determination to her work and stepped up the ladder until she'd become supervisor of eighty girls and women. She'd held that position for years now. Her one sad memory was of the fiancé she'd lost through the boating accident on the Thames. She might have married someone else, being such a cheerful and good-looking woman, but although she was never without men friends, she'd never taken a husband. She lived happily enough, it seemed, in a flat close by Camberwell Green, and the people she most liked to visit were the Andrews family, even if she was never very keen on cousin Maud.

From the doorstep she smiled at Jimmy, a chip off the old block with his grey eyes and a bit of his dad's twinkle.

'Well, young man?' she said.

'You're a nice surprise, Aunt Edie,' said Jimmy. 'Shouldn't you still be at work? Don't tell me your firm's gone bust like mine did.'

'No, I finished early this mornin' because it's Bank Holiday weekend,' said Aunt Edie. 'Look, if you're goin' to keep me standin' on the doorstep like I was someone from the gasworks, I might as well go 'ome.'

'Don't do that, come in,' said Jimmy. She stepped in and he ducked under the brim of her hat and kissed her.

'That's better,' she said. 'Found another job yet, lovey?'

'Not yet.'

'Keep lookin', and if I hear of anything I'll be round double quick to let you know.'

Dad appeared. 'Thought I 'eard you, Edie,' he said.

'Bit of a shock, was it?' smiled Aunt Edie.

'Pleasure,' said Dad, but looked as if his mind was elsewhere, which it was.

'I always get off early Bank Holiday Saturdays,' said Aunt Edie, 'and as I want to go down East Street market, I thought I'd call in 'ere first and give the girls a little treat.'

That was just like Aunt Edie, thought Jimmy. She had never visited without bringing something for his sisters, and him too during his schooldays.

'You're a good sort, Edie,' said Dad, a bit absently.

'Well, I was young meself once,' she said. 'Where's Maud? I'd better pay me respects while I'm 'ere, or I'll get sermonized.' Aunt Edie was inclined to be a bit scathing about her cousin's religious mania.

'Maud's gone over the top a bit,' said Dad.

'Oh?' said Aunt Edie, and went into the parlour with Dad and Jimmy, where Dad put her in the picture. 'She's off 'er rocker,' said Aunt Edie forthrightly, and Jimmy thought there were sparks in her eye. 'What're you doin' about it, Jack?'

'Got to let 'er get it out of 'er system,' said Dad.

'Jimmy,' said Aunt Edie, fishing in her shopping bag, 'take these to your sisters, there's a love.' She gave him two paper bags, each containing half a pound of Walters Palm Toffee. 'I just want to talk to your dad for a bit.'

'Go easy on him,' said Jimmy, and left them to it.

'I'm goin' to do what I shouldn't,' said Aunt Edie, 'I'm goin' to interfere.'

'Help yourself,' said Dad, 'it won't be interference to me, old girl. But watch out for 'er brolly, I've just been poked with it meself.'

'If it comes to a fight,' said Aunt Edie, 'I'll hold me own. She's in the bedroom, is she?'

'She'll be on her way out any minute,' said Dad, who thought a stand-up between his wife and Edie might make Saturday rattle a bit.

'You stay here,' said Aunt Edie, and rustled forth to give battle, with Dad wishing her good luck.

The bedroom door was shut. Aunt Edie knocked and entered. Mother, dressed in her black costume and black hat, was just taking hold of the handle of an old leather suitcase. She looked up. Surprise put a question mark on her face.

'Edie? What're you doin' here?' she asked.

Aunt Edie closed the door. 'I'm not doin' anything yet,' she said, 'but I'm just about to start. I can 'ardly believe what I've just 'eard, that you're goin' off on some religious work, that you're leavin' your fam'ly.'

'The Lord's called me to take up 'Is sword,' said Mother proudly.

'Don't make me spit,' said Aunt Edie.

'Don't you spit in 'ere,' said Mother.

'That's a laugh,' said Aunt Edie. 'Look at it.' The room was untidy. 'You 'aven't even made the bed.'

'I 'appen to have more important work,' said Mother, 'and I'm now goin' out to get on with it.'

'You've been a bit daft for ages,' said Aunt Edie, 'but I never thought you'd go off and leave the kind of fam'ly you've got.'

'Don't you talk to me like that, Edie Harper,' said Mother, taking umbrage, 'I 'appen to have the privilege of bein' accepted into the League of Repenters.'

'Sounds like another name for a loony bin,' said Aunt Edie.

'Oh, what impertinence,' said Mother. 'I'll 'ave you know we've come together by the grace of God.'

'I bet,' said Aunt Edie. 'All right, so God and all 'Is wondrous works are out there somewhere, even if I 'aven't seen many of them meself. But it's no good you bein' in a hurry to shake 'ands with Him. You'll 'ave to wait till you pass on, like the rest of us, and while you're waitin,' Maud Andrews, remember your work's down 'ere on earth with your fam'ly, and don't you forget it.'

'More impertinence,' exclaimed Mother. It was hard to believe just how much impertinence there was about these days.

'You ought to be ashamed of yourself,' said Aunt Edie, her sparks flying. 'Look at you, dressed fit for a funeral, your bedroom not tidied up, the bed not made, and I don't know what else. Nor don't I know how a woman with your kind of fam'ly can talk about 'aving had a call from the Lord. If it was me, I'd tell the Lord to find someone else.'

'Oh, what blasphemy!' cried Mother, and raised her umbrella.

'You poke me with that,' said Aunt Edie, 'and you'll wish you 'adn't. I've watched you for years, you and your silly ways, and you can count yourself lucky you've got a 'usband like Jack. Anyone else would 'ave put you over 'is knees and spanked you long ago. Jack works long hours and 'ard ones, and deserves a bit better than what you're givin' him.'

'Do you 'appen to be referring to Mr Andrews, my 'usband in wedlock?' asked Mother distantly.

'Don't get high and mighty with me, Maud,' said Aunt Edie. 'I know too much about you. Religion's for Sunday church, not for askin' a wife and mother to spend every hour of every day goin' about in a trance.'

'Leave my house,' ordered Mother.

'Not before I've finished speakin' me piece,' said Aunt Edie. 'Your trouble is you don't know when you're well off, you've got what a lot of women would be more than 'appy with, a home, a good 'usband, and a son and two girls that's a credit to any fam'ly. I'll come right out with it, Maud, if Jack, Patsy, Betsy and Jimmy were mine, I'd thank the Lord for me blessings, not go off and leave them. Now what're you doin', what've you got your eyes shut for?'

'I'm prayin',' said Mother. With her eyes still closed, she nodded and murmured. 'Yes, thank you, Lord, yes, all right.' She opened her eyes and gave Aunt Edie a kind look. 'It's come to me, through our Lord, that seein' you're so concerned about my fam'ly, Edie Harper, you could stop being a selfish single woman and come and look after them yourself while I'm away.'

'What?' said Aunt Edie.

'Yes, it come to me in my prayer,' said Mother calmly. 'You can look after them while I'm doin' God's work.'

Aunt Edie, her eyes fiery, said, 'Don't tempt me.'

'Now I've got to be on my way,' said Mother.

'And you don't know when you'll be back?'

'The Lord will instruct me.'

'Poor old Lord,' said Aunt Edie. 'I don't know how He puts up with all you people knockin' Him up day and night, but you're tempting me all right.'

'I'll be 'umbly pleasured if I've shown you 'ow to do your Christian duty,' said Mother graciously.

'If you're not careful, you'll lose your girls,' said Aunt Edie. 'I don't mean they'll leave 'ome, they won't do that, they'll stay with their dad. What I do mean is you'll lose

49

their affection, and when that's gone, Maud, everything that's worthwhile to a mother has gone, I should think.'

'I don't know what you know about being a mother,' said Mother.

'If you think it's all about puttin' religion before your fam'ly,' said Aunt Edie, 'you'll deserve all you get.'

'Kindly keep a civil tongue in your 'ead,' said Mother.

'My 'ead's all right,' said Aunt Edie, 'it's yours that ought to be examined.'

'Oh, what impudence,' said Mother, but Aunt Edie, in a rare paddy, delivered several more home truths. Mother, however, still remained adamant, and eventually departed with her umbrella, her handbag and many of her belongings. First she said goodbye to her family, telling them not to forget to go to church and to give all the food in the larder to the poor. Dad, livid, went over the top then and said bugger the poor. Betsy, unhappy and bewildered, hid her face in his waistcoat. Patsy, angry as well as upset, asked what about the neighbours, what were they supposed to tell the neighbours?

'Tell them I'm doing my Christian duty,' said Mother.

'You'd better get on with it, then,' said Jimmy. And Mother left, much to Aunt Edie's disgust.

Silence descended on the family. Used as they were to Mother's eccentric ways, to have her go off like this was a shock. Aunt Edie was in such a rage about it that she was hard put to contain herself. It was little Betsy who broke the silence, after gulping down a sob.

'Dad, don't Mum really like us any more?'

Dad, knowing he had some cheering up to do, said, 'Course she does, Betsy love.' He gave her a cuddle. 'She's only goin' away for a bit. She'll be back.' She'd bloody better, he said to himself. 'She's just got a few problems, that's all.'

'So 'ave we now,' said Patsy.

'Don't you worry, Patsy, we'll sort ourselves out,' said Jimmy.

'You bet,' said Dad.

'And there's me,' said Aunt Edie, who had already made up her mind about what she was going to do. 'I'd like to talk to you again, Jack.'

'All right, Edie,' said Dad. 'Won't be a tick, kids, then we'll see about gettin' a meal a bit later, eh?'

'I can make some corned beef sandwiches,' said Patsy, 'and we could 'ave a proper meal tonight.'

'Good girl,' said Dad, and took Aunt Edie to the parlour.

There she told him what she proposed to do. She would come and stay every weekend, she said. She'd been with her firm a long time and the manager would let her have some Saturday mornings off. Then she'd be able to come on Friday evenings and leave for her work on Monday mornings. Of course, whenever Maud was home, she would keep out of the way. She said it was only right that Betsy and Patsy should have a woman around some days each week.

'Edie, you can't give up your weekends just for us,' said Dad.

'I don't call it givin' them up,' said Aunt Edie, 'I'm a relative, so I call it bein' a useful member of the fam'ly.'

'But it's not as if they're still young kids, they're all old enough to muck in and—'

'Jimmy's old enough, but Patsy and Betsy are of an age when they're entitled to be out enjoyin' themselves with their friends,' said Aunt Edie. 'I'll do the cookin' and washin', and go over the house, and stop lookin' at me as if I'm incapable.'

'All right, mind my eye,' said Dad with a grin. 'I know you're not incapable.'

'Also,' said Aunt Edie, 'it's not right you gettin' landed with this kind of problem. You've been a good 'usband and father, don't think I 'aven't noticed what's been goin' on between you and Maud since you come 'ome from the war.'

'Still, there's been a few laughs on the way,' said Dad.

'Don't make me spit,' said Aunt Edie. 'Your wife's already been a trial to me. But I'm 'er cousin, and it's up to me to make up for what she's doin' to 'er fam'ly. I wouldn't be much of an aunt to Betsy and Patsy if I couldn't 'elp out a bit at weekends. I'm not goin' to let you say no to me.'

'Stop hittin' me over me head,' said Dad.

'Someone should,' said Aunt Edie. 'Imagine you lettin' Maud do what she's doin', instead of givin' her a good 'iding.'

'I can't do that, Edie, I've never hit a woman in me life, I don't 'old with it.'

'You could 'ave done something to stop 'er goin'.'

'I wasn't goin' to tie her up,' said Dad.

'Pity,' said Aunt Edie. 'Still, she's 'opped it now and it's up to me to 'elp out. Besides, it'll be good for me. I've only ever 'ad to look after meself, and it's got to be good for me to think of others for a change.'

'Well, I feel it's askin' a lot of you,' said Dad.

'Who's askin'? You're not. I'm offerin'.'

'Yes, I know, but—'

'No buts, Jack. I'm goin' down the market now, then I'll go 'ome and pack a few weekend things, then I'll be back 'ere till Tuesday mornin' as it's Bank Holiday. I'll get supper this evenin', and in between I'll see if the 'ouse needs goin' over. Your bedroom does for a start . . . oh, I could 'it that wife of yours.'

'Take it easy, old girl,' said Dad. 'And look, don't be surprised if the neighbours start talkin'.'

'Blow the neighbours,' said Aunt Edie. 'Neighbours always talk.'

'I'm thinkin' of you, Edie, not me.'

'Thanks,' said Aunt Edie, who had very personal reasons for doing what she proposed to do. 'Where's Jimmy? He can come with me and tell me what shoppin' to get for you. Is there a joint of meat in the house for tomorrow's dinner?'

'No, I was goin' out meself with Patsy this afternoon to get a few things for the larder,' said Dad.

'Tell me what you want, and me and Jimmy'll get them.'

'Edie, you're doin' a sergeant-major job on me,' said Dad.

'Is it 'urting?' asked Aunt Edie.

'Not much, I'm used to sergeant-majors,' said Dad, and Aunt Edie gave him a searching look. His wife was being a real headache to him, and a real worry to their children. But he was standing up to it like a man, and she knew him well enough to know he'd fight tooth and nail to do all he could for his upset kids, even if he was reluctant to put his wife over his knees and give her something different to think about. Patsy and Jimmy were both showing a bit of their dad's toughness. It was little Betsy who couldn't hide her unhappiness, although even she had had moments when she was able to giggle.

Aunt Edie couldn't help thinking what a silly bitch Maud Andrews was not to realize exactly what a fine husband and lovely kids she had. Right, thought Aunt Edie, you'd better watch out, Maud.

Aunt Edie had principles, but one or two of them could be stretched a bit.

CHAPTER FOUR

Aunt Edie, sallying forth, entered the East Street market, Jimmy beside her. She had a soft spot for Jimmy. Like his dad, he was good-natured, and was tickled that she'd asked him to go shopping with her. She was an arresting figure in the bright summer dress that shaped her form on this warm August day, and her large flower-bedecked hat was a picture in itself. It caught the eyes of stallholders. It made one call out to her.

> 'Where'd yer get that 'at, love, where'd yer get yer titfer,
> Oh, gawd blimey, are yer sure it fits yer?'

'None of your sauce,' said Aunt Edie and sailed on.

There was something different about her, thought Jimmy. She was always cheerful and outgoing. Today she looked as if she was meeting an exciting challenge. She was going to come every weekend to cook, to do the washing and to go through the house. And she was going to give special attention to Betsy and Patsy. Jimmy didn't think there was anything very exciting about that. It was just housework, and hardly any kind of challenge. But there she was, looking as if she was on top of the world. And she knew how to shop in a market, how to spot a stallholder trying to slip a bruised apple in with good ones.

'Oh, no you don't, me lad.'

'What's that, missus?'

54

'I'll give you what's that if you give me a rotten apple.'

'Eh? Well, blow me, 'ow did that one get in?'

'You slipped it in. I wasn't born yesterday, I'll 'ave you know.'

'Wish you 'ad been, I'd take you 'ome to me missus. Now, 'ow about a nice bunch of grapes, seein' it's 'oliday weekend?'

'Yes, I'll have a bunch of grapes. No, not that one, that one.'

'Grapes, Aunt Edie?' queried Jimmy.

'My treat,' said Aunt Edie.

'You always were a sport,' said Jimmy.

'Now some of them cookin' apples,' said Aunt Edie to the stallholder, 'five big ones.'

'Best in the market, they are, missus.'

'They'd better be,' said Aunt Edie, 'or you'll cop it when I next come round. I want some bananas too. Young bananas, not ones dyin' of old age.'

She was like that with most of her market shopping. In the butcher's shop, she had the butcher swearing his legs of mutton were so fresh they were still nearly walking about.

'Don't make me laugh,' said Aunt Edie. 'Still nearly walkin' about?'

'That's right, missus, they only just stopped.'

'Did you 'ear that, Jimmy?' she asked.

'Yes,' said Jimmy, 'now ask him if that sheep's head over there is still nearly talkin'.'

'Funny you should mention that,' said the butcher, 'it spoke its last words only five minutes ago.'

'All right,' said Aunt Edie, eyeing a generous leg of mutton, 'what did it say?'

''Ello, sailor, 'ow's yer grandma?'

'Just as well it fell dead, then, if it can't talk sense,' said

Aunt Edie. 'Kindly weigh that leg for me.'

'Prime meat, that is, missus.'

'I'll bring it back if it isn't,' said Aunt Edie.

Jimmy thought her a real eye-opener. She made shop-keepers and stallholders sit up and perk up. She left them with grins all over their faces.

'I like you, Aunt Edie,' he said when they had finished the shopping.

'Didn't you like me before, then?'

'Like you more today.'

'That's not a joke?' said Aunt Edie. Jimmy always looked as grave as an owl when he was joking, and he was grave now.

'Well, life bein' serious most of the time,' he said. 'I'm not sure I can make jokes.'

Aunt Edie laughed. 'That's a joke itself,' she said. 'Well, now we've got everything, you can carry it 'ome with you while I – no, wait a bit, you can come to Camberwell on the tram with me. You're a young man now, and it's time you gave me the pleasure of escortin' me. Here, hold the shoppin' bag for me first of all.'

Amid the market crowds Jimmy said, 'D'you mind if I point out that carryin' a shoppin' bag can ruin a bloke's standin', Aunt Edie?'

'Well, dearie me, what a shame,' said Aunt Edie.

'All right, give it here,' said Jimmy. 'I'll risk me standin'.'

Aunt Edie laughed. She handed the laden bag to him, and they made their way through the market to the Walworth Road tram stop. She was happy about her purchases, some of which were the kind of bargains one could always get in the market, even on a crowded Saturday morning. Dad had insisted on giving her housekeeping money for the weekend.

Near the tram stop in the Walworth Road was a group of ex-Servicemen. Forming a little band, they were playing for coppers, coppers that some passers-by tossed into a hat on the kerbside. Aunt Edie found a silver threepenny-bit in her purse and dropped it into the hat.

'Bless yer, lady.'

Aunt Edie and Jimmy went on to the tram stop, Aunt Edie saying, 'That poor mother of yours, Jimmy.' It was the first time she had mentioned her cousin during the shopping expedition. 'Like your dad says, she can't 'elp bein' religious, but if she's that keen on goin' after sinners, she ought to start on the Government first. The war's been over nearly five years, but there's still old soldiers out of work and 'aving to earn a few pennies like those men, by playin' accordions and suchlike in gutters. There can't be anything more sinful than any Government lettin' that 'appen.'

'Good point, Aunt Edie,' said Jimmy. 'I'd like to see Mum chargin' into the Houses of Parliament and settin' about all of them with her umbrella.'

'I don't know about that,' said Aunt Edie, who plainly felt it was her cousin who ought to be set about. She eyed the traffic impatiently. She wanted to get on with things. There were still many horse-drawn vehicles about. The law required them to keep clear of tram tracks, but the drivers of vehicles such as beer drays considered their claim to rights of way went back a bleeding sight longer than electric trams. Accordingly, a tram could often be seen moving slowly along behind a lumbering beer dray, the frustrated tram driver clanging away and looking for a bobby, and the stubborn dray driver taking his time to move over to join traffic on the left of the tram tracks. Street kids always hoped it would lead to a fight. A good pair of fists earned the total admiration of street kids anywhere.

With no tram coming their way at the moment, Aunt Edie and Jimmy spotted a little open cart approaching. It was drawn by a sleek brown pony, and was painted in decorative blue and gold. At the reins sat a pearly king, his cap, jacket and trousers sparkling in the sunshine with a myriad of pearl buttons. He saw Aunt Edie.

'Whoa there, Poppy,' he said to his pony, and pulled up beside the kerb. 'Watcher, Edie, me peach, where yer goin'?'

'I'm just standin' still at the moment, waitin' for a tram 'ome,' said Aunt Edie. 'Had a do this mornin', 'ave you, Joe?'

Joe Gosling's broad and ruddy face spread in a large grin. In the back of his cart sat his daughter, fourteen-year-old Hetty, holding a bunch of flowers. 'Just a bit of a do for some Old Kent Road kids,' he said, 'an' makin' sure all of 'em won a prize. Got time orf from me work.' He was a park attendant, employed by the local council. 'Well, good cause, yer know, Edie. An' they give 'Etty a bunch o' flowers, which she's rapturous about, ain't yer, 'Etty?'

Hetty didn't reply. She was staring woodenly at Jimmy.

'Sweet girl, your Hetty,' said Aunt Edie drily.

'Ain't she just?' said Joe. ''Ere, 'op up, Edie, and I'll ride yer 'ome. 'Oo's yer young man there?'

'Well, 'e's not my young man,' said Aunt Edie. 'Worse luck,' she added, and laughed. 'He's Jimmy, my nephew.'

'Well, good on yer, Jimmy, you 'op up too, along side of 'Etty,' said Joe, 'and I'll cart both of yer to Camberwell. It's yer lucky day, me lad, yer'll like 'Etty.'

Jimmy had reservations about that. But he placed the shopping bag aboard, and while Aunt Edie climbed up to sit beside Joe, he swung himself into the cart by using a wheel spoke as leverage. He sat down on the narrow board seat opposite Hetty. She was in white. Her hat, frock, shoes and stockings were all white, and she looked like a kind of angelic Alice in Wonderland, except that she didn't seem very taken with Wonderland. Joe clucked at Poppy, the pony, and the cart started to run.

'Nice day,' said Jimmy to Hetty. She stared sullenly at him. 'If you like it hot. How'd you feel about August?'

'Mind yer own bleedin' business,' said Alice in Wonderland.

'Well, I thought I'd ask,' said Jimmy amiably.

'No-one asked yer to ask.'

'All right, I'll shut up, shall I?'

'What's yer name?'

'No idea,' said Jimmy who could always play someone else's game.

'Yer bloomin' daft,' said Hetty.

'Well, nobody's perfect,' said Jimmy. 'We've all got some complaint.'

Hetty sniffed and gave up. Joe was talking to Aunt Edie. Jimmy listened.

'Yer a lively one, you are, Edie. Lively as a gel, you always was, and yer still that way. Pearly queen of South Camberwell, you are, and yer got 'igh-falutin' legs.'

'High what?' said Aunt Edie, large hat dancing to the trotting rhythm of the pony.

'I'm speakin' frank of them fancy pins o' yourn,' said Joe.

'Well, you watch I don't pickle that fancy tongue of yours,' said Aunt Edie.

Joe grinned, cracked a playful whip and lightly tweaked the reins. The trotting pony overtook a slow-moving cart piled high with sacks of dry-smelling wheat for a flour mill. They ran along the tram track for a brief while before rejoining the stream of Saturday traffic. They passed two little girls trundling their iron hoops over the pavement. A tram clanged loudly past the cart. It had no effect on the pony.

'Where was I?' asked Joe, putting his whip into its rest.

'Doin' some fancy talk,' said Aunt Edie.

'I tell yer, love, I dunno when you wasn't a real lively sort, and a knockout into the bargain,' said Joe. ''Specially doin' yer turns at our concerts. I seen other knockouts in me day, but I never seen—'

'In case you don't know, Joe Gosling,' said Aunt Edie, 'that's my knee you've got 'old of.'

'Is it?' said Joe. 'Well, I never, so it is. Funny, I never knew me 'and get 'old of a knee before, not down the old Walworth Road.' He took it away. The little cart slowed in thickening traffic. 'Yer know, Edie, since me reg'lar pearly partner, Ma Rawlins, passed on, God rest 'er, I been thinkin' about someone to take 'er place. Someone with an 'eart of gold, just like she 'ad. And could she warble, she was still pipin' away at concerts for kids when she was gone sixty. "I've Got A Lovely Bunch Of Coconuts", that was 'er fav'rite.'

'I know,' said Aunt Edie.

''Ad the figure to go with it, she did,' said Joe.

'Don't look at me,' said Aunt Edie.

'Good old pearly queen, Ma Rawlins was,' reminisced Joe, 'always takin' sweets to orphanage kids, and doin' a knees-up by request. So I been thinkin', Edie, you still bein' a single lady and me bein' a widower, we'd make a rollickin' good team. You can sing like a bird, and my voice ain't one that's 'ad rotten termaters chucked at it yet. So what d'yer think, old gel?'

'I think that's my knee you've got 'old of again,' said Aunt Edie.

'Well, blind me, so it is,' said Joe. 'I dunno what's come

over it today, it must 'ave a temperature or something.' He removed his wayward hand again. In the back of the cart, Jimmy hid a grin and Hetty stared moodily at her flowers. 'I'm embarrassed at the way it's playin' up.'

'Well, talk to it, then,' said Aunt Edie, 'or something sharp will come along and chop it off.'

Joe bawled with laughter. 'You're a card, you are, Edie,' he said.

Jimmy, naturally friendly, tried again with Hetty. 'Are you a pearly?' he asked.

'Am I what?'

'Pearly princess?'

'Me?' Hetty looked disgusted. 'Course I'm not. I'm goin' on the stage, I am.'

'As a comic, tellin' funny jokes?' said Jimmy.

'Doin' what?' said Hetty

'Well, I can see you're a laugh a minute.'

'You daft or something?'

It was Jimmy's turn to give up.

Joe, trying to win Aunt Edie over as they approached Camberwell Green, said, 'You can take yer time considerin' me proposition, yer know, I ain't goin' to rush yer.'

'Well, I can tell you, Joe, I'm not thinkin' about that kind of commitment,' said Aunt Edie.

'Proud and 'andsome, with a mind of yer own, that's what you are, Edie,' said Joe. 'Listen, could yer think about doin' a turn at a concert we're givin' next Saturday week for kids and their parents in St Mark's church 'all? You can choose yer own songs.'

'I'm not sure I'll 'ave time.'

'You can find time, Edie, you got a big 'eart,' said Joe. 'I remember you doin' a turn at the old joanner at me weddin' to Chloe. Yer know, it's still 'ard to believe she's gorn. I been a widower nigh on two year now.' He did more reminiscing as he headed his pony towards Camberwell Grove.

In the back, wooden-faced Hetty said, ''Oo d'yer think you're lookin' at?'

'Can't help meself, can I?' said Jimmy. 'You're sittin' over there and I'm sittin' over here. Does it hurt?'

'I don't know I like it.'

'Well, try fallin' out,' said Jimmy.

'What d'yer mean, fallin' out?'

'Out of the cart.'

'What, and 'it me 'ead on the road?'

'You could try it,' said Jimmy, 'it might not hurt as much as bein' looked at.'

'Yer bleedin' potty,' said the lovable little lady who was going on the stage.

'Whoa there,' said Joe, and the cart came to a halt outside Aunt Edie's flat in Camberwell Grove.

'Thanks for the ride, Joe,' she said, 'and if you'd let go of me knee again, I'll get down.'

'Can't 'ardly believe it, can yer?' said Joe. 'Me mitt's doin' it again. I'll 'ave to take it to the doctor's.'

'Get 'im to give it an operation,' said Aunt Edie, and alighted. Jimmy swung himself down, and lifted the shopping bag out of the cart. He thanked Joe.

'Pleasure,' said Joe, grinning, gleaming and sparkling in his pearlies. 'Keep in touch, Edie, eh?'

'If I've got time,' said Aunt Edie. Joe blew her a kiss and set off again. Jimmy thought he'd better give Hetty a wave, and did. Hetty stuck her tongue out and departed from his life.

'Just as well she's not a pearly princess,' he said, 'or I'd lose me faith in them.'

'Yes, a bit of a brat,' said Aunt Edie. 'Spoiled rotten. Well, let's go up, lovey.'

Camberwell Grove had quite a superior look. Aunt Edie rented the top floor of one of the terraced houses, and enjoyed the privacy of what was a self-contained flat. Jimmy and his sisters knew it well, for Aunt Edie often invited them to Sunday tea. Jimmy liked the bright look of her living-room. She went in for colourful cushions. He meandered about the room while she packed some things in her bedroom. A framed photograph on the mantelshelf was familiar to him. It was of the young man to whom she'd been engaged. Jimmy could never help feeling sorry for him, he'd really missed out. Aunt Edie would have made him a happy bloke.

She did not take long to pack a case, she could be brisk and quick. His mum had got to the stage of being a bit vague about everything except the Lord.

''Ere we are, Jimmy.'

'I'll take the case,' said Jimmy.

'And me the shoppin' bag?' she smiled.

'Good idea,' he said. 'What made you ask me to come with you?'

'What a question,' said Aunt Edie.

'I thought I'd ask.'

'Well, you 'appen to be me fav'rite young man, and I like 'aving a young man like you as an escort.'

'I think I'll come to that concert Joe Gosling mentioned,' said Jimmy, 'you're bound to help out and it might give me a chance to see you doin' a knees-up.'

'You saucebox,' said Aunt Edie. 'I suppose you realize I'm old enough to be your mother?'

'Can't help that, Aunt Edie, I still think you've got good legs.'

'Cheeky monkey,' said Aunt Edie, but laughed.

'I expect Dad'll want to come as well,' said Jimmy, 'you're not old enough to be his mother.'

Aunt Edie actually turned a little pink. 'Well, I don't know,' she said, 'I'll 'ave to watch you, young man. Out you go before you get your ears boxed.' But she was laughing again as she went down the stairs with him.

By the time they got back, Dad and the girls had made their own contribution to the day. The kitchen and scullery had been swept and tidied up, and all the beds made. And Dad had cleaned the kitchen windows. The oil-cloth that covered the kitchen table shone like new, except for cracked corners. The sandwiches were ready, and Dad put the kettle on to make a pot of tea. Aunt Edie, who had bought sausages from the butcher, said she'd do bangers and mash for supper, with fried tomatoes and fried onions, and a banana custard to follow. And for tomorrow's Sunday dinner, she was going to roast a leg of mutton and bake an apple pie.

'Crikey, apple pie wiv custard?' asked Betsy, eyes shining.

'Auntie, you really goin' to do all that?' asked Patsy.

'All that isn't much, lovey,' said Aunt Edie, 'and we've got to eat. Now let's all sit down and 'ave these sandwiches with the pot of tea your dad's makin'. I don't suppose 'e'll take all day.'

From the scullery, where he was pouring boiling water into the teapot, Dad made his response. 'Any moment now, Edie.'

'That's a clever boy,' said Aunt Edie, which made Dad grin. 'Pass the sandwiches round, Jimmy.' Aunt Edie had already decided on how she would approach these weekends. A little authority combined with fuss and affection. But no gushing. She didn't want Dad to think this was just a whim of hers, or Betsy and Patsy to feel it was only Dad who cared for them. Girls their age needed a mum as well as a dad. Or someone who could be a mum.

Dad brought the pot of tea in and sat down. He helped himself to a sandwich.

'Did I 'ear there's goin' to be bangers and mash, banana custard, roast leg of mutton and apple pie?' he asked. 'We'll all get fat.'

'You will if you eat all that lot at once,' said Aunt Edie. 'Shall I be mum? Yes, I might as well.' She poured the tea.

'Patsy's gettin' a bit fat,' said Betsy.

'Me?' said Patsy indignantly.

'I don't see she is, Betsy,' said Aunt Edie.

'Well, she is a little bit,' said Betsy, 'only I best not say where, 'ad I, Dad?'

'Oh, you little 'orror,' cried Patsy. She might have been only thirteen, but she was already budding. Secretly, she was proud, of course. It made her feel she wouldn't take long to be a woman. Like Gladys Cooper, she hoped. Gladys Cooper, a famous actress, was ever so attractive, and during the war soldiers in the trenches asked for picture postcards of her to be sent to them. All the same, a girl didn't want any sister making remarks. 'You Betsy, 'ow would you like me to pull all your 'air out?'

'But I only said a little bit fat,' protested Betsy. 'Didn't I, Dad?' Betsy was always appealing to her dad whenever she needed support.

'Well, I can't tell a lie,' said Dad, 'you did only say a little bit.'

'Point is,' said Jimmy, 'is it true?'

'Don't you start,' said Patsy.

'All right,' said Jimmy affably, 'I'll stay in the dark.'

'Good idea, Jimmy, it's safer,' said Dad. 'Did I ever tell you about the time when me old battalion was in a place called Kut? 'Orrible fly-blown dump, believe me. Didn't 'alf make the old battalion thirsty. The sergeant-major said if 'e caught anybody swipin' the sergeants' beer rations, he'd hang 'em from a coconut tree. We still did a bit of needful swipin', though, through Private Gough bein' able to pick a padlock. Did it at night. Safer in the dark, yer see. I mean, who wants to end up hanging from a coconut tree in a place like Kut?'

'Oh, you're lovely and daft, Dad,' said Patsy. 'Dad's goin' to try doin' some ironing this afternoon, Aunt Edie.'

''E's what?' said Aunt Edie.

'I'll give it a go,' said Dad.

'You won't,' said Aunt Edie.

'Well, durin' me soldiering days—'

'Your soldiering days are over,' said Aunt Edie, 'for which we're all thankful. Never mind that old sergeant-major of yours won't lie down, you're not doin' any ironing. Is it all that stuff out there on the line?'

'Yes, it's what we took to the Bagwash, Aunt Edie,' said Patsy.

'It's a lot of ironing,' said Dad.

'I'll do it,' said Aunt Edie.

'I'll 'elp,' said Patsy.

'No, you and Betsy 'ave got friends you like to go out with Saturday afternoons,' said Aunt Edie. 'Jimmy can help, 'e can fold things and 'e knows where to put them away.'

'Oh, no, don't let 'im,' begged Betsy, ''e'll put apple cores in our fings.'

'Oh, yer silly, that was years ago,' said Patsy.

'Yes, but 'e's grinnin',' said Betsy.

'I'll watch 'im, Betsy,' said Aunt Edie.

'You're a friend in need, you are, Edie,' said Dad.

'I'll share Betsy's room with 'er tonight,' said Aunt Edie.

'All right,' said Dad, 'but no pillow fights, you'll only get licked. Our pickle's dynamite at pillow fights. 'Ere, how about a bus ride to Hyde Park on Bank Holiday Monday? Years since I've been to Hyde Park. Me and Maudie used to go there some Sundays after we were married, and listen to the band. Bound to be a band there on Bank Holiday.'

'D'you fancy that, Aunt Edie?' asked Jimmy.

'Love it,' said Aunt Edie.

'Well, we're not leavin' your aunt out, are we, Betsy?' said Dad. 'It's a fam'ly outin', and your Aunt Edie's fam'ly, specially at weekends. I've just heard she's goin' to do the ironing as well. What a relief.'

'We like Aunt Edie, don't we, Dad?' said Betsy.

'You bet,' said Dad.

And Jimmy thought there was a faint little flush of pleasure on Aunt Edie's face.

CHAPTER FIVE

Father Peter led his troops into Christian Street, White-chapel, into the misnamed heart of the Devil's domain, as befitted the League's guiding light. Here dwelt the drunks and the slatterns, the pickpockets and fly-boys, the striving and the still hopeful. And the ragamuffin kids: unwashed kids, hungry kids, artful kids, verminous kids, nice kids and unholy terrors. Doors stood open, and at the doors stood wives, mothers and the slatterns. The flat-fronted houses looked grimy in the humid sunlight. Chimneys smoked in desultory and limp fashion, as if the kitchen fires were full of garbage reluctant to burn. Even in August some families needed to light their fires for cooking, if they had anything to cook, since pennies for gas meters were better spent on food.

Here and there, a smell of stale cabbage pervaded the air. And the air itself seemed exhausted in its eternal battle with soot and smoke. If the war had brought extra jobs, and also jobs for women, those jobs were gone now, and privation stalked Whitechapel and the rest of the East End. Every London slum was tired out and listless, the people waiting in sour resignation for Lloyd George's promise of a brave new world to come to nothing. Only the kids injected a note of vitality. Some kids, that is. They dashed and darted about, playing their street games or kicking a ball made of rolled rags tied up. The listless ones sat on the edge of the pavements, bare feet in the gutters, looking on with the blank stares of the hungry.

Father Peter, in private life Montgomery Wilberforce, was extraordinarily tall. He was also gaunt and cadaverous, and as dark as the Semitic people of the Holy Land. He wore a top hat of matt black, a black cloak lined with dark grey silk, a black frock coat and black tapering trousers. He seemed in all these garments to feel nothing of the heat. His wide shoulders were straight, his tallness majestic. His fervent soul was full of sorrow for the world and its sinfulness. It was also at times full of God's thunder and lightning. His sorrow showed in his expression, and when there was cause, the thunder and lightning glittered in his dark deep-set eyes. He was the self-ordained minister of the League of Repenters. He had taken up this ministry in the belief that God had called him to it, and had anointed himself in the further belief that this sanctified him according to God's command. His followers, mostly highly religious women, had great faith in him.

Some such women – four precisely – followed him into Christian Street. Mother was there, Mother Mary. Father Peter, in anointing her, had sprinkled a little of the contents of a bottle of bay rum over her head. He had holified the bay rum by blessing it.

Accompanying Mother Mary were Mother Joan, Mother Verity and Mother Ruth. Mother Joan was a fine figure of a woman from Berkshire and had known the humiliation of being thrown by her horse when it refused a high hedge. She fell heavily. There ensued a blinding light and then blackness. When she came to she realized the blinding light had signified a visitation from God. She gave up her horses, her home, her husband and his wealth, and came to London in search of a cause and a leader. Her husband told friends he couldn't do anything with her, her brains had taken a hammering, poor old girl. In London, she found the League of Repenters and its minister, Father Peter, commandingly tall and inspiring. Was the League Roman Catholic? She hoped not. Good plain commonsense Christianity at war with the Devil, that was what she was looking for.

'We are of no denomination,' said Father Peter. 'We are associated with the Lord's prophets and their sisterly brethren. With us,' he declared, 'ye shall be led to righteousness, and ye shall bring that righteousness to sinners.'

'Oh, splendid,' said Mrs Blythe-Huntingdon of Berkshire. 'Righteousness and sinners are just what I'm looking for.' She was forthwith anointed to become Mother Joan.

Mother Verity and Mother Ruth could not claim to have owned horses or wealthy husbands. They were genteel ladies and unmarried, and what they could claim, therefore, were modest means and purity.

Bringing up the rear of the little procession was Father Luke, the first man to be received into the League. Plump and cheerful, he looked not unlike a Friar Tuck. He, too, wore a black top hat, a black frock coat and black trousers. Formerly, he had been Fred Huggett of Hackney, and had been on reverent terms with the Lord all his life. He had taken God's words to work with him, at a jam factory, and had brought them home with him. The walls of his home were adorned with them in capital letters: BY YOUR DEEDS THE LORD SHALL KNOW YE. And so on. In the end, his wife chucked them all out, and him as well. He went to his church and prayed. The Lord answered:

'Fred Huggett, take up thy bed and walk.' He walked, with a tied-up mattress on his back, and met Father Peter, who received him into the League and anointed him as Father Luke. Fred was good at first-aid. He had no money, but nor did several other men and women who had been received into the League. Father Peter, its guiding light, was also its provider of funds and sustenance. He had investments. But he bought no worldly goods.

Down Christian Street he led his Repenters. The Mothers all carried banners bearing the words, REPENT YE SINNERS. Mother Mary was pleased with her banner, it was shining and pristine. She had lost the one she'd carried into battle yesterday, dropping it while fleeing from a mob and a barrage of blasphemies. She had never heard anything more shocking, and that after some awful women had tried to pull her costume off her. Only Mother Verity had been with her. Perhaps they should not have entered the Devil's kitchen on their own, but Father Peter, responding to their enthusiasm, said, 'Go ye, my sisters, seek out the sinners, use the words of God to chastise them and then offer them the joy of repentance.' But the sinners of Whitechapel wouldn't listen. Their language had been something dreadful, and hands had reached to claw at garments. She was lucky she had only lost buttons.

How brave Sister Verity had been, for a tall man, laughing at her, had actually seized her and kissed her. It was hardly believable. Mother Verity flushed deeply at the outrage, but withstood the shock bravely. Then even more bravely she offered the other cheek, suffering another dreadful kiss on her lips. And the Devil's laughing disciple said to her, 'Well, I'll say this much, you're not a complainin' woman, and that's a welcome change in these parts.' Oh, poor Mother Verity, she suffered a third wicked assault on her lips, and she such a ladylike Repenter too. But she fled when a second outrageous man attempted to seize her. Mother Mary, escaping other clawing hands, fled with her. Father Peter boomed with wrath on being told what had befallen them. God's thunder rolled and lightning flashed. It was most awe-inspiring. He vowed he himself would lead a return to Whitechapel on the morrow. He asked for volunteers, and was full of reverent admiration for Mother Mary and Mother Verity when they declared themselves ready to face up to iniquity again.

There he was, a figure of vengefulness but also of compassion, combining the wrath of God with God's willingness to forgive. Mother Verity, steeling herself, hoped she would be afforded the opportunity of persuading her assailant to repent, if he appeared.

Behind them, Father Luke was wheeling a barrow, on which was a huge gleaming urn full of hot soup. Mountains of bread rolls surrounded the urn. The food had been Mother Joan's idea. She was a frank, hearty and practical Repenter.

'Give 'em vittles,' she'd said, 'give 'em fodder. They won't jump the Lord's fences if we don't feed 'em their oats. Can't help a lame dog over a stile without giving it a lift up, you know. Can't chuck it over willy-nilly, it won't like that, it'll bite your hand off. Judging by what happened to Mary and Verity—'

'Mother Mary, Mother Verity,' corrected Father Peter, rolling his r's.

'Oh, deepest apologies, naturally,' said Mother Joan, 'but judging by what happened to them, I'd say that if we don't profit by example, we could all get it in the neck. So could the Lord. In a manner of speaking, of course. So give 'em vittles, Father, give 'em fodder.'

'How compassionate,' said Father Peter.

'Yes, bleedin' good idea,' said Father Luke. Not surprisingly, Father Peter frowned on the comment. 'Beg yer pardon, Father, for me 'Ackney French, but I get carried away sometimes. Will yer grant me penitence?'

'It is done,' said Father Peter, making a forgiving gesture. 'And in penitence, Father, see to the provision of suitable food.'

So Father Luke, in penitence, took up the labour of making the soup, buying the bread rolls and wheeling the barrow.

In Christian Street, the gossiping women turned their heads. Kids at play stopped their play. Seated kids stared. A tousle-haired urchin darted into his parents' house and bawled.

'Dad, they're 'ere again!'

'Eh? What? 'Oo's 'ere?' asked Henry Mullins.

'Them barmy old gels wiv banners, only there's more this time.'

'What, on a Saturday afternoon an' me with me feet up? I'll bleedin' show 'em. Where's me chopper? 'Ere, Nobby, wait. Get the kids, an' see that yer keep yer mince pies skinned for the rozzers, we don't want no flat-feet spoilin' the party. Where's yer mum? Tell 'er I'll 'elp get 'er a new dress or costume if it's our lucky day. All right, scarper, me lad.'

The urchin scarpered. He collected kids. Some ran to one end of the street, some to the other, to watch for coppers. Father Peter, advancing on long dignified legs, came to a halt midway down the street. His followers halted with him, their banners a gentle flutter of blue and gold against the grimy background. A window went up. A woman's voice was heard.

'Oh, gawd blimey, look 'oo's 'ere if it ain't old black Nick hisself and 'is fancy doxies. 'Ere, what's in that barrer? 'Ere, Mrs Burns down there, they got bleedin' bread in that barrer!'

Women in shabby blouses and skirts for the most part began to converge on the Repenters and the barrow from

73

both sides of the street, kids on their heels.

'Peace be with you,' boomed Father Peter, holding up a restraining hand. 'We are here to comfort you, to guide you, and to bring you to salvation by way of repentance. As for all those who are hungered, let them come forth.'

'With soup bowls!' cried Mother Ruth, gentle voice ringing bravely.

'Eat and repent!' cried Mother Mary.

'No, not yet, sister,' said Mother Verity. 'Father Peter first wishes to address them, to beg them to deliver themselves from the wickedness of Satan.'

'Oh, yes, he's such a good man of God and addresses people so dignified,' said Mother Mary, while Mother Verity glanced bravely around to see if that outrageous sinner of yesterday was daring to show himself. Father Peter was beckoning with both hands, encouraging all the people of Christian Street to come and listen to the word of God.

Mother Joan, noting the poverty-stricken look of the women and kids, said briskly, 'I'd say let 'em get to the fodder to start with. Stomachs first, souls after. It always worked splendidly with my husband George.'

The crowd was thickening, men joining it, and every hungry eye was on the barrow. Father Peter, his tall figure and ascetic features impressive, addressed the multitude. 'Welcome, children of God,' he boomed. 'Hear His word and know that in His mercy the wickedness shown here yesterday shall be forgiven. His word surpasses all others, as does His wrath, yet all who ask forgiveness of Him shall receive it. Who among ye desire to repent of yesterday's deeds?'

'Excuse me, guv,' said the man called Henry Mullins, standing forward in his shirt, trousers and braces, 'but 'oo the bleedin' 'ell are you?'

Father Peter replied, 'I am the minister of the League of—'

'Mum, Mum, look at all them bread rolls!' yelled a girl.

The hungry, setting aside restraint, began to push and surge. Father Luke, in charge of dispensing the soup and bread, looked concerned. ''Ere, 'old up now,' he said, 'run an' fetch yer soup bowls first, then line up and I'll be pleased to serve yer some of the Lord's bounty. Blessed are the poor, remember, as long as they don't kick me barrer over.'

'Drop dead, yer silly old bugger,' said a woman. 'Go on, kids, 'elp yerselves.'

Kids pushed, kicked, shoved, reached and snatched.

'Oh, dear,' said Mother Ruth.

'Such nasty language,' said Mother Mary.

'Oh, heavens,' said Mother Verity faintly, for the tall laughing man had appeared. He was on the edge of the crowd, and not hiding his amusement.

Father Peter raised both hands, his arms spreading his cloak. 'Behold the hungered, Lord,' he boomed. 'Place thy hand upon them that they may come peacefully to sustenance.'

'It's just a bit o' bread, guv,' said Henry Mullins. 'There y'ar, look, it couldn't 'ave been much, it's all gorn now.' The mountains of rolls had vanished, much to Father Luke's consternation. The soup urn had a lonely look. Kids were sinking their teeth into the crusty rolls. Mother Mary didn't know whether to be sympathetic or disapproving. She elected for just a little disapproval.

'I wouldn't like to think gluttony's spreadin',' she said.

Father Luke said in a forlorn way, 'Eatin' all that bread up when they ain't 'ad no soup yet.'

The crowd was derisive, waiting for the real palaver to begin, for Henry Mullins to give the word. Henry Mullins was top dog in Christian Street. His fists and his boots had put him there.

'All right, stand back,' he said, his trousers slack, his braces dangling and his shirt sleeves rolled up. 'Stand back, I said.' People still pushed a bit. Every woman wanted to be the first to help herself to the clothes of the female Repenters. 'Now, guv,' said Henry Mullins, 'could yer confide exactly what yer offerin'?'

'Salvation, sir, and with it the Lord's promise that ye shall enter the kingdom of heaven,' said Father Peter sonorously.

'Kind of yer, guv, but we've 'ad some of that. But did I 'ear someone mention soup?'

'You did, sir.'

'Well, we'll be gratified to 'ave that, guv.'

'That's better,' said Mother Mary, more confident today because Father Peter was with them. 'I don't like to 'ear you talkin' unpleasant. I said to my 'usband several times, I said we're all sinners, but we've all got 'ope if we repent.'

'Praise the Lord,' said Mother Joan heartily.

'Praise Him,' said Mother Verity fervently, half an eye on the smiling man while she wondered how she should begin to chastise him. Perhaps Father Peter would give her a lead.

'Yus, and praise yer reverences,' said Henry Mullins, 'we'll 'ave the soup. Cop 'old, Barney, an' you give 'im an 'and, Bill.'

Two men shouldered their way through to the barrow and lifted the heavy urn from it.

''Ere now, wait a minute,' said Father Luke, plump frame quivering. 'Not the urn, you can't take the urn.'

'Now leave orf, mate,' said the man Bill, ''ow can we take the soup what's just been offered by 'is worship if we don't take the urn as well? Soup slips through yer

76

fingers, yer know. Right, orf we go, Barney.'

'Worth a packet, the urn,' said Barney.

'Nickel-plated, I reckon,' said Bill, 'might fetch a quid or two from Solly. Orf we go, then.'

They carried the urn away, with kids running in their wake and Father Peter intoning denunciation of the sin of thievery.

'Damned daylight robbery,' said Mother Joan. 'Still, can't be helped, and it's a good cause. Shall we now pray with you, Father Peter, for the Lord to bring these people to righteousness?'

Father Peter raised his hands again, becoming a dark figure of towering majesty. 'My friends,' he boomed, 'lest ye fall for ever into the ways of Satan, join with us in prayer that ye may be delivered from him. Our Father, which art in heaven—'

'Excuse me, guv, but we've 'ad some of that as well,' said Henry Mullins. ''Ow about that watch an' chain of yourn, could yer consider offerin' us that, say, an' some of the ladies' duds?'

'Duds?' said Father Peter.

'Clobber, guv.'

'I fail—'

'Togs, guv.'

'Clothes?' Father Peter's long gaunt body, sombrely clad, seemed to lengthen and widen and to become a protective shield. 'I believe, sir, that yesterday you made a deplorable attempt to divest Mother Mary of hers, did you not?'

'Not me, guv, I ain't divested no lady in all me life. Female clobber's a mystery to me, always 'as been, always will be. 'Ere, did yer say Mother Mary, guv?'

'This lady is Mother Mary,' said Father Peter, reverently pointing her out. 'She is an anointed sister of the League of Repenters.'

Old women cackled. Men grinned. The tall man, still on the outside edge of the crowd, smiled, his eyes on Mother Verity. Mother Verity trembled.

'Well, I'm blowed,' said Henry Mullins, 'Mother Mary, eh? Well, she's got to be charitable, ain't she? It's like this, guv, me old woman's got 'er poor aunt's funeral comin' orf on Tuesday, an' she ain't got a bit of decent black to wear. Could Mother Mary offer? That costume she's wearin' would fit me old woman a treat.'

'Oh, what a digustin' man,' said Mother Mary, moving closer to Father Peter, her guiding light and shield.

Within Father Peter the thunder was beginning to roll. 'Shall that which belongs to another be taken from her except by her consent?' he asked.

'Just 'er clobber, yer lordship,' said Henry Mullins, 'that's all I'm askin'.'

Women were beginning to flex covetous fingers. The grins on men's faces grew broader. Mother Verity trembled again, for the tall man had edged nearer to her. Courageously, she drew herself up, and her banner grew rigid and unwavering. Mother Ruth emitted a sudden little scream. An urchin's fingers were in her handbag. Mother Joan boxed his ears. He yelped and his fingers came out, clutching a handkerchief. Mother Joan took it from him.

''Ere, you 'it me,' he said. 'Mum – Mum – she 'it me.'

'You were smitten by the hand of the Lord, my boy,' boomed Father Peter. Again he addressed himself to the multitude. The multitude wore a collective look of happy anticipation. The pickpockets were blowing on their fingers. 'My good people, what shall it profit parents if they—'

'Excuse me again, guv,' said Henry Mullins, 'but could yer kindly ask Mother Mary there if she'd consent to donatin' 'er costume immediate? Only we ain't got all day, and it's 'ot out 'ere.'

'Here, you keep away from me, you sinful brute,' said Mother Mary. 'Oh, where's me umbrella?' She had left it at the Bloomsbury headquarters, having decided not to carry that and her banner and handbag as well.

''Ere, 'Enry,' shouted a woman, 'can I 'ave that other lady's outfit?' She pointed at Mother Joan, who was wearing a stylish grey silk blouse and long dark grey skirt, with a black-banded straw boater.

'Bloody cheek,' said Mother Joan.

'I'll 'ave 'ers,' said another woman, pointing at Mother Ruth's sombre grey dress.

'And I ain't goin' to say no to what she's got,' said one more woman, eyes on Mother Verity's dark grey costume.

'You all askin' for their titfers as well?' enquired Henry Mullins, and a ripple surged through pressing bodies.

'Not 'arf, 'Enry,' said his wife, 'be bleedin' posh on Sundays, they would.'

'Smite them, Father Peter, smite them with the word of God,' said Mother Mary.

Father Peter thundered at the multitude, 'Shall ye speak of sin and not know the wrath of God?'

'Course not, guv, course we know 'Is wrath,' said Henry Mullins, 'all our bleedin' 'ouses are near to fallin' down, an' we got an old soldier with a wooden peg on account of God smitin' 'is leg orf on the Somme. Now I'm askin' yer nice, will yer ladies offer their togs or not?'

'Ye gods,' breathed Mother Joan, 'it's war. Chests out, sisters, straighten your backs, prepare to repel boarders, the Lord is with us.'

'And I'm right be'ind yer, ladies,' declared Father Luke.

'Let us pray,' intoned Father Peter. 'Lord, look down

on these thy servants and on these suffering and misguided sinners. Give us strength that we may stand against them, and give us wisdom that we may teach them how to deliver themselves from Satan.'

'Yer playin' about, guv, that's what you're doin',' said Henry Mullins, shaking his head, 'an' yer time's up. All right, gels, in yer go and start 'elping yerselves to what these ladies is refusin' to give yer. But don't tear nothing, an' leave 'em their petticoats, we don't want 'em 'aving to walk 'ome embarrassed. Yus, all right, Effie, you can 'ave the plump gent's trousers for yer old man, if yer want. Right, in yer go.'

Yelling, and eager with a desire to dispossess, women rushed in on the Repenters.

'Father Peter!' cried Mother Mary, aghast as the minister sank to his knees and prayed, leaving her unshielded. The other ladies shrieked. Father Luke pedalled backwards in the direction of Whitechapel's parish church and fell over the barrow. Clawing hands reached for his trousers. Mother Joan struck out with her banner. Mother Ruth dropped hers and did all she could to protect her hat and dress. Mother Verity blushed crimson as covetous hands lifted her skirt and pulled on it.

'Oh, help!' she gasped.

'Oh, what 'eathens!' cried Mother Mary, and smote with her banner.

'Bloody female hooligans, I call 'em,' declared Mother Joan. 'Forgive me, Lord,' she added, and knocked two slatterns off their feet with her banner.

Strong hands delivered Mother Verity from her tormentors, pulling her free from the mêlée and swinging her off her feet to safety. The tall man, in a cap, blue jersey and khaki trousers, gave her a chuckling smile of pleasure. 'Well, if you ain't me sweetheart of yesterday,' he said.

'Help!' gasped Mother Verity.

'Lord, hear thy servant,' intoned Father Peter.

'Hear me, Lord,' gasped Mother Verity, for her deliverer had his eyes on her lips.

'Come back for more, is that a fact?' said the tall man, his rugged masculinity dreadfully menacing. 'Well, you're a sweet surprise and a pretty one.' He wrapped his arms around her. Her banner was gone, her purity defenceless. He kissed her, unmercifully. She flushed and shuddered.

Mother Mary's umbrage was total. She was surrounded by harridans, all of them intent on wresting her costume from her.

'Oh, you wicked women, I'll give you something – oh, if I only 'ad me umbrella. Leave go, d'you 'ear? Oh, I never did know more disgustin' sinning – take that – leave go – oh, dear Lord, I can't 'ardly believe this.'

Mother Verity, dreadfully beset, nevertheless offered the other cheek, and the laughing man kissed her again, such was his indifference to the Lord and his affinity with Satan. She tried to swoon, feeling she must, but nothing happened, except another kiss, and strange dreadful weakness.

Mother Joan was dealing blow after blow. Mother Ruth was clinging on to everything she was wearing. The clawing, pulling and milling were accompanied by shrieks of fiendish laughter. Father Luke had lost his trousers. Father Peter, losing his top hat to a whisking hand, leapt up from his knees and raised both arms to the heavens. His black cloak lifted and spread, and he looked like a dark avenging bird of prey, his great mane of black hair peppered with grey. Thunder rolled up from his chest, and lightning flashes glittered in his eyes. With a roar, he turned on the harridans and flew at them, and the harridans were beset with physical chastisement.

Watching men howled with laughter. On the other hand, one man said to another, 'Gawd bleedin' blimey, Curly, 'e's beltin' yer missus black an' blue.'

'I'd 'elp 'er, only I got a bone in me leg,' said Curly, bald as a peeled potato, 'an' besides, she's been beltin' me for a month.'

Poor Mother Verity, dreadfully flushed and dreadfully outraged, looked up into the face of her smiling tormentor. 'Do your worst, sir, I shall still pray to God to forgive you.' He roared with laughter.

Kids came running from the junction with Commercial Road. 'Rozzers! Flatties!'

Magically, the crowd melted away. The harridans retreated and ran, disappearing into their houses, kids pelting after them. The smiling man strolled away from Mother Verity and entered a house a little farther down the street.

Father Peter's thunder subsided and his heaving chest took a turn for the better. Father Luke, minus his trousers and top hat, staggered to his feet, his long woollen pants dusty and wrinkled. Mother Mary pulled her skirt up from around her ankles. Mother Ruth pushed her dress down. Mother Joan looked down at herself. Her white silk petticoat shimmered.

'Mother Joan, heavens above!' exclaimed Father Peter.

'Hell below, if you ask me, Father,' said Mother Joan. 'Lost my bloody skirt. Can't be helped, small price to pay in the service of the Lord, and I fancy I landed a few telling blows on His behalf.'

'She was 'eroic, Father,' said Mother Mary, 'and so were you, you rose up and smote the 'eathens something godly.'

'The chastisement of the wicked is in our hands through the Lord,' said Father Peter.

'Oh, dear, but poor Father Luke, to have lost his trousers,' said Mother Ruth.

'I grant yer, Mother Ruth, I ain't far short of feelin' uncomfortable about it,' said Father Luke. 'I've also got a hurtful bump on me head. But I'm bearin' in mind the sufferin' need these poor people 'ave for someone else's trousers an' Mother Joan's skirt. Lord above, where've they all gone to?'

The street on either side of the group was empty, except for a few kids. At the junction with Commercial Road stood two uniformed constables, surveying Christian Street and its suspicious air of quiet. Mother Verity rejoined her sister Repenters.

'You saw?' she said. 'What can I say?'

'We all suffered for you, sister,' said Father Peter compassionately.

'I was a bit 'arassed myself,' said Father Luke, 'but the glimpse I 'ad of your ordeal, Mother Verity, told me I was gettin' off light. Father Peter, we've got wickedness goin' on here all right. The Lord's mercy'll be 'ard for this lot to come by.'

'I've never seen such dreadful be'aviour,' said Mother Mary, 'and after yesterday too. Who'd 'ave thought Mother Verity would suffer again?'

'Scoundrel ought to be horse-whipped,' said Mother Joan.

'Vengeance shall be mine, said the Lord,' boomed Father Peter.

The uniformed constables were still surveying the street, and this gave Mother Verity the courage to say, 'Father Peter, something must be done for Father Luke and Mother Joan. They can't possibly return to Bloomsbury as they are. I will go and demand the return of their lost garments.'

'Shall our own Daniel enter the lions' den?' asked Father Peter.

'I'd go meself,' said Father Luke, 'only I don't feel properly dressed for the part.'

'I shall be quite happy to go,' said Mother Verity.

'I will stay and comfort our flock,' said Father Peter.

'I'll go with Mother Verity,' said Mother Mary. 'It's me Christian duty as 'er sister.'

'How kind,' said Mother Verity. She drew her breath, squared her shoulders, and with Mother Mary she crossed the street and knocked on the open door of a certain house. An urchin girl appeared.

'What d'yer want, missus?' she asked.

'Please see if the gentleman in a blue jersey and khaki trousers will come to the door,' said Mother Verity bravely.

'Oh, not him 'imself,' breathed Mother Mary, 'he'll drag you Lord knows where and – oh, think of what 'e might do, sister.'

'No, the policemen are at the top of the street, sister,' said Mother Verity. She looked at the urchin girl. 'Is the gentleman here, my child?'

'No, 'e ain't, we don't 'ave no gents livin' round 'ere.'

'Hullo, hullo,' said a welcoming voice, and the smiling man appeared. 'Well, if it's not me own sweet lady love again.'

'I beg you, sir, not to be importunate, but to consider penitence and the Lord's forgiveness,' said Mother Verity. 'I am here to ask if you'll be kind enough to arrange for a lady's skirt and a gentleman's trousers to be returned. I shall be happy to give you sixpence for them.'

'Well, that's generous, love, I won't deny it. All of a tanner?'

'If you'd be so kind, sir.'

'You're a funny one, missus,' said the man, Will Fletcher. But the light in his eyes was scathing.

'Miss, sir.'

'All one to me,' he said, and Mother Mary thought his smile had something cynical about it. 'All right, wait 'ere.' Off he went, up the street, taking no notice of the watching constables. He turned into a house. He was back quite soon, carrying the trousers and skirt. He handed them over, his blue eyes regarding Mother Verity in curiosity.

'That's very kind of you, sir—'

'I'm not sir, I'm Will Fletcher.'

'Mr Fletcher, you are fully forgiven,' said Mother Verity.

'Am I? What for?'

'Your brutality.'

He laughed out loud. 'Give the tanner to Lulu,' he said, and the urchin girl put out an eager grubby hand. Mother Mary held the garments while Mother Verity opened her handbag and fished for her purse. She fished deeper. She looked at Will Fletcher. His expression was blank.

'My purse has gone,' she said.

'Well, ruddy 'ard luck,' he said.

'Oh,' said Mother Mary, and examined her own handbag. 'Oh, what disgustin' thievin',' she exclaimed. 'I'm goin' to complain to them policemen.'

'Help yerself,' said Will Fletcher, 'but what about Lulu's tanner?'

'Don't go to the policemen, sister,' said Mother Verity, 'go and ask Mother Joan or Father Peter for sixpence. The Lord expects forgiveness of us, we must put aside any bitterness.'

'All I'd got was in me purse,' said Mother Mary, but Mother Verity was right, it wasn't Christian to complain to the law.

Since Mother Joan and Mother Ruth had had their purses lifted too, Father Peter supplied the necessary sixpence. Mother Mary returned to the house with it and gave it to Mother Verity. She handed it to the child, whose fingers closed avidly over it. Will Fletcher looked on silently.

'Is she your daughter, Mr Fletcher?' asked Mother Verity.

'Mine?' He laughed again. 'That she's not. What would I do with daughters or sons, or even a wife, in a place like this? Would I even be 'ere if I had a job? Be your age, lady, or you'll blow me happy memories of you through the ruddy sky. And take my tip, don't come round again. Me kindly neighbours had games with you yesterday, and more games today. Next time—'

'Games?' said Mother Mary. 'I'll 'ave you know it was sinful outrage, and all our purses thieved off us as well. Shameful, that's what it was, shameful.'

'Me heart bleeds for yer, missus,' he said. 'And watch out if there's a next time. Next time me kindly neighbours might just turn unfriendly.'

'Sticks and stones may break my bones—'

'Hoppit, lady,' he said. He smiled at Mother Verity. 'You too, sweetheart. I'll say this much, you're a reg'lar good-looker, even if you are a bit barmy. Here, take a goodbye one for real luck.' And he put his hand under Mother Verity's chin, lifted her face and kissed her. Mother Verity trembled dreadfully. Mother Mary had never seen a more disgraceful kiss, considering how pure Mother Verity was. It was right on her mouth and really shocking. Any other woman would have fainted, but Mother Verity was so brave in enduring it. Her mouth was parted in awful shock when he released her.

'What a disgustin' abomination,' said Mother Mary,

86

terribly shocked herself. 'You won't ever get to the kingdom of 'eaven, you brute.'

He laughed again. 'It's hell for me, is it?' he said. 'Well, I'm used to hell.'

Deeply flushed, Mother Verity said, 'I beg you not to speak like that, salvation is denied to no-one. Again I forgive you. And I shall pray for you.'

Sarcastic laughter followed her as she left with Mother Mary and rejoined the other Repenters. Gratefully, Father Luke restored his rescued trousers to his legs, and with a hearty flourish, Mother Joan pulled on her retrieved skirt.

'Can't blame 'em, I suppose,' she said, 'the Devil's got 'em in his pocket.'

'We shall come again,' declared Father Peter with an awesome glitter of lightning. 'We must. Never have I known people more in need of salvation.'

'That's the stuff, Father,' said Mother Joan. 'By George, sisters, there's the Lord's real work to do here. Never seen such pagan blighters, every last one of 'em needs a lick of fire and brimstone. Not their fault, though. Conditions, you know. A large daily feed of oats and some decent raiment would help to convert 'em.'

'Alas, my funds have some limitations,' said Father Peter.

'Well, we'll get some more,' said Mother Joan. 'I'll pop home to Berkshire and pick up some cheques from my husband.'

'Oh, will he make donations?' asked Mother Ruth, who felt that everything she was wearing needed adjusting.

'I shan't bother about that,' said Mother Joan, 'I'll snaffle some blank cheques and write them out myself, and forge the blighter's signature.'

'Oh, I don't like to 'ear you sayin' things like that,' said Mother Mary.

'Practise truth and honesty in all things, sister,' said Father Peter, placing a gentle hand of reproval on Mother Joan's fine shoulder.

'All in a good cause, Father,' said Mother Joan, 'all in the name of the Lord.'

'Praise 'Im,' said Father Luke.

'But forgery,' said Mother Ruth uncertainly.

'The Lord will forgive,' said Father Luke. ''E's got a noble and understandin' 'eart.'

'Let us return to our temple,' said Father Peter.

'Lead us, Father Peter,' said Mother Mary, thinking she had found her true way in life.

'Yes, lead us, Father,' said Mother Ruth, thinking how magnificent he had been in his chastisement of the harridans, who would surely have ripped her every garment off if he had not risen up in his might.

'I'm right behind yer, sisters,' said Father Luke, feeling much holier now that he had his trousers back on.

'Onward, Christian soldiers,' intoned Father Peter, and led the march back to Bloomsbury, Father Luke bringing up the rear with the empty barrow.

They marched with their banners high and bravely fluttering, Mother Verity thinking something must be done to convert a man whose laughter was false and whose smile hid a bitter soul.

CHAPTER SIX

Aunt Edie had got through her well-planned day without any headaches. She had laid successful siege to a mountain of ironing, cooked and served a supper of sausages and mash, which Dad called zeppelins in a cloud, and given Patsy and Betsy the kind of attention that made them warm very much to her. Betsy said she was glad she wasn't going to have to do the greens at weekends.

The evening became relaxing for everyone, for they all played Banker around the kitchen table, staking their hands with peanuts roasted in their shells. Aunt Edie had bought a whole bag of them. Patsy had acquired the bank and was doing well. A large heap of peanuts belonged to her at this moment, and her natural liveliness was well to the fore. She had been cutting the pack and consistently coming up with picture cards.

'I'm nearly broke,' said Aunt Edie, as Patsy dealt a new round. 'I'm down to four nuts.' She looked at her card, a ten. 'Win or bust,' she said, and put all four nuts beside the card.

'I'm more broker than you, Aunt Edie,' said Betsy. 'I only got two left. I fink Patsy's cheatin' a bit, don't you, Dad?'

'It's a bit suspicious, me pickle, all the kings and queens she keeps cuttin',' said Dad, and backed an eight with three nuts.

Betsy gave a wail as she looked at her card, a mingy

three. 'I'm only puttin' one nut on that,' she said. 'I got to keep the other one.'

Jimmy backed a jack with six nuts. 'Oh, cocky, are we?' said Patsy, and cut the pack. Her luck ran out. She showed a four. 'Blow that,' she said, and Betsy wailed again. She was the only one who'd lost. She broke open her last peanut and ate the two kernels.

'What's the rule?' asked Dad.

'You can't eat any till the game's over,' said Patsy, paying out.

'Well, I ate me last one in case I lost that too,' said Betsy.

'Have some of mine,' said Dad, and gave her six from his heap.

'Oh, yer awful good to me, Dad,' she said.

'All right, give us a kiss, then,' said Dad, and Betsy, sitting next to him, gave him a moist smacker on his cheek.

After three more rounds, Aunt Edie was also bereft of nuts. 'Have some of mine, Aunt Edie,' said Jimmy, and gave her six.

'Well, ain't you a young gent, Jimmy?' she said.

'All right, give us a kiss, then,' said Jimmy.

'What?'

'It's custom'ry,' said Jimmy.

'That's news to me,' said Aunt Edie, 'but I'd better be custom'ry, I suppose,' and she kissed Jimmy on his cheek. Betsy and Patsy looked on in delight. Aunt Edie was fun.

'Mum 'ud have a fit, us gambling and kissin' and everything,' said Patsy.

'What's everything?' asked Jimmy. 'I think I might like some of that.'

'That boy,' said Aunt Edie, and laughed.

Betsy and Patsy stared at her. Imagine Aunt Edie

laughing like that, out loud, as if it didn't matter that Mum had gone religious. The girls smiled.

Later that evening, Aunt Edie said good night to Dad and went up to the bedroom she was to share with Betsy. She took a lighted candle in its holder with her, and placed it on the mahogany chest of drawers. She moved quietly about. Betsy was sound asleep, lying on her side, face cuddled into the pillow, hair loose and softly at rest. Aunt Edie looked down at her.

'Bless you, sweet,' she whispered. 'I'd like to have all three of you if that mum of yours goes and spends the rest of her life repentin'.'

The house in Bloomsbury was large and many-roomed. On the ground floor, two spacious rooms had been knocked into one to create a chapel of worship. It was actually described by the League as the Chapel of Penitence. It was very simple, its walls unadorned, its windows draped by medium grey velvet curtains, its floor uncarpeted, as was its dais, and only an oak crucifix hung on the wall at the back of the dais denoted its religious significance. Also on the ground floor were a dining-room, a kitchen, a scullery, an office, a room for quiet meditation and a small library.

On the first and second floors there was sleeping accommodation for twenty resident Repenters, with space for more if extra beds were required. Women who had given up their worldly goods and departed their homes to join the League of Repenters, were offered residence in the minister's house. Father Peter, who had his private quarters on the first floor, had a compassionate under-standing of the needs of women. Male members of the League were expected to stand on their own feet, except for Father Luke, whose circumstances were beggarly and who had, accordingly, been given residence. The house itself, as a plate on its front door disclosed, was known as the Temple of Endeavour. Father Peter felt that that embraced all things relating to the purpose of the League.

It had been a trying day for God's servants, but at least Father Peter had made good the money four of his followers had lost to pickpockets. Except for himself, all residents, fifteen in number, had retired. He came from the chapel into the hall carrying a candle lantern, and made his way up the staircase, his tread measured and stately. In the corridor of the first floor he knocked on a bedroom door.

'Enter,' called a woman.

He opened the door, but did not enter. He stood there, the lantern's pale flame casting light and shadow over his gaunt face. The room was in darkness, and two lady Repenters lay abed.

'Good night, my sisters,' he intoned, 'and may the blessing of God be upon you.'

'Good night, Father Peter,' they both murmured.

He withdrew, closing the door gently. He went the rounds of other bedrooms, to bestow his nightly blessing on the women residents. It pleased their Christian souls to have the minister in such religious care of them.

He knocked on one more door and opened it. 'Oh, Father Peter – oh, my goodness—' Mother Joan was in bed. Mother Mary was not. She was standing by the plain simple dressing-table in her corset, drawers and stockings, exposed to the minister's dark eyes in the light of a globed gas mantle.

'Ah, my dear sister, a hundred pardons, so sorry . . . but bless you, bless you both . . . good night.' He disappeared and the door closed. Mother Mary stood burning.

'Was that Father Peter?' asked Mother Joan, coming up to a sitting position in her bed.

'Oh, lor' . . . oh, dear . . . I'm afraid so,' blushed Mother Mary. 'Oh, I don't 'ardly know where to look now.'

'Jumped the jolly old starter's flag, did he?' said Mother Joan. 'Can't be helped, sister. He means well, his nightly blessings come from his heart, and he's a fine figurehead in our fight against that ghastly bounder Satan. Thought this afternoon that if anyone looked capable of invoking the Day of Judgement, he did. Awesome, I thought. Don't stand there like a dummy, sister, get your things off and get into bed. I'm exhausted. Great Scott, you're not blushing, are you? He was only there a couple of seconds. Just one of life's little happenings. Buck up now.'

'Yes, sister . . . oh, lor',' breathed Mother Mary, 'I never been more embarrassed in all me life.'

'Think nothing of it,' said Mother Joan, 'let me tell you what happened to Lady Carrington-Cummings, a friend of mine. I kept warning her, and so did my husband George, that her country house was going rotten for lack of repairs. Wouldn't listen. She was there one weekend, and taking a bath. The floor gave way under the bath, and it dropped straight through and landed in the main kitchen, with her still in it. Peach of a woman, too. Magnificent body. Damned lucky she wasn't hurt, but very unfortunate that all the servants were present. Her butler was never the same man. So there you are, sister, you've nothing to worry about by comparison. Turn the light out before you get into bed, it's been a long day on behalf of the Lord.'

'Amen,' said Mother Mary, hoping she hadn't sinned by being caught in her private underwear. She turned the gas down until the revealing brightness of the mantle expired.

*

Aunt Edie was first down on Sunday morning. She went to work with the frying-pan. Dad showed his face.

'Like some 'elp, Edie – hullo, what's that?'

'Eggs and bacon for everyone,' said Aunt Edie.

'Eggs and bacon?' said Dad.

'My treat,' said Aunt Edie.

'What a woman,' said Dad. Eggs and bacon for breakfast represented a real treat. 'You're spoilin' us.'

'Oh, go on with you,' said Aunt Edie, turning rashers. ''Ere, what's goin' on upstairs?'

'Pillow fights,' said Dad. Upstairs at the moment was a battleground. Betsy was yelling, Patsy shrieking, Jimmy calling for help. 'Patsy and Betsy are usin' pillows to knock Jimmy out of his bed.' A thump sounded. 'That's it, he's out of bed.'

'It's not what Maud would stand for,' said Aunt Edie.

'By a fortunate coincidence, she don't 'appen to be here,' said Dad.

Betsy yelled down from the landing. 'Dad, Dad! 'Elp! Jimmy's tryin' to chuck Patsy down the stairs!'

'I'm on me way,' called Dad, and up to the landing he went, collecting a cushion from the parlour on the way.

Aunt Edie heard yelling, joyous sounds from Betsy and Patsy as their dad entered the fray. The cat was away, and all the mice were playing. Aunt Edie silently laughed. What a family, she thought. Just my kind of people.

Mother had a religious morning. After a simple breakfast, Father Peter conducted a service in the Chapel of Penitence. Thirteen lady residents were present, so was Father Luke, and so were some non-resident members of both sexes. Mother Joan was absent, having popped home to Berkshire to see about acquiring some blank cheques that could be put to good Samaritan use. A whole mountain of decent clothing was needed for the poor of Whitechapel, so was some decent food. All the same, as Father Peter said, even the neediest people must not have their sins condoned. The campaign in Whitechapel would continue. Whitechapel was to be the League's proving ground, their first real field of battle, and when that battle was won and Satan despatched, they would carry the fight to other fields with hard-won confidence. Father Peter intoned praises for Mothers Mary, Joan, Ruth and Verity, all of whom had participated in yesterday's brave endeavours.

'Amen,' said Father Luke, 'and didn't the Lord give me the privilege of bein' right be'ind them? But it grieved me to see Mother Verity in such sore travail and me not bein' able to lift even me little finger to 'elp her.'

'I never saw no woman stand up braver to outrage,' declared Mother Mary. 'I just wish I'd had me umbrella with me. If it's all the same to you, Father Peter, I'll take it to Whitechapel next time instead of a banner.'

From his Bible rostrum on the dais, Father Peter regarded her benevolently. Mother Mary coloured as she remembered how she had come to his eyes last night, in her underwear. Lord, could anything have been more intimately sinful? Jack had been a bit larky during their first years of marriage, but later, as a respectable wife and mother, she'd put a stop to it. It just wasn't decent.

'Mother Mary, you may carry whatever you wish into battle,' said Father Peter.

'Thank you, Father.'

'I am in admiration of you,' said the minister.

Oh, lor', thought Mother Mary, I hope he don't mean the way I looked in me corset.

'Praise her,' said Mother Verity.

'Indeed,' boomed Father Peter. 'Now let us prepare for

the market. We will go in pairs and hand out the pamphlets that arrived yesterday from the printers. They contain the word of God and details of our intentions to do His work.'

'Praise Him,' intoned the Repenters.

Petticoat Lane, in the east of the City of London, was a market into which hundreds of cockneys and other people poured on Sunday mornings. Almost any kind of curios, except stuffed elephants, were on offer. The secondhand clothes stalls were legendary, and one could fit oneself out like a king or queen if one didn't mind setting the lot off with a cardboard crown. It was always crowded and was more so these days, with the war over and people looking for the kind of antique that could turn out to be worth far more than the price a stallholder asked for it.

Mother Verity stood with her banner. Beside her was Mother Mary, with her umbrella. They both handed out pamphlets. The pamphlets introduced the reader to words of the Lord, and invited enrolment with the League of Repenters, whose religious objectives were set out. Warnings followed concerning the fate of all who sided with the Devil. The final sentence in bold capitals was an unmistakable warning: BEHOLD, THE DAY OF JUDGEMENT IS AT HAND!

Not all recipients of the pamphlets were too overcome to comment. 'It's bleedin' barmy,' said a man in a choker to Mother Mary, 'an' why ain't you at 'ome, lookin' after yer kids?'

'The Lord's called me, that's why,' said Mother Mary, 'and I wouldn't be surprised if 'E wasn't callin' you.'

'An' what would 'E be callin' me for, if I might be so bold as to ask?'

'To bring you to repentence.'

'Me? What've I done?'

'We're all sinners,' said Mother Mary.

'Yes, an' some of us is orf our bleedin' 'eads as well,' said the cockney gent, and went on his way.

Mother Verity was spoken to by a lady who, having read the pamphlet, handed it back and said in a Belgravia accent, 'Really, my good woman, I am as ready as you are to face the Day of Judgement.'

'Oh, how happy I am for you,' said Mother Verity, 'although as a weak and unworthy woman myself, I fear I shall be found wanting.'

'Then I should avoid the Day of Judgement, if I were you,' said the lady.

'Don't stand about, missus, you're in me way,' said a cockney woman.

'You're mistaken, my good woman, it's these people who are standing about.'

'So are you, an' you're the one that's in me way.'

'Really,' said the lady, offended, and lost herself in the clamouring crowds.

Then there was the flashy young woman who, having read the pamphlet, or some of it, said to the two Repenters, 'Doin' this for a livin', are yer, dearies?'

'For the Lord,' said Mother Mary.

'I've 'eard about 'Im, I'm Gloria Mayfair.' She was actually Gladys Higgs. ''Ow much d'yer get paid?'

'We ask for no payment, only for the Lord's blessing,' said Mother Verity, and Gloria looked her over, and Mother Mary too.

'Well, yer can't live on that, duckies. I've 'ad blessings meself, from all sorts, but I can't say they've done me as much good as fried cod'n chips. Look, dearies, 'ow would yer like to come to a knees-up tonight? I can see yer both nice ladies, an' there'll be some obliging gentlemen present that'll pay gen'rous. Course, you both need to do yer faces up a bit, then could yer do a good knees-up an' some of the other for gents that's gen'rous? You'd like a bit of 'ard cash on top of the Lord's blessin', wouldn't yer?'

''Ere, what d'you mean?' asked Mother Mary in sudden dreadful suspicion.

'That's it, love, you've got it,' said Gloria, and winked.

'Oh, 'ow dare you, that's disgustin',' said Mother Mary, outraged.

''Ere, mind that umbrella,' said Gloria.

'I'll give you mind it,' said Mother Mary.

'Well, there's gratitude, I don't think,' said Gloria, pushing the point of the umbrella away from her valuable bosom. ''Ere's me tryin' to do both of yer a good turn—'

'Please go away,' said Mother Verity gently, 'and leave us to pray for you.'

'Bless yer, duckie, but don't do that, the last time someone prayed for me, me gentleman friend 'opped it while 'e still 'adn't paid me.'

'Disgustin',' said Mother Mary.

A policeman arrived, bringing ponderous but benevolent authority with him. 'What, might I ask, is all this 'ere, ladies?'

'We're giving out the Lord's pamphlets,' said Mother Verity, her banner at rest.

'Well, that's as maybe,' said the arm of the law, 'but it's me duty to advise you ladies you're causin' an illegal hobstruction.'

'Not me, dearie,' said Gloria, and whisked away.

'I don't see 'ow we're an obstruction here,' said Mother Mary. 'It's all obstruction.'

'No standin' impediments allowed,' said the constable, 'I'll 'ave to hask you ladies to move along.'

'May we give out pamphlets while we're moving?' asked Mother Verity.

'I don't see as you can't do that,' said the officer, 'as long as there's no stoppin', loiterin' or hobstructin' for the purpose of makin' a gatherin', which if there is will require me to arrest both of yer.'

'What impudence,' said Mother Mary. 'I never been arrested in all me life, I've a good mind to teach you 'ow to talk proper to respectable ladies.' She shook her umbrella threateningly.

'Now, missus, that won't do, yer know,' said the constable. A small crowd was collecting.

'Go it, missus,' called a boy.

'No riotin', incitin' or shoutin' the odds, me lad,' said the policeman, 'or I'll 'ave you down at the station, too.'

''Ow dare you threaten that young boy,' said Mother Mary, ''e's a child of the Lord.'

'No, he ain't,' said a man, ''e's a bleedin' rip, and 'is dad's Albert Cope.'

'Move along, move along,' said the constable.

'Obstructin', well, I don't know,' said Mother Mary.

'Come along, sister,' said Mother Verity, and took her gently by the arm and led her away. 'You have a wonderful enthusiasm, and no fears. How weak I am, I'm all fears. I fear for the world and for that misguided man who crossed my path in such a bruising way yesterday and Friday. I must do what I can to save him from his godless waywardness.'

'I'll save him,' said Mother Mary as they threaded their way in and out of the crowds. 'I'll give him the sharp end of my umbrella.'

'You're a tower of strength, sister,' said Mother Verity, 'but I don't feel that's quite the right way to help him.'

*

A bell tinkled cheerfully in the street. 'That's the muffin man, Dad,' cried Betsy.

They were all in the parlour, except for Patsy, who was out with friends. Aunt Edie, who had served up a lovely roast leg of mutton for dinner, with apple pie for afters, was now doing some invaluable darning for the family. Jimmy was making a list of firms and factories to call on about a job, and Dad was reading the Sunday paper. He'd informed Aunt Edie that to give her a break, he and Patsy would get the tea later on. Aunt Edie said she was obliged by the offer, but was looking forward to getting it herself. The bell of the muffin man alerted the family to his wares.

'He won't have crumpets, not in August,' said Jimmy.

'But 'e'll 'ave shrimps an' winkles,' said Betsy, who adored both.

'All right, me pickle,' said Dad, 'we'll have some, shall we?'

The bell tinkled again. 'I'll go,' said Jimmy, and Dad gave him enough money for a pint of winkles and a pint of shrimps. That would make Sunday tea a real cockney treat.

Jimmy caught the muffin man up on the corner of Crampton Street, where he was serving a small boy with a pint of winkles, their blue-black shells moistly shining. In the winter, a muffin man's baize-covered tray was laden mainly with crumpets. In the summer, toasted crumpets usually gave way to shellfish.

'There y'ar, little 'un,' said the Walworth muffin man, and added two extra winkles to the pint pot. He emptied them into a bag. ''Ow about a tanner for that lot?'

'Mum's 'ad an 'ard week, mister,' said the boy, 'so she says d'yer mind ten 'apennies an' four farvings?'

'Not if it all comes to a tanner,' said the muffin man, which it did, and off went the small boy with his bag of winkles. 'Now, me lord,' said the muffin man to Jimmy, 'what can I do for you?'

'Pint of shrimps and a pint of winkles, if you'd be so obliging,' said Jimmy.

'If I wasn't obligin', where would I be?' said the genial street purveyor. 'In the work'ouse. Same the other way round. If you wasn't obligin' by not buyin' me perishables, I wouldn't 'ave the pleasure of sellin' 'em to yer, would I? And if no-one else obliged me likewise, it 'ud be the work'ouse again, wouldn't it? There y'ar, young feller, pint of winkles in a bag, and now for yer shrimps.' The muffin man heaped shrimps into the pewter pot. 'Got a basin? No, I see you ain't. Shall I tip 'em into yer pocket?'

'D'you mind if you don't?' said Jimmy. 'Me Sunday suit'll smell fishy if you do, and people'll think I was born under a Billingsgate stall.'

'Well, some young fellers might not mind,' said the muffin man. 'Some young fellers might be proud, 'specially if they liked kippers.' He poured the shrimps into a paper bag. 'Me Uncle Stan was born under a mulberry bush, so I 'eard, so of course 'e 'ad a mulberry 'ooter when 'e grew older. There y'ar, yer young comic, and that lot'll cost yer a bob. 'Aving a party, are yer?'

'No, just Sunday tea with Aunt Edie.' Jimmy handed over the bob.

'Who's yer Aunt Edie?'

'A pearly queen.'

'Ah, that's a lady after me own 'eart,' said the muffin man. 'Give 'er me love.'

Jimmy carried back the shrimps, the winkles and the message. 'What?' said Aunt Edie when the message was delivered.

'Yes, sent you his love,' said Jimmy. 'You're a lady after 'is own heart, he said.'

101

'Saucy devil, I don't even know 'im,' said Aunt Edie.

'No, but I told him you were a pearly queen,' said Jimmy. 'His eyes lit up like fireworks and he nearly dropped all his winkles. I thought about tellin' him you were rollickin' good at doin' a pearly knees-up, and that you were goin' to do a turn at a pearly concert next Saturday week.'

'Jack Andrews,' said Aunt Edie, 'I'm goin' to 'ave to box your son's ears.'

'All right, Edie, help yourself,' said Dad. 'Mind, I'm not sayin' I disagree with 'im, or that I don't 'ave hopes of seein' you performin' a rollickin' knees-up, which pleasure 'asn't come my way before.'

Aunt Edie looked at him over her darning. Dad hid himself behind his paper. Aunt Edie smiled. 'You're a pair together, you and Jimmy,' she said, 'aren't they, Betsy?' Betsy giggled.

'Tell you what, Betsy love,' said Dad, 'let's all go and see Aunt Edie doin' her turn at this concert, shall we?'

'Crikey, could we, Dad?' asked Betsy.

'Now look 'ere,' said Aunt Edie, 'I didn't tell Joe Gosling I'd do a turn for certain.'

'Joe Gosling?' said Dad. 'I've 'eard of him. Is he the pearly king of South Camberwell?'

'He's Aunt Edie's lovin' admirer as well,' said Jimmy.

'Well, is that a fact?' Dad smiled at Aunt Edie. 'Good on yer, Edie, and good luck, time you got fixed up in romantic style, old girl.'

Aunt Edie didn't seem to like that at all. In fact, she got quite shirty. 'I'll please myself about that, Jack Andrews, if you don't mind. I don't 'appen to be the sort that gets fixed up with any man just because 'e fancies me.'

'I know you're not, Edie,' said Dad, 'I only—'

'Kindly mind your business,' said Aunt Edie.

Betsy cast a look at her dad. He gave her a wink. 'Someone's knocked over the milk bucket, me pickle,' he said.

'Yes, I fink it was you, Dad,' said Betsy.

'What a life,' said Dad.

Aunt Edie bent her head to her darning. A little sound escaped her. Jimmy knew she was trying not to laugh. Aunt Edie never had the rats for longer than a few minutes.

When Patsy arrived home, Aunt Edie was beginning to get the tea. Patsy went upstairs, then called down, 'Can you come up a minute, Jimmy?' Jimmy went up. He and Patsy were pals.

'What's up?' he asked.

'That Lily Shaw,' said Patsy, wrinkling her nose. 'D'you know what she's just been sayin' to me?'

'Well, no, I don't,' said Jimmy. 'I wasn't there, was I?'

'That's it, talk barmy,' said Patsy. 'She said she'd 'eard that our mum 'ad gone away, and that our Aunt Edie 'ad come to take 'er place. Honest, the way she said it, I bet she's been listening to 'er mum an' dad, you know 'er dad thinks Mum's a loony. I said Aunt Edie was just thinkin' of visitin' at weekends, and she gave me one of 'er clever looks and said she'd 'eard that when the cat's away the mice start playin'. I bet that's what she 'eard her mum say.'

'Well, Dad's not a mouse,' said Jimmy, 'he's an old soldier, he's got rules.'

'But Aunt Edie's still ever so good-lookin',' said Patsy, 'and she's lively as well, and Mum's not been much fun for ages.'

'No, Dad won't play games with Aunt Edie,' said Jimmy. He thought. 'Anyway,' he said, 'it's against the law.'

Patsy gave a muffled little yell of laughter. 'Ain't you a scream?' she said.

'Not as much as you are,' said Jimmy. 'Here, Patsy, did you know the Walworth muffin man's uncle was born under a mulberry bush?'

'No, course I don't know, and 'ow do you?'

'He's got a mulberry nose. That's a sign of bein' born under a mulberry bush, didn't you know that, either?'

Patsy, shrieking with laughter, chased him down the stairs.

Tea, with the shrimps and winkles, was served in the parlour, with Aunt Edie presiding as if she'd been born to the role of a warm-hearted cockney mum. Jimmy mentioned the forthcoming pearlies concert again, and Patsy couldn't wait to hear more when Aunt Edie said yes, she probably would do a turn. She could sing a bit, she said, and often had at a pearly concert for charity.

'I don't remember us ever seein' you, Auntie,' said Patsy.

'Nor can I recollect you ever invitin' us, Edie,' said Dad.

'I was not encouraged to be invitin',' said Aunt Edie.

'Ah,' said Dad, knowing that Mother considered the pearlies common and a knees-up vulgar, even though she'd been born a cockney. Mind, she'd only started to think like that in her twenties, when religion was getting a real hold on her. 'Anyway, we'll all come and see you this time, Edie.'

'Honoured, I'm sure,' said Aunt Edie.

'Lovely,' said Patsy.

'Spiffin',' said Betsy.

'Knees-up?' said Jimmy.

'Not likely,' said Aunt Edie, 'not with you and that dad of yours lookin'.'

'Edie,' said Dad, 'did I ever tell you about me old sergeant-major givin' a turn at a battalion concert in Kut?'

''Ere we go,' said Aunt Edie.

'You ain't ever told me, Dad,' said Betsy.

'Well, me pickle,' said Dad, 'it was a soldiers' concert, and we fixed up a stage and so on, with a joanna. The sergeant-major did 'is turn, he sang "The Road To Mandalay". Fav'rite with soldiers, that is. There he was, singing away and marchin' up and down in 'is boots, and what 'appened? The stage fell apart, the joanna fell through it and so did the sergeant-major. "Who done that?" he roared up from down below. And someone hollered, "You done it yerself, sergeant-major, you made a hole in the road to Mandalay and fell through it." You ought to 'ave heard what come up from down below then, I couldn't even tell it to sailors, and most sailors 'ave heard everything. Still, he was all right once we'd lifted the old joanna off him.'

'I don't know who's the real turn at this table, Jack Andrews,' said Aunt Edie, 'you or that chronic sergeant-major of yours.'

'Dad's funny, though, ain't 'e, Aunt Edie?' said Betsy.

'I'll give 'im funny, Betsy, if he comes up with any more stories about 'is sergeant-major,' said Aunt Edie.

'Aunt Edie,' said Jimmy, 'how about you and me doin' a duet at your concert? How about "If You Were The Only Girl In The World And I Was The Only Boy"?'

'I never know if that young man is serious or not,' said Aunt Edie, but with a little sparkle of fun in her eyes. 'Who'd like more tea?'

'Me, please,' said Betsy, and Aunt Edie refilled all their cups.

Patsy thought oh, I really like Aunt Edie, she's a lot more fun than poor old Mum.

'I'm willin', y'know, Aunt Edie,' said Jimmy.

'Well, we'll see, Jimmy, we'll see,' said Aunt Edie.

'I 'ope Aunt Edie don't fall through the stage like Dad's sergeant-major did,' said Betsy.

Aunt Edie laughed so much then that she nearly cried. Which made everyone else laugh their heads off. The upsetting nature of Mother's absence was forgotten again.

CHAPTER SEVEN

During dinner in the Temple that evening, Father Peter expressed satisfaction at the day's work of distributing pamphlets. A number of possible followers had been recruited. There had been a few minor embarrassments due to irreverence, but on the whole much of the seed they had cast had borne fruit.

'The Lord's been with us,' said Father Luke, 'givin' us 'Is blessin'. Which reminds me, Father Peter, I'd take it kindly, like, if Mrs Murphy could bless the potatoes with a bit more salt.' Mrs Murphy was the Temple cook, and came in daily.

'I'll speak to her,' said Father Peter.

After dinner, he addressed himself to Mother Mary, who had expressed a wish to do some confessing. He said he was always available to hear confession, it unburdened his followers, especially the ladies, of anything that lay a little heavily on their consciences. Mother Mary said that was ever so kind of him, and went up with him to his private quarters on the first floor. In his study, with the curtains drawn to, the gas mantle turned low to cast subdued and discreet light, he sat with his back to that light so that shadow veiled his face, and Mother Mary knelt on a hassock at his feet.

'I've only been to confession once, Father,' she said, 'after I was confirmed. I didn't go any more, it was a bit embarrassin'. And I wasn't a sinful girl, anyway, my mother brought me up very religious. Mind, since gettin' married, I won't say I 'aven't been a bit irritable with me fam'ly sometimes.'

In a low and kind voice, Father Peter said that that wasn't a sin, merley a small human failing. Mother Mary had a bit of a think and said she'd once hit a noisy barking dog with a stick.

'An unhappy gesture towards a dumb animal, perhaps, sister, but—'

'It wasn't dumb, I can tell you that,' said Mother Mary, adjusting her knees on the hassock. 'Bark bark all the time. So I gave it a bit of a whack with a stick.'

Father Peter said the Lord would not regard that as a great sin. There were sins far more serious. Was the sin of the flesh on her mind, perhaps?

Mother Mary looked askance. 'Oh, I couldn't confess nothing like that, Father.'

'But have you been guilty of such a sin, Mother Mary?'

'I'm a married woman,' said Mother Mary offendedly. 'It's my opinion that it's only men that's guilty of that kind of sin.'

'Be assured you are confessing to the Lord, sister, not to me. I am only the medium. You may, without worry, speak of these things.'

'What things?' asked Mother Mary.

'Sins of the flesh.'

'I already said I couldn't confess nothing like that, Father. What I want is to go among sinners and feel I'm not one meself, so I thought I'd purify meself by tellin' you that before I was actually married . . . well . . .' Mother Mary had another think. No, she just couldn't. Still, there was something else. 'Well, perhaps I was a bit sinful when I used to think about men and women gettin' married. You know.'

'Tell me, sister,' said Father Peter with gentle insistence.

'Like what they did together on 'oneymoon,' said Mother Mary in a muffled tone.

'Ah, and what did you imagine they did, sister?'

'I can't remember what I imagined.'

'Was your sin in the thoughts you had about it?'

'Oh, the very idea. I just wondered what 'appened and how babies were made. That's what's on me mind now, Father, thinkin' it might 'ave been a sin to wonder about it.'

'I understand. However, having taken your marriage vows, what were your thoughts when you came to . . . ah . . . when it happened?'

'Oh, I'm not tellin' about that, Father, it's private.'

'Marriage and its consummation are blessed by God, sister, and you may confess your thoughts and feelings.'

'No, I couldn't,' said Mother Mary. 'I'll just 'ave to ask God's pardon that I couldn't.' Nor could she confess the worst, that she'd let Dad fondle her in dreadfully intimate ways before they were married.

'My child.' Father Peter's hand alighted gently on her bent head. His touch was a blessing. 'Perhaps some other time. There can be sin in one's thoughts and feelings. These should be confessed.'

Mother Mary wondered again if it had been a sin to have been caught in her underwear. But she just couldn't mention that, either.

'Well, if I feel I'd like to talk to you again—?'

'Of course, some other time. Your faith is very strong, sister.' The gentle hand touched her shoulder. 'It gave you courage to leave your home and enter the service of the Lord. You are absolved of your small sins.'

'Thank you, Father, I feel I can go pure among sinners now.'

109

At home, after a Sunday supper of cold lamb, fried potatoes and pickled red cabbage, Aunt Edie was a further delight to the family. She did a turn at the piano. Mother had played a bit, but only hymns in recent years. It drove Dad back to his Sunday paper, and it drove Jimmy and his sisters out of doors. Aunt Edie didn't play hymns. No sooner was she at the keyboard than the parlour was alive with music hall songs. One followed another, and she sang them all, 'Cockles and Mussels', 'Daisy Bell', 'Lily of Laguna' and 'It's A Long Way To Tipperary'. They all sang 'Tipperary', Dad with the strong voice of an old soldier. Aunt Edie followed that with 'Any Old Iron', Harry Champion's famous cockney song. And she sang it with gusto.

'Encore, Auntie!' cried Patsy.

So Aunt Edie sang it again. Well, if anyone in Walworth didn't like 'Any Old Iron', then he or she needed to see a doctor.

After that, Jimmy suggested 'If You Were The Only Girl', and that he and Aunt Edie should sing it together.

'Made up your mind, 'ave you, Jimmy?' she smiled.

'Let's give it a go,' said Jimmy.

'Yes, come on, Aunt Edie, you and Jimmy,' said Patsy.

'I 'ope I'm not lettin' myself in for something that's goin' to finish up a dead duck at the concert,' said Aunt Edie. Jimmy got up to stand beside her at the piano. 'No, face the audience, Jimmy,' she said.

'Crikey,' said Betsy, who couldn't remember any Sunday evening as rousing as this. 'We're the audience, Dad.'

'So we are, me pickle,' said Dad, 'except we don't want you chuckin' any bad eggs at your brother, they might end up all over Aunt Edie's Sunday dress.'

'Quiet in the stalls, if you don't mind,' said Aunt Edie. 'All right, then, Jimmy. You know all the words?'

'I'll break my leg if I don't,' said Jimmy.

'Off we go, then,' said Aunt Edie, her mood irrepressibly infectious, and she rippled along the keyboard in the introductory chord. Then she and Jimmy sang the song together, Jimmy going solo when required and she likewise. She discovered he had a very good young baritone. 'Well, bless us, Jimmy,' she said at the end, with the select audience clapping. 'That wasn't 'alf bad.'

'Ruddy good, if you ask me,' said Dad.

'Language, Jack Andrews, language and little children,' said Aunt Edie.

'Me, Aunt Edie?' said Patsy.

'Me?' said Betsy.

'Bless you, duckies,' said Aunt Edie. 'Want to go through the song again, Jimmy?'

They went through it again, and then did 'Let's All Sing Like The Birdies Sing' as another duet. Betsy giggled herself hysterical at Jimmy's 'tweet tweet'. It made her gasp, 'Aunt Edie, stop 'im, or I'll 'ave an accident.'

'Here, you better not come to the concert, then,' said Patsy.

'No, nor had any other girls your age, Betsy,' said Dad. 'We don't want accidents all over the hall.'

Aunt Edie's laughter pealed around the parlour.

The following day, Bank Holiday Monday, saw them all aboard a bus. The weather was fine, and they rode on the open top deck, from where one had a lofty view of sooty old London and felt high above the Thames as the vehicle chugged over Westminster Bridge. Aunt Edie said she was risking getting her large white Sunday hat dusty.

'Of course, Betsy, it's not really an 'at, yer know,' said

111

Dad. 'It's what ladies like Aunt Edie call a creation, and if it blows off we're goin' to be in 'orrible trouble for makin' her ride on top with us.'

'You're right, Jack Andrews,' said Aunt Edie. 'You won't live to see the day through.'

Her hat had a white gauzy veil that protected her face, and Patsy thought she looked grand. She always dressed well, specially in summer. It often made Mum sniff a bit. She'd say it was all vanity. Dad said once that a bit of vanity was what made a lot of women look a bit of all right, and Mum took umbrage at that, saying a bit of all right was low and common. She said pearly queens were common too. Patsy didn't think so herself, she thought pearlies were jolly, hearty and entertaining, and fond of doing charitable works.

Hyde Park was green, the dry green of August, and the sun of August gave it large splashes of gold. Patsy and Betsy were in their best Sunday frocks, short-skirted, Patsy wearing imitation silk stockings and Betsy white socks. Jimmy wore a white open-necked cricket shirt and grey flannels. So did Dad. Jimmy was bare-headed and Dad wore a straw boater tipped over his eyes. Patsy said he looked cheeky. Dad winked. Aunt Edie wore a waisted lemon-coloured dress and patent white leather shoes fastened with buttons. Betsy said she bet her aunt would get off with a bloke.

'I'll do me best, love,' said Aunt Edie, 'but he'd better be a rich bloke.'

In the bandstand, uniformed soldiers were playing lively music and people were paying threepence to sit in deckchairs and listen in comfort. Dad and Aunt Edie decided they'd like some of that, although she did say Dad was welcome to wander around with Jimmy and the girls if he preferred. Dad said he didn't prefer, he said wandering around with his lively lot would wear his feet out. Could he accordingly have the pleasure of treating her to a deckchair and listening to the band with her? Jimmy said, 'Treat yourselves to two, why don't you? You and Aunt Edie will make just one chair look a bit crowded.'

'Hoppit,' said Aunt Edie.

Jimmy and the girls wandered off. They found the Serpentine. The shimmering water of the lake looked magical, and there were young men rowing their young ladies around it in boats. The spectacle held Patsy and Betsy. Jimmy told them to stay there while he did some strolling. He'd pick them up later. Off he went, reaching Speakers Corner, where all kinds of people, some barmy and some intense, stood on soap boxes or mobile rostrums and made speeches about things like the rich grinding the poor, the advantages of doing away with kings, queens and grand dukes, the awesome might of an avenging God, the iniquity of throwing people into workhouses, and so on. Anarchists argued for the assassination of everyone except themselves, and a policeman paraded around to make sure that such freedom of speech was not interfered with, and that hecklers only heckled. Pelting speakers with rotten fruit was forbidden. Jimmy stopped for a minute or so to listen to a self-proclaimed Bolshevik denouncing the capitalist profiteers of Britain and urging the workers to strike. Knowing he couldn't go on strike himself, because he had no job, Jimmy moved on to where hecklers were having a high old time at the expense of another speaker, a very tall dark-faced man in a black cloak and with a great mane of grey-peppered black hair. He was thundering at the hecklers.

'I say unto you that God's anger will blast all who mock Him!'

'Now don't upset yourself, Moses,' called one heckler. 'I only asked can 'E make custard.'

'Miserable unbeliever, did not God create the whole world aₙd all its wonders?' boomed Father Peter, the man on the rostrum.

'Praise Him,' sang several lady Repenters, who were standing around the rostrum, banners high.

Jimmy's eyes opened wide. Mother was among the banner-bearers, except that she carried only her umbrella. She looked holy, her eyes were shining, her expression just the kind she always wore in church.

'Did He not create Adam, and from Adam did he not create Eve, and did He not send Joshua to smite the unbelievers?' thundered the speaker, arms lifted high and cloak spreading like black wings.

'Yes, but can 'E make custard?' asked the heckler, and the crowd tittered.

'Shall ye come to the Day of Judgement with mockery on your lips?' Father Peter's eyes glittered. 'What shall it profit a man to deride the Lord?'

''Ere, leave orf, mister,' said another heckler. 'Me friend's only askin' about custard.'

'Yes, I like custard,' said his friend, and the crowd yelled with laughter. Jimmy saw Mother's expression change, and he knew she was beginning to fume. Her umbrella quivered.

'By your words the Lord shall know ye,' declaimed Father Peter, 'and by your deeds He will judge you. We who serve Him through the League of Repenters offer you redemption and salvation. Repent!'

'Yer got me there, old cock,' said the second heckler. 'D'yer mean me mate's got to repent because 'e likes custard?'

The crowd howled. Jimmy saw Mother advance, her umbrella raised.

'I'll give the pair of you something, you and your custard!' she cried. 'What disgustin' impudence!'

'Mind yer eye, Fred,' said the first heckler, 'old Mother Riley's after givin' it a poke.'

The umbrella struck, thumping his shoulder. 'Take that!' cried Mother ringingly, and the crowd roared in delight.

'Go it, missus!'

'Sister, sister, come back!' begged Mother Verity.

'Take that!' cried Mother again, and thumped the other man.

'Thus were the Philistines smitten,' boomed Father Peter in exaltation.

'Now, missus,' said the first heckler, 'it ain't exactly Christian, yer know, to go about wallopin' people.'

The crowd roared again. 'Give 'im another go, missus!'

'I will if he don't keep quiet,' shouted Mother, and Jimmy thought, poor old Mum, Dad's got a real problem with her.

'The Lord's enemies shall reap the whirlwind,' declared Father Peter.

'Ruddy 'ell,' said the heckler, 'all I asked was can 'E make – 'ere, missus, I just thought, 'ow about blancmange, then, can 'E make blancmange? Me kids is 'ighly partial to blancmange.'

'Take that!' cried Mother yet again, and once more her umbrella smote. Mother Verity and Father Luke hastened forward and drew her gently back to the rostrum. Father Peter began to launch a variety of awesome warnings at the crowd. Jimmy retreated before he was spotted by Mother. He suspected he might get thumped himself, for not being at home repenting of Sunday's roast. He felt she really had gone potty.

He thought he'd better rejoin his sisters at the Serpentine, but glimpsing horses and riders as he approached Rotten Row, he went to have a look at them. A girl wandered across the sandy riding track. He yelled and rushed at her. A rider's horse reared up before her. Jimmy pulled her out of its way and dragged her clear. The rider delivered some loud, bitter and pungent comments, and people shook their heads at the girl. She took no notice, she was far more interested in her deliverer.

'Golly, you were quick,' she said.

'Well, I didn't want you finishin' up flattened, it would've spoiled your Bank Holiday,' said Jimmy.

'What?' she said. She was about fourteen, he thought. She was dressed in a white frock and a round white straw hat. The hat was now a bit crooked. She had light brown hair tied, like Patsy's, with ribbon. Her eyes were round and brown.

'In case you don't know, horses can flatten people,' said Jimmy, always willing to stop for a chat with the man in the street or a girl in a park. 'My dad saw it 'appen to a soldier in Mesopotamia. Knocked down and flattened by Turkish 'orses, y'know, and when they dug him up he was just like a pancake. You don't want to go home to your mum and dad lookin' like a pancake, do you?'

'Well!' Thirteen-year-old Sophy Gibbs drew a deep breath. 'Of all the cheek, who'd you think you're talking to, you rotten boy?'

'Don't know, do I? Never seen you before, have I?'

'You've got a nerve,' she said. 'I'm not somebody's left-over washing, you know. Just because you saved my life, don't think you can give me all this cheek. I've a good mind to push your face in.'

116

A string of riders trotted by. 'I didn't exactly save your life,' said Jimmy, his solemn expression hiding a mental grin.

'Yes, you did,' said Sophy. 'I suppose you go about saving every girl's life so that you can lecture them.'

'No, not much—'

'Don't make excuses,' said Sophy, 'just tell me your name and address, and I'll ask my father to send you a postal order.'

'What for?' asked Jimmy.

'For saving my life, of course. Will a sixpenny postal order do?'

'As much as that?' said Jimmy. 'What about just a penny stamp and an empty jam jar?' Grocers offered a penny for an empty jam jar.

'My life's worth more than a stamp and a jam jar,' said Sophy.

'All right, tell you what,' said Jimmy, 'ask your dad to give sixpence to some poor old lady in a work'ouse, and we'll call it quits.'

'Yes, all right,' said Sophy.

'Well, so long,' said Jimmy, 'don't go gettin' in the way of any more horses.'

'Oh, no you don't,' said Sophy, grabbing his arm. 'You can't just push off after saving my life, I bet even criminals wouldn't do that, I bet they'd at least buy me an ice cream wafer. We can get one at the kiosk by the tea rooms.'

'Well, I'd like to,' said Jimmy, 'but I can't afford it. Still, all right—'

'Oh, I've got some money, I'll pay, and you can owe me,' said Sophy, used to having her own way. 'Come on.'

'No, I've just remembered, I've got to go and find me sisters by the Serpentine.'

'Never mind them,' said Sophy imperiously, 'just come on. What's your name? I'm—'

'Hullo, what's going on?' A man had arrived, a rugged-looking man in a grey summer suit and light trilby hat, an elegant lady beside him.

'Daddy, I've just had my life saved,' said Sophy.

'Really?' said the elegant lady. 'I suppose that means you've been up to something again. But at least your frock is still clean. Who's this young gentleman?'

'Mummy, he's the one who saved my life, from a galloping runaway horse,' said Sophy, 'but I wouldn't call him a young gentleman, you should have heard the cheeky beast lecturing me.'

'It wasn't a runaway horse,' said Jimmy, and Sophy's parents, Mr and Mrs Gibbs, took a good look at him. Mr Gibbs had a slight smile on his face, as if his daughter was an amusement to him. Mrs Gibbs looked as if Sophy could be a trial to her.

'I'd like to have heard the lecture,' said Mr Gibbs.

'So would I,' said Mrs Gibbs, a lady of refined looks.

'I didn't exactly save her life,' said Jimmy, 'just from gettin' herself knocked down.'

'He's going to buy me an ice cream wafer now, at the kiosk,' said Sophy.

'Shouldn't you be buying him one?' asked Mr Gibbs.

'Oh, I'm going to pay,' said Sophy, 'and he's going to owe me.'

'That doesn't sound right,' said Mrs Gibbs.

'Actu'lly,' said Jimmy, 'I've got to join my sisters at the Serpentine, they're waitin' for me.'

Liking his looks, Mr Gibbs said, 'Well, bring them along and I'll buy ice cream wafers for everybody.'

'Tea for me, Frank,' said Mrs Gibbs.

'I'll go and help this boy bring his sisters,' said Sophy.

'Not by the Serpentine you won't,' said Mrs Gibbs. 'I know what will happen, you'll fall in and your father will have to come and pull you out. You'll come with us.'

'Oh, blow,' said Sophy, adventurous, capricious and headstrong.

'All right, I'll bring my sisters,' said Jimmy, and off he went.

'Who is he, what's his name?' asked Mr Gibbs.

'He didn't say,' said Sophy. 'Don't some boys make you want to spit?'

'You terror, I'll give you spit,' said Mrs Gibbs.

Sophy rolled her eyes.

'What d'you mean?' asked Patsy.

'Yes, her dad's goin' to buy us all ice cream wafers from the kiosk,' said Jimmy, who'd given a sensible account of the incident. 'You go on to the tea rooms with Betsy, while I tell Dad and Aunt Edie where we'll be, then I'll catch you up.' Off he went to the bandstand, the afternoon concert still going on. Dad and Aunt Edie were enjoying the music. Jimmy explained the situation.

'Oh, you met a girl, Jimmy?' Aunt Edie showed the natural interest of a woman who held her nephew and nieces in affection. 'Is she nice?'

'Barmy,' said Jimmy. 'Still, we can't say no to ice cream wafers.'

'Go ahead,' said dad, 'and I'll bring your Aunt Edie over for a cup of tea in a while.'

'See you in the tea rooms, then,' said Jimmy. 'Aunt Edie, you don't half look peachy.'

'That boy,' smiled Aunt Edie, watching him go.

'He's got taste,' said Dad, 'I'll say that much.'

'I wonder who 'e gets it from,' said Aunt Edie.

'Me?' said Dad.

'Don't make me laugh,' said Aunt Edie, who had long wondered what he saw in her cousin Maud. The band launched itself into the 'Radetzky March', and at once her feet began to tap. She liked a military band and its rousing music.

Jimmy, catching his sisters up, took them on to the tea rooms where Sophy and her parents were waiting. Patsy saw at once that the girl's dress and hat were posh and expensive, and that her mother's summery outfit was ever so elegant. Crikey, she thought, Jimmy's met rich people.

'Hullo again,' said Mr Gibbs, 'are these your sisters?' He smiled. 'You didn't tell us they were pretty. Sit down and I'll get the wafers and then order some tea. I'm Mr Gibbs, and this charming lady is my wife.'

'This is Patsy,' said Jimmy, 'and this is Betsy. We're Andrews.'

'I'm Sophy,' said Mr Gibb's daughter, a law unto herself if she could get away with it. 'You haven't said your own name.'

'He's Jimmy,' said Patsy, with Betsy hanging shyly back.

'Sit down,' said Mr Gibbs again, then went to the kiosk. Everyone else sat down, Mrs Gibbs viewing Jimmy and his sisters with a little smile. She had seen their like in Brixton, the birthplace of her husband.

The tea rooms were crowded. There were cockney families, middle-class families, and a small group of ladies with Belgravia accents. In such a cosmopolitan atmosphere, the post-war depression seemed a lot less depressing. Cockney dads were in form, threatening their kids with the belt if they misbehaved. Cockney mums were making tart comments to waitresses about the shocking price of currant buns. Bright little bunches of cherries or grapes splashed their large hats with colour. A single glossy white feather adorned Mrs Gibb's small hat.

'Did your brother tell you he saved me from being trampled to death by a runaway horse?' asked Sophy of Patsy.

'Crikey, did yer really, Jimmy?' asked Betsy, coming out of her shyness at this breathtaking news.

'He just said he'd met a girl in Rotten Row,' said Patsy. 'He said she was standin' in front of a horse.'

'A moving horse?' smiled Mrs Gibbs.

'Moving?' said Sophy. 'It was jolly well galloping. And foaming at the nostrils,' she added for good measure.

'Oh, crikey,' breathed Betsy.

'I think I'd better make it clear that Sophy has a habit of exaggerating everything,' said Mrs Gibbs.

'Dad says vinegar on the tongue is a good cure for that, Mrs Gibbs,' said Jimmy, 'but you have to catch the tongue while it's still young.'

'Perhaps I'll try that,' said Mrs Gibbs.

Mr Gibbs returned with five wafers, one each for everybody except his wife. He handed them out with a smile. A waitress arrived and he ordered a pot of tea and fruit cake for six. The waitress said she didn't know if the wafers ought to be eaten at the table, but as they were ordering tea and fruit cake perhaps it was all right.

'There's a nice girl,' said Mr Gibbs with a smile, and that did the trick, it made the waitress feel she was special.

Mr Frank Gibbs was a man of enterprise and initiative. Born of cockney parents in Brixton, he had pulled himself out of the rut to become a skilled carpenter, joiner and furniture designer. He worked for high-class manufacturers, but by the time he was twenty-five he had started his own business. It had expanded rapidly. He was forty-seven now and the owner of two factories. His wife, Elizabeth, had a middle-class upbringing. Needing someone to supervise his office staff and to act as his secretary, he advertised and she applied for the job. She was twenty-one then, he was twenty-seven, and in a week he was in love with her. He married her six months later. He still had a few rough edges and knew it, so he made his proposal prepared for her to turn him down. But she accepted without hesitation. She liked his masculinity and his vigour. She turned him into a man with no rough edges at all, but changed nothing of his enthusiastic approach to life and to business. She gave him three children, twin boys first and then a girl. Both boys at eighteen had entered the Army, both had wanted a military career. Sophy, their daughter, was her father's one weakness. She could get anything she wanted out of him. He spoiled her day in, day out. Only his wife stood between Sophy and domestic anarchy.

An outgoing man, Mr Gibbs engaged himself in conversation with Jimmy and the boy's sisters. The wafers finished, a large pot of tea arrived with a plate of fruit cake slices. While Mrs Gibbs looked after the wants of the young people, Mr Gibbs talked and listened. He soon found out that Jimmy was in need of a job.

'I can give you something to do until one turns up,' he said.

'Yes, he can come and do things for me,' said Sophy, who was presently looking for a kindred spirit.

'I forbid that here and now,' said Mrs Gibbs.

'But, Mummy—'

'Never,' said Mrs Gibbs. 'I don't want the responsibility of having to tell Jimmy's parents that he's died a sudden and violent death.'

'Crumbs,' said Betsy through her fruit cake. 'Our mum an' dad wouldn't like that.'

'No, I suppose it's not popular,' said Jimmy gravely. 'Mr Gibbs, can you really give me something to do till I get another job?'

122

'Twice over,' said Mr Gibbs, and went on to say that he and Mrs Gibbs had just purchased a house in Anerley, not far from the Crystal Palace. It was an old but impressive property with several acres of grounds that had been left to run wild. The house itself had been fully redecorated and essential repairs carried out, and the family was in occupation. During the last week, landscape gardeners had begun a massive clearance of the overgrown grounds. All kinds of work needed to be done. Could Jimmy use a saw? Jimmy could.

'Well, that's fine,' said Mr Gibbs. 'If you'd like to come every day, there's work for you for quite a while.'

'Yes, and I'll help,' said Sophy.

'I think not,' said Mrs Gibbs.

'Mummy, you do fuss,' said Sophy.

'It's just as well I do,' said Mrs Gibbs amid the enjoyable clatter of Bank Holiday tea, 'someone has to make sure you stay alive.'

'Well, I'll just tell him what to do,' said Sophy, 'that's all.'

'Your father will do that,' said Mrs Gibbs, and took fresh stock of Jimmy. Along with her husband, she liked the look of the boy. He had to be saved from Sophy. 'Would you like to do the work?' she asked him.

'I'm all for it, Mrs Gibbs,' said Jimmy.

'I'll pay you, of course,' said Mr Gibbs.

'How much, please?' asked Patsy, pleased for her brother but impulsively wanting to find out if he was going to be slave-driven.

'How about four bob a day?' said Mr Gibbs.

'Four bob a day?' said Jimmy. At this particular moment in his life, that sounded highly profitable.

'Fair do's, I hope, Jimmy?' said Mr Gibbs.

'I'll come tomorrow, on an early tram,' said Jimmy.

'Patsy's on her school holidays, so I'll ask her if she can do the rounds of some firms for me, to see if there's any job on offer.'

'Me do what?' said Patsy.

'I like Patsy,' said Jimmy. 'You could ask some sisters favours and all you'd get would be a poke in the eye. But Patsy's kind and obligin'.'

'I can't remember she's obliged me,' said Betsy.

'Yes, I 'ave,' said Patsy indignantly.

'Yes, but not much,' said Betsy, and Mrs Gibbs laughed. She recognized the typical cockney liveliness of these two girls. Sophy was watching Jimmy, a little hint of wickedness in her eyes.

Dad and Aunt Edie entered the tea rooms and came over. Jimmy did the introductions, and Mrs Gibbs, of course, wondered about the presence of the boy's handsome aunt and the absence of his mother. Dad shook hands with Mr Gibbs, and Aunt Edie said hullo to Mrs Gibbs, who thought her large hat spectacular. Aunt Edie thought the single feather in Mrs Gibb's small hat very stylish, and she observed with interest the lady's daughter, the girl Jimmy had met in Rotten Row. My, what a poppet, Jimmy already knew how to pick them. With a name like Sophy too, just about the most teasing name a girl could have. Aunt Edie felt there was a very teasing minx behind the girl's demure look. And didn't Jimmy look at home. Mr and Mrs Gibbs were obviously well-off, but Jimmy was so cool anyone would have thought he mixed with rich people every day. Well, it took a lot to put Jimmy out of his stride. He was like his dad. Bless them all, thought Aunt Edie.

No-one quite knew the extent of Aunt Edie's affection for Jimmy and his sisters, or the contempt she felt for their mother's cranky self-indulgencies. Their dad, she felt, deserved a far more loving wife than Maud had become.

Mr Gibbs ordered more tea and fruit cake, and Aunt Edie and Dad joined the little party. Chatter chased itself around the table. Mrs Gibbs, who liked men in a sensible way, which meant she found them entertaining enough to overlook their faults, engaged Dad in conversation. Discovering he had served in the Army during the war, she told him that her twin sons had joined the regulars six months ago. Dad said he hoped they wouldn't run up against his old sergeant-major, who'd been known to eat recruits. Mrs Gibbs laughed. Dad said no laughing matter, it can be seriously painful. What was his sergeant-major's name, then? George Frederick Hobbs, said Dad. Mrs Gibbs said she'd write to her sons and ask them if that's the name of their sergeant-major. Well, said Dad, if it is, your letter might not arrive in time. There might only be bones left. Mrs Gibbs laughed again. Dad had already passed the test of being entertaining.

Aunt Edie was chatting with Mr Gibbs, and Sophy was doing her best to monopolize Jimmy. She asked him if he liked chopping trees down.

'I'm choppin' them down all the time,' he said, 'about fifty a day.'

'That's a fib, no-one could chop down fifty a day,' said Sophy.

'All right, say forty a day.'

'What a fibber,' said Sophy, 'you'd have to have hundreds of trees in your garden to chop down even ten a day.'

'We only got a back yard,' said Betsy, 'we don't 'ave no trees.'

'No, well, I've chopped them all down,' said Jimmy.

'How many did you have, then?' asked Sophy.

'About a thousand,' said Jimmy.

'Oh, you flabbergasting fibber,' said Sophy in delight.

'You'd best not believe 'ardly anything my brother says,' advised Patsy.

'How old is he?' asked Sophy.

'About six or seven,' said Patsy.

'Course 'e ain't,' said Betsy. 'Jimmy's sixteen,' she added proudly. Well, small girls were proud when they had a sixteen-year-old brother who could flabbergast posh girls like this one.

'I'm thirteen.' Sophy made an impressive declaration of her years, as if at that age she was already superior to the rest of civilization. 'I'll help your brother when he comes to work for my father.'

'I think your mum said you're not to,' remarked Patsy.

'Oh, I shan't tell her,' said Sophy. 'She gets the wind up as soon as I put my foot outside the door. I can't do anything with her sometimes. Is your mother like that?'

'Well, sometimes she's a bit like it,' said Patsy cautiously.

'Girls have awful problems with mothers,' said Sophy.

'I heard that,' said Mrs Gibbs.

'Well, that's jolly well not fair,' said Sophy, 'you're not supposed to be listening when we're talking privately about parents.'

'Oh, dear me, I am sorry,' said Mrs Gibbs drily.

'I bet Jimmy's mother doesn't listen to private conversations,' said Sophy, 'does she, Jimmy?'

'Oh, we don't 'ave private conversations in our house,' said Jimmy. 'You can't when you've got sisters that like to listen to everything.'

'I like listenin',' said Betsy. 'Dad says funny fings, don't you, Dad?'

'Never mind what Dad says,' said Patsy, 'listen to what that Jimmy's sayin', he's 'aving a go at us, Betsy.'

'Shall we kick 'im?' asked Betsy ingenuously.

'We can't, not now,' said Patsy, 'we're in company.'

'Don't mind us,' said Mr Gibbs, 'go ahead.'

That aroused laughter. More conversation followed before the two families went their separate ways, Jimmy with the address of Sophy's parents tucked into his pocket and an animated goodbye from Sophy ringing in his ears.

'That girl likes you, Jimmy,' said Patsy, as they made their way to the bus stop.

'Not too much, I hope,' said Jimmy. 'I've got a feelin' it could mean an early death. Well, from what her mum said it could.'

'I think you'll win, Jimmy,' said Aunt Edie.

'Made a conquest, 'ave you, Jimmy?' smiled Dad.

'I never heard of any feller my age makin' a conquest,' said Jimmy. 'And I don't know it would make sense to chase after a rich girl, anyway.'

'I suppose there's other ways of makin' your fortune,' said Dad, 'like findin' a goldmine.'

'A rich girl's a goldmine,' said Aunt Edie, 'and nicer to cuddle, I should think.' And she laughed.

Patsy thought, ain't it lovely having our Aunt Edie with us?

Aunt Edie served up a supper of fried eggs, bacon and tomatoes with bread and butter. And afterwards, she played the piano again and sang again. And she practised the duets with Jimmy again. It all added up to a lovely Bank Holiday weekend.

Mother had been absent throughout, but Aunt Edie had come up trumps. Jimmy had said nothing about Mother being at Speakers Corner supporting a dark-looking large bloke who was even barmier about religion than she was. He didn't think it would help if Dad knew she had set about hecklers with her umbrella.

Last thing, just before Aunt Edie went up to bed, Dad said, 'You've been a champ, Edie old girl, thanks.'

'Yes, well,' said Aunt Edie, and seemed stuck for words for once.

'Jimmy an' the girls enjoyed 'aving you here,' said Dad.

'They're not 'elpless kids, I'll say that, Jack,' said Aunt Edie. 'You've done a good job with them.'

'Yes, Maudie's always—'

'Not her,' said Aunt Edie, 'you. I haven't been blind all these years, 'specially not since you come 'ome from the war. I'll be goin' straight to work in the mornin' after I've got breakfast, and I'll be 'ere again next Friday evenin', unless you let me know that Maud's come back.'

'I'll be gone early meself, I've got to be in by eight,' said Dad.

'I'll get your breakfast,' said Aunt Edie, lighting the candle that was to see her up to bed.

'No, I'll manage—'

'I'll do it,' said Aunt Edie, 'someone's got to remember you spent all those years fightin' in the war and gettin' yourself wounded.' And she went up to the bedroom before Dad could say any more. But he grinned. Aunt Edie was a woman and a half.

CHAPTER EIGHT

The house in Anerley was called The Beeches. It stood almost alone, for the immediate houses on either side were both a long stone's throw away. The wide front garden was all lawn except for two giant beech trees that soared massively upwards. Double wrought-iron gates set into a high brick wall opened on to a gravel drive and a spacious forecourt fronting the handsome house. On the forecourt stood a horse-drawn van on which was painted the name of a firm of landscape gardeners in flowery script. There was also an open motorcar, a 6 hp De Dion Bouton, a gleaming yellow two-seater, with black fenders and huge brass lamps.

Jimmy, entering through the open gates, stared at the motorcar, a sign of real riches. Crikey, what a machine! He walked up the drive to the forecourt. The shafts of the van rested on the ground, and he supposed the horse was cropping away somewhere. He approached the large front door set inside an arched stone frame. He pulled on a metal bell handle and heard the bell jangle.

A young maid, dressed in dark blue with a white lacy front and a white cap, opened the door. Crikey, what a corker, thought Jimmy. She had shining black hair, bright eyes and vivacious looks.

'Well, you're early,' she said.

'You knew I was comin'?' asked Jimmy.

'I was told by madam that a boy was. Are you a boy?'

'Well, yes, as far as I know,' said Jimmy. 'I think you're a girl.'

'Oh, you're a clever boy as well?'

'No, I'm just Jimmy Andrews.'

'I think you're cheeky,' she said, looking him over. ''Specially usin' the front door and not the side. Well, madam and young madam's still at breakfast. The master's out and about, though, givin' orders to the workmen. D'you want a cup of tea and a bit of toast before Mr 'Odges takes you to report to Mr Gibbs? Come on, this way.'

She led Jimmy through a hall larger than his Dad's house in Manor Place, then down a passage to the main kitchen. It was hung with pots and pans, and a huge range was slowly burning coal. At a large table sat a dignified-looking man, a woman and another maid.

'Here's the boy, Mr 'Odges, he'd like a cup of tea and a slice of that toast. That's Mr 'Odges, that's Mrs Redfern, the cook, and that's Ivy, who does the dusting, lights the fires and 'elps Mrs Redfern.'

Mr Hodges, the butler, was stout as well as dignified, Mrs Redfern was a widow but plump and jolly for all that, and Ivy was a bit skinny.

'Hullo, I'm Jimmy Andrews, I've come to help Mr Gibbs.'

'I'm Ada,' said the young maid.

'Bet your dad likes you,' said Jimmy.

'I think we've got a cheeky one 'ere, Mr 'Odges,' said Ada. 'Still, you can sit down, Jimmy.'

Jimmy sat down, all eyes on him, and Mrs Redfern poured him a cup of tea and Ada gave him a slice of toast from a dish. Ivy pushed butter and marmalade across. Jimmy thanked her.

'Might I henquire as to your age, young man?' asked Mr Hodges.

'Sixteen,' said Jimmy, buttering his toast.

'Poor young feller, what a shame,' said Ivy, 'it don't seem right, anyone your age perishin'.'

'Beg your pardon?' said Jimmy.

'Ain't you seen outside, ain't you seen what it's like?' said Ivy. 'Talk about jungles, everything's bigger than you are, and you ain't little. It's nearly bigger than Mr 'Odges and even the master. You only want some of it to fall on you an' you won't ever be seen again, will 'e, Mr 'Odges?'

'I am in 'ope that the lad is sharp,' said Mr Hodges.

'Some of it nearly done Mr 'Odges last week, nearly done 'im for good,' said Ivy, 'and I just don't know 'ow the young madam ain't disappeared for ever.'

'Take no notice, Jimmy,' said Ada, who was just sixteen. She'd been in service with the Gibbs since she was fourteen. 'Ivy's always the life an' soul, 'specially at funerals.'

'Well, I'm not keen on lettin' things fall on me,' said Jimmy, enjoying the toast and marmalade. 'In fact, I made up my mind yesterday that at my age I'd like to stay alive. I've 'ardly done any real livin' yet.'

'I hadmire a boy that can think about things,' said Mr Hodges.

'Some people wander about like they was blind to what might fall on them,' said Mrs Redfern. 'I'm that pleased this boy looks as if he can see what's comin'. Can you see like that, young man?'

'I've not had much trouble so far,' said Jimmy.

'That's good,' said cook. 'Well, he seems a sensible boy, Mr Hodges.'

'Granted, Mrs Redfern,' said the butler.

'I heard something about him savin' the young madam from being run over by a horse. Did you do that, young man?'

'I just pulled her out of the way,' said Jimmy.

'She's got nine lives, the young madam,' said Ivy.

'Madam says she needs them all,' said Ada.

'I'll keep out of her way,' said Jimmy. 'I don't want to 'elp her use one of them up.'

'You'll be lucky,' said Ada.

'Lucky?' said Jimmy.

'If you can keep out of young madam's way,' said Ada.

'Poor young feller,' said Ivy. 'What with things that might fall on 'im, an' what the young madam might do to 'im, 'is fate don't bear thinkin' about.'

'I think it's bein' so cheerful that keeps Ivy goin', don't you, Mr 'Odges?' said Ada.

'I am in fits,' said Mr Hodges. He rose from the table. A buzzer chirruped. He looked at the indicator box mounted on the wall. 'Madam's finished breakfast. Clear the breakfast room, Ada. Come along, my boy, and I will take you to the outer world and to the master, Mr Gibbs.'

'Good luck, Jimmy,' said Ada. A bright little smile surfaced. 'At least you got a nice sunny day for things to fall on you.'

'Yes, what a blessin',' said Jimmy, and followed Mr Hodges out of the main kitchen into a smaller one with a large sink and storage bins.

Mr Hodges led the way along a corridor to a side door of the house. He turned right along a path and came round to a large conservatory at the rear of the mansion-like residence. The conservatory looked as if it contained its own jungle. From a magnificent paved terrace, Jimmy saw the main jungle. Just beyond the terrace overgrown ground had been cleared to a depth of thirty yards. The clearance was some sixty yards wide, and on either side were huge piles of brambles, twigs, leaves and small tree branches. Beyond the clearing was the jungle. Lofty beeches and huge spreading oaks reached for the sky, and in between slender saplings fought to reach the light. The trees looked as if they were bedded in a tangled mass of hawthorn, bramble, wild roses and the like, and these were sprouting high in their battle to escape enveloping weeds and tall grasses. Above the jungle, Jimmy glimpsed sunlight flashing on the vast curved glass roof of the Crystal Palace, nearly a mile away. The terrace was bounded by stone balusters supporting a stone coping. A central opening led to six shallow paved steps, balustrated on either side, and the steps took one down to the clearing. In the quietness of the morning, Jimmy heard the sounds of axes and saws away to the left.

Mr Hodges blew a whistle and waited. 'Might I hask if you have brought an apron, young man?' he enquired.

'Me? An apron? I hope you're jokin', Mr Hodges.'

'A workman's apron. Protection for your jersey and trousers. Mr Gibbs won't want to send you 'ome looking ruined. Ah, here he is.'

Mr Gibbs emerged from the left of the jungle and walked over the clearing. He was wearing old corduroy trousers and an open-necked brown shirt. His head was bare, his face brown from the sun. He reached the steps and smiled up at Jimmy.

'So there you are, young 'un. Good.' It wasn't yet nine o'clock, but Mr Gibbs looked as if he'd been at work for hours. 'Come on.'

'Might I suggest he needs an apron, sir?' said Mr Hodges.

'So he does. One of the calico ones, Hodges. D'you mind?'

'I will hadvance back to the kitchen, sir,' said Hodges, and did so. He returned with a light brown calico apron and gave it to Jimmy, who put it on and tied it. It was a thick, coarse protective garment.

'Right, this way, Jimmy,' said Mr Gibbs, and Jimmy went down the steps and followed him across the clearing. Mr Gibbs bore left. A line of beeches appeared, the ground between them cleared. 'I'm working myself, I'm taking a week off from my business. I like this kind of work, it's preparation for another kind of work, creating something.'

'A garden?' said Jimmy.

'I've twelve acres here, Jimmy, enough to create a large garden and a park.' Mr Gibbs broke through the line of beeches. Jimmy followed and saw another clearing. Mr Gibbs stopped. 'I'm a Brixton man, Jimmy, born and bred in the smoke, so I like parks and green grass. How do you feel about that?'

'Well, I like Ruskin Park and Hyde Park, Mr Gibbs.'

'Don't we all. Right, this is your starting pitch, Jimmy.'

The large clearing was littered, not only with hacked undergrowth but with felled bush and shrub. In the middle a large bonfire had been constructed. Felled saplings and the trunks of dead trees were piled to one side. Close to the pile were sawn-off branches. In the jungle beyond the sounds of axes and saws came clearer to Jimmy's ears.

'There doesn't seem any end to the jungle, Mr Gibbs.'

'It's like this over most of the acres, Jimmy.'

'You goin' to saw everything down except this line of trees, Mr Gibbs?'

'Not on your life, Jimmy. Most of the saplings, yes. They don't belong, except in a few places. They're trying to pinch air from established trees. Getting rid of them is like a pruning operation, and you need to do it to keep the established trees healthy and vigorous. As it is, some trees

134

have died. They'll have to come down too. Now, over there are wheelbarrows, rakes, pitchforks, saws, the lot. Your job is to clear up, first to saw those branches up, to rid all major branches of smaller branches. Everything's going to be burned. Tons of stuff. See that bonfire over there? That's ready for lighting. I want you to build others just like it. But we shan't be putting a torch to them by day, we'll smoke out the whole of Anerley if we do. We'll light them at night. In one of those wheelbarrows is a thick pair of industrial gloves that'll protect your hands, otherwise you'll tear your fingers to pieces when you're gathering up all this hacked bramble. Can you make bonfires, Jimmy, building a cradle first so that there's air to help the fire get started?'

'Layers of twigs, Mr Gibbs?'

'That's the stuff, Jimmy. Can I leave you to it? Oh, there'll be some lemonade for you about mid-morning. Go up to the terrace for it, one of the servants will call you. How's that?'

'I'm followin' you, Mr Gibbs.'

'Leave any timber that's too heavy. I'll get the men to throw it on when the bonfires are going tonight. Now I'm off to supervise them. That's the advantage of being the gaffer, they work and you supervise.' Mr Gibbs smiled and left Jimmy to it. Jimmy decided on clearing work first, on building bonfires of all the hacked stuff and sawing up branches later. He found the gloves, pulled them on, took hold of a rake and began to clear an area for the building of the first bonfire. The day was warm, the air sweet with the scent of scythed grass and chopped blackthorn. Jimmy whistled. It exhilarated him to be working out of doors and in country-like surroundings such as these. He raked away, using his gloved hands to move large tangles of hacked bramble.

Eyes watched him, eyes full of mischief. She appeared, summery in an apple green frock, her hair ribboned. Jimmy sensed trouble.

'Hullo, Jimmy.'

'Yes, good morning,' said Jimmy. 'I won't keep you and I'm a bit busy.'

'You're all over bits,' said Sophy.

'Can't stop,' said Jimmy, raking away.

'I'll help,' said Sophy.

'You're not supposed to.'

'Oh, Mummy said it's all right, she said I ought to come and say hullo to you, she said she'd feel ashamed if I didn't. I suppose any mother would feel ashamed if her only daughter didn't come and say hullo to someone who saved her life. I'll go and get another rake.'

'You're on school holidays, I suppose, are you?' said Jimmy, pulling a heap of bramble free of the ground. 'Don't you have some dolls you can go and play with?'

'Dolls? Dolls? Me?' Sophy split her sides. 'I'm not seven years old, you know, you impertinent beast. I'll get a rake.' Off she went, treading a path through the debris. Back she came, bearing a rake. 'Now, I'll help you.'

'Excuse me, but you can't,' said Jimmy, now at work in the middle of his cleared area. He had an armful of leafy twigs and was making a cradle.

'I'm going to,' declared Sophy.

'Not in your frock,' said Jimmy.

'Oh, it's just an old thing. What are you doing?'

'Buildin' a bonfire.'

'Oh, I'll bring more sticks and stuff,' said Sophy, dropping the rake.

'Look, you sure your mum said it'll be all right?'

'Of course I'm sure,' said Sophy, pulling twigs free of debris.

'Wouldn't you like to go and say hullo to your dad?' asked Jimmy hopefully.

'I said hullo to him before breakfast. Oh, do wake up, Jimmy. Here.' She showered twigs on to the cradle.

'I think I've got trouble,' said Jimmy under his breath.

Sophy was insistent, and they worked together building the bonfire, Jimmy using his gloved hands to cope with thorn and bramble, Sophy pulling at less harmful stuff. The bonfire began to mount. Jimmy went for a pitchfork at that stage. Sophy called to him to bring her one too. Resigned, he did so. They used the pitchforks to dig into the raked mounds of debris and to add them to the growing mountain. Jimmy was quick and efficient, Sophy exuberant and careless.

'Up she goes!' she cried, showering debris.

'Look, d'you mind not chuckin' it over me?' said Jimmy, brushing stuff from his hair.

'Don't be cheeky,' said Sophy, 'and don't stand in my way.' She brought more tangled debris on her pitchfork. A girl of the outdoors, the sun had turned her face golden. She jerked upwards with the pitchfork. Twigs, grass and other stuff went up into the air and fell back over her.

'That's clever, that is,' said Jimmy.

'Oh, blimey,' said Sophy, and brushed bits and pieces from her hair and frock leaving dust marks on both. 'Oh, well, never mind, all in a day's work.'

Jimmy brought a large forkful and neatly deposited it. Sophy chucked her next load all over the place and yelled with laughter as scythed hay landed on Jimmy's head.

'Well, thanks for your help,' he said. 'Now go and have a nice time somewhere and I'll carry on.'

'I'm having a nice time here,' she said. She wouldn't go, she stayed with him, worked with him, bossed him about, ran around picking up light broken branches, tossed them on to the mountain of debris, talked all the time and got in his way. There was grass in her hair, dust on her face and a tear in her frock.

'Oh, crikey,' said Jimmy, taking a look at her.

Her eyes bright, she said, 'It's jolly blissful, messing about. I like messing about, don't you?'

'I'm not messin' about,' said Jimmy. 'I'm workin'.'

'Sophy?' A voice called. 'Are you down there, doing your sketching?'

'Oh, corks,' said Sophy, and ran towards the line of beeches. Coming to a stop, she called, 'Is that you, Mummy?'

'Oh, you are there. Are you doing your sketching?'

'Pardon, Mummy?'

'Come up here, where I can see you.'

'I'm all right, Mummy.'

'Are you with your father?'

'Daddy's with the men sawing, I don't want to get in the way and get sawn up.'

'Thank God for that. What are you sketching?'

'Pardon, Mummy?'

'What are you sketching?'

'Well, there's lot of things, wild flowers and everything.'

'If you see the boy Jimmy, keep out of his way.'

'Yes, he's ever so busy, Mummy. I don't mind helping him, if you like.'

'God help him if you do. Just get on with your sketching.'

'Yes, Mummy, I'll go and look for my sketch book, I put it down somewhere. Can I have some lemonade later?'

'When the whistle blows. Behave yourself now, and don't get your frock grubby.'

'No, Mummy.'

When she rejoined Jimmy she had a thick sketch book and a box of crayons with her. She put them down on the ground. Jimmy looked at her. The ribbon in her hair was loose and dangling, her hair itself all over the place, her frock covered with bits and pieces.

'I think you'd better do some sketchin', like your mum says.'

'Yes, in a minute.' Sophy was quick to engage herself again with a rake.

'It sorrows me that you're a fibber,' said Jimmy, working on a new area.

'Blessed impudence,' said Sophy. 'I didn't fib to Mummy.'

'You did to me. You told me your mum said it was all right for you to 'elp me.'

'Oh, that,' said Sophy. 'Well, I can always tell Mummy you made me.'

'Oh, crikey,' said Jimmy, 'I knew I'd got trouble. Listen, you'd better do a bit of sketchin', your mum's bound to ask to see some.'

'All right,' said Sophy, and sat down on the ground. She opened up the sketch book and the box of crayons, looked up at Jimmy, saw him start work again, and began to sketch.

Jimmy enjoyed a quiet fifteen minutes. Then, at ten-thirty, a whistle blew.

'Is that for the lemonade?' he asked.

'Yes,' said Sophy, head bent over her sketching. 'Jimmy, could you bring mine, I don't think I'll go up, in case – yes, you bring mine. There'll be biscuits as well. Ask for a tray.'

'Don't fall down a hole while I'm gone,' said Jimmy, and he heard her giggle as he went up through the paths to the terrace. It wasn't Mr Hodges who was there with the lemonade, it was Mrs Gibbs, looking corking, he thought, in a lovely lilac summer dress.

'So there you are, Jimmy,' she said, smiling down at him as he came up the steps.

'Hullo, Mrs Gibbs,' he said. There was a tray on an ornamental garden table. He saw two glasses of home-made lemonade and a plate of biscuits.

'You look very workman-like, young man,' said Mrs Gibbs.

'Yes, I've only tripped over the apron once, Mrs Gibbs, I think it must've been made for a six-feet-six bloke, don't you?'

Mrs Gibbs smiled again. What a very nice boy he was. He came from Walworth, he looked a growing young man, and his frank and open grey eyes gave her the impression that far from being afraid of life, he'd fight it all the way. Just like her husband, a Brixton cockney, who'd challenged life at every turn and made of himself the kind of man she admired. Mrs Gibbs took very warmly to Jimmy at that moment.

'Well, any old apron will do to prevent you tearing your jersey to pieces, won't it?' she said. 'There's your lemonade and biscuits, and where's that harum-scarum daughter of mine? Climbing a tree, I shouldn't wonder.'

'I saw her doin' some sketchin', Mrs Gibbs.' Jimmy knew Sophy was going to be in the soup on account of the state of her frock, and dirt all over her hair and face, but one principle was sacred to Walworth boys: if someone was going to be in the soup, you did your best either to keep them out of it or to make sure the soup wasn't too hot. 'Oh, and I think I've got to apologize, Mrs Gibbs. She just came to say hullo to me, which was nice of her, I must say, but I didn't see 'er comin', I crossed her path and accident'lly tripped her up. I'm very sorry, Mrs Gibbs.'

Mrs Gibbs gave him a searching look. Jimmy was as grave as an owl. 'I see, Jimmy. You tripped her up. Is her condition fatal?'

'Beg your pardon, Mrs Gibbs?'

'Never mind.' Mrs Gibbs smiled again. 'Where is she? Why hasn't she come up for her lemonade?'

'Oh, she's probably gone deaf from concentratin' on her sketchin',' said Jimmy. 'I go deaf myself when I'm doin' something I've got to think seriously about. I just 'ope I'm not in a deaf condition if our house ever catches fire and I don't hear the fire engines. I don't like thinkin' about that sort of thing, do you, Mrs Gibbs?'

Mrs Gibbs laughed. 'I'm an optimist myself, Jimmy.'

'Yes, I think you make a very nice optimist, Mrs Gibbs. Shall I take Sophy's lemonade to her? I think I know where she is, I think I know where to find her.'

'Very well, Jimmy, and when you do find her tell her if she returns to the house looking like last year's ragbag, I'll sell her to the dustmen when they next call.'

'Yes, I'll tell 'er that, Mrs Gibbs. Shall I take the tray?'

'Do that, Jimmy,' said Mrs Gibbs and stood on the terrace watching him as he carried the tray down the path and disappeared into the jungle. She heard him whistling, and felt rather touched that her husband had given the boy the chance to earn himself some money. Sophy was down there with him, of course, and doing her precocious best to torment the life out of him. Mrs Gibbs hoped Jimmy would give as good as he got. She had a feeling he would.

'You haven't been very quick,' said Sophy as Jimmy arrived with the tray.

'Well, your mum and me had a talk,' said Jimmy. He put the tray down on the ground and gave the girl a glass of lemonade. She was sitting with her sketch book on her lap.

'You didn't tell her where I was, did you?' said Sophy.

'I said I thought I knew where to find you, so she let me bring the tray. And I gave her a sort of warnin' that you might look a bit of a shock to 'er when she next sees you.'

'Listen, you blessed boy, don't you tell my mother things like that.'

'Listen, faceache, your mum's goin' to sell you to the dustmen if you go back to the house lookin' like a ragbag.'

'Excuse me,' said Sophy, 'if you call me faceache again, I'll kick you silly.'

'Yes, you would, too,' said Jimmy, drinking his lemonade. 'I bet you're a danger to human life. I told your mum I accident'lly tripped you up, so she'll expect you to look a bit of a ragbag. Just don't get to look like last year's, that's all.'

'You cheeky beast,' said Sophy.

Jimmy ate a biscuit, then went back to his work. He began to build a pile for another bonfire, as Mr Gibbs had told him to. He liked the work, he liked the activity of it. Sophy appeared beside him, stooping to pick up the heavier debris and to throw it on the pile.

'No, not yet,' said Jimmy, 'I'm buildin' a cradle first.' He showed her: one layer of sticks first, then another layer crossways over it, and so on.

'Oh, I'll get bits of branches like sticks,' said Sophy, and off she went to search and rummage. Jimmy made a wide sweep of the littered clearing, finding his own kind of kindling.

He heard a yell. 'Jimmy, come here!' He took a look. There she was, trapped in a tangle of stuff. Away to the left, axes and saws were at work, weedy saplings falling. He walked up to her. Her legs were buried in a forest of ferns, the skirt of her dress caught by smashed bramble.

'I don't think that looks too good,' he said.

'Oh, really?' said Sophy. 'What a blessed clever boy, what a shame you look like a boiled cauliflower. Well, don't just stand there, do something!'

'I'm sorry,' said Jimmy. 'I've got to say that, I've got to say I'm sorry, because I'm afraid you're stuck. Never mind, when I've finished me morning's work, I'll go and find your dad. I expect 'e'll be able to do something.' And he went back to his work, Sophy left in a state of disbelief.

'Oh, you rotten boy! Come back, do you hear? Oh, crikey, you wait, I'll hate you for ever, Jimmy Andrews, I'll never speak to you again, so there!'

'Is that a promise?' called Jimmy, piling debris over the cradle.

'Yes, it is! Oh, I've never met a rottener boy, I feel sick at letting you save my life.' Sophy was sure she was sinking deeper, chopped bramble taking hold of her frock.

'Well, all right, if it's a promise,' said Jimmy. There was a pair of heavy secateurs in a spare wheelbarrow. He slipped off his right glove, picked them up and returned to the trapped girl. He began to cut the clinging pieces of bramble to bits, pulling them away.

'Oh, my hero,' said Sophy wickedly.

'You promised you wouldn't speak,' said Jimmy.

'Well, I'm not going to, I'm not going to actually speak to you, I'm just going to say things, that's all.'

'Stand still,' said Jimmy.

'Well, I like that,' said Sophy. 'If I could stop standing still I could get out, couldn't I? Look what you've done to my frock.'

'Listen, faceache—'

'I'll kick you.'

'Your frock's had too many fights with thorny bits,' said Jimmy, 'it's nothing to do with me.' He cleared away the

143

bramble. Sophy didn't step free from the ferns, she jumped free. The skirt of her frock ripped.

'Oh, help,' she said, 'now look what we've done.'

'Now look what you've done, you mean,' said Jimmy.

'Mummy's going to have something to say to you. Oh, well, it can't be helped, let's get on.'

Jimmy was already getting on. Sophy began to dart about again, to drag and haul broken branches. Jimmy hauled larger ones. He'd done his best to discourage her, but Sophy had no intention of being left out of activity like this, especially not when she had as a companion a boy even more active than she was. She acquired another tear in her frock.

The several acres had become a woodland run wild. The landscape gardeners called in to tame it and make a parkland of it had an immense task on their hands for months. The sounds of their saws and axes was constant.

A voice broke through. 'Heavens above, can this be true?'

They turned. Sophy's mother was there. Mrs Gibbs had been unable to resist coming to investigate.

'Oh, crikey,' said Sophy. Her hair was a mess, her ribbon gone, her frock torn and grubby, and there were smuts on her face.

'You horror,' said Mrs Gibbs.

'Me?' said Sophy.

'Can that be the frock you put on this morning?'

'It's only an old one, Mummy.'

'This is only the second time you've worn it. What's happened to it, have you been attacked by tigers? Are there tigers in this jungle?'

'Mummy, of course not, and they're only little tears.'

'I'm sorry, Mrs Gibbs,' said Jimmy, 'but when I accident'lly tripped her up, there was bramble in the way.'

'Yes, honestly, Mummy, it's all over the place, you'll have to speak to Daddy about it.'

'Yes, there is a lot of it, Mrs Gibbs,' said Jimmy.

'Yes, isn't there?' said Mrs Gibbs, quite aware that the boy was trying to protect her daughter. 'Please carry on, Jimmy. You come with me, miss.'

'But, Mummy, we're busy,' protested Sophy.

'You're a horror,' said Mrs Gibbs, 'and you're destined for the dustbin. Pick up your sketch book and come with me.'

'Oh, corks, it's the lash, I bet,' said Sophy, and went with her mother, picking up her sketch book and box of crayons on the way. Following her, she said, 'I don't know how Jimmy's going to manage without me, Mummy. I mean, what's Daddy going to say when he finds out I've had to stop helping?'

'I've no idea what he's going to say, I'm hoping he'll smack your bottom.'

'I'll leave home,' said Sophy.

'Good,' said Mrs Gibbs. They reached the terrace. 'Sophy, I despair of you. Heavens, you're thirteen, not nine, you dreadful girl. What am I going to do with you?'

'Oh, I don't suppose there's much you can do now, Mummy, I suppose I'm going to be a dreadful girl all my life.'

'Over my dead body, you are,' said Mrs Gibbs, who always had a terrible problem trying to keep a straight face whenever she had this kind of dialogue with her irrepressible daughter. 'You're going to turn over a new leaf this holiday, and go about with girls who have managed to become acceptable young ladies.'

'Ugh,' said Sophy. 'I don't like girls, they're soppy, can't I go about with Jimmy? After all, he did save my life.'

'That young man comes from a family not as fortunate as ours, Sophy, and your father is giving him a little work here. It's not very fair of you, is it, to make yourself a nuisance to him because you want him as some kind of toy. I'm not going to let you do that, he's too nice a boy to be used for your amusement.'

'Mummy, what an awful thing to say, I don't know how to forgive you, but I'll have to, all girls have to forgive their mothers.'

'I'm grateful, of course,' said Mrs Gibbs, 'but you're going to spend the rest of the day up here, where I can keep my eye on you. Go and change that frock, and wash your hands and face, then do some serious sketching. What have you done so far?'

'Well, I kept getting interrupted, so I've only done one,' said Sophy, 'it's nothing much.'

'Show me.' Mrs Gibbs knew the necessity of being firm with her daughter, who was spoiled outrageously by her doting father. A little reluctantly, Sophy opened her sketch book and showed her mother a black crayon drawing of the boy she'd been having fun with. Mrs Gibbs regarded it with a little shock of instant pleasure for her daughter's undoubted talent. It was a gifted black and white impression of Jimmy's head and shoulders.

'Darling, that's lovely,' she said. 'Don't throw talent like that away.'

Sophy was a reluctant scholar. 'Mummy, I don't have to be up here sketching all day, do I? Not all day.'

'You can do other things, but you're not to lose yourself in that jungle again,' said Mrs Gibbs.

'Oh, lor', what a life,' said Sophy.

CHAPTER NINE

'That's the spirit, Father,' said Mother Joan. She was back from Berkshire, with several blank cheques in her handbag. 'No point in making the battle more difficult. A rattling good nosebag and—'

'Nosebag, sister?' queried Father Peter.

'Bags of fodder,' said Mother Joan, 'and clothes as well. No good ignoring their stomachs and backs. Remember how our Lord fed the five thousand, and I daresay He'd have provided them with winter vests too, if necessary.'

'Ah, to the poor shall be given the sustenance and warmth that will mellow their hardened souls,' said Father Peter.

'My idea precisely,' said Mother Joan.

'Some of their souls need a good hidin',' said Mother Mary.

'We must be charitable, sister,' said Mother Verity.

''Ear, 'ear,' said Father Luke, 'I'm all for the Lord's bounty bein' provided to the poor through the charitable 'ands of Mother Joan, and to us through the charitable 'ands of Father Peter. Ah, them 'ardened souls, don't the Lord say judge not and you won't be judged yourselves? I wasn't too 'appy about them thievin' our new urn, the price of which came out of Father Peter's gen'rous pocket, but then I said to meself, Father Luke, I said, we put temptation in the way of people who don't 'ave urns, which was a sin.'

'For which we are duly penitent,' said Father Peter.

'Mind, I was a bit vexed,' said Mother Mary.

'A human emotion under the circumstances, sister,' said Father Peter gently, laying a warm hand of understanding on her shoulder.

'Leave everything to us, Father,' said Mother Joan, 'we'll arrange the supply of food and clothing. Saddle up, sisters, and let's head for the fences with Father Luke.'

'It's condonin' sin to deal with fences, sister,' said Father Luke. 'They 'andle stolen goods.'

'No, no, the Lord's fences, you chump,' said Mother Joan. 'The challenge He offers for us to jump them and keep us on the right path.'

'I bless your excursion, sister,' said Father Peter. 'I have work to do here, examining and instructing new members. Our work in Hyde Park has borne precious fruit.'

'West End shops, sister?' enquired Mother Verity. She and the others, Mother Joan, Mother Mary, Mother Ruth and Father Luke, were on their way.

'Not likely,' said Mother Joan. 'They'll rob us blind. No, East End shops, sister. Best prices and a knowledge of the kind of food that's most suitable. They'll sell us tinned calves' tongues cooked in jelly in the West End. I'd say bully beef would be a lot more welcome, by George. Forward, sisters.'

'I've got my umbrella,' said Mother Mary.

'Keep it at the ready, sister,' said Mother Joan, 'a few noddles might need to be thumped.'

'Could yer repeat that, lady?' asked the grocer in Commercial Street.

'I asked what food you'd supply to a family in need,' said Mother Joan, vigorously buxom.

'On tick, yer mean?'

'Certainly not. State the suitable commodities, enough to go in a large carrier bag. And if your price is right, we'll want enough for fifty bags.'

'Gawd stone the crows,' said the grocer, a little man with a large moustache. ''Ow many?'

'Fifty.'

'Full up? Fifty carrier bags full up?'

'Yes, and full up with what, may I ask?' Mother Joan was in a formidable mood.

''Ere, give us 'arf a mo' to get me breath back, lady. Let's see. Flour, sugar, dried fruit, bakin' ingredients, tinned corned beef, bread, marge, potatoes – I got potatoes – porridge oats, eggs, condensed milk—' The grocer paused. 'Excuse me, lady, but who's payin'?'

'I am. With a cheque.'

''Old it, lady, it don't become me business to take cheques. It ain't Christmas, yer know, an' nor ain't I Santy Claus. Fifty carrier bags full up with me goods an' yer offerin' a cheque? 'Ave a 'eart, lady.'

'The Lord shall know you for your miserable distrust,' said Mother Joan. 'Where can I cash a cheque hereabouts?'

'Ah, well, I might be able to 'elp yer there. Charlie, look after the shop a bit.'

'I gotcher, Dad,' said a young man in a white apron. He looked as if he was guarding the open sacks of comestibles that lined the floor against the counter.

The grocer took the lady Repenters and Father Luke to a watch and clock shop two doors down. It was dark, dusty and ancient, and crammed with timepieces of every kind. Behind the counter and under a small gaslight sat the proprietor, a glass in his eye, through which he was peering at the dismantled works of a pocket watch. He looked up, took the glass from his eye, and his dark beard came apart to reveal white smiling teeth.

'Vell, vell, vhat a pleasant day to be sure,' he said, rising. 'Good afternoon, ladies, and velcome to my shop. Vhat can I do for you?'

'Meet me friend, Mr Solly Rubenstein,' said the grocer. 'A cheque, Solly, they'd like you to cash a cheque. If I could leave you ladies to it, I'll work out a price for a full carrier bag times fifty, though I'll tell yer now, it's likely to come to nigh on a quid a bag.'

'What discount?' asked Mother Joan.

'Eh?'

'Don't fiddle about.'

'Well, I won't say it ain't a fairish order, lady, very fairish, nor can I say it ain't worth a bit of discount. I'll work that out too. Give 'em yer best quality service, Solly.' The grocer disappeared.

'A cheque, vas it, lady?' asked Solly Rubenstein.

'Can you cash me a hundred pounds?' asked Mother Joan.

Solly Rubenstein blinked and coughed.

'My dear, vhat vas that figure?'

'A hundred pounds,' said Mother Joan.

'Vhat a painful day,' sighed Mr Rubenstein. 'Five pounds, who vould argue over that? Ten pounds, vell, that might raise a small argument for the good of my health, but a hundred pounds, my dear? Tck, tck, do you vish me to fall ill?'

'Why should you fall ill? That's ridiculous. You're in business, aren't you?' Mother Joan was in a no-nonsense mood. 'And you have just been recommended to me by the grocer.'

'True, true, lady, but a hundred pounds and not having

the pleasure of being acquainted vith you, vell, that's awkward, on my vord it is.'

'I don't like unobligin' men,' murmured Mother Mary.

'Patience, sister,' whispered Mother Ruth.

'Come along, Mr Rubenstein, yes or no, I won't stand for hedging and muttering,' said Mother Joan.

Solly Rubenstein looked her over. A lady, of course. 'Vell, your name and address, perhaps?' he ventured.

'Georgina Blake-Huntingdon, the Temple of Penitence, Bloomsbury,' said Mother Joan crisply. That, she thought, would do nicely, even though her name was Honoria. She had already signed the cheques with her husband's name, G. Blake-Huntingdon. The forgery was a Christian gesture in view of the cause.

'Ah,' said Mr Rubenstein. A sect, of course, and they all looked like highly respectable ladies, except for the plump gent in a top hat. He looked like their portly shepherd. 'Vell now, madam, for a hundred pounds might I mention collateral?'

Collateral sounded indecent to Mother Mary, and she took a firmer grip on her umbrella. But Mother Joan, because of her faith in the objective, took off a glove and slipped a diamond ring from a finger. She placed it on the dusty counter. Mr Rubenstein put the glass into his eye socket and examined the ring.

'Well?' said Mother Joan.

He removed the glass. 'Should I argue with a ring like this?' he said.

'I don't advise it,' said Mother Joan. 'I'll call the police if you attempt to defame its value.'

Mr Rubenstein looked at her in horror. 'Should ve even mention such a thing, madam? Vhy, that vould make us all ill. I vill accept the collateral and cash your cheque for a small charge.'

'How small?' demanded Mother Joan.

'Vell, no more than ten per cent, and who could say fairer?'

'Ten per cent is ten pounds, Mr Rubenstein.'

'Disgustin',' said Mother Mary. 'I'll give 'im ten per cent.'

'Five per cent,' said Mother Joan.

'Dear my soul,' said Mr Rubenstein, 'that's hard, madam, hard.'

'Five per cent,' said Mother Joan, 'and I'm in a hurry, too much so to go to the City branch of the bank. Yes or no, Mr Rubenstein?'

'Vell,' said Mr Rubenstein cautiously.

'Done,' said Mother Joan briskly.

'I vill accept the loss,' said Mr Rubenstein.

'Fiddlesticks,' said Mother Joan, and took a cheque from her handbag, with a fountain pen. She filled it in, copying her husband's scrawling handwriting to match the signature, already forged. Mr Rubenstein examined the cheque. 'I'll return for the ring in five days,' said Mother Joan.

'Vhen perhaps I might have the pleasure of offering for it?'

'Perhaps. We'll see. Now give me ninety-five pounds, please.'

When they were out of the shop, Father Luke said, 'Well, I can't say I ever saw a more Christian performance than that, Mother Joan, and I've seen some in me time. Mind you, I got to thinkin' suppose it bounces?'

'Bounces, Father Luke?' said Mother Verity.

'He means if the bank refuses to honour the cheque,' said Mother Joan.

'Oh, dear,' said Mother Ruth, a little askance at the act of forgery.

'So embarrassing,' said Mother Verity.

'Bang goes yer ring, Mother Joan,' said Father Luke, shaking his head.

'Can't be helped,' said Mother Joan. 'Count it that we fell at one fence. We shall remount unhurt. Worldly goods are expendable. Come, back to the grocer.'

The street was dingy. Even the traffic looked limply dingy. But the grocer was cheerful and welcoming. Even his moustache looked perky.

'Me friend Solly obliged yer, ladies?' he asked.

'He did,' said Mother Joan.

'Ain't it a kind world, lady? Now, I've got a list made out of a boxful of goods, which'll be times fifty—'

'A boxful?'

'Well, a carrier bag's limitin', like, and yer'll get squashin' and squeezin', which won't do the eggs no good, and if yer mean to be really good-'earted, eggs'll be like Christmas 'as come for the fam'lies concerned. I can supply the boxes, grocery cardboard boxes, which I won't charge yer no more than a penny each for, and 'ere's me list of 'ighly recommended contents.'

Mother Joan studied the pencilled list: flour, a two-pound bag, sugar, a two-pound bag, four pounds of rice, pound of tea, four tins of condensed milk, two pounds of mixed dried fruit, a large tin of corned beef, two pounds of margarine, a large packet of porridge oats, a dozen eggs, two large loaves and other items. The cost of a boxful came to sixteen shillings and sevenpence. The grocer pointed out the gross cost was actually seventeen and sevenpence, that he was giving a bob discount on every boxful.

'Sixpence, I fancy,' said Mother Joan.

'Eh?' said the grocer.

'Nearer sixpence.'

'Well, I did it approximate, like, an' you could say it's somewhere near to a bob.'

'I'll pay sixteen shillings and sixpence for each boxful,' said Mother Joan. 'It's the Lord's bounty.'

'Eh? Well, yes, see what yer mean, lady, the Lord's charity, eh? They could do with a lot of that round 'ere. When d'yer want all the stuff ready? Yer got certain perishables to think about. And I got one or two items to order on account of yer large an' valued commission.'

'Friday, I think,' said Mother Joan. 'Have them all ready by mid-morning on Friday.'

'Right y'ar,' said the grocer. 'Would yer kindly do me the honour of showin' me the colour of yer money, and offerin' twenty-five per cent in advance to show a bit of goodwill, lady?'

'Very well,' said Mother Joan, and took the roll of banknotes from her handbag. 'Ten pounds, I think, would be fair enough.'

'Yes, that's fair do's, lady, and I'm obliged to yer. 'Ere, where you off to, Charlie?'

'Just got to see a man about a dog, Dad,' said Charlie, and slipped out of the shop.

Mother Joan inspected a sample cardboard box of a size that would comfortably contain the goods, thanked the grocer and asked him if he could recommend a good clothier's where comfortable and durable overcoats could be purchased for adults and children, jerseys for boys, frocks for girls and boots for everyone.

'Isaac's, High Street, missus. Isaac's Ware'ouse, fit the Chinese out from 'ead to 'eel, he could, an' there's a hundred million of them, I've 'eard.'

'Good. Splendid. And if you've sinned, repent and you shall find the kingdom of heaven.'

'Kind of yer, lady, I'll 'ave some of that when I've got time from earnin' me livin'.'

The ladies, escorted by a beaming Father Luke, left the

shop and went on to Whitechapel High Street. There they found Isaac's Warehouse, and the amiable proprietor himself, a gentleman who regarded every customer as the joy of his life. Nothing was too much trouble for him in his desire to satisfy, and the only time joy departed from him was when he failed to satisfy and the customer left without buying anything. That did not happen too often. What did happen, often, was a customer going off wondering why he'd bought three pairs of braces and a pair of trousers when all he'd wanted was a belt. Isaac Sutch was an endearing salesman. He was delighted to meet the ladies of the League of Repenters, and to congratulate Father Luke on his well-fitting frock-coat. He could offer him an even better-fitting one at cut price. He was overwhelmed with happiness to know what Mother Joan was after. Overcoats by the dozen for adults and children? Boots? Jerseys? Frocks? Moses be praised. All prices would be slashed. No, no, he would ask for no money until the order was delivered to Bloomsbury, except perhaps for a small deposit. He could recognize ladies when he saw them, and a gentleman. Ladies from everywhere were his customers. A cheque? Of course, of course, Lady Roseberry always paid by cheque. He would only ask for delivery to be made when the cheque had been cleared, purely as a matter of friendly business, of course. What a day of joy to be of service to such customers, the details would be written down immediately. The whole cheque would be paid now? What could be happier than settlement before delivery? Such trust was of a kind to bring tears to the eyes. So, to the details.

They emerged eventually in satisfaction. Father Luke declared himself a total admirer of Mother Joan and her sister Repenters. Mother Mary declared things were improving, she hadn't had any call to use her umbrella.

'I'd like to mention that Mrs Murphy could do with improvin',' said Father Luke, as they made their way to the London Underground, 'she still ain't saltin' the potatoes, yer know, sisters.'

'A small thing, Father Luke,' said Mother Ruth. 'Let us be grateful for all that we receive at the table.'

'Amen,' said Mother Mary, 'we don't want gluttony raisin' its sinful 'ead.'

Street kids scurried about, darting between the ladies, and Mother Verity sighed at their thinness and shabbiness, but marvelled at their energy and at the giggling laughter of little girls being chased. A man, bare-headed and in a blue jersey, his trousers threadbare, approached, carrying a young girl. She was giggling, too, at him. Mother Verity quivered. He glanced at her as he passed the walking group. A cynical smile showed. Mother Verity went impulsively after him.

'Sir,' she called. He stopped and turned. The girl, face smudged but hair brushed and shining, stared at her. 'Sir, pardon me, please, but may I ask you a question?'

Will Fletcher, tall but lean with privation, said, 'Gawd help us, don't tell me you've been carryin' the 'oly word to Christian Street again.'

'No, there are things we must first do for the people before we go there again, Mr Fletcher.'

'Hear that, Lulu? I'm Mr Fletcher to this 'oly lady.'

'She give me sixpence,' said Lulu.

'The girl is not your daughter, you said?' enquired Mother Verity.

'I lodge with 'er fam'ly, that's all,' said Will Fletcher, and his smile was there, a smile she'd come to recognize as mirthless. 'Look, lady, I'm sorry I was a bit rough with yer, but I happen to be out of patience with your kind. You can believe in the goodness of the Lord as much as you like, but don't expect me to, even if I don't feel proud of meself for man'andling yer. You go your way, lady, just let me go mine.'

'I believe most of all in helping the suffering,' said Mother Verity, a little flush on her face because his blue eyes seemed so cynical and searching. 'Mr Fletcher, may I ask if you served in the war?'

'It shows, does it?'

'Yes, Mr Fletcher, it does, and I think one of the reasons why it shows so bitterly is because the country has already forgotten you, and hasn't even bothered to reward you with a job. Is that so, Mr Fletcher?'

'Well, hell an' the devil,' said Will Fletcher, 'you're speechifyin' me.'

'I am only trying to say I understand.'

'After what I did to you in front of all those people?' he said.

'That is forgotten and forgiven,' she said, although it was not forgotten.

'You're a funny woman.'

'I should like to talk to you sometimes about the consolation the Lord can bring to all of us,' she said.

'Oh, my achin' ribs,' said Will Fletcher, and laughed. Lulu, finding the laughter infectious, giggled. 'You're on a hidin' to nothing there, lady.'

'I am Miss Celia Stokes.'

'Well, good for you, Miss Celia Stokes, but do me a favour an' don't come round offerin' me the Lord's consolation. Say goodbye, Lulu lovey.'

'Goo'bye,' said Lulu.

'I wish yer well,' said Will Fletcher, and off he went, Lulu joggling in his arms.

Mother Mary arrived. 'That was that disgustin' brute,' she said. 'Oh, you poor thing, sister, I was sure 'e was goin' to be outrageous again, but I 'ad me umbrella ready.'

'He's a man who needs help, sister.'

'I'll give 'im help,' said Mother Mary. 'Still, I suppose the Lord does expect us to do what we can even for him.'

'I'm sure He does, sister. Come along, let's catch the others up.'

They renewed contact at a moment when two men, one short and thin, one large and thickset, approached in a talkative vein. The large man suddenly veered, shouldering Father Luke and Mother Ruth aside. The short man darted and made a lightning grab at Mother Joan's handbag, who was being momentarily isolated. Father Luke, outraged at finding himself sprawling on the pavement, jumped up.

''Old on, sister, 'old on, I'll go an' find a copper!' And off he went, as fast as his plump legs would carry him.

Mother Joan struggled to retain her handbag.

'The very idea! You scoundrel! Let go!' The strap of the handbag was slipping down her left arm, she clutching the bag itself with her right hand.

'Give it 'ere, yer fat old cow!' hissed the thief.

Mother Mary sprang into action. She dealt the sinful villain a punitive blow over his capped head. Her umbrella shivered and descended again. The large man went for her. She stopped him by ramming the point of the brolly into his breadbasket. People in the street looked, walked on and did nothing. A shopkeeper, standing at his open door, retreated to the interior. A woman, entering Isaac's, informed the proprietor that a robbery was taking place, at which Isaac deplored what the world was coming to and asked for the happiness of serving her.

Mother Mary laid about her. Mother Joan held on. The short man took a fearful bash on his head. The large man made another rush. Mother Verity, praying to the Lord to forgive her, put out a foot and tripped him up.

'Oh, dear,' breathed Mother Ruth as he crashed.

The short man ran off then. The large man, bruised and winded, got up and followed him, swearing his head off. Will Fletcher arrived, little Lulu coming at a scamper from some way down the street. Mother Mary, seeing the man who'd assaulted Mother Verity with disgusting kisses, thought she might as well set about him too. It was a good opportunity, and her mood was right. Down came the umbrella. Will Fletcher took the blow on a raised arm.

'Leave off, will yer?' he said. 'Didn't I tell yer not to come this way again?'

'None of that, my man,' said Mother Joan. 'The Lord is our guide and protector.'

'Some protector,' said Will Fletcher, and took a look at people who had stopped now that there wasn't anything to bear witness to. 'Hoppit,' he said, and they moved off. 'I'll 'and it to this lady, she clouted a sight harder on your account than the Lord.'

'That's the Lord's sword she wields,' said Mother Joan.

'Well, take it back 'ome, and her with it. 'Ave you got money in that 'andbag of yours? I mean real money, seein' you were the one they went for.'

'Well, bless my soul,' said Mother Joan, 'what a quarrelsome chap you are.'

'That means you've got money. Where're you goin' with it?'

'To the London Underground station.'

Lulu pushed in. Will Fletcher took hold of her hand. 'All right, ladies, I'll walk you to the station,' he said.

'Hope we can trust you,' said Mother Mary.

'Thank you, Mr Fletcher,' said Mother Verity.

'Well, go on, then,' said Will Fletcher curtly. 'I'll follow.'

They walked to the station. Father Luke made a reappearance.

'Me 'eart's bleedin',' he said. 'I've been all over an' not seen a single copper.'

'Never mind, Father Luke,' said Mother Ruth. 'It was good of you to go looking. We're quite all right, and the misguided gentlemen ran off in the end. Mother Joan still has her handbag.'

'The Lord be praised,' said Father Luke, taking his top hat off and wiping his brow.

Will Fletcher parted from them at the Underground station. Mother Verity begged him to allow her to give Lulu another sixpence.

'That's it, lady, chuck your Christianity about,' he said. Mother Verity winced. 'All right, sorry, give Lulu the sixpence, then. She's not proud, and nor am I, am I?'

'You are very proud, Mr Fletcher, but the child likes you, obviously so, and accordingly there's hope for you.'

He laughed. She gave the girl a sixpence, and this time Lulu thanked her. Will Fletcher was still laughing as he went off with the girl trotting beside him.

Aunt Edie, home from her work, let herself into her flat. For the first time ever its silence displeased her. There was not a sound. Even the noise of Camberwell traffic did not penetrate. She had come home to four walls and nothing else. For three days she had lived amid the sounds of a small child, a growing girl and a growing boy, in a house that was alive, not only with them but her cousin Maud's husband. That woman, some Christian. How could any woman walk out on dear little Betsy, darling Patsy and that endearing boy Jimmy? What did it mean, her feeling of flatness? It meant she could hardly wait for next weekend. But suppose Maud was back?

160

'I'll knock her head off,' said Aunt Edie out loud.

She went out later to the pub. She did not often go to a pub on her own unless it was to meet someone. Joe Gosling was there.

'Well, Edie me old love, sit down. What would yer like, a drop of Guinness?'

'I'm not your old love, but yes, I'd like a small Guinness.'

He got her one and sat down beside her. 'Yer a fine figure of a woman, yer know, Edie.'

'Eyes off,' said Aunt Edie.

'Me? Eyes orf what?'

'What's mine, what's private.'

'I'll grant yer it's yer very own, Edie, but I put it to yer, ain't it been private a bit long? Bein' a widower and eligible accordin', I take it on meself to suggest it just ain't sociable to keep a fine figure like yourn all to yerself all yer life.'

'Let go of my knee,' said Aunt Edie.

'Eh? Well, I'm blowed, that 'and o' mine just slipped under the table, like. It must've known something.'

'Yes, it knew my knee was there.'

'Like you say, Edie, so it did. 'Ave yer thought any more about you and me bein' pearly partners?'

'I've thought about that concert. All right, Joe, I'll do a turn, and I'll bring a young man to do a couple of duets with me.'

'Yer a sport, love, yer me 'eart's delight. Drink up, and I'll treat you to another.'

'You won't,' said Aunt Edie. 'I'm not that kind of drinker.'

'Just as yer like. 'Oo's this young man?'

'My nephew Jimmy.'

'Oh, 'im that was ridin' on me cart with you last week. Lively lad, that one.'

'Yes,' said Aunt Edie, and wondered how Jimmy had got on helping Mr Gibbs today.

Jimmy was home a little late. He'd worked past his time and Mr Gibbs had said carry on if you want to, stop when you've done enough, and I'll pay you daily, sixpence an hour, and that includes time for breaks. You've got to have breaks, lad.

Jimmy had enjoyed the work. Sophy had remained absent after being hauled off by her mother. That left him free to get on with things. Not that he didn't like her. You couldn't not like a girl as pretty as she was. But she was a wild one all right, you couldn't tell where the next fateful happening might come from, or when. And besides, she was rich. Jimmy wasn't without sense, he knew she simply wanted to make use of him for playing games.

He told his dad and sisters about his day, about the acres of jungle, high enough and thick enough to get lost in, and that his job was to clear littered ground and build bonfires.

'Did you see her?' asked Patsy.

'Sophy, you mean?' said Jimmy.

'Did you see her?' Patsy was more interested in relationships than jungles.

'I saw her this mornin'. She got 'erself into a mess and 'er mum gave her a rollickin' and took her indoors.'

'Bit of a tomboy, is she?' asked Dad.

'Well, a bit dangerous to human life, I suppose,' said Jimmy.

'Crikey,' breathed Betsy, 'like cannibals?'

'Patsy, did you go and call on some of the firms I listed, and ask if there were any jobs goin'?' Jimmy had his future on his mind.

'Yes, I did, I walked me and Betsy off our feet,' said

Patsy, 'and there wasn't one job goin'. I ain't doin' it any more.'

'Nor me,' said Betsy. 'I nearly wore me boots out, an' me feet as well, didn't I, Dad?'

'Hard luck, me pickle,' said Dad, 'but all in a good cause.'

'Well, look,' said Jimmy, 'Mr Gibbs paid me for today, five bob because I worked on. Here's sixpence each for you an' Betsy, even if you didn't come up with any prospects, and if you do go again, I'll give you sixpence each again, out of me wages as a woodland worker.'

'Oh, Jimmy, thanks ever so,' said Patsy, and Betsy goggled at a whole shining tanner. 'Sixpence is doin' us proud. We don't mind goin' again and askin', do we, Betsy?'

'I wish Dad could get me some new feet,' said Betsy.

'What's a woodland worker?' asked Patsy.

'A young bloke that clears up the sawdust,' said Dad with a grin.

'I wish Aunt Edie was 'ere,' said Betsy, ''cos I don't fink Mum's comin' 'ome a lot, do you, Dad?'

'Give 'er time, Betsy love,' said Dad. If he and his kids were coming to terms with Mother's absence, there were still moments when emotions showed.

CHAPTER TEN

'Hullo,' said Ada the next morning.

'Hullo,' said Jimmy.

'You've come again, then,' said Ada.

'Yes, and I've arrived as well,' said Jimmy.

'Cheeky again,' said Ada.

'Not much, though,' said Jimmy.

'Kindly step in,' said Ada, and Jimmy entered. She looked up at him. He was only six months older than she was, but inches taller. He wore a solemn expression, but it wasn't in his eyes. There was a joker in his eyes, she could tell. 'You're laughin' at me,' she said.

'Me?' said Jimmy.

'I'm important in this 'ouse, I'll have you know,' said Ada.

'All right, I'll call you Lady Ada,' said Jimmy.

'I knew it, you are cheeky. Kindly follow me.' Ada took him through to the kitchen, where the staff were finishing their breakfast.

'Well, look 'oo's 'ere,' said Ivy, ''e's still alive.'

'Good morning, my boy,' said Mr Hodges.

'Morning, Mr Hodges.'

'Like a nice cup of tea and a slice of toast again?' invited cook.

'Well, bless you, Mrs Redfern, that's really kind of you,' said Jimmy.

Ada, laughing, said, 'He's showin' off this mornin'.'

'It's the relief at not 'aving 'ad anything fall on 'im yesterday,' said Ivy.

'We are 'appy you survived, young man,' said Mr Hodges as Jimmy sat down to tea and toast.

'Mind, I don't know 'e'll last the week out,' said Ivy.

'That Ivy,' said Mrs Redfern, shaking her head at Mr Hodges. 'She'll have us all in our graves before we're ready to go.'

'I am not amused,' said Mr Hodges.

'We 'eard that the young madam made 'er fatal mark on you,' said Ivy.

'Who said?' asked Jimmy.

'The young madam,' said Ada, and laughed. 'Got you there, Jimmy,' she added.

'Mr Hodges,' said Jimmy, 'I might have to see to young Ada before the day's out.'

'I 'ope it won't be injurious,' said Mr Hodges.

'Young Ada? Told you he was showin' off,' said Ada.

'May I ask 'ow you propose to see to her, young man?' asked Mrs Redfern.

'Well, I'll give it serious thought, Mrs Redfern,' said Jimmy. 'Mind, a kiss usually does it. It sort of numbs them, and they don't give you any sauce any more.'

'Well!' exclaimed Ada. 'Mr 'Odges, did you ever hear the like?'

'I have not 'ad hoccasion to in this kitchen,' said Mr Hodges.

'And I don't know a kiss will work with Ada,' said Mrs Redfern, her plump face wreathed in a smile.

'Well, I'll give 'er another,' said Jimmy, 'two kisses really give 'em something to think about. Thanks a lot for the toast an' marmalade, I'll get movin' now, I know the way.' He heard Ada shrieking with laughter as he made his way out.

The ground he had worked over yesterday was patterned with large heaps of white ashes that were still faintly smouldering. Mr Gibbs appeared, emerging from the trees and crowded undergrowth on the left. Jimmy went to meet him.

'Hullo, Jimmy, glad to see you again. You did a fine job yesterday. There's a similar clearing through here. The landscape gardeners are working to their own design. You'd think they'd simply make a sweep from east to west or north to south. No, they're going to leave some areas untouched for the time being and tidy them up later, and make a coppice of each. They're the areas where they won't take out all the saplings, they'll thin them out, they'll design each coppice individually. Come this way, Jimmy.'

Mr Gibbs led Jimmy through flattened undergrowth and out to a clearing similar to yesterday's, but larger. And there was far more sawing to be done. The landscape men had taken out a host of saplings, diseased trees and dead trees. The trunks were piled at one edge, the lopped branches lay in thick array. Jimmy's job was to saw up those branches for burning. The rest of the clearing was a mangled bed of chopped undergrowth.

'Lord above,' said Jimmy.

'Yes, there's work here for a week,' said Mr Gibbs.

'I think I could do it in three days, or four, Mr Gibbs.'

'Good for you, if you can, Jimmy. Same procedure. Build bonfires and we'll fire them tonight. Is the bramble giving you any trouble?'

'It put up a fight yesterday,' said Jimmy. 'The big stuff can wrestle like a gorilla, y'know. Tried to down me once or twice, so I used the cutters to get my own back. I'd get sorry for meself if I let bramble down me.'

'Well, shout if it does,' said Mr Gibbs, and again left him to it.

Jimmy went to work. It was another warm day, and the sky hung blue above Anerley, remote from the crowded streets of Walworth. And the morning was peaceful. There was no sign of Sophy. At half-past ten a whistle called him up to the terrace. Mrs Gibbs was there. On a table stood a cup of tea and a plate containing a fresh jam doughnut.

'Here you are, Jimmy, tea this morning, and a doughnut.'

'Well, I don't know how to thank you, Mrs Gibbs,' he said, his forehead bedewed with perspiration, his hair tousled and damp. 'Jam doughnuts 'appen to be my favourite partiality.'

'And mine, when I was your age,' smiled Mrs Gibbs. 'Ada's just come back from the baker's with two dozen, and Ivy took a plateful down to the men, with a pot of tea.'

'I must say, Mrs Gibbs, it's like bein' in the country here, and you're like the squire's wife.'

'Oh, I'm playing the grand lady, am I?'

'Well, you look like one, Mrs Gibbs,' said Jimmy, seating himself on the top step.

'I hope I don't,' she said, 'grand ladies are toffee-nosed, aren't they?'

'I don't think you are, Mrs Gibbs,' said Jimmy. She handed him the cup and saucer and the plate containing the doughnut. 'And I don't think squires' wives are, either. Squires' wives take baskets of eggs round to poor village people and sit with sick ones to make sure they take their medicine.'

'Fascinating,' said Mrs Gibbs.

'Pardon, Mrs Gibbs?'

'Yes, quite delicious.'

'You come across that sort of thing in books,' said Jimmy, and began to eat the doughnut.

167

'Do you read lots of books, Jimmy?'

'As many as I can get hold of.'

'I wish Sophy read a lot more and messed about a lot less,' said Mrs Gibbs.

'If I might say so, Mrs Gibbs, Sophy's still a bit young,' said Jimmy. 'Not many boys and girls read a lot until they get to my age.'

'Oh, dear, poor old Methuselah,' said Mrs Gibbs, finding the boy appealing.

'Me?' he said.

'So old,' she said.

'I suppose I am gettin' on,' said Jimmy, washing the last of the doughnut down with tea.

'Oh, my word, how depressing, Jimmy.'

'You have to face up to that sort of thing, Mrs Gibbs.'

'Yes, we must all attack the dread years bravely,' said Mrs Gibbs. 'Well, finish your cup of tea, and Ada will see that you get some sandwiches at midday.'

'Yes, Mr Gibbs said not to bother to bring my own, like I did yesterday.'

'Quite right. You need not bother, Jimmy. Well, I must go now.' Mrs Gibbs entered the house by way of the conservatory.

Ada appeared. 'I left a doughnut here,' she said.

'Glad you did,' said Jimmy.

'Who's eaten it?' asked Ada.

'Me,' said Jimmy.

'There's a good boy.'

'I heard that,' said Jimmy.

'Just havin' my own back,' said Ada, her little white maid's cap perky. 'We all had a doughnut this mornin', except Mr 'Odges. He says it's not dignified for butlers to eat doughnuts.'

'I don't think I'll be a butler, then,' said Jimmy.

'What d'you want to be?' asked Ada, collecting the cup, saucer and plate.

'Well, I've thought about bein' a husband and father,' said Jimmy. 'Not this week, of course.'

Ada laughed. 'No, nor next week, I shouldn't think,' she said.

'I thought about later on,' said Jimmy. 'Well, it's been nice talkin' to you, Ada, but I've got to get on, I'd better go and join the other men now.'

'Other men?' Ada laughed again. 'Jimmy, you're potty.'

'You're nice too,' said Jimmy, and went whistling on his way. Ada watched him go, a smile on her face.

Jimmy resumed his work, mashing bramble to pieces with a long pair of secateurs and building up bonfires. He could hear the landscape gardeners working farther down. The twelve acres of ground were on a gentle slope, and Jimmy could imagine that when everything had been cleared except little woods, the view from the house would be marvellous. He did some sawing after a while, and placed manageable branches on top of the high heaps of debris, creating pyramids. A little after twelve, the whistle blew again, and he found Ada standing on the bottom step of the terrace. On a tray in her hands was a glass of ginger beer, two ham sandwiches and a slice of cake. The sandwiches were large, the bread fresh and crusty, the filling generous.

'Here we are, Buffalo Bill,' said Ada, 'something to keep you goin'. How you gettin' on?'

'Fine,' said Jimmy, taking the tray, 'and I must say I'm bein' treated handsome.'

'Master and madam don't believe in starvin' the workers,' said Ada. 'Have you seen the young madam?'

'No, not this mornin',' said Jimmy.

'She's slipped her 'andcuffs,' said Ada.

'Help,' said Jimmy, 'does Mrs Gibbs have to handcuff her?'

'Good as. It never works. That's why she's called the young madam. If you see her, Jimmy, bring her back up 'ere.'

'Me?' said Jimmy.

'It's an order from Mr 'Odges,' said Ada. 'He's in charge of the young madam while Mrs Gibbs is out. Of course, if she's down there with 'er father, you don't have to worry, but if she's not, well, Mr 'Odges said tell that young boy Jimmy to bring her back to the house.'

Jimmy eyed her gravely. Ada put on a demure look.

'Supposin' she won't come?' said Jimmy, ignoring the little arrow.

'Throw her over your horse,' said Ada.

'I'll have to find one first. D'you live here, Ada?'

'Of course,' said Ada, perkily proud, 'we're not common dailies, we're proper staff. 'Ope you enjoy the sandwiches, cook did them for you. You're a nice young boy, she said.'

'I'm really goin' to have to see to you, Ada.'

'Percy will dot you one in the eye if you do,' said Ada.

'Who's Percy?'

'My young gentleman.'

'What a sickenin' blow,' said Jimmy. 'I might as well go and let something 'eavy fall on me now.'

Ada laughed and Jimmy took the tray down to his work area. He sat down on a tree trunk, took a swig of the ginger beer and began to make healthy inroads into the sandwiches. The ham had been sliced off the bone and mustard applied. Jimmy ate with relish. Mr Gibbs insisted he took thirty minutes break at midday.

A voice reached his ears the moment he'd finished his snack. 'Jimmy!'

'Oh, help,' he muttered.

'Jimmy!'

'Yes?' he called.

'Come down here.'

'What for?'

'Just come, will you?' Sophy's voice emanated from the jungle below.

'I'm busy, and you've got to go back to the house.'

'I'll kick you if you don't come when you're called!'

Resignedly, Jimmy went. He crossed the clearing and entered the jungle by way of a trampled path between high grasses and rampant ferns. It sloped downwards. Sophy appeared. Holy Moses, thought Jimmy, she'll catch it. She was bare-legged and her feet were black with wet mud. Her white blouse was spotted with mud and her blue skirt was tucked up high above her knees. A blue hair ribbon was loose and dangling, and her eyes were accusing.

'You're for it,' he said.

'I called you six times—'

'Twice.'

'Don't argue,' said Sophy, 'just turn around.'

'What for?'

'So I can kick you.'

'Excuse me, but I'm not keen on bein' kicked by girls,' said Jimmy. 'It's not good for me self-respect, and what d'you want to go around kickin' people for, anyway?'

'Not people,' said Sophy, 'you. You didn't come when I called you and you're a cheeky beast as well.'

'All right,' said Jimmy, 'let's get it over with, then, or you'll stand there hollerin' at me. It beats me, the way girls holler if you don't do what they want. But I'm not turnin' round. Just kick me this way.'

'I will too,' said Sophy, and kicked at him with a muddy right foot. She missed. Jimmy wasn't there any more. It unbalanced her completely, and she fell over. A little shriek escaped her. 'Oh, you rotten boy!'

'Not rotten,' said Jimmy, 'just a bit of quick footwork on my part, and if you don't mind me sayin' so, you're not much good at kickin'. I'd give it up if I was you. I mean, if you like goin' around kickin' people, what's the good of it if it only makes you fall over?'

Sophy, coming to her knees in trampled ferns, stared up at him. Jimmy looked as grave as an undertaker, but she didn't see him as that, she saw him as a kindred spirit. Suddenly, she was bubbling with giggles. 'Oh, I like you,' she said, and came to her feet. 'But I've still a good mind to push your face in.' She laughed. 'But I won't this time. Come down here.'

'Where?'

'To the pond. I've lost Ferdy. You can help me find him.'

'Who's Ferdy?' asked Jimmy.

'My frog. Didn't you know there was a pond down here?'

'No, and I didn't know there were any frogs, either. Ada says you've got to go back to the house.'

'Oh, not yet, Mummy's out till one o'clock. I'll go up then and have lunch with her, honest. Come on, it's your break time.'

'Yes, but I've only got about ten minutes left. Then you've got to go back.'

'Jimmy, don't fuss, just come on.'

He took his workman's apron off and followed her down the beaten track to the edge of what she called a pond but looked like a bog to him. A large wet surface was thick and green amid sprouting water grass. Trees surrounded it.

'Some pond,' he said.

'Oh, look, there's Ferdy, get him for me!'

172

A frog's head was above the green slimy surface, a head with two round heavy-lidded eyes. Jimmy, further resigned, took his shoes and socks off.

'How d'you know that's Ferdy?' he asked, rolling his trousers up.

'Of course I know. Get him for me.'

'All right,' said Jimmy. The fact was, young Sophy's high spirits and sense of adventure were infectious. He moved forward, his feet sinking a little. He had frog-hunted in London ponds with friends in his younger days.

Sophy darted, bare feet entering the morass, and her hand reaching. The frog vanished. 'Oh, bother,' she said.

'That's no way to catch a frog,' said Jimmy. 'You wouldn't even catch an elephant like that.'

'Oh, you daft boy, who wants to catch an elephant? Jimmy, look, he's there again.'

The frog's head had made a reappearance, and was closer. Jimmy silently stooped. The bulbous eyes of the frog were unblinking. He trailed his hand across the surface of the green slime, dipped it and scooped the frog up. It came alive in his hand. Sophy shrieked with joy as he held it firmly.

'There you are,' said Jimmy, and transferred the creature to her hands. 'Now you'd better go back.'

Sophy laughed, held the frog in one hand and gave him a playful push with the other. With his feet slightly sunk in the boggy ground, Jimmy fell backward, landing on his bottom. He felt the wetness of the earth transfer itself immediately to the seat of his trousers.

'Crikey, what're you sitting down for?' asked Sophy and burst into laughter.

'That's done it,' said Jimmy. He got up, shifted his feet to firmer ground and said, 'You goin' back, Miss Gibbs, or not?'

'Miss Gibbs?' Sophy, frog still in her hand, her feet muddier, her skirt still tucked up into the legs of her short drawers, stared at him like a girl delighted that he really was a kindred spirit. 'Oh, aren't you funny? And I'm not going back, I'm going to climb trees with you. There's apple trees up on the other side of the pond – oh, you beast, you rotten rotten boy!'

She was off her feet and over his right shoulder. Jimmy, supple and strong, had her in a fireman's lift. Her head hung down over his shoulder, his arm was around her skirted thighs, and her bare legs were kicking. She'd lost the frog, and her fists were pummelling his back.

'This way,' said Jimmy, and began to carry her back over the trampled path to the clearing. He carried her across the clearing, Sophy shrieking.

'Oh, you wait, you horrendous boy, you wait! I'll never speak to you again, never, never, never! I'll ask Daddy to throw you in the pond, I'll kick you till you're dead! Beast, beast, beast!'

'It's for your own good,' said Jimmy, who had learned at school that you could only talk for so long, and then you had to take action. That is, if you wanted to settle an argument. 'I've got to hand you over to Ada before your mum gets back.'

Too late: as he carried her over towards the terrace steps, Mrs Gibbs came out on to the terrace from the conservatory. In a full-skirted dress that floated lightly around her ankles, and a summery white hat, she stood to observe the spectacle, her face a study in astonishment.

Oh, gawd, thought Jimmy, that's done it, I'll get the chopper for sure. He released Sophie, setting her down on the edge of the terrace as carefully as he could. She straightened up, face flushed, eyes alight. She had never enjoyed herself so much in all the harum-scarum years of her young life. About to launch herself at Jimmy, she saw her mother out of the corner of her eye. She turned. Her mother looked at her, then at Jimmy, and then at her daughter again. She was almost lost for words.

'I don't believe it,' she said. Her daughter's feet were wet with black mud, her bare legs splashed with it, her crumpled skirt partly tucked-up, partly hanging, her hair a mess and her blouse marked. 'Is this possible?'

'Yes, would you believe it, Mummy, this blessed boy carting me like that?' said Sophy.

'Is it my own daughter I see?' asked Mrs Gibbs. 'Is it you?'

'Mummy, of course it's me.'

'Is it? I see only a frightful object. Look at you.'

Jimmy coughed and said, 'Well, I'll get back to my work, Mrs Gibbs.'

'Stay where you are, young man.'

'Yes, Mrs Gibbs,' said Jimmy, and stood there on the terrace steps resigning himself to the chopper.

Mrs Gibbs regarded her daughter again. Sophy would be fourteen in November. Most other girls with her background would now be pictures of sweet, growing charm. Not Sophy. Sophy the Dreadful, her brothers called her.

'I accept that you must be Sophy. I shudder, but I accept it. Where are your shoes and socks?'

'I wish I knew,' said Sophy. 'I put them down somewhere, but—'

'What is your skirt doing most of the way up your legs?'

'Oh, it's all right, Mummy, it's tucked into my you-knows. Well, some of it is. I had to get into the pond to look for Ferdy.'

'That's all too obvious, and am I to understand you were going to bring that hideous frog into the house again?'

175

'I could put him in a cardboard box, if you like, Mummy, and keep him in my wardrobe.'

'Not while I'm still drawing breath, you won't.'

'I can't think why you don't like him, Mummy,' said Sophy, eyes innocent beyond belief. 'Oh, Jimmy found him for me—'

'May God forgive him,' said Mrs Gibbs.

'Then we lost him again,' said Sophy, 'and then that blessed boy had the cheek to pick me up and throw me over his shoulder. Don't boys show off? Did you see what a bundle he made of me?'

'So, young man, you helped my daughter find that repulsive frog and also helped her to cover herself in mud,' said Mrs Gibbs. 'What have you to say for yourself?'

'Yes, I know I'm done for, Mrs Gibbs, I can see that,' said Jimmy. 'I'll just go off home, shall I?'

'You'll do no such thing,' said Mrs Gibbs.

'I should say not, I owe him one first, Mummy,' said Sophy.

'Hold your tongue, you horror,' said Mrs Gibbs, and neither Jimmy nor Sophy knew how she was struggling to contain herself. The sight of her demon daughter meeting her match at last, yelling and kicking over the boy's shoulder, had been astonishing but utterly laughable. Yet she dare not laugh. 'Young man, explain yourself.'

'Yes, Mrs Gibbs,' said Jimmy. 'Well, I was havin' my break, so I went down to the pond with Sophy. Mrs Gibbs, if you don't mind me sayin' so, it's more like a swamp than a pond, and Sophy shouldn't go down there in case she gets sucked under. I read a Sherlock Holmes story once in which a feller disappeared in a Dartmoor swamp, he was sucked all the way under. I wouldn't like Sophy to get sucked under down there, Mrs Gibbs. Where was I?'

Mrs Gibbs quivered. 'Yes, where were you?' she asked with an effort.

'Oh, yes, about goin' down there with Sophy in my break time,' said Jimmy, grave as an owl as usual. 'Well, she was potty about findin' this frog, so I scooped it up and gave it to her and said she'd got to go back to the house. Unfortunately—'

'Pardon?' said Mrs Gibbs, wondering how much longer she could preserve a calm front.

'Yes, unfortunately, Mrs Gibbs, I 'ad to carry her. I didn't have a horse, so I carried her over me shoulder, I couldn't think of any other way.'

'A horse?' Mrs Gibbs's pleasant voice had a slightly strangled sound.

'Yes, I was told to throw her over my horse if I had to, and bring her back that way, but not havin' a horse—' Jimmy stopped. Sophy was shrieking with laughter, and her mother looked as if she didn't know exactly what was happening.

Drawing breath, Mrs Gibbs said, 'Who told you to throw my daughter over your horse?'

'Well, now you come to ask, Mrs Gibbs, I think I forget.'

'Was it her father?'

'I just can't think who it was, Mrs Gibbs.'

'I bet it wasn't Daddy,' said Sophy. 'Daddy wouldn't stand for me being thrown over any horse, nor over anyone's shoulder. You can see what an impossible boy he is, Mummy. I should think he's going to turn out to be a problem, don't you?'

'Oh, one problem can recognize another, can it?' said Mrs Gibbs.

'It's all right, Mrs Gibbs,' said Jimmy. 'I know I've done it in, I didn't stop to think, I just chucked her over my shoulder. You can give me my marchin' orders.'

'It's the sack for you from this work, is it?' said Mrs Gibbs.

'Mummy, you can't,' protested Sophy, 'you can't sack him just because he showed off. I can see to him, Daddy often says a good punch in the eye does wonders for some people.'

'Your father needs speaking to, you deplorable girl. So do you, and in no uncertain terms. Jimmy, go back to your work.'

'You're not goin' to give me the push, Mrs Gibbs?' said Jimmy.

'Not this time,' she said.

'You're a sport, Mrs Gibbs,' said Jimmy, and went gratefully back to his work.

Mrs Gibbs eyed her daughter. Her daughter offered a sweet smile. 'You were supposed to spend the morning reading *Oliver Twist*,' said Mrs Gibbs.

'Oh, I did,' said Sophy. 'I got up to where he asked for more, then I thought about Ferdy being lost and starving.'

'No, you didn't, you thought about roping Jimmy in for larks during his break time. Aren't you an utterly disgraceful girl?'

'Yes, I suppose so,' said Sophy.

'I wonder, could you try improving yourself?'

'Yes, I'll read some more of *Oliver Twist*, shall I, after lunch?'

'Get Ivy to bring you a bowl of water. Wash your feet before you come into the house.'

'Yes, Mummy, and it's ever so good of you to put up with me.'

Mrs Gibbs made an abrupt departure. Entering the house through the conservatory, she picked up her skirts and flew up to her bedroom in a desperate attempt to reach it before her control cracked. She failed.

'What's that?' asked Ivy in the kitchen.

'Lordy,' said the cook, 'it sounds like madam 'aving hysterics.'

CHAPTER ELEVEN

After lunch in the Temple on Thursday, Father Peter received, by appointment, a prospective Repenter in his private sitting room. The ladies were in hope for him, because the young woman's entry into the League would represent a very Christian triumph for him. Miss Kitty Drake, alas, was a fallen woman. She lived in Soho, and entertained men there in the unmentionable way. Recently, however, she had been to a church to see a friend of hers married to a dear old gentleman of wealth. It was a love match. He loved her saucy prettiness and she loved his money.

The church and the service affected Kitty in the most unexpected way, making her silently groan and worry about the life she was leading. She came across the pamphlet issued by the League of Repenters, which in no uncertain terms told her she was heading for fire and brimstone. She had a terrible attack of religion, and went to see Father Peter. He was so kind and understanding that she promised to think seriously about giving up sin and becoming a Repenter. She admitted she was sinning twice over. In the first place she was fornicating, and in the second place she was enjoying it.

'It's me body, yer see, Father, it gets terrible passionate.'

'Ah, the lusts of the flesh are indeed troublesome, Miss Drake. Rest assured we here will do our utmost to help you achieve self-denial and redemption so that you may work with us for the Lord.'

'But I won't earn no money.'

'You will receive free board and lodging, my child, and I will see to it that there is always a little money in your purse.'

'Oh, it's terrible temptin' to give up me life of shame an' come an' join you. I'll let yer know tomorrer afternoon, will that be all right?'

'I hope I shall have the pleasure of receiving you into the fold, my child.'

So on Thursday afternoon, Kitty was in dialogue again with Father Peter in his private sitting room. She informed him that she just couldn't stop feeling chronically needful of repenting, that she wanted to reform and to join the League. Father Peter, impressive in his majestic understanding, said he would commence at once to instruct her in the first essentials of self-denial, that when today's catechism was over he would receive her into the Temple as a resident Repenter, and continue instructing her until full self-denial had been achieved. Undoubtedly, she was indeed in need of redemption. After all, he said, there was a third sin. The sin of fornication and the sin of enjoying it had been spoken of. But there was also the sin of being paid for it.

'Prostitution, my child, is very wrong.'

'Oh, I never call meself one of them, Father Peter, I call meself obligin'. I know it's still sinning to oblige gentlemen, but I don't like to think I'm common, like all them others are.'

'My child, that shows admirable sensitivity.' Father Peter's deep voice was murmurously understanding, his dark eyes gentle in their regard of the obliging young woman. Her white blouse was doing its best to cope with her fulsome bosom, her black skirt encircling the lacy frills of a red petticoat. The skirt, calf-length, revealed her long lace-up black boots, shining with polish. It was a pleasure to see she had pride in her appearance, and that she was attractive in her looks, even if her lips were a little too moistly bright with carmine. 'Sensitivity is a virtue.'

'Oh, d'yer think so?' Kitty looked pleased, for her new-found religiousness really was chronic, and she needed to be told she had some virtues. She only liked to oblige nice gentlemen, for instance.

'Sensitivity is a virtue blessed by the Lord,' said Father Peter and went on with his catechism concerning the necessity of self-denial, and how it could be overcome by a surfeit of that which was not self-denial.

'What's a surfeit, Father?' asked Kitty.

'An abundance, my child.'

'Oh, d'yer mean too much of a good thing?'

'Indeed. You have seen the light. Come, let us first pray together in the other room.'

The other room was his bedroom. There, he offered up a prayer for her sinful body, while Kitty lay, as instructed, on the bed, and delivered the required amen. Then he lay down with her. After a little while, Kitty groaned, 'Oh, yer undoin' me all over, Father.'

He explained reassuringly that the aforesaid surfeit must be undertaken with a man of Christian understanding, and that although it might trouble his soul a little, he was taking on the responsibility himself. Kitty said that was so good of him. The instruction proceeded.

After a further while, Kitty breathed, 'Oh, yer gettin' me terrible passionate, Father.'

The afternoon proved most satisfying. Kitty partici-pated in an abundance of that which was not self-denial. Father Peter said although his soul was indeed troubled by his own participation, he would ask for the Lord's blessing. 'As for you, my child, I shall now take you down to the Chapel of Penitence, receive you into the League and anoint you as Mother Magda. You may then bring your belongings into the Temple and become a resident. My task in helping you to achieve full self-denial will continue.'

'Oh, yer mean until I don't enjoy it no more?' asked Kitty, who had spent two hours intermittently groaning with pleasure.

'Exactly, my child. Did I not say you have seen the light?'

Most of the lady Repenters had been out during the afternoon, going about the work of distributing pamphlets in and around the City. Only Father Luke was present at the anointing of Miss Kitty Drake, who emerged from the sprinkled drops of holified bay rum as Mother Magda, short, of course, for Mother Mary Magdalene.

Mother Verity had gone on a private visit to the City, to see an uncle of hers, a director of a firm dealing in exports and imports.

Uncle Harold was fond of his niece, exceptionally so, which was why she went to him. He received her with pleasure, and she explained the reason for her visit.

'Good God,' he said.

'Praise Him.'

'Yes, amen, I daresay, but Celia, my dear, all this damned devotion—'

'Uncle Harold?' she said in gentle protest.

'Well, I said it and I meant it. Has there been a time when you haven't devoted yourself to vicars and parsons and churches? I'll never believe that God intended a sweet woman like you to become as good as a nun. I don't hold with nuns, anyway. Not natural for a woman. Not natural for you.'

183

'Was the war natural, Uncle Harold, in depriving women of millions of men? The alternative for me is devotion to the Lord through the medium of the League of Repenters, led by a man of dynamic vision.'

'Poppycock,' said Uncle Harold, a man of practical vision himself. 'Sounds like a charlatan to me. People like that end up in the *News of the World*, but you never could resist a cause. What a waste. And now what, you've found some good-for-nothing who needs a job, and you're asking me to find one for him?'

Mother Verity, used to frankness and bluntness from her favourite uncle, smiled gently and said, 'Not a good-for-nothing, a man who fought in the war and who is bitter because his country has forgotten him.'

Uncle Harold mumbled and muttered at that, knowing thousands of needy ex-soldiers were receiving no help from the Government. 'Are you sure he's a deserving case, Celia?'

'All men who spent years in the trenches are deserving cases, Uncle Harold, even those whose characters may be dubious. I want you to find a job for this one. Have I ever asked anything of you before?'

'Never. I wish you had. You're the only relative who's never plagued me. But conditions are bad, Celia, there simply aren't jobs to hand out.'

'I know you'll find him one,' said Mother Verity.

'Damn me, you mean it,' said Uncle Harold. His sharp eyes searched her from beneath bushy brows. Her expression, serene, remained so. 'Well, I can't find him work in the docks, unless he has a docker's card, which he obviously hasn't. And the dockers will only work with their own kind. The only possibility is as a loader or checker in our Spitalfields warehouse, although I tell you frankly, my dear, that we don't need extra men.'

'I'm sure you need one, Uncle.'

'Is there something special about this man, Celia?'

'Only the Lord knows that, Uncle Harold.'

'Not necessarily. I've known one or two special people in my time, including you. Well, what's the fellow's name, and how am I expected to get in touch with him?'

Mother Verity said on no account should the offer of a job to Will Fletcher of Christian Street, Whitechapel, come from her uncle or any of his managers. If it did, Mr Fletcher would know someone had spoken for him, and she did not want him to find out it was her.

'I see. You're to remain an anonymous Christian well-wisher, are you?'

'You can put it like that if you like, Uncle,' she said, and went on to suggest that a constable from the local police station, one who possibly knew Mr Fletcher, should casually advise him of a job that was going. Did her uncle know anyone of authority in the police, someone who could contact the Whitechapel station and ask for this to be done?

'That won't be a problem,' said Uncle Harold. 'You've thought this all out, haven't you? I fancy there's more to it than your devotion to – what was it?'

'The League of Repenters and its work among the poor.'

'Damned if I can understand how an intelligent woman like you, Celia, can attach yourself to something that's for cranks and eccentrics.'

'The Lord works in many different ways,' said Mother Verity.

'Well, I can't say no to you, I'll do what you want in respect of this fellow, Will Fletcher. Right away.'

'Bless you, Uncle Harold.'

*

Friday was a busy day for some Repenters. The new incumbent, Mother Magda, in need of activity of a Christian kind, willingly volunteered to help distribute boxfuls of food among the poor of Whitechapel. A horse and van had been hired, and was driven by Mother Joan to the grocer with Father Luke and Mother Mary ensconced in the van. To Father Luke's suggestion that he should drive, Mother Joan said, in her straightforward way, not bloody likely, Father. Good of you to offer and all that, but if there's a horse around that has to be handled, permit me. I've been handling them since the day I left my cradle.

Father Peter and Mother Magda went on ahead to Christian Street in a hansom cab, preferable to a taxi. Father Peter, not unreasonably, considered motor vehicles and internal combustion the work of the Devil.

Mother Verity had decided not to go to Christian Street on this occasion, and accompanied Mother Ruth to Soho to distribute pamphlets.

The Whitechapel grocer had the boxes of food ready, as promised. It had been a lot of work, he said, a bit like a shipping order, but wouldn't deny it was a welcome slice of business for a struggling Christian shopkeeper like him. He almost bowed to Mother Joan in his gratitude when she settled with him, after checking the contents of one box at random. He'd been sorely grieved, he said, when he'd heard she'd been jumped by some thieving coves from Shoreditch after she'd placed the order with him, but when he also heard they'd been sent packing he was, he said, overcome with relief. The geezers had to be from Shoreditch, he said, as there hadn't been any flash Harries like them in Whitechapel since Dick Turpin had last rode in. You can ask me son Charlie, he said, and his son nodded in vigorous confirmation.

He and Charlie helped Father Luke and the ladies to

186

load the boxes on to the van. It was strenuous work, but heartening and satisfying to know they were bringing manna to the desert. Then they set off for Christian Street where Father Peter, as mighty as Goliath but not a worshipper of false idols, was waiting with Mother Magda, the latter in a palpitating state of religious fervour in her desire to help feed the starving poor and so begin atonement. Father Peter was going to hear confession from her after dinner in the evening, although she didn't know what she was going to confess when she'd already told him so much of her sins.

When Mother Joan brought the van to a stop, the street kids swarmed around it, rather as if the Lord had already brought them news of what it contained. Mother Mary, clutching her umbrella, joined Father Luke in the glad business of knocking on doors to announce there was a box of food for every house. Out came the slatterns and the hopeful wives and mothers, and out came some men.

Father Peter lifted his hands in blessing. 'My friends, rejoice in the Lord's bounty we bring you.'

'Oh, don't 'e talk lovely?' said Mother Magda to Mother Joan.

'A splendid leader and minister, a reincarnation of John the Baptist himself, by George,' said Mother Joan heartily. The adults were advancing to join the swarming urchins. 'One box of food for each house!' she declared in a ringing voice.

'Place a pamphlet in each box, sister,' said Father Peter to Mother Magda.

'Be a pleasure,' said Mother Magda who, at his behest, had taken a vow of silence concerning that which was the opposite of self-denial. ''Ere, give over, you lot, stop pushin'.'

The van, its tailboard down, the mountain of food boxes

187

visible, was under siege, and so were the Repenters. The swarm of kids and adults turned into a swarm of locusts.

'Stand back,' boomed Father Peter, 'let the servants of the Lord deliver the boxes, one each into the hands of the head of every household. I command you.'

'Knock it orf, guv,' said one man, 'we'll do our own deliv'ry,' and he climbed up into the van, followed by a second man. The swarming locusts went to work. Mother Mary began to take umbrage. Mother Joan tried to put her buxom firmness in the way of the locusts. Father Peter's thunder began to roll. Mother Magda quivered at its sound. Father Luke put in his own protest.

''Ere, turn it up, ladies an' gents,' he said, 'we've come to serve yer an' redeem yer from 'unger. Turn it up.'

'Aincher a dear?' said a woman, and kissed his plump cheek.

'Oh, 'elp,' groaned Father Luke, 'get thee from me, yer wickedness.'

Mother Mary, furious at such sinful divestment of the van and its contents, set to work with her umbrella.

'Take that! An' that! I'll give you 'elp yourselves!'

'Stand back, you bounders!' cried Mother Joan.

Boxes of food were disappearing, the men in the van pushing them forward. Scores of hands were pillaging and plundering.

'Stone the crows,' breathed Father Luke, 'it's bleedin' robbery.'

Mother Magda was doing her best to hand out pamphlets. Someone pinched her bottom. 'Oh, they ain't no gentlemen 'ereabouts,' she gasped.

'I'll give them gentlemen!' cried Mother Mary. Her own bottom was pinched. She yelped in outrage and swung round. She saw a man's back. 'Take that, you disgustin' creature!' She thumped his shoulders.

The Repenters, hemmed in, were hustled and bustled. Father Peter loomed above all. He swung his arms and gathered Mother Mary and Mother Magda to the protective shield of his chest, enfolding them. Their religious fervour summited within his devoted guardianship. He boomed warnings to the looting sinners of God's vengeance. It made no difference. The locusts picked the van clean and melted away, and the van stood empty. The only evidence of its former contents lay in the sight of half a dozen cardboard boxes, crumpled and trampled in the gutter.

'Shall the Lord forgive this?' boomed Father Peter.

'Can't be helped,' said Mother Joan in practical fashion, 'we brought 'em fodder and they've got fodder.'

'But some was for the next street,' gloomed Father Luke. 'It don't 'ardly bear thinkin' of, the need these people 'ave got for Christian ways.'

'Cheer up, Father Luke,' said Mother Joan, 'they're not yet past redemption. They're learning. Didn't you notice they made no attempt to pinch our clothes? That's a little light of hope, what? Well done, Father Peter, in plucking our sisters from the mob. What bounders. I've been nipped in places I can't mention.'

'We shall return,' said Father Peter, gauntly stern as he released Mothers Mary and Magda. 'Even here, in Satan's own kitchen, mine eyes have seen the glory of the Lord.'

'Magnificent,' said Mother Joan, 'I saw it too, when my horse threw me. Yes, we shall return, Father, we shall return yet again.'

'You're goin' to bring 'em the clothes?' said Father Luke.

'Of course.'

'I am 'umble in the sight of such forgiveness and perseverance,' said Father Luke.

'I'll give them something next time,' said Mother Mary.
'I'll give them more than shoes an' boots.'

'I commend your spirit, sister,' said Father Peter.

'They wasn't no gentlemen,' said Mother Magda. 'I'm
used to only meetin' gentlemen. Still, it's me serious wish
to go among the poor with you, Father, and do me
penitence by 'elping them.'

'Bless you, my child,' said Father Peter.

'Back to the Temple, everyone,' said Mother Joan.

'I just remembered, I've got to go 'ome for a bit,' said
Mother Mary, frowning vaguely. 'I'll come back later.'

The man Will Fletcher had not appeared, nor had the
small girl Lulu. Will Fletcher had gone to Spitalfields, to
enquire after a job that a local bobby had mentioned to
him earlier in the day. He had taken Lulu with him. She
was one of five children. Her mother had hopped it with a
sailor five years ago. Lulu clung to the affection the
lodger, Will Fletcher, gave her.

It was four o'clock in the afternoon. Patsy and Betsy had
been home for half an hour, and Patsy had news for Jimmy
when he came home himself. A factory in Bermondsey
wanted a boy as a workshop runabout and to make tea for
the men. For seven and six a week. Patsy didn't think
much of a job like that for her brother, but it was a start.

'Will Jimmy give us anuvver tanner each?' asked Betsy.
Patsy was peeling potatoes.

'Course he will,' said Patsy.

'Lily Shaw likes our Jimmy,' said Betsy.

'I know she does,' said Patsy, 'but she's not goin' to
have 'im. I like that other girl best.'

'What uvver one?' asked Betsy.

'The one he met in Hyde Park,' said Patsy. 'I liked 'er
mum an' dad as well.'

'She looked a nice mum,' said Betsy, sorrowful that her own mum didn't seem a proper one any more. 'But they're awful rich, I fink.'

'Yes, but you can't blame them for that,' said Patsy, 'people get left money, but it don't mean they're not nice – who's that?' The sound of the front door opening and closing was followed by the sound of footsteps. Mother entered the kitchen and gazed at her daughters at the scullery sink.

'Mum!' cried Betsy.

'Who's that?' asked Mother.

'It's me an' Patsy.' Betsy and her sister entered the kitchen. Mother regarded them vaguely.

'Shouldn't you be at school?' she asked.

'It's summer 'olidays,' said Patsy. 'Don't you want to give us a kiss?'

Mother pecked at their cheeks.

''Ave you come 'ome, Mum?' asked Betsy.

'Mother, if you don't mind. I've come to get some more things. Where's your father?'

'He's at work,' said Patsy.

'That's just like 'im,' said Mother. 'He's never 'ere when he's wanted.'

'That's not fair,' said Patsy, 'Dad's here when *we* want 'im.'

'Don't you have a brother?' asked Mother.

Patsy, rebellious, said, 'What a daft question.'

'What impertinence,' said Mother.

'Jimmy's workin' for rich people,' said Betsy, watching her mum cautiously.

'He's always doin' something he shouldn't,' said Mother.

'No, 'e's not,' said Patsy.

'I don't want no answering back,' said Mother. 'Now

I've got to get more things.' She went to the downstairs bedroom, leaving Patsy in a temper and Betsy uncomfortable.

'Mum's gone all funny, ain't she?' said Betsy sadly.

'Well, she'd better get over it,' said Patsy, 'or I'll ask Aunt Edie to come an' live with us for good.'

'But Dad likes our mum, don't 'e?' said Betsy.

'He puts up with 'er, you mean,' said Patsy, and went back to the potatoes. Betsy followed. She felt more secure staying close to her spirited sister.

'D'you like Aunt Edie, Patsy?'

'Yes, lots,' said Patsy.

'Patsy, I fink I like 'er lots too.'

'She'll be 'ere this evening, for the weekend,' said Patsy.

'Will it be nice, like it was last weekend?' asked Betsy.

'I bet Dad'll be lots of laughs, like last weekend,' said Patsy, potato peel dropping into the bowl. 'And I bet Aunt Edie'll tell 'im off again.'

'Why's she tell our Dad off?'

'So's he won't know she likes 'im.'

'Why?' asked Betsy.

'Well, ladies like Aunt Edie mustn't let married men like Dad know they like them.'

'Crikey, mustn't they?'

'Course they mustn't. So they tell them off.'

'Our mum ain't goin' to stay the weekend, is she?' said Betsy.

'We've got to put up with it, Betsy.'

'I don't mind as long as Aunt Edie's 'ere,' said Betsy.

Mother reappeared, an old Gladstone bag accompanying her umbrella. 'What's that you're doin' out there?' she asked.

'Peelin' potatoes,' said Patsy, finishing the chore.

'I 'ope you're not goin' to eat sinfully,' said Mother.

'There's been too much of that.' She put the Gladstone bag down and opened the larder door. 'What's this?'

'Liver an' bacon,' said Patsy. 'Dad asked me to get some for supper.'

'It's gluttony,' said Mother. 'I'm goin' to give it to that poor Mrs Dobson.' She drew out the plate of liver and bacon. The liver was fresh and shining, the bacon rashers looking succulent.

Patsy drew a breath. 'Put that back,' she said.

'No cheek, my girl,' said Mother.

'Put it back,' said Patsy.

'I'll give you put it back,' said Mother, and gaped vaguely as Patsy took the plate from her and restored it to the larder, Betsy watching with wide-open eyes.

'We're not givin' Dad or Jimmy bread an' water when they come 'ome from work,' said Patsy, 'nor—' She stopped, feeling it wiser not to mention Aunt Edie. Mother intervened telepathically.

'Where's your Aunt Edie?'

'Workin', of course, like she always is this time of day,' said Patsy.

'She ought to be 'ere. What a selfish woman. I told 'er what 'er duty was. I know me own duty, which is a Christian one, 'elping sinners to repent. I 'ope there's been repentin' goin' on in this house while I've been away.'

'Oh, you can't hear nothing in this 'ouse except repentin',' said Patsy.

'I'm pleased to know it,' said Mother. 'Well, I've got to go now.'

'Shall we give your love to Dad?' asked Patsy, a little fire in her eyes.

'Who?' asked Mother.

'Goodbye, Mum,' said Patsy.

'Yes, I've got to go. I'll pray for all of you.' She left.

Betsy looked doleful. Patsy grimaced.

Aunt Edie arrived just before five-thirty. She had got off early, and having taken her weekend case to work with her in the morning, she came straight from the factory at Peckham. She let herself in using the latchcord.

There they were, the girls, in the kitchen, the table laid for supper, the potatoes cooking on the gas stove and tinned peas ready to be heated. They smiled to see her, and Aunt Edie warmed to them.

'Hullo, me pets, how's tricks?' she said, her own smile cheerful.

'We're ever so glad you've come, Aunt Edie,' said Patsy.

'We like it you're 'ere,' said Betsy, and Aunt Edie hugged them both before getting down to the homely task of cooking the liver and bacon, with fried onions.

'Where's Jimmy?' she asked from the scullery.

'Oh, he's doin' that work that Mr Gibbs said 'e could,' replied Patsy.

'And 'e's been givin' me an' Patsy a tanner each every day for goin' out to look for a job for 'im,' said Betsy.

'Well, that's a lovely brother you've got.'

'We went into a firm this afternoon that said they've got a job for a boy,' said Patsy. 'I expect Jimmy'll be 'ome about the same time as Dad, about six, Aunt Edie. I expect they'll be ever so pleased to see you. Mum come 'ome for five minutes this afternoon, she took more things with 'er.'

'She's gone away again, 'as she?' Aunt Edie's voice sounded as if it was having trouble getting past her tonsils.

'Yes, I fink so, Auntie,' said Betsy. 'She said we wasn't to eat sinful.'

'I'll give her sinful,' muttered Aunt Edie.

194

'Beg your pardon, Auntie?' said Patsy.

'It's all right, darlings, don't you worry, we'll have a lovely weekend,' said Aunt Edie.

Patsy and Betsy looked at each other. Fancy, Aunt Edie calling them darlings now. She must like them.

Patsy smiled.

CHAPTER TWELVE

'Snap,' said Dad.

'What d'you mean?' asked Aunt Edie.

'We've both got two rashers of bacon,' said Dad.

'We've all got two rashers, except Betsy, who only wanted one,' said Aunt Edie.

'All right,' said Dad, 'snap with everyone except Betsy.'

Betsy giggled.

'Time your dad grew up, Betsy,' said Aunt Edie, 'time he started to improve.'

Betsy cast a look at Patsy. Patsy winked.

'I don't know what the world's goin' to do with some dads, do you, Aunt Edie?' said Patsy.

'Drown 'em,' said Aunt Edie, and Patsy thought their aunt looked kind of specially attractive this evening. She had a lovely blouse on, with a high crinkly collar and pearl buttons down the front. It showed she had an awfully nice figure. And her hair looked as if she'd just had it styled.

'You've got room for improvement, Dad,' said Jimmy, who was getting tanned from his outdoor work.

'That's what me old sergeant-major kept tellin' me,' said Dad.

'Not him again,' said Aunt Edie.

'"Corporal Andrews," he kept sayin', "it's me painful duty to hinform you you'll cop it if you don't keep yer ruddy noddle down. You get it shot off by Johnny Turk and I'll put you on a charge for bein' careless while on duty. There's room for improvement," he'd say.'

'Well, you must have improved, Dad,' said Jimmy, 'or you'd be sittin' here eatin' liver and bacon with no head.'

Aunt Edie burst into laughter. Everyone looked at her. 'Now what've I done?' she asked.

'Nice you're here, Aunt Edie,' said Jimmy. 'I've been thinkin'. About that Bermondsey firm, Patsy. I think I'd better go straight there in the mornin'. Then if I get the job, I'd best go up to Anerley an' tell Mr Gibbs I'm fixed up.'

'For seven an' six a week?' said Dad. An unusual frown creased his forehead. 'Daylight robbery. It's near to forty-five hours a week at tuppence a ruddy hour.'

'Still, it's a job, Dad.'

'Yes, if it's not a dead end one, Jimmy lad,' said Dad, 'and Bermondsey's full of jobs like that. I'm goin' to leave it to you to make up your own mind about it, but I want you to know we're not too badly off. I get a decent wage an' grocery perks into the bargain, and besides – no, well, I'll leave it to you to decide.'

'I think your dad means you're bringing 'ome good money from Mr Gibbs,' said Aunt Edie, 'that you're earnin' four bob a day and that you'll be earnin' it for weeks.'

'Yes, you could give yourself a bit of time, Jimmy,' said Patsy, who wanted her brother to have the kind of job that could make him hold his head high among the young men of Walworth.

'Well, tell you what,' said Jimmy, enjoying his supper, 'I think I'll call on the firm and see if there's decent prospects. Yes, I'll do that. I don't suppose I'll ever build railways or undergrounds, and I don't suppose I'll ever play centre-forward for Tottenham 'Otspur, either – not that I wouldn't like to, I would, in fact, I'm fond of football – where was I, Aunt Edie?'

'Gettin' there,' said Aunt Edie, who was discovering exactly how much she loved Jimmy and his sisters.

'Yes, gettin' nearly up the chimney,' said Patsy.

'What's Tot'nam 'Otspur?' asked Betsy.

'I'm sorry for you, Betsy, if you don't know about Tottenham 'Otspur,' said Jimmy.

'I can't know everyfing,' said Betsy, 'not when I've only been goin' to school a few years.'

'Bless yer, me pickle, you're good enough for me just as you are,' said Dad.

'Well, I was sayin' that even if I never get me name in the newspapers, I'd like a job with some prospects,' said Jimmy.

'Right,' said Dad, although with things as they were, he thought good prospects hard to come by. 'You stick to that line of thought, Jimmy. By the way, Patsy, didn't yer mum say anything at all about how long she'd be away?'

'No,' said Patsy.

Aunt Edie gave silent vent to her anger by grinding a piece of liver into annihilation.

'Oh, well,' said Dad. 'How about a tram ride to Peckham Rye on Sunday afternoon, an' takin' a picnic tea with us?'

'Wiv Aunt Edie?' asked Betsy.

'Oh, I think we could always find room on a tram for Aunt Edie, yer know,' said Dad.

'I'm honoured, I'm sure,' said Aunt Edie.

'That's settled, then,' said Dad. 'We'll take Jimmy's cricket bat and get Aunt Edie to do some wallopin'.'

'Who's goin' to bowl to me?' asked Aunt Edie.

'Betsy,' said Dad. 'She'll bowl you some dollies for wallopin', then we'll put Jimmy on to get you leg before.'

'Wait a minute, Jack Andrews,' said Aunt Edie, 'what's leg before? You're not gettin' me playin' cricket with me skirts up on Peckham Rye.'

'Auntie, you don't 'ave to show your legs,' said Patsy, 'it's just if the ball hits you there.'

'Don't take any notice of that, Aunt Edie,' said Jimmy. 'Of course you have to show your legs, or the bowler won't know where they are.'

'What?' asked Aunt Edie, who could do a lovely pearly knees-up but knew little about cricket.

'Only to your knees,' said Jimmy, 'it's not fair on the bowler otherwise. You can tuck your skirts up, Dad won't mind—'

'I bet he won't,' said Aunt Edie.

'I won't, either,' said Jimmy.

'Jimmy Andrews,' said Aunt Edie, 'd'you think I was born yesterday?'

'Glad you weren't,' said Jimmy, 'you'd 'ardly have any legs at all if you had been.'

Betsy giggled. Patsy shrieked. Dad coughed. Aunt Edie looked him in the eye.

'That boy of yours,' she said. 'I'm goin' to have to watch him this weekend.'

'Oh, I watch 'im all the time, Aunt Edie,' said Patsy, 'but it don't do me much good.'

They enjoyed an entertaining evening. Patsy had meant to go out and join some street friends, but stayed in because there were lots of laughs with Aunt Edie there. Aunt Edie was in lovely form, so was Dad. His jokes made her give him laughing looks, except that Patsy thought she pulled herself up every so often to say something like, 'That's enough of that, Jack Andrews, we don't want to 'ear any more about Arabian concubines, if you don't mind.' It was as if she was reminding herself she mustn't

199

come between Dad and Mum, that it wouldn't do for her and Dad to get too familiar with each other. Fancy her not being married, thought Patsy, she'd have been a lovely mum herself.

'Well, I don't know any more I could confess, Father,' said Mother Magda, who had recounted much of her ways of obliging nice gentlemen.

'All that you have confessed is now a closed book, except to the Lord, my child,' murmured Father Peter, 'and be sure that by confession and repentance He will absolve you in the end.'

'Oh, won't 'E absolve me now?' asked Mother Magda.

'Be sure His absolution will come when you have achieved the blessedness of self-denial. Shall we go into the other room, sister, and pray?'

'Oh, do we 'ave time before I go to bed, Father?'

'An hour, my child, an hour.'

In the other room, his bedroom, she said, 'Shall I lie down?'

'Do so, yes,' said Father Peter, and she placed herself on the bed. He said a prayer for her, and she said amen.

'How do you feel after confession, sister?'

'Oh, it's give me a terrible temptation to sin.'

'We shall fight such temptation together, it's the only true way to reach eventual purity of mind and body.'

'Oh, I'm chronic about gettin' to be pure.'

It was hardly a curative hour. There was such a lot of that which made sin dreadfully enjoyable.

When Aunt Edie came down the next morning, Saturday, Dad was in his cap, jacket and hard-wearing corduroy trousers. He was just about to leave for his morning's work.

'What about your breakfast?' asked Aunt Edie.

'Had it. Cup of tea and a slice of toast. Thanks for bein' here again, Edie.'

'Yes, off you go, then, I'll see to the children's breakfast.'

'Bless you, old girl. So long.'

'Don't call me old girl.'

She left a little later to go to her own work for the morning, and she meant to inveigle her boss into letting her off early. Then she could make a start on the week's washing as soon as she got back. Patsy said she'd prepare a light midday meal.

Jimmy went off to Bermondsey, but found the job for a runabout tea boy had gone. It had been filled yesterday afternoon, subsequent to Patsy's call on behalf of her brother. All the same, Jimmy asked the foreman if the job had had prospects. Prospects? Course it had, the men would always want their tea and there'd always be running about to do. Jimmy said he didn't think that amounted to prospects, more like a blank wall. 'Hoppit, cocky,' said the foreman.

Jimmy hopped it, and with no regrets. It was nearly ten o'clock when he reached the handsome house in Anerley. Ada opened the side door to him.

'Oh,' she said in relief. 'We thought – oh, you've come, then?'

'Yes, I've arrived, Lady Ada,' said Jimmy, 'I—'

'Cheeky again, are we?' said Ada. 'No wonder you make the young madam giggle. But you're late as well as cheeky. You'll cop it.'

'Is Mr Gibbs shirty about me not bein' here on time?'

'We thought you'd give us up,' said Ada. 'Mr 'Odges said he was grieved that some young gents could turn out disappointin'.'

'I wouldn't give people up without sayin', or without a good reason,' said Jimmy.

'There, I said you wouldn't,' smiled Ada. 'You'd better go through, Mr Gibbs is on the terrace, I don't suppose he's spittin' nuts and bolts yet.'

Jimmy went round to the terrace, where Mr Gibbs, brown-faced and husky-looking in shirt, trousers and belt, his sleeves rolled up, was listening to his precocious daughter.

Sophy was saying, 'Let that be a lesson to you, Daddy, giving work to boys who don't turn up, what a rotter, doesn't it make you want to spit? Wait till – oh, look, he's here.'

Mr Gibbs turned. 'Sorry I'm late, Mr Gibbs,' said Jimmy.

'Blessed cheek, where've you been all this time?' asked Sophy.

'Thought we'd lost your services, Jimmy,' said Mr Gibbs.

'Well, it was like this,' said Jimmy, and explained exactly why he was late. He finished by saying, 'I had to go after the job, Mr Gibbs, I like what I'm doin' for you, I could do work like this all me life, but—'

'Understood, Jimmy,' said Mr Gibbs. 'The firm called it a job, did they? I know about jobs like that. Don't fall into one of them, or you'll disappoint me. On the other hand, you might come back at me and ask what's the alternative these days. That's the big problem, lack of real jobs, isn't it? It's our government, Jimmy, they won't accept they can get the economy moving by funding a countrywide building programme – houses, new roads, improved roads and more railway systems, as well as new schools.'

'Daddy, you boring old thing,' said Sophy. 'Anyway, can I help Jimmy now he's here?'

'I think you'd better ask your mother,' said Mr Gibbs.

'But you've already said I could help as long as I wear my new dungarees and the gardening gloves. Oh, come on, Daddy, you can't expect Jimmy to do everything by himself, you don't want him to go home looking as if you've slaved him to death, do you?'

'It's not a good idea, no,' said Mr Gibbs.

'Then I won't be a tick, Jimmy,' said Sophy, darting away.

'Let your mother know what's happening,' called her father.

'Yes, I will if I see her,' called Sophy, 'but she's ever so busy this morning, so if I don't see her I won't actually go and interrupt her.' She disappeared. Mr Gibbs smiled.

'I'll get on, shall I, Mr Gibbs?' said Jimmy. 'I think I can finish that clearin' today, I've only got a few big branches left to saw up. That's if I can cope with any problems that might come along.'

'Problems?' said Mr Gibbs. He smiled again. 'Yes, I see. Well, I must get back to the men.' Off he went, very much as if it was wiser not to hang around and not to ask about problems. He knew that his irrepressible daughter had a new interest, Jimmy. Jimmy's company was her current hobby. It might last the summer out. Then she would find something else. It was all part of the years of growing up, when girls like Sophy were butterflies. There was no point in trying to turn a thirteen-year-old girl into a steadfast woman. Sophy would acquire that quality later. It was a quality that her mother had.

Jimmy set to with a saw, a long sharp saw. The ashes of burned bonfires marked the clearing. One bonfire, only half-built, was to be completed and piled with light sawn branches, to be burned tonight. That would finish this clearing, and on Monday he would start on another. The work really exhilarated him, and he was beginning to see factory work as dull and boring.

Sophy arrived: clad in brown dungarees and wearing thick gardening gloves, she looked like a young female navvy. Her spirits high, she set to, holding each small branch firmly while Jimmy sawed them from the main branch. She carried each one to the bonfire to chuck it on. Jimmy called to her to just put them down beside the mound, he'd come and place them on later.

'I can put them on as good as you,' she said.

'Well, if you could I'd let you,' said Jimmy, 'but you can't, so I won't. It's no good just chuckin' them on, you have to build a bonfire, not knock it about.'

'Cheeky impertinence you've got,' said Sophy, but her spirits were high and she did as he wanted. She was biding her time, of course, waiting until she could trip him up and jump on him. She liked his impertinence, his challenging way of dealing with her, and gave no thought at all to the fact that he came from a cockney family.

Jimmy was on the lookout for larks from her, but she behaved as if the activity was enough. Mind, he couldn't stop her talking. She talked all the time.

Eventually and inevitably, her mother appeared on the scene.

'Oh, hullo, Mummy,' said Sophy, sweet with innocence.

'I thought so,' said Mrs Gibbs.

'Daddy said I could help as long as I wore the new dungarees he bought for me,' said Sophy, looking warm from work and the sun.

'Those dungarees were bought because I seem unable to stop you galloping off into these jungles, to prevent you ruining your clothes and getting yourself scratched to death, not to get in Jimmy's way. Good morning, Jimmy.'

'Hullo, Mrs Gibbs,' said Jimmy, resting the saw.

'You managed to get here, then?' said Mrs Gibbs, smiling.

'Yes. I was late because—'

'He went after some rotten job,' said Sophy, 'for seven and sixpence a week. Seven and six. Mummy, doesn't that make you want to spit?'

'Did you take it, Jimmy?' asked Mrs Gibbs.

'No, they'd already given it to someone else,' said Jimmy, 'but I wouldn't have taken it, anyway, it didn't have any prospects.'

'Very wise. Sophy, come here.'

'Yes, Mummy?' Butter wouldn't have melted in Sophy's mouth as she came to look up at her mother.

For her daughter's ears alone, Mrs Gibbs said, 'What are you wearing under those dungarees?'

'Oh, just my Liberty bodice and you-knows, Mummy.' Sophy's smooth young shoulders were bare except where the wide braces of her dungarees lay over them, covering the straps of her vest.

'You shocker,' said Mrs Gibbs.

'But, Mummy, you can't wear a frock under dungarees, 'specially on a hot day like this.'

'Precocious child,' said Mrs Gibbs. 'Well, behave yourself now, do you understand?'

'I don't know why you think I won't,' said Sophy.

'Jimmy,' called Mrs Gibbs, 'if Sophy gives you any trouble, tie her up and sit her in that wheelbarrow.'

'I'll do that,' said Jimmy.

'Good,' said Mrs Gibbs, and left them.

It was a day of high summer, and to Jimmy as good as being out in the country. Felled saplings and mown grasses offered all the heady aromas of the countryside. In her delight at being out of doors with him, Sophy curbed her penchant for monkey tricks. At eleven-thirty, Ada brought them each a glass of cool lemonade.

'Well, thanks, Ada,' said Jimmy.

'You haven't brought any biscuits,' said Sophy.

'No, your mother said it would spoil your lunch, Miss Sophy.' Ada looked at the girl. What a ravishing young creature she was for her age, even in dungarees. And she had her eye on Jimmy all right, Jimmy with his young manly growing-up look, and clear grey ears that looked you straight in the face.

'That's all, Ada, you can go now,' said Sophy.

Ada, recognizing that the girl wanted Jimmy to herself, turned and left. She heard Jimmy say, 'You shouldn't speak like that to Ada.'

'Blessed cheek,' said Sophy, 'why not?'

'Because she's nice,' said Jimmy, and Ada went smiling on her way then.

At one o'clock, Jimmy was invited to eat a lunch of cold chicken and salad at a table on the terrace with Sophy and her mother. And Mr Gibbs joined them, Mrs Gibbs insisted. She said she'd divorce him if she had to eat every lunch alone with Sophy the Dreadful, while he ate bread, cheese and pickled onions with the men. Mr Gibbs asked if it was wise to have Jimmy sit down with them. Mrs Gibbs said she liked the boy and that he was good company.

When they were at lunch, she asked her husband why he'd given Sophy permission to turn herself into a labourer.

'Did I?' said Mr Gibbs cautiously.

'So she said.'

'I've been absent-minded lately,' said Mr Gibbs.

'Oh, you bought the dungarees in an absent-minded moment, did you?' said Mrs Gibbs.

'I get like that sometimes,' said Sophy, 'and it makes life jolly trying. I've had a trying life altogether, falling down the stairs when I was seven, then getting the measles when I was nine, and having to put up with the war all those years, and now having my headmistress, Miss Mortimer, getting a down on me.'

'All that lot's the reason why you're a monkey, is it?' said Mr Gibbs.

'I expect it was the fall down the stairs that did it,' said Jimmy. 'I expect she landed on her head. It turns girls a bit funny when they land on their heads. Well, that's what I've 'eard. You just have to be patient and hope for the best, Mrs Gibbs.'

'And what happens when patience goes through the roof?' asked Mrs Gibbs.

'I suppose you just have to grin and bear it,' said Jimmy. 'And get the roof repaired,' he added.

Mrs Gibbs smiled. Jimmy was very good company. He went back to his work after lunch, and Sophy was again allowed to join him. She was frisky in the afternoon sun, helping Jimmy to pile dry leaves into a wheelbarrow. Jimmy was using them to rim the foot of the huge bonfire. Nothing untoward happened until Sophy chose to enjoy a diversion. The young hoyden came out in her, she showered Jimmy with leaves, then darted away in escape. She leapt on to a pile of stripped tree trunks on the edge of the clearing. The top trunk rolled, Sophy leapt off and ran forward. Her feet tangled themselves in a bed of chopped undergrowth. Jimmy rushed the wheelbarrow towards the rolling trunk. The trunk struck it, the wheelbarrow jumped and turned over, spilling a river of leaves. Jimmy was thrown over with it. Sophy was on her hands and knees. The fallen wheelbarrow stopped the progress of the trunk, a foot in diameter, only inches from her. She pulled herself free and ran over to Jimmy, who lay on his back.

'Blessed earthquakes,' she said, 'would you think that rotten log would have chased me like that?'

'Well, it was behavin' itself until you jumped on it,' said Jimmy. 'Who tripped me up?'

'The wheelbarrow did it. Jimmy, you're not hurt, are you?'

'Don't know yet,' said Jimmy, and climbed to his feet. 'Well, I think I'm still alive.'

'Gosh, I'd have caught it if you weren't,' said Sophy. 'You won't tell Mummy, will you? She'll fuss like anything.'

'I'll just tell her I've had a bit of a tryin' day,' said Jimmy, 'but I think your dad'll want to know how that log got there. It's too heavy to roll back to the pile.'

'Oh, I'll tell Daddy it just rolled off, which it did, didn't it?'

'Best thing, I suppose,' said Jimmy. 'He'll get the men to move it. D'you want to go an' do some quiet readin' now?'

'I should say not,' said Sophy. 'Jimmy, you just saved my life again.'

'All right, send me a postal order.'

Sophy bubbled into laughter.

Mr Gibbs paid Jimmy at the end of the day and told him that if a job didn't come along, he at least had months of work here, which Jimmy thought cracking.

Ada saw him out. 'You're gettin' ever so brown,' she said.

'Give me best wishes to Percy,' said Jimmy.

'Who? Oh, you dotty thing,' said Ada. 'See you Monday?'

'I don't know I'll live that long,' said Jimmy, 'not now you've broken me heart.'

'You're a joker, you are, Jimmy.'

'I'm kind to old ladies as well.'

'I bet. What d'you think of the young madam?'

'Well, I'm thankful I'm still able to walk,' said Jimmy. 'Still, she's pretty, and lively too, and game for anything that's a laugh.'

'Oh, you're fallin' for her, are you?' said Ada.

'What's the use? So long, Ada.'

''Bye, Jimmy.'

By evening, Aunt Edie had done the week's washing and cooked the supper. The family marvelled at her, she did everything so cheerfully. Over supper, Jimmy said it didn't matter about that job being taken, he wanted one that had prospects, anyway. And he was all right for the time being, working up at Anerley for Mr Gibbs. He'd give Dad something out of the wages Mr Gibbs was paying him, something towards family expenses. Dad said just put it aside as savings for the moment.

'Yes, that's sensible,' said Aunt Edie.

'Betsy,' said Jimmy, 'I'll take you and Patsy for a walk after supper, and we'll see if the toffee-apple shop's open in King and Queen Street.'

'I like toffee-apples,' said Aunt Edie.

'Bring you one back, then,' said Jimmy.

Out he went with his sisters after the washing-up had been done, leaving Dad to his daily paper, while Aunt Edie went into the yard to lift the washing off the line. Dad went out to help her.

'I can manage,' she said.

'So can I,' said Dad.

'It doesn't need two of us.'

'Halves the work, though,' said Dad cheerfully. ''Ello, what's this pretty thing?'

'Eyes off, if you don't mind,' said Aunt Edie. 'I brought some of my own things to put in the wash. Go an' read your paper.'

'I didn't know pillow cases were like this,' said Dad.

'Leave it be,' said Aunt Edie, 'it's not a pillow case, and you know it.'

'Can't be, now I come to give it a proper look,' said Dad. 'It's got holes both ends.'

It was a waist petticoat, Aunt Edie's. She gave him a look. He gave her a grin.

'D'you want your ears boxed, Jack Andrews?' she said.

'Lace too,' said Dad, 'it looks a bit sinful to me.'

Aunt Edie, suppressing her true feelings, said, 'I suppose Maud wears flannel, does she?'

'Couldn't say,' said Dad, unpegging sheets. 'I 'aven't seen anything of Maudie's for years.'

'Well, all those years you were away in the Army, you didn't see anything of her, either.'

'You could say that,' said Dad.

Suspecting what he really meant, Aunt Edie said through gritted teeth, 'Time you stood up like a man, Jack Andrews, and gave 'er a good hidin'.'

'Now, Edie—'

'I've a good mind, next time I see 'er, to do it for you. It's all very well bein' peaceable, but what about your kids? What do they think about you lettin' their mother walk out on them and not liftin' a finger to stop her?'

'Best way,' said Dad, his arms full of dry washing.

'Easiest way, you mean.' Aunt Edie gave him another look. A man like him, she thought, still healthy and vigorous, and that wife of his probably hadn't let him touch her since little Betsy was conceived. She hadn't liked having a third child, especially a whole four years after Patsy was born.

'The kids'll manage, Edie,' said Dad pacifically.

They probably would too, thought Aunt Edie, because of him. They liked their dad, they knew about the war and were proud of him. He took the dry washing in. She followed with an armful. They placed it in the tin bath for her to go through when she was ready to iron. Dad sat down at the kitchen table and picked up his paper again.

'Sorry,' said Aunt Edie abruptly.

'What for?' asked Dad.

'Sticking my nose in.'

'Well, I like it,' said Dad. 'You always did 'ave a good-looking nose, Edie old love.'

'Oh, blow you, Jack Andrews,' she said in an angry little way.

'What for?' asked Dad again.

'Never mind,' she said, 'just never mind.'

Lily Shaw, button-eyed and a growing young busybody, latched herself on to Jimmy, Patsy and Betsy as they crossed from Manor Place into Browning Street.

'Where yer goin'?' she said. 'I'll come with yer, I ain't doin' nothing else. 'Ere, we 'eard yer Aunt Edie's stayin' with yer again.'

'I expect everyone's heard,' said Jimmy. 'Dad's been standin' in our doorway shoutin' it through a trumpet. He doesn't want anyone not to hear, like the people in Crampton Street and the Walworth Road. Still, if they didn't, perhaps you'd go round an' tell 'em, Lily.'

'Yes, it wouldn't be right if there was people who 'adn't heard,' said Patsy.

'Oh, I'll ask me mum,' said Lily, 'she'll be pleased to oblige yer. 'Ere, don't Jimmy look all brown, Patsy? Where's 'e been goin' to?'

'Oh, ain't you heard?' said Patsy. 'Betsy, fancy that, Lily's not heard about our Jimmy.'

'Crumbs, what a shame,' said Betsy.

'Don't bein' all brown make Jimmy look 'andsome?' said Lily. 'Come on, where you been goin', Jimmy?'

'Tell you what, Lily,' said Jimmy, 'I'll get Dad's trumpet out tomorrow, and holler it through that.'

'Oh, would yer, Jimmy?' said Lily. 'I ain't never seen yer dad's trumpet.'

'I ain't neiver,' said Betsy.

'Mind, you could tell me now, if yer like, Jimmy,' said Lily, 'only me mum's been sayin' where's that Jimmy Andrews goin' off to every day. Well, we ain't 'eard you've got a job yet. 'As 'e got a job, Patsy?'

''Ave you got a job, Jimmy?' asked Patsy.

Browning Street was quite balmy in the evening sunshine.

'Have I got a job, Betsy?' asked Jimmy.

Betsy thought as she trotted beside her brother. ''E's met a girl,' she said.

'What girl?' asked Lily jealously.

''E met 'er in 'Yde Park,' said Betsy, 'she's ever so pretty. 'Er name's Soapy. Or somefing like that.'

They turned into King and Queen Street. People were at their open doors, catching the evening air and gossiping. Street kids were about, coming from the East Street market. Not all the stalls had packed up for the day. The kids were carrying specked or overripe fruit stallholders had let them have.

''Strewth,' said Lily, 'fancy 'aving a name like Soapy, and I bet she ain't as pretty as I am. What yer all goin' down 'ere for, are yer goin' to the market?'

'What we goin' down here for, Jimmy?' asked Patsy.

'Well, now you come to ask,' said Jimmy, 'I forget.'

'Toffee-apples,' said Betsy.

'Are yer well orf, then?' asked Lily.

'Not yet,' said Jimmy. The shop was open and there were trays of upside-down toffee apples in the window. Jimmy bought a dozen for sixpence, gave two to Lily and carried the rest back home. Lily was ecstatic, her long pink tongue going rapturously to work on the darkly golden toffee. She wanted to come in with them when they got back home, but Patsy said their dad wasn't having visitors this evening, he'd got a bone in his leg that was playing him up. It was one of his wounded bones, she said, and it would get a headache if visitors came in.

They all enjoyed the toffee apples, Dad and Aunt Edie as well.

Sunday was cloudy and not as hot, but they enjoyed the day. Aunt Edie, busy, cheerful and mothering, did roast beef with Yorkshire pudding for dinner, and another apple pie. Everyone had seconds of the apple pie, except Dad.

'I suppose your Dad doesn't like it,' said Aunt Edie.

'You 'appen to have given me a slice as big as my loaf of bread,' said Dad.

'Well, fancy that,' said Aunt Edie, 'I didn't know there was anything as big as your loaf of bread, Jack Andrews.'

Dad roared with laughter. Betsy burst into giggles. Aunt Edie gave Dad one of her old-fashioned looks.

'Aunt Edie, you're funny,' said Jimmy.

'So's my apple pie,' said Aunt Edie.

'I think I'll 'ave seconds, after all,' said Dad. 'Seems a shame to let that last piece sit there all by itself.'

'You don't 'ave to have it,' said Aunt Edie.

'I'll 'ave it,' said Dad.

'You sure?' said Aunt Edie. 'I mean, if you don't like it—?'

'Me old sergeant-major once said—'

'I'll give you your seconds up your waistcoat if you bring that old sergeant-major of yours in again,' said Aunt Edie.

Dad roared with laughter again. Patsy and Jimmy joined in. Betsy giggled through pie and custard.

'You're a born pearly queen, you are, Aunt Edie,' said Jimmy.

'Here,' said Aunt Edie and served Dad the last piece of apple pie.

Dad looked at it. 'Is that all?' he asked. 'You sure you ain't robbin' me, Your Pearly Queenship?'

Aunt Edie brought the house down then. She leaned across the table and pushed a spoonful of custard into his mouth. She did it as if she wanted to do it, as if suddenly she couldn't resist the fun of it.

Then she was laughing.

Crikey, thought Patsy, our mum was never like this.

Later, they all took a tram to Peckham Rye, Aunt Edie carrying a shopping bag containing food for a picnic tea, Dad carrying a carpet bag containing an old primus stove, a tin kettle, a teapot and a large bottle of water. The sun came out and the warm afternoon light flooded the Rye and the rooftops of Peckham. Patsy thought Aunt Edie looked a picture in her large white Sunday hat and full-skirted white dress. Cockney women had a great liking for white on summer Sundays, as if they were in defiance of what smoky London could do to it. They dressed their daughters in it, and wore white blouses themselves.

Jimmy brought his cricket bat and ball, with stumps, and despite Aunt Edie saying she hadn't played cricket since she was a little girl, she had to play this afternoon. Everyone insisted. Betsy wanted to bat first, so they let her. Patsy bowled underarm to her, Betsy aimed to biff it

214

and missed. She lost her balance and fell on the stumps.

'Out first ball, you pickle,' said Dad.

Betsy wasn't having that. Nor was Aunt Edie. 'It ain't fair,' said Betsy, 'I'll scream.'

'So will I,' said Aunt Edie.

'What a palaver,' said Dad.

So Betsy had another go. Her biff connected this time. But Jimmy caught her out. Betsy yelled in disgust.

'You're in, Aunt Edie,' said Patsy.

'Oh, lor',' said Aunt Edie, but took the bat and stood at the wicket. Her hat was off, her piled hair shining in the light. She walloped the first ball from Patsy and laughed in triumph.

'Run, Auntie, run!' cried Betsy, and scampered after the ball.

'All right,' said Aunt Edie. Hitching her dress with one hand and carrying the bat with her other, she ran to the bowler's mark. Dad grinned, so did Jimmy. Aunt Edie running, skirts tossing, was a cracking Sunday afternoon sight. She missed the next ball from Patsy and it struck the skirt of her dress.

'Was that lbw?' asked Dad.

'What's lbw?' asked Aunt Edie. 'Some of your French?'

'Leg before wicket,' said Jimmy.

'Yes, was it?' asked Patsy.

'Told you we'd have problems,' said Jimmy. 'I mean, where's her legs? Can you see 'em, Dad?'

'Not from 'ere,' said Dad.

'The ball hit her just there,' said Patsy pointing.

'Is that where 'er right leg is?' asked Jimmy.

'Could we 'ave a look, Edie?' asked Dad.

'Yes, could we, Aunt Edie?' asked Patsy, one with her dad and brother when larks were on. 'It's only fair.'

'Think I'm daft, do you?' said Aunt Edie. 'That's it,

215

gather round, the lot of you, but you'll be lucky, young Jimmy, an' you Jack Andrews, if you think I'm goin' to show my legs to the whole of Peckham.' The Rye was the playground this afternoon of scores of families.

'Not fair, yer know, keepin' yer hidden talents covered up at cricket,' said Dad.

Aunt Edie went for him. Amid Betsy's shrieks of joy, she lifted the bat and rushed. Dad turned tail and ran. Aunt Edie chased after him. A frisky dog joined in. Dad fell over it. Aunt Edie caught him. Patsy yelled with laughter as her dad took a thump from the bat on his backside.

'Ruddy sergeant-majors,' said Dad.

'I'll give you sergeant-majors,' said Aunt Edie, and gave him another thump.

'That's done it,' said Dad, and with a quick supple movement of his long wiry body he was up. Aunt Edie dropped the bat, picked up her skirts and fled, putting herself behind Jimmy.

'Stop 'im, Jimmy!' she gasped.

'Go it, Dad, go it!' cried Patsy.

'Patsy, oh, yer demon!' gasped Aunt Edie, and ran round and round Jimmy, with Dad at her back, a huge grin on his face. He didn't catch her, of course. It was the threat that governed the spirit of the moment.

'Keep goin', Aunt Edie,' said Jimmy, 'good game of cricket you're playin'.'

It was all part of the best Sunday afternoon the family could remember. And everyone told Aunt Edie what a good sport she was. Dad boiled a kettle of water on the primus stove, and they made tea to have with the picnic. Jimmy and Patsy noted that Aunt Edie hardly told Dad off at all. She wanted to know how long Jimmy's work at Anerley would last. Jimmy said until sometime in November, according to Mr Gibbs. Aunt Edie said she'd keep an eye open in Camberwell for a job for him.

'Bless yer, Aunt Edie,' said Jimmy. 'I wouldn't mind givin' you a kiss and a cuddle for that.'

''Elp yerself, Jimmy,' said Dad, 'it's a nice afternoon.'

'Who's laughin'?' asked Aunt Edie.

'Me,' said Patsy.

Later, on the way to the tram home, Patsy spoke to Jimmy.

'Has that girl give you a kiss and a cuddle yet?'

'What girl?' asked Jimmy.

'Sophy Gibbs,' said Patsy, her best Sunday frock lightly rippling around her legs.

'Oh, only when I arrive and when I go, and in between,' said Jimmy. 'She's a bit reserved, yer know.'

'Hark the 'erald angels sing,' said Patsy.

At Speakers Corner in Hyde Park, Father Peter was declaiming to a crowd, his voice booming above the heckling. Lady Repenters handed out pamphlets, while Mother Mary guarded herself and her sisters with her umbrella, and Mother Magda quivered a little sinfully to the rolling thunder that rose up from the minister's deep chest whenever a heckler derided the word of the Lord. The policeman on duty kept his ear open, as usual, for any incitement that would lead to a riot, but intervened only once, and that was to advise Mother Mary she was disturbing the peace a bit.

'It's that there brolly of yours, madam. Once you start trying to poke people's eyes with it, you're making an unlawful weapon of it, which means you'll have to come along to the station with me.'

'What impertinence,' said Mother Mary, 'I've met your kind before. I'll 'ave you know it's the Lord's 'and that

217

guides me umbrella, and I don't know what I'd do without it when there's all them disgustin' blasphemers interruptin' our minister something shockin'.'

'I'll see to them,' said the constable, 'you see you just use your brolly for keeping off the rain.'

'Well, all right,' said Mother Mary, 'but I'll give them something if they don't pay no attention to you.'

On Sunday evening, Aunt Edie entertained the family by playing the piano again. It was not the only parlour piano that was being used in Walworth. Relations like uncles and aunts and grandmothers and grandfathers visited on Sundays, and such days finished with songs around family pianos. Even some of the poorest families owned a piano that dated from Victorian times.

Aunt Edie was a gem at a keyboard. Astonishingly, many cockney men and women had a natural gift for understanding a keyboard without ever having had a single lesson. Aunt Edie loved music and song, and she and Jimmy practised their duets again. After which, she said yes, he could sing with her at the concert next Saturday.

''Ooray,' said Patsy.

'We'll all be there,' said Dad.

'You don't have to be,' said Aunt Edie.

'All right,' said Dad, 'just me an' Patsy and me little pickle. We won't ask old Mother Huggins.'

'Who's she?' asked Patsy.

'Never 'eard of her,' said Dad, 'so we can't ask her, can we?'

Patsy yelled with laughter, Betsy giggled and Jimmy grinned. Aunt Edie kept a straight face.

'Life an' soul of the party, you are, Jack Andrews,' she said.

CHAPTER THIRTEEN

Will Fletcher was up in his room, cleaning his boots for Monday morning, when ragged little Lulu put her head round his door.

'Hullo, fatty,' he said. It was a joke between them. Peaky Lulu was far from fat. 'What's up?'

'It's 'er,' said Lulu.

'Who's her?'

'The lady,' said Lulu.

'Not her, not that barmy one.'

'She wants yer,' said Lulu.

'Come to stick 'er finger in the eye of me conscience, 'as she, Lulu?'

'She said only if yer don't 'ave comp'ny.'

'Gawd save Ireland, and I tell yer, it needs savin',' said Will, smiling. It was a natural smile, it was a smile for Lulu, the youngest and most neglected child of Bert Rogers, the man whose wife had hopped it. 'Fine place I've got 'ere for entertainin' company, don't yer think, me little sweet'eart? All right for you an' me an' snakes an' ladders – well, you're me best company, ain't you? All right, I'll come down and face me conscience.'

'She's nice,' said Lulu, as he picked her up and carried her down the narrow stairs.

'Barmy, Lulu, that's what she is,' said Will Fletcher.

Outside, Mother Verity was waiting, Mother Ruth beside her.

'Good evening, Mr Fletcher,' said Mother Verity, noting his unbuttoned shirt, his strong throat and his old Army trousers.

'Evenin'. Is this another conversion job?'

'Conversion?' she said, and he wondered what it was about religion that could turn a woman good-looking and intelligent into a case for a loony bin.

'Have you come to have another go at savin' me soul?'

'I can only pray, Mr Fletcher,' said Mother Verity with a faint smile, while Mother Ruth quivered at all the hard, cutting edges to the man who held a thin-looking waif in his arms. 'No, I've come to ask for your help. You are the only one I really know around here. You see, we wish to—' Mother Verity faltered a little because of his very direct blue eyes and because she felt he was already thinking she was here to be graciously kind and holy. 'Mr Fletcher, boxes of food were brought a few days ago.'

'So I heard. And they pinched the lot. What else did you expect? They don't mind the Salvation Army, they do mind preachers, even preachers who bring food.'

'We don't wish to preach, Mr Fletcher, only to help. If we have the means to help, should we stand aside? I will admit that in bringing help, we also hope to bring recognition of a different kind of help, that which only the Lord can give.'

'You're an odd woman,' said Will Fletcher.

'So you've said. Mr Fletcher, we know these people are terribly in need of clothing. Will you tell us the best way of distributing garments without risking a riot? Of giving them out so that everyone has something? They are new clothes and durable. Overcoats, frocks, jerseys, blouses, boots. Can you tell me how we can be certain that the child in your arms will receive a frock and boots, Mr Fletcher?'

Will Fletcher stared at her. She met his eyes, she stood

up to his intimidating masculinity. His tight mouth broke apart. He smiled.

'You win, lady,' he said. 'Bring the stuff one evenin'. Knock me up. I'll see there's no shovin' and grabbin'.'

'Thank you, Mr Fletcher.'

'I'm licked,' he said, 'by charity.'

'You despise charity, Mr Fletcher?'

He laughed, but good-naturedly. 'Charity keeps some people alive round 'ere,' he said.

'But you despise those who bring it?'

'Give over, lady, am I sayin' that? I'm not. I'm sayin' I'm up to my ears with not likin' conditions that mean the people in these streets can't do without charity.'

Mother Verity hesitated before asking, 'Mr Fletcher, are you in need yourself?'

'I was,' he said bluntly, 'I'm not now. I've just landed a job, as a loader in a Spitalfields warehouse.'

'I'm glad for you, Mr Fletcher,' said Mother Verity.

'I'm licked again,' he said.

'What do you mean?'

'Go on, Lulu, tell the lady what we mean,' he said, smiling at the girl.

'Yer nice,' said Lulu, 'yer nice, missus.'

'That's it,' he said. He laughed, 'That's a real lickin', don't yer think, Lulu, findin' out that Sister Charity's nice?'

Mother Verity showed faint colour.

'It don't 'urt,' said Lulu.

'Well, we can take that kind of a lickin', can't we, me sweet'eart?' said Will Fletcher.

'We'll bring the clothes and boots one evening, then,' said Mother Verity.

'Right. But give me a knock first, before Henry Mullins sets 'is harpies on the goods. Durin' the day I'll be conspicuous by me absence, due to the job, d'y'see?'

221

'Yes, Mr Fletcher. Thank you for being so kind and helpful.'

'Barmy,' he said.

'Pardon?'

'Beats me,' said Will Fletcher.

'Good night, Mr Fletcher, good night, child,' said Mother Verity.

He and Lulu watched the two ladies go. 'Well, what d'yer think, Lulu,' he said, 'are we barmy too? Come on, come up and put some spit on me boots and we'll give 'em a real shine, eh?'

Aunt Edie was up very early on Monday morning, and when Dad came down he found there was a breakfast of fried bacon and egg ready for him.

'Edie—'

'Sit down and get on with it.'

'Well, I don't know when I last 'ad egg and bacon to start me arduous week,' said Dad. 'Where'd it come from?'

'Out of the frying pan.'

'I mean—'

'I like to contribute something while I'm 'ere,' said Aunt Edie, and poured him a cup of steaming tea.

'God bless yer, Edie.'

'Don't go mad,' said Aunt Edie, 'and don't you chase me again, Jack Andrews, in front of the kids an' the public like you did yesterday.'

'Didn't catch you, though,' said Dad, 'not like you caught me.'

'You asked for that. You and your 'idden talents.'

'Not mine, yours,' said Dad.

'I don't want any of that from you, you're a married man.'

'Can't 'elp that,' said Dad. 'Next time we play cricket, it's got to be fair do's, legs before wicket without skirts in the way.' He looked up as Aunt Edie rushed into the scullery. 'What's up, Edie?'

'Nothing.' Her voice was muffled. 'I'm startin' the kids' breakfast, that's all.'

She was having a terrible job holding back laughter.

Jimmy began a new week at Anerley. Mr Gibbs was back at his business, leaving the landscape gardeners' foreman in full charge of the men. The jungle was gradually thinning, the brush and undergrowth collapsing square yard by square yard, the sawn or axed saplings falling.

Mrs Gibbs saw to Jimmy and to paying him at the end of each day. She liked the boy and his attitude, he went willingly about his work. She made sure Ada took refreshments to him mid-morning and midday, and she had him come up to the terrace each afternoon to share a pot of tea with her. But she kept Sophy away from him as much as she could. She knew her precocious daughter and how forward she was. She was quite capable, even at thirteen, of enslaving Jimmy and then making a huge joke of his infatuation.

Restriction on her activities put Sophy in a fiendish mood, so that she played up on the few occasions when she was able to be with Jimmy.

'I'm goin' to have to wallop you,' he said one afternoon.

'Some hopes,' said Sophy, 'bet you couldn't even lick a stamp.'

'Well, let's find out,' said Jimmy. 'Bend over.'

'What for?'

'Don't know, do I? Not until I find something to wallop you with.'

Sophy shrieked with laughter.

Ada did not miss the fact that the young madam was prettying herself up every day. Little minx, thought Ada. At her age and all.

Jimmy was a welcome guest in the kitchen when he arrived each morning. There was always a cup of tea and a slice of toast for him. Mr Hodges always said good morning, my boy, Ivy always said he was lasting out something miraculous, Mrs Redfern always said he was a real young gent, and he and Ada always teased each other. It was a game they'd developed.

One morning a young man came in by way of the side door and the smaller kitchen. A black cap sat on his thatch of fair, curly hair, and he wore a blue striped white shirt, a black waistcoat with shining metal buttons and black trousers. It was a manservant's uniform. He had freckles, blue eyes and a happy grin.

'Watcher, sports,' he said, 'lordin' it, are yer, as usual? Takin' yer time over yer porridge? Dunno as that 'ud do in our place. My, yer on a cushy number 'ere, Mr 'Odges. 'Ullo, Ada me sweetie – 'ere, 'ullo again, who's this? Yer new bootboy?'

'This is Jimmy, he's helpin' the gardeners,' said cook.

'That is correct,' said Mr Hodges, 'and might I hask you, young Mr Hunter, to kindly hobserve your manners by knocking before you enter?'

'Righty-oh, Mr 'Odges, 'ow's this?' Percy Hunter, eighteen years old, knocked on the table with his knuckles. 'There y'ar, me manners is observed. 'Ere,' he said to Jimmy, 'what yer sittin' next to Ada for? That's my chair.'

Ada let a little annoyance show, and Jimmy said, 'Well, I suppose I'm just keepin' it warm for you. Could I 'ave the pleasure of knowin' who you are?'

''Ullo, 'ullo, we got a young lordship 'ere, 'ave we?' said Percy.

'That's Percy 'Unter, Jimmy, 'e's Ada's young man,' said Ivy.

'I 'ave that honour,' said Percy, 'and Ada 'as the pleasure.'

'Pleased to meet you,' said Jimmy.

'Yer still sittin' in me chair,' said Percy, grinning, and Ada wrinkled her nose. Suddenly, she didn't feel very keen about him. Suddenly, he seemed a bit loud and brash. He was in service with the Wheeler family on the other side of Anerley, and he hoped to save enough money to open a shop by the time he was thirty. He had lots of dash and go, and was always ready to treat her when they went out together on their Sundays off. When they visited her parents' home in Peckham, he'd take her mum a bunch of flowers and buy her a bunch too, and they'd have Sunday dinner and tea with her family. Mind, her dad had said she didn't have to be serious about a feller at her age. Ada thought now that perhaps her dad meant don't get serious about Percy, even if he did treat her and her mum to flowers. Ada found it uncomfortable to suddenly realize there was someone else she liked a lot better than Percy.

'Have you called special?' she asked him.

''Appening to be in this 'appy locality,' said Percy, 'I find I got time for one of yer refreshin' cups of tea.'

Mrs Redfern lifted the pot. 'Well, that's a shame,' she said, 'it's empty.'

'And I have to hinform everyone it's back to their duties,' said Mr Hodges.

'I been diddled,' said Percy, 'this 'ere young lordship's collared me custom'ry chair and 'e's 'ad me cup of tea.'

'Well, I'd better get on,' said Jimmy, 'thanks for me

extra breakfast, Mr Hodges, thanks, Mrs Redfern.' He got up. 'You can have your chair now,' he said to Percy.

'It ain't 'is chair, it's just where 'e puts 'is bottom when 'e pops in,' said Ivy. Jimmy gave her a wink, smiled at Ada and went out to his work.

The evening was heavy. An August thunderstorm seemed to be brewing. Unemployed men sat on their doorsteps watching the street kids. A horse-drawn van appeared. Mother Verity, in company with Mother Mary and Mother Ruth, was talking to Will Fletcher, a mellower man now that he had a job. He beckoned, and the van came on, Mother Joan pulling up alongside the group. Father Luke descended from the back of the van. Father Peter had put him in charge, for the minister was hearing confession this evening from Mother Magda. Father Luke thought she'd got the Lord in her soul all right, this was her third time of confessing.

Adults and kids began to gather. Will Fletcher put himself at the back of the van and told the adults to line up, then they'd get clothes and boots for their families. A woman said young Eddie Mullins had gone to fetch his dad. The urchin boy came out of the house, followed by the brawny figure of his father, Mr Henry Mullins, who came sauntering up to the van.

'Watcher, Will old cock, what they brought this time?' he said.

'Clothes and boots,' said Will.

''Ello, Porky,' said Henry Mullins to Father Luke, 'yer come with more offerings, 'ave yer? Well, I tell yer what, you buzz orf while yer still in one piece an' take yer funny old gels with yer, and I'll look after the offerings an' the 'orse an' cart as well. Looks like a nice bit of 'orsemeat, that nag does, once we get it to the knackers' yard.'

'Excuse me,' said Father Luke, 'but—'

''Oppit,' said Henry Mullins.

'It's not your evenin', Henry,' said Will Fletcher. 'I'm in charge this time.'

'Yer what?'

'Not your evenin', I said. Everyone's goin' to line up, and these ladies will hand out clobber for every fam'ly. No arguments, it'll only get untidy.'

'Oh, yer got a job, so yer chuckin' yer weight around, are yer?' said Henry Mullins. 'Well, I still ain't got no bleedin' job meself, so it's my weight that counts.'

There were men around the van now, as well as women and kids.

'Not this time, Henry,' said Will Fletcher, and Mother Verity, watching and listening, stiffened at the sudden tension. Henry Mullins was not a man to back off. His word was law in Christian Street.

'More over, Will,' he said, his fists bunching.

'Get in line, Henry, you or yer missus,' said Will.

Henry Mullins swung a fast fist. Will, knowing it was bound to come, blocked it with an upraised arm.

'The blighters,' said Mother Joan, 'there's going to be blood, by George.' Mother Joan was in fine fettle. The cheques hadn't bounced, they'd been debited to her husband's account and she had her ring back, much to the sorrow of Solly Rubenstein.

'Give over, Henry,' said Will. 'I told you, it's not your evenin'.'

The hard fist swung again. Will put up another block with his left arm and delivered a straight right. It put Henry Mullins on his back in the gutter. 'Oh, yer bleedin' dummy,' Henry roared, 'yer signed for yer own funeral!' Up he came, tearing in, and down he went again.

Will caught the eye of his barmy lady. There was a flush

on her face, even a little excitement in her expression. 'Oh, Mr Fletcher,' she breathed.

Henry Mullins staggered to his feet, drew several breaths, squared his shoulders, put up his fists and bored in. He had to. He was cock of the walk round here. He closed fast with the challenger, but parted from him even faster as Will delivered an uppercut. His head jerked up, his eyes rolled, and down he went for a third time. No-one interfered. No-one would.

'Jolly bruising,' said Mother Joan, who understood this man-to-man stuff.

''Ow disgustin',' said Mother Mary, who had a good mind to give both men a taste of her umbrella.

'How magnificent,' breathed Mother Verity, and Mother Ruth looked at her in astonishment. How flushed she was, how strangely excited she seemed. Oh, dear, whatever was happening?

Henry Mullins rolled over and stared dizzily at the gutter. 'Bleedin' done me,' he groaned.

''Ard luck, Henry,' said Will. 'Help 'im up, Sid, give 'im a hand to get home.'

And that was it. Will Fletcher took charge, making one person from each family line up, then watching while Father Luke and the ladies handed out clothes and foot-wear to these people and to other family representatives from adjoining streets. It took some time, but Will stayed to see that there was no trouble, little Lulu beside him. Once only, he said to the queueing people, 'Never mind it's not the Salvation Army, it's the right kind of charity.'

At the end, when the van had been emptied, Mother Joan strode briskly up to him and clapped him heartily on his shoulder. 'Good man, well done,' she said, 'the Lord bless you.'

'Praise 'Im,' said Mother Mary.

228

'Hear that, Lulu? It's praise the Lord,' said Will, hand on the child's thin shoulder.

'An' yer give Mister Mullins an 'eadache,' said Lulu proudly.

Mother Verity came up with a frock, socks, vests, coat and a small pair of boots. 'Mr Fletcher, I think these will all fit the girl,' she said.

'Special for Lulu, are they?'

'Her brothers and sisters all have something, but yes, perhaps there should be one special child, Mr Fletcher,' said Mother Verity, and handed the items to him. 'Oh, I took the liberty of telling my sisters in charity that you were to have nothing. No overcoat, I mean.'

'Kind of yer,' said Will drily.

'You are a man able to stand on your own feet, Mr Fletcher. I'm proud of you.'

'Knock it off, Sister Charity.'

'Also, you have a job. I'm so pleased. But I will see you again, I hope.'

'Now listen,' said Will, 'I'm not 'aving it, I'll look after me conscience, I don't want it comin' after me. You're a nice woman, and I ain't too pleased with meself for what I did, but—'

'You kissed 'er,' said Lulu, 'I saw yer, Uncle Will.'

'Well, so I did, sweet'eart, so I did, but sometimes a woman's there, and sometimes you've got to kiss 'er. It might not make much of a man of you, but some women rouse the old Adam in some of us. It didn't please Sister Charity too much, because she's a nice woman, but there it is, it was done and it can't be undone. Only we don't want 'er hauntin' me, do we, Lulu?'

'I'm not given to haunting people, Mr Fletcher,' said Mother Verity, 'but our work is here in the East End, so I'm sure we'll see each other again.'

'I'm movin',' said Will.

The air was heavier, the clouds dark and brooding.

'Oh,' said Mother Verity.

'Well, the job's come with a fair wage, and I don't aim to stay around 'ere much longer, not now I can afford some decent lodgings. One of the other loaders knows of some.'

'Where?' asked Mother Verity.

''E'll let me know. Bethnal Green, I think he said. I want a couple of rooms, I'm takin' Lulu with me. She's all I've got—'

'But she's not yours, Mr Fletcher.'

'She's me little mate, me little pal, and 'er dad couldn't care less about her. I've told him I'm takin' 'er. It'll cost yer half a crown, he said, and he's got it, and I've got Lulu.'

'Mr Fletcher, I thought you didn't believe in God.'

'Give over,' said Will.

'But God has touched you.'

'Is that a fact?' Will laughed. 'He'll come to tea with me and Lulu next?'

'If you take the child into your care, Mr Fletcher, the Lord will always be present.'

'I can't make you out,' said Will. 'I thought you were barmy, then I thought you weren't, now I don't know what to think.'

'We're ready for the off, sister,' sang out Mother Joan.

'Yes, come on,' called Mother Mary, 'we're all goin' back in the van.'

'Good night, Mr Fletcher, thank you for all your help,' said Mother Verity, 'you were magnificent.'

'Would yer mind leavin' off, Sister Charity?' said Will.

'You're a man, Mr Fletcher. Good night.'

Will, holding Lulu's new clothes and boots, watched

the van move off, Lulu still beside him. 'Well, she's a funny one, Lulu, and no error, eh?'

'Is she a lady?' asked Lulu.

'A lady? Yes, I reckon she is, sweet'eart. A lady. Come on, let's see what you look like in yer new togs.'

In the pocket of the little winter coat they found a shining new florin.

The thunderstorm broke. The sky roared and bellowed, the lightning flashed, and the rain sheeted down to swamp the streets and to pierce the waters of the Thames like glittering stair rods.

CHAPTER FOURTEEN

On Friday evening, Lily Shaw's mother just happened to accidentally come out through her open front door and bump into Dad on his way home from work.

'Oh, 'ullo, Jack,' she said, 'fancy it bein' you.'

'Yes, what a coincidence, Ivy,' said Dad, 'seein' it's you.'

'Yes, I just come out. I must say yer lookin' real fit an' manly, considerin' all them years of yourn away at the war. Yer a credit to yer fam'ly – oh, we 'eard Maud's cousin Edie's come for the weekend again. My, ain't she a kind, obligin' woman with Maud bein' away? I can't say 'ow sorry I am about Maud 'aving to go away, it must be something really chronic, is it?'

'Fairly chronic,' said Dad.

'She's gorn to a home for the chronic, I suppose?'

'I suppose you could say so,' said Dad, cheerfulness covering up his reticence.

'Don't that seem 'ard luck when she's been such a good religious woman all these years?' said Mrs Shaw. 'Makes yer think, don't it? Mrs Johnson said she 'opes it wasn't religion that took Maud orf.' She paused, waiting for a response, but Dad just smiled. 'It must be 'ard on you an' yer fam'ly, Jack. Still, with Maud's cousin Edie comin' reg'lar to look after yer, what a blessin'. Ain't she an 'andsome woman, an' still single too. I said to me old man, I said what a blessin' Jack's got cousin Edie with 'im at

232

weekends, a kind woman like that. It makes up for Maud 'aving to be away, I said. And Mrs Johnson was sayin' just the same thing to me only yesterday.'

'Well, I'll let you all know if there's any other news,' said Dad.

'What other news?' asked Mrs Shaw with interest.

'No idea,' said Dad, 'not till it 'appens, Ivy. So long.'

Aunt Edie had arrived. She was with Betsy and Patsy, and they were all chattering. Dad said nothing about Mrs Shaw and the gossip. If things got troublesome, however, he'd have to do something. As it was, Aunt Edie seemed so determined that Betsy and Patsy shouldn't miss their mother at the weekends, that at the moment it was their feelings that counted far more than gossip. His conscience was clear. So was Aunt Edie's.

And when Jimmy arrived home from Anerley, his pleasure at seeing Aunt Edie again was so obvious that there was no question of disturbing the present order of things.

On Saturday, Mr Gibbs left his business at twelve-thirty to get home in time for lunch. His wife was her usual pleasant self. His daughter, however, was mutinously inclined.

'Sophy's going to leave home,' said Mrs Gibbs.

'Are you, monkey?' asked Mr Gibbs. 'Where you off to?'

'Beachy Head,' said Sophy.

'Well, take care. Beachy Head's dangerous. You can fall off it.'

'Fall off? I'm going to jump off,' said Sophy. 'Daddy, it's Saturday, but all I've been allowed to do is help Jimmy for just a measly half-hour and take him some sandwiches for his lunch. All that work he's got to do, there's tons of it, and I said to Mummy supposing he breaks his back?

233

You won't like it, because you'll be the one to have to tell his parents. And d'you know what Mummy's done? She's invited some girls over for this afternoon and I've got to entertain them. Girls, would you believe, they'll just talk about boys and frocks.'

'Frocks for boys?' said Mr Gibbs, admiring the oak panelling of the handsome dining room.

'No, you silly, just frocks. And boys. I don't know why I've got to spend a Saturday afternoon in agony.'

'It's to help you to become a little more ladylike than you are,' said Mrs Gibbs.

'Ugh,' said Sophy.

'They're all nice girls,' said her mother.

'I hate girls. Except me. I like me.'

'Yes, I like you too, darling,' said Mrs Gibbs, 'and so does Daddy.'

'Oh, jolly good,' said Sophy, 'can Jimmy come to Devon with us?' She and her parents were due to go to a rented cottage in Devon for ten days, commencing the last week in August.

'Pardon?' said Mrs Gibbs.

'I'll ask him after lunch, shall I, Mummy?' said Sophy. 'He ought to have a holiday before he dies doing all that horrific work for Daddy.'

'I don't think that's a good idea, pet,' said Mr Gibbs.

Mr Hodges looked in. 'Everything to your satisfaction, sir?' he enquired.

'Fine,' said Mr Gibbs.

'Then staff will proceed with their own lunch, and by your leave, madam.'

'Of course, Mr Hodges,' said Mrs Gibbs, who had a polite and friendly relationship with the servants.

Mr Hodges retired. Sophy said, 'What's wrong with us asking Jimmy to Devon?'

'Because there'll still be work for him to do here,' said Mr Gibbs.

'Oh, you're mean, Daddy. If those agonizing girls ask me this afternoon about you, I don't know how I'm going to face up to having to tell them you're mean.'

'Well, tell 'em I'm perfect.'

'They won't believe me,' said Sophy, 'they'll see the twisted look on my face.'

'I'd like to see that myself,' said Mrs Gibbs.

Sophy did her best.

'I like it,' said Mr Gibbs. 'D'you like it, Elizabeth?'

'Sweet,' said Mrs Gibbs.

'What a life,' said Sophy the Dreadful.

The concert at St Mark's Hall in Camberwell that evening went with a swing before an audience of parents and their children. It started at six-thirty and finished at eight-thirty. The pearlies were in their element with their turns. The audience rocked and little girls giggled themselves into fits.

Aunt Edie appeared in a white pearly queen dress and hat, and she sparkled from head to foot. Dad thought her a figure of animated colour, with a smile as brilliant as a shining star on her face as she addressed the audience.

'Who's afraid of the big bad wolf, kiddies?'

'I am!'

'I ain't!'

'I am!'

'Well, not to worry, my little loves, because the big bad wolf won't be appearin' this evenin', he had a crocodile for 'is dinner and don't feel very well.'

Shrieks.

'Crumbs, our Aunt Edie,' whispered Betsy proudly.

'Don't she look a real pearly queen, Dad?' said Patsy.

When the laughter had died down, Aunt Edie said from the stage, 'As the big bad wolf can't come, I'm here instead, I'm Red Ridin' Hood's big sister.'

'Oh, d'yer get ate up sometimes?' called a boy.

'Not often,' said Aunt Edie, giving her pearly dress a saucy little twirl. 'I've got me own ways of dealin' with big bad wolves. I caught one in the thunderstorm the other night, and 'e's still out in me back yard, hanging up to dry. Who's that laughin'?'

'We all are, missus!'

'That's enough of that, we don't want all that laughin', you'll all choke on yer acid drops.'

Patsy was near to hysterics. Dad was wondering why Maud's cousin hadn't ever taken up with a decent bloke and got herself married. Losing her fiancé years ago had been tragic, but she'd got over it, she'd come up smiling. Why wasn't she married, a lovely-looking woman like her?

'Oh, Dad, ain't she funny?' gasped Patsy.

'Now how about what I'm here for,' called Aunt Edie, a glittering pearly flamboyance, 'how about a song? What would you like as a start?'

'"Pack up yer troubles!"' The request was from a man.

Standing in the wings, Jimmy thought his aunt hesitated for a moment, as if she didn't want to be reminded of the war, and a little picture flashed into his mind of her walking in a stiff and vexed way from the hospital in which his dad had been recuperating from a serious wound. She hadn't liked what the war was doing to soldiers.

'All right, old soldier,' she called in response to the request, and sat down at the piano. 'I'll sing it first, then all join in, an' that includes the lady with toffee-apples in her hat. Here we go, then.'

And she played and sang 'Pack Up Your Troubles In Your Old Kitbag'. And then the audience joined in. Except Dad. Dad was thinking of Johnny Turk, and the flies and the heat, and of blood that turned black inside a minute. The audience was carried along by Aunt Edie's infectious performance especially when, after two more numbers, she played and sang 'I've Got A Lovely Bunch Of Coconuts'.

Then she introduced Jimmy. 'Mums, dads and kids,' she said, 'it's me great honour an' privilege to present me young man to you, name of Jimmy Andrews, who comes from down the road in Walworth, where the gels follow him about – only I saw 'im first. Come on, Jimmy.'

Jimmy showed himself. The audience clapped and the kids cheered.

'Cor, aincher luvverly!' called a girl.

'Not all the time,' said Jimmy, 'sometimes I'm just ordinary. But not often.'

Patsy curled herself up into a shrieking ball.

'Crikey, our Jimmy,' said Betsy.

Dad was grinning.

'Jimmy and me's got a romance goin',' called Aunt Edie from the piano, 'so we're going to sing romantic together. Off we go, Jimmy love.'

They sang the duet, 'If You Were The Only Girl In The World'. Jimmy had no stage fright, he took it all in his stride and he had a very pleasant voice. In any case, Aunt Edie took him along in the song in a way to ensure he didn't fail her. They followed with 'Let's All Sing Like The Birdies Sing', and Jimmy's tweet-tweets brought the house down.

Aunt Edie finished her turn with a request from the audience, 'Any Old Iron'. The audience joined in and stamped their feet as well, and Aunt Edie departed from the stage, arm in arm with Jimmy, to a standing ovation.

Waiting for her off-stage was Joe Gosling, a resplendent pearly king.

'Told yer, Edie, told yer,' he said with a broad grin of delight. 'Yer a born natural. Ain't she that, Jimmy, a born natural?'

'Yes, and she's good too,' said Jimmy.

'Well, I said that, didn't I? A born natural, I said.'

'Yes, and she can sing as well,' said Jimmy.

'Eh?' said Joe. 'Course she can sing as well, I wasn't excludin' nothing. Yer Aunt Edie's good all over.'

'Keeps you guessin', though, when she's leg before wicket at cricket,' said Jimmy.

Aunt Edie burst into laughter. 'I'll give you leg before wicket,' she said.

'You're the best, Aunt Edie, you are,' said Jimmy, 'and that's a fact.' And he gave her a kiss and a cuddle. Aunt Edie's eyes suddenly went moist.

'Take yer to the pub soon as the show's finished, Edie me darling,' said Joe.

'Kind of yer, Joe, but no thanks.'

'Yes, sorry, Mr Gosling,' said Jimmy, 'but she's with me.'

'Strike a light,' said Joe, 'done in me eye by a young cockalorum.'

'I'll go and get changed,' said Aunt Edie.

She went back to Walworth with the family. When they got off the tram at Manor Place, Jimmy said as he was flush from working for Mr Gibbs, he'd treat everyone to fish and chips. The shop was only a few yards away and was exuding an irresistible aroma. Aunt Edie walked on with the others while Jimmy went to the shop.

'That boy,' she said.

'Our Jimmy?' said Patsy.

'I don't know who's goin' to be able to say no to 'im when he's older,' said Aunt Edie.

'Well, after that concert,' said Dad, 'I don't know meself who can say no to you. Mind, it depends on what you ask for. What d'yer think, Betsy me pickle, an' Patsy me love, now that you've seen your Aunt Edie bring the 'ouse down?'

'Oh, she was so good, Dad, that I don't know what to think,' said Patsy. 'Couldn't you ask your old sergeant-major?'

'Not a bad idea, that, Patsy,' said Dad.

'Don't mind me,' said Aunt Edie, who still seemed to have a glow about her. 'I'm only someone walkin' with you.'

'You're our star turn, proud to 'ave you walkin' with us,' said Dad, 'only Patsy reminded me of the time me old battalion reached Damascus an' Johnny Turk was chuckin' down his arms. The sergeant-major celebrated by showin' he knew a bit about 'ow to treat a star turn. He got off with a female Syrian tummy wobbler—'

'What's one of them, Dad?' asked Betsy.

'They're dancers,' said Dad, 'an' when they're dancin' they wobble their tummies, they're all star turns. Well, me old sergeant-major spoke this one some choice words that were 'ighly complimentary, and you know what she did? Filled his face full of Turkish Delight. Ruddy whole boxful landed in his cakehole.'

They turned in at the house, with Betsy giggling. 'Any more of that sergeant-major stuff,' said Aunt Edie, 'and a whole 'elping of fried cod and chips is goin' to land on your head, Jack Andrews.'

That brought the house down again.

Father Peter was most impressed by the successful

distribution of clothes and footwear, and of its mellowing effect on the people of Whitechapel. He expressed his admiration of the way it had been done. He and Father Luke were at dinner with the resident lady Repenters.

'Softening 'em up, Father,' said Mother Joan. 'Best way, you know. They're heathens, of course, but you can't drill Christian ways into 'em until they're receptive. But we can't fit all the East End out with new clothes, the money wouldn't run to it, not by a long chalk. Ye gods, those poor little devils running about in their bare feet. Now my idea is that we go collecting clothes and footwear, from districts more affluent than the East End. There's a year's work in that, the Lord's practical work.'

'Praise Him,' said the Repenters.

'That's the stuff,' said Mother Joan.

'Your suggestion does you credit, sister,' said Father Peter.

'Very sound, Father, very sound,' said Father Luke. 'Mind you, there's still 'ardly any salt in the potatoes. 'As anyone noticed Mrs Murphy still don't seem to be bothering?'

'A small thing, Father Luke,' said Mother Ruth, an uncomplaining woman.

'We shall concentrate on clothes collections,' said Father Peter.

'I was prayin' last night,' said Mother Mary, 'and I think the Lord said something to me about it wasn't right for the poor to wear only sackcloth.'

'His word is our command,' said Father Peter, 'and I concur with Mother Joan in that to supply the poor with necessities is to begin the process of making them receptive to the ways of Christianity. While their state is wholly parlous, they will remain heathens. Their hardened souls must be softened. I fear that in going among them

240

with anger I have lacked understanding, but with the Lord's help I shall redeem myself.'

'Amen,' said the Repenters.

'It was Mother Verity, I believe, who softened the soul of the man who outraged her in the beginning and whom we all thought past redemption,' said Father Peter, gaunt face benign of expression.

'Even in the beginning, Father, I did not think him quite past redemption,' said Mother Verity.

'Praise 'er faith,' said Father Luke.

'And her forgivingness,' said Mother Mary. 'I don't know I could ever 'ave forgive 'im myself.'

'Her lips,' said Father Peter, shaking a sad head, 'to take her lips so brutally.'

Colour touched Mother Verity's cheeks.

''Orrible,' said Mother Mary.

'We must all be forgiving, sister,' said Mother Ruth.

'Still, the Lord's fire an' brimstone can't be for nothing,' said Mother Mary.

'True, my child,' said Father Peter, 'that is for those who have sold their souls to Satan. For them the Lord has neither forgiveness nor mercy. For others, for people who have misguidedly sinned, there is always forgiveness.'

'Well spoken, Father,' said Mother Joan.

'I have seen the light,' said Father Peter.

'So have I, by George,' said Mother Joan, 'damn nearly blinded me.'

'Jimmy . . . lunch . . . slice of veal and ham pie, oh—' Ada blinked. There was Jimmy in the sunshine, sawing up a large branch, clearing it of smaller branches. He was wearing just shoes and an old pair of Scout shorts. His chest was bare and browning. Perspiration bedewed his forehead and glistened in his hair. Ada blinked again.

After all, a girl didn't often see a boy half undressed, specially a boy with such a firm body. 'Oh,' she said again.

'What's all this ohing?' asked Jimmy.

'Hoeing?'

'No, ohing.'

'Where's your shirt and apron?' asked Ada.

'Don't need 'em for this work,' said Jimmy. 'Crikey, is all that for me, Ada?' It was a large slice of pie, and there were slices of tomato and some lettuce with it. And a pint mug of lemonade, home-made by Mrs Redfern. A whole pint. 'Ada, you're all doin' me proud, I don't know I've met kinder people, nor a nicer girl.' He put the saw down, came up to her and took the tray from her. Ada gulped a little. 'It's all right, is it, me not havin' me shirt on?'

'Yes . . . no . . . I don't know, I suppose so,' said Ada. It was all right, of course it was. The landscape gardeners were working in their vests. It was just that she felt startled, and a little bit funny. 'There's a pickled onion hidin' under the lettuce, if you like pickled onions,' she said, by way of returning to normal.

'What a treat,' said Jimmy, 'it'll help me to keep cheerful. Me broken heart needs a pickled onion or two and some veal and ham pie. I was pleased to meet Percy the other mornin' – well, perhaps not pleased, seein' what a lucky bloke he is, but I was interested, of course.'

'You're goin' dotty,' said Ada, 'you're havin' me on, I know you, Jimmy Andrews. And look, I'm not engaged or anything, my dad wouldn't let me get engaged to anyone when I'm only just sixteen.'

'No, you'll 'ave to wait a bit,' said Jimmy, seating himself on a log and placing the tray on his knees. 'Percy's a handsome feller, I noticed.'

'Handsome?' said Ada, who had begun to feel Percy

242

was a bit ordinary except for his non-stop tongue.

'I'm hopin' to be handsome meself when I'm older,' said Jimmy. 'I've heard it's better than lookin' like the back end of a horse and cart.'

'Yes, keep tryin',' said Ada, 'you don't want to look like that all your life. Oh, I've got to go or Mr 'Odges will be after me.'

'What, at his age?' said Jimmy. 'Saucy old devil. Still, can't blame him, I suppose.'

'Oh, 'elp, you'll be me death, you will, Jimmy,' said Ada, and rushed off. She had laughing hysterics on the way.

Sophy appeared at two o'clock, a summery enchantment in a frock of azure blue. 'Gosh, look at you,' she said, 'you're hardly dressed.'

'Hullo, Mr Thorpe,' said Jimmy. Mr George Thorpe was the landscape gardeners' foreman who'd talked to him about how to tame and shape nature's tendency to run wild.

'How can anyone be soppy enough to think I'm Mr Thorpe?' said Sophy in disgust.

'Me, I suppose,' said Jimmy, 'when the sun's in my eyes. Oh, it's you, Sophy.'

'Yes, and I can't stay and help you,' she said.

'That's good,' said Jimmy.

'But I can stay long enough to kick you.'

'Long enough to fall over, you mean, like you did before. That won't do your frock any good, there's some thorny bits and pieces lyin' about round here.'

'Yes, that's why I can't stay and help you,' said Sophy, 'it's a new frock and Mummy says she'll pack me off to a boarding school if I ruin it. D'you like it?'

'Looks nice,' said Jimmy guardedly. The girl herself looked corking.

'Would you like to come to tea on Sunday?' asked Sophy.

'Pardon?' said Jimmy, picking up the saw.

'I'll tell Mummy you're coming,' said Sophy, 'then she won't be able to say no.'

'You can't invite me to tea without askin' your mum first,' said Jimmy. Commonsense surfacing, he added, 'And I can't come, anyway.'

'Why can't you?'

'Because your mum 'asn't asked me, that's why, and because you're posh and rich as well, and I'm not.'

'Oh, don't be soppy,' said Sophy. 'I'm not rich, I only get a few shillings pocket money a week from Daddy.'

'I mean your fam'ly's rich,' said Jimmy, going to work with the saw.

'Oh, you rotter,' said Sophy. 'Daddy was born poor, I'll have you know.'

'But he's not poor now, he's got all this and servants. Besides, my Aunt Edie will be with us.'

'Well, the Sunday after, then,' said Sophy.

'No, my Aunt Edie's comin' for the weekend as well, and the next.'

'Well, I don't think much of any aunt who's as inconvenient as that,' said Sophy. 'Jimmy, stop sawing. You can kiss me, if you like.'

'Don't be daft,' said Jimmy.

'I don't let every boy kiss me, I—' Sophy stopped. Her mother was calling her, and from not far away. 'Coming, Mummy.' She went off at a hasty run. Jimmy grinned. Saved by the gong, he thought.

That day, Patsy and Betsy were in Ruskin Park with two street friends, having enjoyed a little picnic of bread and marge, bits of cheese and a juicy red tomato each. Then they had afters of roast peanuts. Along came a park-keeper to cast his eyes over the four girls seated on a bench.

''Ullo, 'ullo, what've we got 'ere, then?' he asked.

'We ain't got nothing, mister,' said Lucy Lee, Patsy's friend, 'we've ate it all.'

'Except we got two monkey nuts left,' said Betsy.

'D'yer want one, mister?' asked Harriet Jones, Betsy's friend.

'I'm not desperate,' said the park-keeper, looking very official in his brown uniform, 'and you sure that's all you got left? What's that on me clean floor, might I ask?'

'Oh, they're just the shells,' said Patsy.

'What, on me clean floor?'

'Oh, crumbs,' said Harriet.

'You're right, crumbs as well, I see,' said the park-keeper. 'Crumbs an' peanut shells on me clean floor is against the law.'

'Oh, 'elp,' said Lucy.

'Now who's going to clear 'em up before I fall down in a faint, eh, me young girlies?'

'We all will,' said Patsy.

'Will yer now?'

'Honest,' said Patsy, and the park-keeper smiled. Who wouldn't when eye to eye with a girl whose hair was the colour of August gold and whose face looked as clean as a primrose washed by April showers?

'On yer school holidays, are yer?'

'Yes, mister,' said Betsy.

'All right, don't you worry,' said the park-keeper. 'I'll get me brush an' pan an' clear up when you've all kindly vacated the bench.'

'We don't mind doin' it,' said Patsy.

'Don't you worry, only watch me clean floor next time, eh?'

'Yes, mister,' said Lucy, and the park-keeper strolled away smiling. After all the years of horrible war, four girls happily eating roast monkey nuts on a park bench were worth a smile or two.

A horse-drawn van turned into the Walworth Road from Manor Place, Father Luke at the reins, Mother Mary and Mother Magda sitting in the back. As it entered the traffic, four girls turned into Manor Place from the opposite corner, having just got off a tram. They walked home, Lucy and Harriet separating from Patsy and Betsy.

When they were indoors, Patsy said, 'Shall we 'ave a cup of tea, Betsy?'

'I'm faintin' wiv thirst,' said Betsy, and went upstairs while Patsy filled the kettle. When Betsy came down she was a dumbfounded little girl.

'Patsy, Patsy, we ain't got no clothes left, they're all gorn.'

'Oh, you daft ha'porth,' said Patsy.

'Patsy, we ain't, I been in your room as well. They're all gorn. I fink we been burgled.'

Patsy rushed upstairs. Her chest of drawers was empty of clothes and underwear, and her little wardrobe was as empty as Mother Hubbard's cupboard. It was the same in Betsy's bedroom, and Jimmy's. Footwear as well had gone. She came pell-mell down the stairs and ran into her parents' bedroom. All her dad's clothes were missing, although there were a few things of her mother's still around.

Aghast, Patsy said, 'Someone's pinched everything, Betsy, everything.'

'Yes, I fink burglars 'ave been in,' said Betsy. Tears began to spill from her eyes.

'Don't cry, Betsy, we don't 'ave burglars round here, it's someone else,' said Patsy.

They found the answer in the form of a note on the kitchen mantelshelf. It was from Mother.

I've taken everyone's things to give to the poor, don't forget that from them that hath shall be taken all of it. I hope you're all going to church and that your Aunt Edie is doing her duty and looking after you.

Mother

'Told you it was mortal,' said Dad, home from his work and looking into Betsy's woebegone face and Patsy's angry eyes. 'Your mum could be the death of me, but I'm strictly against that. And I'm even more strictly against 'er upsettin' you two. You're me own angels. I'm goin' after her, I know where that place in Bloomsbury is. 'Ullo, that's Jimmy comin' in. I'll take 'im with me. Can you manage to get a bit of supper goin' while we're gone, Patsy?'

'Yes, course I can, Dad. You'll get our things back, won't you?'

'If I couldn't, I wouldn't be able to look me old sergeant-major in the eye, would I?'

It didn't take Dad and Jimmy long to get to Bloomsbury. They rode on an open bus operated by the London General Omnibus Company. It took them over Waterloo Bridge and up through Kingsway and Southampton Row to land them in the heart of Bloomsbury. Dad was silent as he walked fast to Bedford Way, and Jimmy knew that for once he was ready to lose his temper. Arriving at the large house now named the Temple of Endeavour, Dad thundered on the huge iron knocker. Half a minute elapsed before someone opened it. It was Mother Ruth, the gentle and uncomplaining Repenter.

'May I help you?' she asked.

'I'm Jack Andrews,' said Dad. 'Where's my wife?'

'Sir?'

'My wife, Maud Andrews, where is she?'

'Oh, yes, Mother Mary. I'm so sorry, but she's out at the moment. She's been out all day, collecting clothes for the poor.'

'That's a fact, is it?' said Dad. 'Well, when will she be back?'

'We're expecting her and Father Luke and Mother Magda any moment – oh, I think this may be them.'

The horse-drawn van, ambling down the street, pulled up. Father Luke descended, put a nosebag on the horse, then went round to the back of the van to help Mother Mary and Mother Magda alight.

Dad and Jimmy were there in a flash.

'You silly woman,' said Dad.

Mother stared at him. 'What're you doin' here?' she asked. 'And who's that boy with you? Don't I know him?'

'I'm not 'ere to answer daft questions,' said Dad. 'Who are you?' he asked Father Luke.

''Umbly, sir, I announce myself as Father Luke of—'

'Hoppit,' said Dad.

''Ere, I say—'

'Push off,' said Dad, and Father Luke took a look into glinting grey eyes and retired into the Temple with a portly dignity and an air of injury. 'And who are you?' asked Dad of Mother Magda.

''Ere, I don't like the sound of you,' said Mother Magda, 'you ain't a nice gentleman.'

'Right first time,' said Dad. 'Hoppit.'

'It's me bounden duty to talk to Father Peter about you,' said Mother Magda.

'Don't bring 'im out here,' said Dad, 'or I'll stuff 'im down a manhole.'

'Well, I don't know, what a coarse brute,' said Mother Magda, and hurried away to search for Father Peter.

Dad looked Mother in the eye. 'You came 'ome and pinched all our clothes,' he said.

'I'll give you something you talk to me Christian friends like that,' said Mother, and shook her umbrella in his face.

Dad pushed it aside. 'It's all in the van, is it?' he said. 'Right, tailboard down, Jimmy, and up you get.'

Jimmy let the tailboard down and swung himself into the van. There were a dozen large tea chests, all full of clothes or footwear.

'Clothes for the five thousand here, Dad,' he said.

'Which is the one our stuff's in?' asked Dad of Mother.

'Don't you come it with me,' said Mother, and set about him with her umbrella, much to the open-mouthed astonishment of passers-by. Dad did lose his temper then. He took the umbrella from her, smashed it over his knee, flung it into the gutter, picked her up and carried her into the hall of the Temple, Mother Ruth looking on in faint shock. Dad dumped Mother into a chair.

'Oh, you sinful 'eathen,' she gasped.

'Stay there,' said Dad, 'I'll be back in a few minutes to tie you up and carry you 'ome.' He returned to the van. He climbed up and joined Jimmy. Jimmy had upended two chests, and there was a heap of spilled clothes. 'That's the ticket, Jimmy.'

Together they upended another. And another. And a fifth. Out spilled an overcoat and a jacket, and then the family's clothes and footwear, a great mound of items.

'Poor old Mum,' said Jimmy.

'Gone potty, Jimmy, poor old gel,' said Dad. 'Right, put all our stuff back in that chest. I'll go an' get her.'

'You bringing her home, Dad?' asked Jimmy.

'Thing is, will she act up?'

'Bound to, if she can do a thing like this,' said Jimmy. 'Like makin' off with everything except what we're standing up in, an' that includes what Betsy and Patsy are standing up in as well. Betsy's upset, and Patsy's spittin'.'

A shadow fell across them. The tall, gaunt and wide-shouldered minister of the League of Repenters loomed at the open back of the van. 'Vandals!' he boomed.

'Who are you?' asked Dad.

'The minister of the League of Repenters.'

'Oh, you're bloke in charge of the loony bin, are yer?' said Dad. 'Well, back off a bit, because I'm comin' down to knock your bleedin' 'ead off.'

'Heathen!' boomed Father Peter, and the thunder rumbled in his chest.

'Watch out, mister,' said Jimmy, 'Dad's had more boxin' belts than hot dinners.'

'Miserable young man, know ye not that enemies of the Lord shall fall like corn before His reapers?'

'I fancy doin' a bit of reapin',' said Dad, and jumped down. Father Peter at his height and in his rumbling thunder may have been awesome, but Dad shoved him aside and strode back into the Temple. The hall showed a group of women, all in prayer for his soul, but Mother wasn't among them.

'Where's my wife?' he asked.

'She has gone, sir,' said Mother Ruth.

'Gone upstairs, you mean?'

'She has gone from our Temple, sir, to pray elsewhere for you.'

'Holy ruddy mackerel,' said Dad, 'tell 'er to do some praying for herself, and tell 'er the Lord's waitin' for her at 'ome, with an umbrella twice as big as her own.'

'Repent, yer brute, repent,' said Mother Magda.

Father Peter appeared, his hands crossed over his chest, his gait slow and reverent. Silently he entered the Chapel of Penitence.

'Barmy,' said Dad, 'and if I don't get out of 'ere quick, I'll be off me ruddy chump meself.' He went back to the van. Jimmy was out of it, guarding the tea chest and its contents. He looked at his son. Jimmy grinned. Dad grinned. 'Jimmy lad,' he said, 'when you next go to church give thanks that you, Patsy, Betsy and me are all granted the privilege of bein' sane. Up with that chest.' They took hold of it together and walked away, carrying it between them. 'It's a funny thing, yer know, son, but we don't realize how well off we are for bein' sane till we bump into people all as barmy as one-eyed parrots with a twitch.'

'And what about Mum?' asked Jimmy.

'Scarpered.'

'Dodged you, did she, Dad? Didn't want to come home?'

'Didn't seem like it, Jimmy.'

'Best thing, really,' said Jimmy. 'I don't think she's ready to come back yet. And besides—'

'Besides what?' asked Dad.

'She wasn't dressed for it, you ruined 'er umbrella.'

Dad laughed.

They took the tea chest on to a bus, and the bus carried them home.

''Oo wants to know?' asked Bert Rogers, chin unshaven, braces dangling, a bottle of beer in his hand, and addiction to drink making a bleary man of him.

'A friend,' said Mother Verity. She was by herself, the evening was cloudy, the street dull and dingy, urchins roaming the gutters. The basic picture never altered. Even

251

when the sun shone, its light only accentuated the dinginess, and the raggedness of the urchins.

'A friend?' Bert Rogers looked her over. 'That's you, is it, missus? Comin' up in the world, is 'e?' Two men passed by, glanced at her handbag and then at him. A sly bleary grin distorted his red face for a fleeting second. 'Posh, are yer, lady?' The men went on, turning into Ellen Street.

'Has Mr Fletcher moved or not?' asked Mother Verity. 'If so, could you give me his new address?'

''E's down there.' Bert Rogers jerked a thumb. 'Ellen Street. Talkin' to 'is mates.'

'Thank you,' said Mother Verity, although that was not what she wanted. What she wanted was to know Will Fletcher's new address without having to ask him herself. Nevertheless, she walked down to Ellen Street. Turning into it, she was at once confronted by the two men, their caps now pulled low down over their foreheads. Women at open doors turned their backs immediately.

Will Fletcher, striding up Christian Street from Commercial Road, saw a woman emerge in haste from Ellen Street, only to be pulled back by long arms. He had sight of her only for a second, but he recognized her. He heard a cry that was instantly shut off.

'Christ,' he breathed, 'is she as daft as that?' He ran. Turning into Ellen Street, he pulled up, for there she was, one man behind her, left arm around her waist, one hand clapped over her mouth. No-one was looking, every back was turned. Even the kids showed their backs. That was the way of it in this area. No-one bore witness. A second man was trying to prise her handbag from her. Will reached and spun him aside.

'What the bleedin' 'ell—'

'Give over, yer silly buggers,' said Will, 'that's a sister of charity you're manhandling, not a condescendin' female

252

with 'er nose in the air. Let go of her, Lenny. If you've not recognized 'er, then shift the mud out of yer mince pies.'

The man, Lenny, released her. Quite calmly, Mother Verity straightened the jacket of her grey costume and righted her partly dislodged hat.

'Is it our fault she come lookin' like a bleedin' duchess?' said Lenny, growling the question.

'Don't get me riled,' said Will, 'just shove off.'

'I got an appointment, anyways,' said the other man, and the two of them left.

Will regarded Mother Verity sternly. 'You're hauntin' me,' he said.

'Thank you for your kind help, Mr Fletcher.'

'That's no answer.'

'Did you ask a question, then? I didn't think so. You made a comment, I thought.'

'Now listen,' said Will, 'I'm not takin' another lickin' from that tongue of yours. If you want a question, I'll ask one. What d'you mean by bein' daft enough to come round 'ere all by yourself? And what d'you mean by bringing your 'andbag with you?'

'That's two questions,' said Mother Verity with a gentle smile.

'Gawd give me strength,' said Will. Everyone was looking now, of course. 'Can't I get it into that crazy 'ead of yours that you're a sittin' duck in these streets?'

'I thought the people in this place had begun to recognize me as a friend, Mr Fletcher.'

'That's goin' to take a lot longer than a few weeks, Sister Charity.'

'That's your name for me?' she asked.

'Am I talkin' to meself?' said Will. 'Are you listenin' or not?'

'Yes, of course.'

'Then next time you come, bring a copper with you, not your 'andbag.'

'There's very little in my handbag, Mr Fletcher.'

Will took his cap off and ran an exasperated hand over his thick, wiry hair. 'It makes no difference if you're only carryin' a few bob. A few bob is enough. An' don't ever come by yourself again, not for any ruddy reason. What made you come this evenin', anyway?'

'I was passing and thought it only polite to come and say hullo.'

'Oh, you thought I'd be sittin' in Bert Rogers's drawin'-room with me velvet smokin' jacket on and admirin' 'is silver candlesticks, did yer? And all ready to make you a polite pot of tea, I suppose?'

Mother Verity, losing none of her ladylike calmness, said, 'I simply thought you might consider it unfriendly of me not to have stopped to ask how you were, or to find out if you had moved and taken that little girl with you.'

'I'll start swearin' in a minute,' said Will, relieved that at least the people in the street were keeping themselves at a respectful distance. 'I'll go off bang and swear me 'ead off. All right, yes, I've made me move to new lodgings, I made it when I got back from me job early this evenin'. I'm 'ere now because I came back to get something Lulu forgot. She was a bit excited an' forgot 'er rag doll, which she always takes to bed with 'er. Me new landlady's lookin' after her at the moment.'

'So she is with you, Mr Fletcher, you're going to take care of her?'

'Lulu's goin' to be me life's work, Sister Charity.'

'Would you like me to—'

'Keep off,' said Will. 'If you come knockin' at my door in Bethnal Green to see if me Christianity is improvin', I won't be responsible for the consequences.'

'I only have a Christian wish to—'

'Well, I won't 'ave any wishes like that meself,' said Will, 'all I'll have if I see you on me doorstep will be an improper attack of the old Adam.'

'Whatever do you mean, Mr Fletcher?'

'I mean you shouldn't ruddy well look the way you do look, should you?' Will thought her looks, especially her fine mouth, near to criminally provoking. 'Now listen, I'm goin' to get Lulu's rag doll, then see you safely out of 'ere. I'm goin' to take you to a tram and throw you aboard. You got that, Sister Charity?'

'Thank you, Mr Fletcher, that's very kind of you, I've felt all along you're essentially a good man.'

Will laughed. A little smile touched Mother Verity's mouth.

He saw her aboard a tram. She was still standing on the platform when it moved off, looking back at him, he with a battered old rag doll in his hand.

She wondered in bed that night how she could find out his new address and why Mother Magda found it necessary to go to confession so often with Father Peter. Father Peter was impressive in the strength and character of his faith, but even he must be feeling embarrassed. Poor Mother Magda, her sordid past lay heavily on her conscience, perhaps.

A gentle knock on the bedroom door made Mother Verity call, 'Who is it?'

The door opened. 'Good night, my sisters, and may the blessing of God be upon you.'

'Good night, Father,' said Mother Verity. In the other bed, Mother Ruth was already asleep.

The door closed and the minister went on his way. It occurred to Mother Verity then that this custom of bestowing a good night blessing wasn't really necessary. It

255

even had a little impropriety to it. One might not be in bed, one might be undressing.

One could only suppose that in his Christian goodness the minister simply did not think of that.

CHAPTER FIFTEEN

On her way to the Andrews house in Manor Place on Friday evening, it was Aunt Edie's turn to be accidentally bumped into by Mrs Shaw.

'Oh, it's you, Miss 'Arper, well, I never,' said the friendly neighbourhood gossip, glancing at Aunt Edie's weekend suitcase. 'I expect you've come to be a kind 'elp again.'

'Hullo, Mrs Shaw, yes, it does 'appen to be me,' said Aunt Edie.

'I must say, yer a good soul in Jack Andrews's hour of trial,' said Mrs Shaw.

'Oh, he can stand on his own feet, Mrs Shaw, it's his children who need a bit of care and fussin'.'

'I was sayin' to me old man, I was sayin' you've got an 'eart of gold, Miss 'Arper, and 'e said 'e was very admirin' of yer. It's a shame yer cousin Maud's not 'erself. I expect it's all them years of Jack bein' away at the war and 'er 'aving to care for Jimmy and 'is sisters all by 'erself, I expect it's give 'er a breakdown. Mind, we did 'ear she come 'ome in a van the other day, but only for about 'alf an hour, so I suppose she's improved a bit. Is she in one of them 'omes where they look after people 'aving breakdowns? Only we 'aven't 'eard if she is or where it is.'

'I expect Mr Andrews doesn't want friends an' neighbours goin' to visit,' said Aunt Edie, no more disposed than Dad himself to let anyone know his wife had gone chronically religious. 'You know how kind friends an' neighbours can be, and I expect Mr Andrews thinks it's best for her not to 'ave visitors.'

'Yes, 'e's a nice man,' said Mrs Shaw, 'and 'e's come out of the war still lookin' fit and 'andsome. It's a shame—'

'Not half,' said Aunt Edie briskly. 'Well, it's been nice talkin' to you, Mrs Shaw, I'll go an' see if the girls are in.'

They were, and they'd done something towards preparing the supper. Patsy had peeled the potatoes and Betsy had done the broad beans. They greeted Aunt Edie happily, and she gave them a hug and a kiss. She asked if they'd seen their mum during the week. Patsy said no. Her mum had been, she said, while she and Betsy were out, and Mum had taken everyone's clothes away.

'What?' said Aunt Edie, and Patsy put her in the picture. Aunt Edie looked as if her sparks were going to fly. Patsy said Dad was nearly spitting blood for once. 'I'm not surprised,' said Aunt Edie, controlling her anger to make a careful comment. 'Your mum's not very well, we've all got to be a bit understandin', loveys.'

'But all me clothes, Auntie,' said Betsy. 'I didn't 'ave anyfink.'

'Never mind, your dad brought them back,' said Aunt Edie, 'and we'll all 'ave another nice weekend, you'll see. 'Ow's my young man?'

'That boy,' said Patsy, and Aunt Edie smiled. Jimmy was getting to be quite a character these days. 'He comes home lookin' as if he goes on holiday to Southend every day, or as if he's been hop-pickin' down in Kent.'

''E's disgustin' brown,' said Betsy.

'Pardon?' said Aunt Edie.

'That's what Patsy told 'im 'e was,' said Betsy.

'Well, I'll 'ave a good look at him when he comes in,'

said Aunt Edie. 'Now I think I'd better help with the supper.'

Dad arrived home. Aunt Edie was frying plaice fillets, bought fresh from the market fishmonger by Patsy earlier in the day.

''Ullo, 'ullo, 'ow's our pearly queen?' he asked.

'Leave off,' said Aunt Edie, 'I'm nobody's pearly queen.'

'Well, watch out for Joe Gosling,' said Dad, 'he's got both 'is eyes on you.'

'Is that supposed to be funny?' said Aunt Edie.

'Nothing funny about it,' said Dad. 'He told me after the concert last Saturday that 'e was inclined very serious towards you.'

'D'you mind gettin' your dad out of this scullery, Patsy?' called Aunt Edie. 'I'll 'it him with this fish fork if you don't.'

'That plaice looks good, Edie,' said Dad.

'Hoppit,' said Aunt Edie brusquely.

Jimmy came in, looking as brown as a berry. 'Watcher, fam'ly. Watcher, Aunt Edie. How's me pearly queen?'

'Don't you start, young Jimmy,' said Aunt Edie, 'or you an' your dad'll both get your ears boxed.'

'Crumbs,' whispered Betsy to Patsy in the kitchen, 'd'you fink Aunt Edie's got the rats?'

'No, course she 'asn't,' whispered Patsy. 'She likes it.'

'Why does she sound as if she's got the rats, then?'

'She's a grown-up, and all grown-ups act a bit silly.'

'I ain't goin' to be a grown-up, then,' whispered Betsy, 'are you?'

'I'll 'ave to be when I'm married.'

'But will yer 'usband like yer bein' silly?'

'He won't know, 'e'll be silly himself. Well, more silly, seeing 'e'll be a man.'

259

There was another dialogue between Dad and Aunt Edie in the parlour after supper. Aunt Edie wanted to know exactly how he'd handled his wife when he'd gone to get the family's clothes back. He told her.

'You did what?' asked Aunt Edie.

'Broke 'er ruddy umbrella,' said Dad.

'You actually stood up to 'er?' said Aunt Edie.

'Well, she needs a new umbrella, if that's what you mean,' said Dad, 'but I wouldn't say it's a question of standin' up to her, Edie, more like tryin' to make her see the fam'ly's only goin' to put up with so much.'

'Not good enough,' said Aunt Edie, who was getting a little edgy with Dad lately. 'Bring 'er back 'ome and show 'er who's boss. Sometimes a man's got to be the boss. Maud's got to be cured before it's too late. Comin' here and cartin' off all 'er fam'ly's clothes to give to the poor, that's tellin' me she's nearly over the top.'

'Well, I suppose she thought—'

'I'll spit if you keep makin' excuses for her, Jack. What's goin' to 'appen if she goes right over the top, and gets put in an institution? It would leave young Patsy 'aving to be mum to all of you. You don't think I'll stand for lettin' Patsy take on that sort of responsibility, do you? A girl 'er age? It would take all the fun out of 'er life. I'd give up me job first, I'd—' Aunt Edie stopped and bit her lip.

'Now, Edie—'

'Don't you now Edie me. You're a man, Jack Andrews, you've always been a man, only you've forgot it's the duty of a husband an' father to see his wife don't play up at the expense of 'is kids. Don't you know young Betsy has got so that she's afraid of 'er mother? Don't you know Patsy can't stand 'er barmy ways, and that Jimmy couldn't care less if she comes back 'ome or not? Well, if she don't come back, and if she gets carted off to a loony bin, this fam'ly's not goin' to be without a mum. If Jimmy, Patsy an' Betsy were all grown up, all of an age to get married, it would be different, but they're not, and they've got to 'ave someone who'll be a mum to them.'

Dad, shaken by her flying sparks, said, 'You mean yourself, Edie?'

'There's not goin' to be anyone else, except over my dead body,' said Aunt Edie, who could have told him that for years she'd wanted to take Maud's place. 'So you'd better bring Maud 'ome and cure 'er before it's too late, because the neighbours will 'ave something to talk about then.'

'Edie, I couldn't ask you to do a thing like that, give up your job and take the fam'ly on,' said Dad.

'No, you wouldn't ask, would you? So I'd 'ave to volunteer, wouldn't I?'

'But, Edie old girl, you'd get talked about something rotten,' said Dad.

'Then you'd 'ave to move, wouldn't you?' said Aunt Edie, all sparks.

'Ruddy coconuts,' said Dad, 'you're a pearly queen and a sergeant-major all rolled into one.'

'Oh, I am, am I?'

'You bet you are,' said Dad, 'and I like you for it. That's the trouble.'

'What d'you mean?' A little flush appeared on Aunt Edie's face.

'Never mind,' said Dad.

'I do mind,' said Aunt Edie, 'I want to know what you mean.'

'Well, I'm not sure you'd be safe, love, if you set up 'ome with me and the kids.'

'Why wouldn't I?' The flush deepened. Aunt Edie knew

exactly what he meant, of course, but she wouldn't have been the woman she was if she hadn't wanted him to spell it out.

'You're special to this fam'ly, Edie, and to me, and I always did go for pearly queens.'

'Say what you mean,' said Aunt Edie.

'I've said what I mean.'

'Not in plain words, you 'aven't.'

'Listen, Edie, if there's one thing I don't want to do, it's something that would make a mess of our friendship,' said Dad. 'You've been a friend to me for as long as I can remember, the very best friend, and that's it, I'm not sayin' any more, except if you came and lived with us, it could all go up the spout.'

'I see.' Aunt Edie drew a breath, knowing what she had accomplished. She had found out that her cousin Maud's husband, the secret love of her life, wanted her. There were no more sparks. Her eyes were warm and melting. She might not ever get him, but it was a lovely feeling, knowing he wanted her. 'Well, I think I'd best start sortin' out the week's washin'. I'll be doin' it first thing after breakfast tomorrow. I've got the mornin' off.'

'How'd you manage that?' asked Dad, a little rueful because he knew he'd said far more than he should.

'I asked for it.'

'Edie, you'll get docked a morning's pay,' he said, 'and on our account.'

'On account of your son an' daughters,' said Aunt Edie. 'I wouldn't want you to think it was for you as well, would I?'

Trying to make light of things, Dad said, 'You're a star turn, Edie, and that's a fact.'

'So's your old sergeant-major,' said Aunt Edie.

★

Saturday was an uninterrupted day for Jimmy. Mrs Gibbs kept a tight rein on Sophy, she knew what was happening. Sophy had taken a fancy to Jimmy, and was trying to add him to her belongings. It was all too preposterous, but utterly typical. She'd been like that with her brothers. By the time she was eleven, she'd made them her errand boys.

At five o'clock Mr Gibbs went down to see Jimmy who had carried out all his work with willing enthusiasm from the day he'd started. The cleared areas, divided by lines of trees or specified copses, were all patterned with the ashes of bonfires Jimmy had built. George Thorpe, the landscape man in charge, had spoken well of him.

'How's it going, Jimmy?' asked Mr Gibbs.

'I keep thinkin' it's all a bit slow, Mr Gibbs.'

'It's that kind of work, Jimmy, so don't worry, I like the way you're tackling it. Have you managed to get a job yet?'

'Not yet,' said Jimmy.

'Well, I'm off to Devon tomorrow with my wife and our young monkey. We'll be back next Wednesday week. It's as long as I can afford to be away. You can carry on here while we're away, Ada will look after you and Mr Thorpe will be around if you want him. Now, I've got a proposition for you. On the Monday after we're back, would you like a job at my factory in Peckham as a junior hand among wood and sawdust, and an apprenticeship in furniture manufacture? You'd learn about wood and sawdust at first, you'd be at the bottom end of things, but you'd have prospects. Or, alternatively, you can continue here, as a help to the landscape gardeners, with a view to staying on after their work is finished and becoming one of my permanent gardening staff. For the factory job, I'd pay you a pound a week to start with. For the job as a junior gardener, well, I'd discuss your wage with you.'

'A pound a week at the fact'ry, Mr Gibbs?' Jimmy knew that was a good wage for an unskilled hand of his age.

'Well, you could give the factory a go, Jimmy, and if it didn't suit you, the job as a gardener here would still be open, as long as you didn't take too much time to decide.'

'Crikey, that's really good of you, Mr Gibbs, but who's goin' to do the work I've been doin' here if I try the fact'ry job?'

'The landscape people. It was going to be done by them originally. Then I thought you might like the work until you found a job. Well, what d'you say, young 'un?'

'I'll give the fact'ry a go, Mr Gibbs.' Jimmy knew Mr Gibbs, he knew him for a man who'd been born in Brixton and come up in the world. Brixton was a mixture of cockneys and other people, and theatre people had houses on Brixton Hill. Sometimes you could tell who Mr Gibbs had belonged to when there was just a trace of cockney in his voice. He'd be a good boss, Jimmy was sure of that. But he was also sensible of the fact that Mr Gibbs wouldn't treat him at the factory as he treated him here. 'I've got to thank you, Mr Gibbs.'

'Well, fair do's, Jimmy, I'm counting on you becoming an asset, whatever you end up doing in my employ. Right, then, you start at eight o'clock Monday fortnight. The factory's in Canal Head, Peckham. And here's your money for today's work.'

'Thanks, Mr Gibbs, thanks for everything.'

'You'll do, Jimmy.'

'Hope you enjoy your holiday.'

'I'll be in trouble if I don't,' said Mr Gibbs.

Jimmy made his way up to the house at five-thirty, his finishing time. There was still no sign of Sophy. He put his head into the kitchen. Only Mrs Redfern and Ada were there.

'Hullo, I'm off now. 'Ave a nice Sunday tomorrow. See you Monday.'

'You'll see Ada and Mr Hodges,' said cook with a plump smile. 'Ivy and me will be in Devon with the family.'

'Well, you're lookin' happy as usual, Mrs Redfern,' said Jimmy.

'I always try not to look as if I'm goin' to my own funeral,' said Mrs Redfern.

'That's good,' said Jimmy. 'Young Ada there, she always looks as if Christmas has just come. Some fellers have all the luck, don't they? Well, I'd better get off home.'

'Yes, you'd better,' said Ada, 'or you'll get us so we won't know what you're talkin' about. I'll come and see you out.' At the front door, she said, 'Stop sayin' things like some fellers have all the luck.'

'All right,' said Jimmy, 'a joke can wear a bit thin, can't it? I'll give that one up.'

'You don't actu'lly 'ave a broken heart,' said Ada.

'Tell you what I have got,' said Jimmy, 'a job. At Mr Gibbs's Peckham fact'ry, starting Monday fortnight. And if I don't like it, he said I can 'ave a permanent job here as a gardener.'

'Oh, that's nice,' said Ada, 'except if you worked 'ere as a gardener, would I have to put up with you pullin' my leg every day?'

'Well, I expect you've got legs worth pullin', Ada, I expect—'

'Oh, cheeky devil,' said Ada.

'You're a nice girl, Ada. See you Monday, then.'

'So long, Jimmy.'

She watched him go. Then, about to close the door, she saw a figure dart into view. That young madam. She'd been lying in wait for Jimmy.

Sophy, catching Jimmy up, said, 'Well, I like that, going off without saying goodbye to me when we're off on holiday tomorrow.'

'All right, have a nice holiday,' said Jimmy. 'Don't get lost round the haystacks, don't fall out of trees, don't let farm dogs chase you, don't muck about in ditches and be a good girl to your mum. Oh, your dad's offered me a job in his Peckham fact'ry, I'm startin' the Monday after you get back.'

'I know that,' said Sophy, looking wickedly pretty, 'but you don't want to work in a factory, not when Daddy's said you can work here. We can still have fun together here.'

'I'm givin' the fact'ry a go,' said Jimmy. 'I'll be safer there.'

'Jimmy, you're just the rottenest boy ever sometimes, but I bet you won't like factory work, I bet you'll come back here.' Sophy cast a winsome glance. 'Still, you can kiss me as I'm going on holiday tomorrow.'

'Not likely, I don't want to get the sack before I've started – here, hold off—'

Sophy, arms around his neck, came up on her toes and kissed him. Oh, the little minx. Ada closed the front door and went back to the kitchen in a temper.

'Gosh,' said Sophy, 'don't you kiss nice, Jimmy?'

'I'll wallop you,' said Jimmy. 'Not now. When you come back. You wait.'

Sophy was laughing as he ran for the gates.

CHAPTER SIXTEEN

Aunt Edie brought enjoyment to the weekend, as usual. She liked jokes and laughter and fun. Betsy and Patsy loved the attention and affection she gave them. Some people might have said she was undermining the standing of her cousin Maud with the family. Aunt Edie would have said she was doing her best to make life happy for them. Actually, she was behaving as she'd often wanted to, by taking the family to her heart. It was a joy to her to be so close to them and to be looking after them, Dad as well. Dad especially sometimes.

'Now don't get under my feet, Jack Andrews.'

'I thought I'd give you a bit of help.'

'Why don't you sit down and read your paper, and have a smoke of your pipe? Or give Betsy a tickle? You know 'ow much Betsy likes a tickle.'

'Got to catch 'er first,' said Dad.

'Bet you can't, Dad, bet you can't!' cried Betsy, and off they went, Betsy shrieking in and out of rooms, and up and down the stairs, Dad chasing her and letting her escape until the moment was right and Betsy had collapsed in yelling delight.

Everyone was happy, of course, about Jimmy's new job. Aunt Edie gave him a kiss for being a clever young man. Jimmy asked for an encore.

'That boy,' said Aunt Edie, shaking her head. 'He'll be askin' to take me out next.'

'Crikey,' said Betsy, 'Jimmy can't go out wiv Aunt Edie, can 'e, Dad? She's older than 'im, ain't you, Aunt Edie?'

'Not much older,' said Dad, 'say a couple of years or so. And what's more, me pickle, our Jimmy's growin' older all the time, as you can see, and your Aunt Edie's growin' younger, which is as plain as me old sergeant-major's hooter.'

'Lor', fancy that,' said Betsy, astonished at the news. 'Could our Jimmy marry our Aunt Edie, then?'

'He'd 'ave to ask her first,' said Dad.

'Yes, you 'ave to propose,' said Patsy.

'Crumbs, would yer, Jimmy?' asked Betsy.

'D'you fancy a honeymoon in Brighton, Aunt Edie?' asked Jimmy.

'I know what I fancy,' said Aunt Edie, 'a saucepan lid. I could do some people a lot of good with a saucepan lid. I'm livin' in a monkey house at weekends, and I know who the chief monkey is, Jack Andrews. You and your sergeant-major's hooter.'

'Yes, plain as the nose on 'is face, it was,' said Dad. 'Still is, probably.'

'Who's laughin'?' asked Aunt Edie.

Everyone was. So Aunt Edie went for Dad with a saucepan lid.

'Crumbs, it ain't like this when Mum's 'ere,' said Betsy to Patsy in a whisper.

'What a palaver,' said Patsy, 'and we don't 'ave to repent, either.'

Nothing that related to the Lord's work was too much trouble for the members of the League of Repenters. While Father Luke or Mother Joan drove the horse and van around districts inhabited by people more affluent than those of the East End, and accompanying Repenters knocked on doors and asked for clothes for the poor, others went different ways. They worked in pairs, pushing handcarts or barrows. Mother Mary's endeavours were more notable than ever, for Father Peter had bought her a new umbrella and bestowed it with a blessing, a gentle touch of her shoulder.

She was out with Mother Magda one day, Mother Magda pushing a barrow on which lay clothes donated by householders approving the cause. Owning a splendid body, Mother Magda was suitably equipped to do the pushing. They were in Hampstead Road, about a mile from their Temple, and some of the houses looked as if they were overflowing with affluence.

'Stop,' commanded Mother Mary, slender and bossy.

'All right,' said Mother Magda, fulsome and friendly, although she was repentant of what these characteristics had led her to in her recent past.

'I'll knock,' said Mother Mary, 'you stay with the barrow, we don't want sinful 'ands thievin' what we've collected so far.'

'Yes, all right, ducky, but would you mind addressin' me more friendly, like?' said Mother Magda. 'I ain't used to bein' bossed about.'

'We won't 'ave no arguments, sister. The Lord's spoken to me an' told me what me duties are.' Mother Mary approached the door of a promising-looking house and used the shining brass knocker. No answer. She knocked again. The door opened, disclosing a man in a dark blue dressing-gown. He had a five o'clock shadow and looked as if he'd only just got up, although it was past eleven in the morning.

Reprovingly, Mother Mary said, 'I had to knock twice.'

'Sorry, no servants here at the moment,' he said, and

blinked as he saw her black costume. 'Damn me, what's this? The funeral's not until Thursday.'

'What funeral?' said Mother Mary. 'I 'aven't come about any funeral. Still, will it be a Christian burial?'

'The old bitch'll kick the coffin to pieces if it isn't,' said the man who was raffishly masculine.

'I don't like to hear anyone speakin' like that of the dead,' said Mother Mary.

'Well, take it from me, she never said anything good about anyone herself, the old biddy.'

'All the same,' said Mother Mary sternly, 'kindly don't speak ill of the dead.'

'Who the devil are you? A distant relative on the distaff side?'

'I'm from the League of Repenters, collectin' clothes for the poor an' needy,' said Mother Mary. 'I'm sure you'll give something, that's a nice dressin'-gown you're wearin', it would be just right for someone that feels the cold.'

'I'll give you the shirt off my back as well, of course,' said the man.

'No, we don't want shirts straight off backs,' said Mother Mary primly. 'We only want clean shirts and other clothes. I'll be pleased to come in and 'ave a look at what you've got.'

The man cast a speculative eye over her. 'Yes, come in,' he said, 'don't wait for an invitation. You can take what you want from the old girl's wardrobes. Not the furs, though. This way.' He led her through the hall and up the stairs, whistling as he went, which Mother Mary thought a bit disrespectful to the departed. He took her into a palatial bedroom. She blinked at its opulence. He opened up two wardrobes, disclosing an array of coats, dresses, costumes, blouses and skirts. And furs.

'Well,' said Mother Mary reprovingly. 'I never saw

anything more sinful. What these things must've cost. I don't know we want such sinful clothes for the poor. Still, our minister can say a blessin' over them before we give them out, so I don't mind unburdenin' you of them. 'Ave you got a large cardboard box or something?'

The man, looking amused, took a leather suitcase from the bottom of a wardrobe. 'Here you are, you can have that as well,' he said, 'it's been to Nice and back a few times.'

'That's more sin,' said Mother Mary, and poked the suitcase with her new umbrella. 'I don't know, wherever a Christian body turns, there's more sin. Perhaps you'd kindly pass me the clothes one at a time, it's all for the Lord.'

'Frightful thought, that, the Lord wearing these things,' said the man. Mother Mary gave him a stern look. He grinned and began to unload the wardrobes.

Outside, a lady of haughty looks approached Mother Magda and the barrow. 'Pardon me, my good woman, but you can't sell second-hand clothing here, nor stand your barrow there. Take it away at once.'

'What a sauce,' said Mother Magda. 'If I wasn't a lady, and a repentin' one, I'd 'ave something to say to you.'

'No hawkers or pavement traders here, if you don't mind,' said the toffee-nosed lady.

''Ere, I'm not 'awking or tradin', I'm 'elping to collect clothes for poor people,' said Mother Magda, 'so don't give me none of them 'aughty looks or I'll belt yer one. Well, I would if I wasn't a Christian woman with charity and kindness in me bosom. 'Ere, you better 'ave one of our pamphlets.' She thrust one at the lady, who took it and read it.

'Heavens, how stirring,' said the lady.

'Yes, our minister's exaltifying,' said Mother Magda,

who had picked that word up from Mother Althea. ''E's our guidin' light, an' doin' 'is good works for all of us.' She wondered how long Father Peter would be doing his special good works for her. She didn't feel that three or four times a week was much of an abundance of sinfulness, that it was getting to be too much of a good thing. It just made her feel terrible passionate.

'I shall go to Bloomsbury and see him,' said the lady, overcome by the message of the pamphlet.

''E'll be pleased to see yer, I'm sure,' said Mother Magda.

Upstairs in the house, Mother Mary was setting about the man with her new umbrella. Of all the horrid impudence, he had put his arm around her waist and said something about one good turn deserving another. Then he'd kissed her, and on her mouth. Outraged, Mother Mary dealt whacks and blows.

'Damn me, you're off your silly topknot—'

'I'll give you good turn – take that – and that!'

'You crazy old cow—'

'Oh, what disgustin' impudence! Take that!' The umbrella whacked him over his head. 'I'll have the law on you, an' the Lord's vengeance as well. I've a good mind not to take all these clothes – stand back, d'you 'ear?' The umbrella poked his navel. 'Now you just carry that case down to the street, go on. Do a bit of penitence for your sinfulness or I'll give you a lot more of what you've just 'ad.'

The man, grinning, said, 'Well, old girl, there's room for improvement, one kiss wasn't very much. A lot more could square things up, y'know.'

'Well, of all the sauce! The Day of Judgement's waitin' for you, and the Devil! Take that!' But the umbrella missed for once. The man shouted with laughter.

'You're first cousin to Aunt Agatha, the old bitch,' he said.

'Oh, I never met more sinning than's in you,' said Mother Mary. 'You just carry that case down, you 'ear?'

Laughing, he carried it down and with Mother Mary at his back, umbrella at the ready. He deposited it on the barrow and still laughing, went back into the house.

'What's 'e laughin' about?' asked Mother Magda.

'I'll give 'im laugh,' said Mother Mary. She went to the closed front door, pushed the flap of the letter-box open, then stooped and shouted through it. 'Be sure the Lord witnessed your abomination!'

'Oh, did 'e abominate yer, sister?' asked Mother Magda, imagination suddenly running riot.

'I gave 'im something to remember it by,' declared Mother Mary.

'No wonder you was up there a long time,' said Mother Magda. 'Oh, yer poor woman, I was never done wicked by meself, me gentlemen was always nice to me.'

'Now you 'ush about them sinful days of yours, sister, you're in Christian penitence now,' said Mother Mary, primly straightening her costume jacket.

'Still, I was never abominated,' said Mother Magda, 'me 'eart bleeds for yer, sister.'

''Ow kind,' said Mother Mary. It was all going over the top of her head, her head being what it was these days. 'Never mind, 'is deeds will find 'im out, and I did get a big suitcase of lovely clothes from his passed-on aunt that's lately deceased, poor woman. Look.' She opened the lid of the large suitcase. It was packed with expensive clothes.

'Oh, my,' breathed Mother Magda, 'ain't they ravishin'? You can't 'elp sayin' get be'ind me, Satan. I mean, there's some women that wouldn't mind bein' done wicked by for 'alf this lot. Does it make yer feel better, sister? I mean, 'e was that dark and 'andsome, wasn't 'e?'

'I'll give 'im dark and 'andsome next time I see 'im,' said Mother Mary. 'Well, come along, sister, there's other nice-lookin' houses down 'ere.'

The two batty women pushed on, Mother Magda's imagination making her feel so terrible passionate that she silently groaned for help from above.

When the long day was over for the Repenters and they were gathered at dinner with their minister, the news that Mother Mary had been abominated while doing the Lord's work caused outcries of consternation. It was Mother Magda, of course, who spread the news.

'Oh, dear.'

'How dreadful.'

'Poor, dear Mother Mary.'

'Such brutality.'

'But she carried on with 'er work so brave,' said Mother Magda.

'Well, I gave the brute something chronic to think about,' said Mother Mary, 'with me umbrella. 'E won't lay 'is wicked 'ands so ready on another woman.'

Mother Verity looked at her. Mother Mary seemed very self-satisfied. 'Was it outrage at its dreadful worst, sister?' asked Mother Verity.

'I never met a more dreadful sinner except the one that treated you so abominable, sister,' said Mother Mary.

'Oh, dear,' sighed Mother Ruth.

'First-class soundrel,' said Mother Joan, 'needs hanging. Bear up, Mother Mary, the Lord will avenge you. He'll drop the blighter in the soup, mark my words.'

'My child,' said Father Peter, 'be very sure we all grieve for you.'

''Ow kind, Father,' said Mother Mary.

'My blood's boilin',' said Father Luke. 'I just wish I'd

been there, I'd've 'ad the coppers on him quicker than the faithful can say the Lord's prayer.'

'Oh, I gave 'im what for, Father Luke, I can tell you,' said Mother Mary.

'My child,' said Father Peter, 'perhaps I should hear confession from you this evening.'

'Thank you, Father, I'd best unburden me soul,' said Mother Mary.

'I'm troubled meself, Father,' said Mother Magda.

'Yes, of course,' murmured Father Peter, a figure of looming compassion at the head of the table. 'I will receive you after Mother Mary, sister.'

Mother Verity experienced her first doubts.

'A kiss, my child?' said Father Peter gently.

'Yes, the impudence, would you believe,' said Mother Mary, head reverently bent in the faint glow of light. 'An' the sinfulness, which was worse, it makes you think Satan's got 'old of you. I couldn't 'ardly credit I was bein' taken advantage of when I was only there out of Christian charity, and 'im with a funeral only two days away.'

'That was all, a kiss?'

'Oh, I've got to confess 'is arm was around me waist as well. I wish I could also confess I turned the other cheek, like Mother Verity did those times, but I just didn't feel like it, I felt more like castin' 'im into the pit, Father.'

'He did not – ah – interfere with your clothing?'

'Pardon?' said Mother Mary, shocked but still in reverence to her confessor.

'He did not attempt to – ah – lift your skirts?'

'I'd like to see any man try that, I'd make 'im wish he'd never been born.'

'Did you perhaps have forbidden thoughts while he was kissing you?'

''Ow can you ask such a thing, Father?'

'Satan is always close to every one of us, my child, tempting us into sinful thoughts, even if we're strong enough to resist the deeds.'

'Well, I kept 'im from gettin' close to me, Father, all I thought about was where was my umbrella, an' then I let the man 'ave it, I can tell you, and if I ever see 'im again I'll let 'im 'ave more of it.'

A hand touched her hair in gentle benediction. 'You are absolved of the sin of losing your temper, my child.'

'Thank you, Father, amen.'

Mother Magda's confession was lengthy. It was all about the sinful thoughts she had concerning how Mother Mary had been abominated and done wicked by, and how such thoughts had made her terrible passionate.

Father Peter absolved her of her thinking sinfulness, and dealt with her forbidden feelings in his usual willing way. He reassured her in respect of her doubts concerning whether or not she was receiving the necessary surfeit of sinfulness. It would simply take time, he said.

'Oh, that's all right, then,' she said.

CHAPTER SEVENTEEN

It was a bit quiet at Anerley without Sophy. It meant Jimmy was able to work without the young madam creeping up on him. Mr Thorpe, who looked like a ruddy-faced farmer, had some kind and instructional words for him now and again, but he wasn't dragged into any potty conversations with Sophy. The weather wasn't as hot as it had been, September was on the edge of August and bringing cool evenings. Ada teased him when he arrived each day, and he responded in kind over the customary cup of tea and slice of toast. Mr Hodges was gracious to him and paid him at the end of each day. Ada gave him his refreshments, he came up to the terrace for them, and had his habitual exchanges with the young maid. She usually retired back to the kitchen giggling or having hysterics.

'I don't know why you're so good to me, Ada,' he said one afternoon, when he was enjoying a cup of tea and a slice of cake.

'I don't, either,' said Ada, 'you're a terror, you are. Bet your girl can't make you out.'

'What girl?'

'How many 'ave you got, then? Six?'

'I'm savin' girls up till I've got decent money in me pocket,' said Jimmy. 'Best thing, that is. Well, accordin' to how my dad has informed me. You've got to be able to treat girls, he said. If you can't, best to lay off till you can. Girls are made to be treated, Ada.'

'Why?' asked Ada, thinking him full of young manliness with his tanned face and sunburned arms.

'Because girls are nice,' said Jimmy. 'My sister Patsy's nice, so's my other sister, Betsy. So are you. Mind, I don't want to pay you compliments, I don't want Percy to come and break me leg.'

'Leave off about Percy,' said Ada. 'I suppose you'd like to take the young madam out an' treat her, would you?'

'Sophy? What, at her age? Her dad would chuck me in the pond. Besides, I wouldn't take a rich girl out. Be daft.'

'I bet you know some pretty girls,' said Ada.

'I know one,' said Jimmy.

'Who?'

'Ta for the cake an' tea, Ada. I'd best get back to work now.'

'Oh, come on, who is she?' asked Ada.

'She's engraved on me heart,' said Jimmy.

'Jimmy, you're so dotty you're makin' me jump up an' down.'

'Well, don't fall over,' said Jimmy, and went back to his work.

Uncle Harold had given his charming niece all kinds of bushy-browed looks, but after talking to a clerk in the appropriate department, had come up with the address of Will Fletcher, now employed in the firm's Spitalfields warehouse. Mother Verity thanked him.

'What's it really all about, Celia?' he asked.

'Goodwill towards the deserving, Uncle Harold.'

'Damned if I like the sound of that,' said Uncle Harold.

Mother Verity smiled and left.

Now she was in Underwood Road, Bethnal Green, and it was twenty-five to four in the afternoon. She walked to the corner, reaching Vallance Road, and waited there, occasionally glancing at a house in Underwood Road, number fourteen. Children under school age were playing around the doorsteps of other houses. The neighbourhood was a visible improvement on Christian Street, Whitechapel. The houses were better. Doorsteps looked cleaner. There was more pride here.

At four o'clock, a nearby school began to disgorge noisy boys and girls. Mother Verity heard them. One could always hear children in school playgrounds or coming out of school. She stayed where she was, waiting.

Lulu appeared. She was wearing a brown tam-o'-shanter, a new pinafore frock and shining little boots. She was with another girl, and they were both giggling. They stopped in Underwood Road, outside number fourteen, talking and giggling. Then the other girl went on, and Lulu turned into number fourteen, pulled a latchcord and entered the house. The door closed.

Mother Verity, satisfied, turned and left.

Lulu would now be waiting for Will Fletcher to come home.

Aunt Edie arrived again at the weekend. She gave Betsy and Patsy hugs and kisses, and quickly got to work on Friday evening's supper. When Dad and Jimmy came home, she announced over supper that she was going out later.

'Good for you,' said Dad.

'Joe Gosling is callin' for me,' she said.

'Oh?' said Dad.

'Yes,' said Aunt Edie. Dad gave her a look. She returned it. Dad suspected then that she was letting him know that if she took up with Joe Gosling, neighbours wouldn't talk about her in dubious terms. 'I'm 'aving the pleasure of bein' taken to the Camberwell Palace music 'all.'

'He's after you, Aunt Edie,' said Jimmy.

''E's that Camberwell pearly king,' said Patsy.

'Aunt Edie, you goin' to marry 'im?' asked Betsy excitedly.

'No, I'm just goin' to the music 'all with him,' said Aunt Edie.

'Well, that's good,' said Dad, but didn't sound overjoyed. And Jimmy hoped Aunt Edie wasn't getting serious. Joe Gosling was all right, a cheerful and hearty bloke, but not Jimmy's idea of a happy-ever-after for Aunt Edie.

''Ave a lovely time, Auntie,' said Patsy, ''ope you get treated swell.'

'Don't stay out all night,' said Jimmy, 'or I'll come after you.'

'Now then, cheeky,' said Aunt Edie.

Dad came out of a thoughtful moment to say, 'That reminds me of 1918, when we were knockin' Johnny Turk for six, and me old sergeant-major—'

'That old sergeant-major of yours wants hanging on the line,' said Aunt Edie.

'After you've put 'im through the mangle first, Aunt Edie?' said Patsy.

Aunt Edie burst into laughter.

Dad went thoughtful again.

Aunt Edie had quite a late night out, Joe Gosling not bringing her back until well after eleven. Dad was still up.

''Ere she is,' said Joe cheerfully, 'all in one piece, old soldier.' His hearty smile hid the fact that he thought Jack Andrews was taking advantage of Edie's generous nature by having her look after his family at weekends. 'Some rare turns at the Palace tonight. 'Arry Champion hisself, talk about any old iron, what a performance, brought the 'ouse down. Anyway, 'ere's yer 'andsome cousin-in-law. We 'ad a couple in the pub after we come out of the Palace. Are yer standin' up all right, Edie?'

Aunt Edie blinked. Dad, looking at her, thought she might have had more than a couple.

'What's that you said, Joe?' she asked.

'Standin' up all right, are yer, me old love?' asked Joe.

'The day I can't stand up, Joe Gosling, will be the day I'm in me coffin,' said Aunt Edie. Joe grinned and gave her a friendly kiss on her cheek. 'Who did that?' she asked. 'Who's takin' liberties?'

'Well, I got certain 'opes, Edie, concernin' what might be a lucky day for me in me near future,' said Joe, and gave Dad a wink.

'Ta for me night out,' said Aunt Edie, and Joe said good night to her and Dad, and left. Dad closed the front door. Aunt Edie peered at him. 'Are you lookin' at me, Jack Andrews?'

'Well, yes, I am,' said Dad, and Aunt Edie swayed.

'I am now goin' up to bed,' she said.

'I'm not sure you'll get there,' said Dad.

'What d'you mean?'

'You're 'aving trouble standin' up,' said Dad.

Aunt Edie had had three halves of Guinness. She liked the occasional half, that was all, but tonight she'd felt she needed a cure for her emotional problems, which hadn't been helped by the heart-tugging rendering of sentimental music hall songs. But even though she liked the occasional Guinness, a whole pint and a half had been a little too much for her. She blinked again.

'Take your 'ands off me, Jack Andrews, you don't want the neighbours talkin', do you?'

'Not touchin' you, Edie,' said Dad, feeling a bit shirty with Joe Gosling for letting her have one too many. She had never been a woman for drink. She was a lively, rousing pearly queen on occasions, but not the kind to be seen in pubs.

'Would you mind gettin' out of me way so's I can go up to bed?' she said.

'You 'appen to be standin' right next to the stairs, old girl,' said Dad. The gas lamp cast light over the passage and stairs. Aunt Edie carefully turned. She swayed. Dad put a helpful arm around her waist.

'What's goin' on?' she asked.

'Come on, I'll see you up to your room,' said Dad.

'What about—' Aunt Edie groped for words. 'What about the neighbours?' That was on her mind, even though her mind was a little dizzy. It was on her mind because he kept making a thing of it.

'Never mind the neighbours,' said Dad. 'Let's get you up the stairs.' He helped her to begin her upward climb, his arm around her. 'Can't 'ave you fallin' down me own stairs.'

He reached the landing with her. She swayed inside his arm and turned. The passage lamp gave some light to the landing, but not much, and her face beneath her hat looked a bit misty to Dad. And her mouth looked soft and dark. He nearly lost his head. He nearly kissed her. It was a shock to find out how much he wanted to, how much he wanted to hold her. More than that, how much he wanted her. Ruddy hell, he thought, that's done it, Jack Andrews, you're in trouble now. His deep liking and fondness for his wife's cousin, which he had known were dangerous under the circumstances, had suddenly become much more than that, much more dangerous. He couldn't remember the last time he had made love to Maud. She hadn't wanted him to, and he'd become indifferent. She'd forgotten she was a wife and a woman. Edie was all woman.

'What's goin' on?' asked Aunt Edie in a faint husky voice. She had her own emotions to cope with, as well as unsteady legs.

Dad took a grip on himself. 'You're all right now, Edie,' he said, 'there's your room.' He took his arm away and opened the door to Betsy's bedroom. Aunt Edie turned again and swayed again. A warm bosom brushed his arm. 'In you go.'

'All these years,' she sighed, and Dad guided her through the door. He closed it and went downstairs. What a woman, he thought, I'm in the ruddy cart now. And wait till I see Joe Gosling again, he'll get an earful and a bit for pouring drink into her. On the other hand, would it be the best thing that could happen if Joe and Edie got spliced?

Oh, hell, I don't like the sound of that.

When Jimmy arrived at Anerley the next morning, Mr Hodges solemnly proffered a letter that lay on a silver tray.

'For you, your young Lordship,' he said.

'Me?'

'Your name is J. Andrews Hesquire?' said Mr Hodges.

'Care of The Beeches, Anerley?' said Ada. 'And postmarked Salcombe in Devon?'

'Well, who'd 'ave thought it?' said Jimmy. He took the letter and opened it. Inside was a picture postcard of Salcombe, and on the reverse were pencilled lines from Sophy.

Dear Blessed Boy,

I hope you're behaving yourself, we're having a lovely time here, except I did knock a gate down, well it came off its hinges or something, and Mummy said I'll turn her grey before her time. I've met some soppy girls and a boy who says he wants to marry me when I'm older. Ugh. It's a relief you're not like that.

Hundreds of kisses, Sophy.

'She's barmy,' said Jimmy.

'Why, what's she said?' asked Ada.

'That she's met a boy who wants to marry her, and that she's glad I don't.'

'The young madam is in form,' said Mr Hodges.

'Young pickle, she is,' said Ada, 'talkin' about marriage at her age.'

'What a girl,' said Jimmy with a grin.

'Can't 'elp laughin', can you?' said Ada.

'How's Mr Hunter?' asked Jimmy.

'Who?' said Ada.

'Percy,' said Jimmy, and Ada wrinkled her nice nose.

'I have forbidden that young gentleman hentry into this 'ouse on account of his hinterfering ways concerning the duties of Miss Ridley,' said Mr Hodges.

'Who's Miss Ridley?' asked Jimmy.

'Me,' said Ada.

'Well, that's a shame, Mr Hodges,' said Jimmy, 'no wonder she's not lookin' very happy.'

'You fibber,' said Ada, 'you're tryin' to say I'm lookin' mis'rable. I'm not, am I, Mr 'Odges?'

'I am glad to say, Ada,' said Mr Hodges, who had a fatherly fondness for her, 'that madam and I myself 'ave never known you suchlike. You are our singing nightingale.'

'So there, Jimmy Andrews,' said Ada.

'Mind you, Mr Hodges,' said Jimmy, 'if Mr Percy Hunter has been chasin' our singing nightingale around the house while Mr and Mrs Gibbs have been away, I can't say I blame 'im, but I can see why you've had to put your foot down – oh, 'elp—'

Ada had seized a rolling-pin and was after him. She chased him out of the kitchen, through the smaller kitchen, out of the side door and round to the terrace. Jimmy hurtled down the terrace steps. The rolling-pin hurtled after him, just missing. He stopped and turned. Ada was on the terrace, looking for something else to throw.

'You wait!' she called.

'Excuse me,' said Jimmy, 'but could you give us a song, me precious nightingale, instead of another rolling-pin?'

Ada doubled up, and Jimmy went down to his work.

When Dad got home from his Saturday morning stint with his delivery van, Aunt Edie steered him into the parlour for a stand-up.

'Just what 'appened last night, Jack Andrews?' she asked. She felt embarrassed because she was foggy about last night, she could only remember Joe Gosling saying good night and Dad being on the landing with her. She was never going to touch drink again, not like that. It had been emotion and frustration that made her accept Joe's invitation to the Camberwell Palace and give Dad something to think about. Blow the neighbours, that was what she'd felt, even though she knew Dad was right. 'Come on, what 'appened?'

'Nothing,' said Dad, deciding not to look at her in case he had another attack of what wasn't good for him. 'Except you'd 'ad a drop too much, Edie.'

'That's a lie,' said Aunt Edie, proudly good-looking in a lacy white blouse and long navy blue skirt. 'I've never 'ad a drop too much in me life, I'd lose me job if the manager thought I was a drinkin' woman. I just 'ad a Guinness. What I want to know is did you lay your 'ands on me?'

'I 'ad a good mind to,' said Dad unthinkingly.

'What?'

'Eh?' said Dad, suffering want and confusion.

'What did you say?' demanded Aunt Edie, who didn't quite know where she was because of wishes, hopes and fogginess.

'Me?' said Dad, shifting his gaze from a chair to the pearl buttons of her blouse. They ran in a curving line from her neck to her waist, which hardly helped. His gaze wandered elsewhere, his feelings alarming him. Aunt Edie watched his wandering eyes in astonishment. She had never known him unable to look anyone straight in the eye.

'Did you take liberties with me, Jack Andrews?'

'Me?' said Dad, fighting to get on an even keel.

'What's up with you?' she asked. 'You're usin' words like a ten-year-old 'aving a bad five minutes with 'is schoolteacher. I want to know, did you take liberties with me?'

'Like what?' asked Dad.

'How do I know? I wouldn't be askin' if I knew, would I?'

'Look, all I did was 'elp you up the stairs,' said Dad, 'you bein' a bit sideways on.'

'A bit what?' said Aunt Edie. 'Jack Andrews, I'll box your ears for you. All I 'ad was a Guinness. It must've been a bit strong. Well, I might 'ave 'ad another, Joe Gosling keepin' me lively company at the time.'

Blow Joe Gosling, thought Dad, I suddenly don't feel too keen on that bloke.

'Just because I got a bit clouded up didn't give you no right to take liberties.' Out of the fog something came to her. ''Specially seein' you're so concerned about the neighbours.' Yes, she'd had to say something like that last night, she remembered now.

'It beats me you thinkin' I'd take liberties with you, Edie,' said Dad, now looking at the fireplace.

'Look me in the face,' said Aunt Edie.

'That fireplace is ornamental, considerin',' said Dad. 'It's Victorian, y'know, and the Victorians liked bein' ornamental.'

'I'm on to you, Jack Andrews,' said Aunt Edie. 'Did you kiss me last night?'

'I don't know why you're goin' on, Edie old girl. I told you, I just gave you a bit of 'elp gettin' up to the bedroom. Well, I 'ad a responsibility to see you didn't fall elbow over bottom down the stairs.'

Suddenly, Aunt Edie wanted to smile. She knew why he wouldn't look her in the eye. Not because he'd taken liberties, but because of his feelings for her. That Maud, what a disgraceful ingrate of a woman, she didn't deserve Jack, a lovely old soldier and all of a man. You wait, Maud, if I'm given only half a chance, I'll be the kind of pleasure to him I bet you've never been. And I won't be hypocritical enough to ask the Lord to forgive me. Falling elbow over bottom down the stairs? 'Is that supposed to be funny?' she asked.

'Funny?' said Dad. 'You can end up seriously hurt fallin' down the stairs. You're a lovely pearly queen, you are, Edie, and I don't want you breakin' a leg in my 'ouse. Not when you've got—' Dad checked.

'When I've got what?' asked Aunt Edie.

'Can't remember what I was goin' to say.'

'Were you goin' to make remarks about my legs?'

'Now how could I?' said Dad. 'I've never seen 'em. Well, I've seen your ankles, but I've never seen you do a knees-up. I'll just 'ave to keep hopin'.'

Aunt Edie laughed. 'You silly old thing, Jack,' she said.

'Well, I've got to admit, I do feel a bit half-and-half at the moment.'

'What's that mean?'

'Well, due to certain circumstances,' said Dad, 'I don't know if I'm comin' or goin'.'

Aunt Edie gave in to her own feelings then. She put her hands on his shoulders, lifted her face and kissed him, on the mouth. 'There,' she said softly. 'It's up to you, Jack. Anytime.'

'Jesus, Edie, have a heart.'

'You know where I live,' said Aunt Edie

'Lord give me strength,' said Dad.

Jimmy, Patsy and Betsy thought Aunt Edie a really warm and lovely woman that weekend. She went about singing, she did the washing, she did the cooking and she fussed everyone, including Dad. And when they all went strolling around Ruskin Park on Sunday afternoon she looked the handsomest and most mellow woman there, her hat sailing serenely along with her. The funny thing was, Dad kept frowning a lot, as if he didn't approve of Aunt Edie looking a real picture.

CHAPTER EIGHTEEN

It was remarkable how Father Peter's darkly gaunt face could express the kind of reassuring benevolence that induced so much faith and devotion in his lady followers. It was a smiling benevolence he bestowed on Mother Verity one morning when she said she would like to go about her charitable work independently some days.

'Sister, you are entirely free to come and go,' he said. 'Just as you have been doing of late.'

'My own personal endeavours accord with the work of the League,' said Mother Verity, whose doubts about the organization were not directed at the minister's followers. 'They concern redemption.'

'Splendid,' said Father Peter. 'Go your way, sister, whenever you feel the need to. I hope, however, you will be among us when we make our distribution of clothing and footwear. It will be on a grand scale. Our collections are bearing magnificent fruit.'

'I know, and am happy about it,' said Mother Verity, and made her way out of the Temple, leaving Father Peter sighing over her charming nature.

'Well, I tell you what, missus,' said the Bethnal Green newsagent, 'if there's nothing on any of the window cards with a suitable address, you might try Mrs Hitchins. I believe she's thinkin' about lettin' a couple of rooms.'

'Do you know this lady's address?' asked Mother Verity.

'Fifteen Underwood Road.'

'Thank you,' said Mother Verity, elated at such good fortune.

Mrs Hitchins was a jolly person, whose only real grumble was about the fact that winning the war hadn't done the country much good, or the people, either. 'I mean, when you think about it,' she said, leading the way up the stairs of her house. Only a few minutes conversation with the lady caller had helped her to make up her mind to let the two rooms that weren't being used. Such a nice lady. 'All that money and all them soldiers' lives spent on beatin' that German Kaiser, an' look where it's got us. Goin' backwards, me 'usband says. We was thankful we only 'ad daughters and no sons, specially as our daughters 'as all been married since the Armistice. We're grandparents now, which we wouldn't 'ave been if they'd all been sons and all been killed in the war. Well, that's the bedroom I'm able to offer, it's at the back, and the room you can use for livin' in, it's at the front.'

Both rooms were clean and well-kept. Mother Verity had an aversion to anything that spoke of dirt and spiders, although she could face up bravely to the task of eliminating same.

'How very nice, Mrs Hitchins,' she said, glancing around the furnished bedroom.

'Well, I hope so, Miss Stokes, you bein' a lady, as I can see.'

As for the living room, which at present had a bed in it in addition to suitable furniture, its position could not have been better. Through its window it looked directly on to the house opposite, number fourteen.

'May I take the rooms, Mrs Hitchins?'

'A pleasure, I'm sure,' said Mrs Hitchins, 'you don't mind seven an' six a week for the two? Me an' me 'usband won't disturb you, we sleep downstairs, so we won't be comin' up and down. It's only our youngest daughter that comes and stays sometimes, with 'er 'usband. Well, they live up in Essex, so they stay the night when they come at weekends, usin' the third room up here. When would you like to move in?'

'I'm not quite sure,' said Mother Verity, 'but I must be fair, I'll start renting the rooms from tomorrow and perhaps use them occasionally before I move in permanently.' She had a small independent income that would easily take care of the rent.

'Oh, I don't know as I should charge you if you're not here,' said Mrs Hitchins.

'But you must, that's only fair.'

'You're a lady all right, Miss Stokes, and I'm that pleased to 'ave been able to oblige you.'

Mother Verity was extremely pleased to have found such suitably located rooms and to discover the landlady such an agreeable person. They settled the matter very amicably, and Mother Verity paid the first week's rent in advance, as was customary.

And Bethnal Green itself really was an improvement on Whitechapel.

'She's home,' said Ada when she opened the door to Jimmy on Thursday morning.

'Pardon?' said Jimmy cautiously.

'The young madam. The roof's not fallen in yet, but it won't be long. Madam and sir arrived back with her last night, and it's sounded ever since as if there's a train engine in the house.'

'I'd better keep out of its way, then,' said Jimmy,

following Ada through to the kitchen. 'I'm not ready at my age to be run over. You can die from bein' run over, Ada.'

'I bet it hurts too,' said Ada. 'Here's our young lordship, Mr 'Odges, all ready to be eaten alive.'

'Nice and early, I see,' said Mr Hodges.

'Mornin', everyone,' said Jimmy. 'Hullo, Mrs Redfern, hullo, Ivy, did you have a good time in Devon?'

'Heavenly, for about five minutes a day,' said Mrs Redfern, and laughed. 'And how's our toast and marmalade boy? Give him a slice, Ivy, and I'll pour him a cup of tea.'

''E'll need more than a cup of tea,' said Ivy, ''e'll need the last meal of the condemned. Up at six she was this mornin', the young madam. Six, would yer believe, and I 'ad to get up and do a breakfast for 'er. Ate it in 'ere, she did, talkin' all the time, and jumpin' up an' down till the kitchen looked like the wreck of the 'Esperus. I dunno that that girl's ever goin' to grow up.'

The servants' bell buzzed. Mr Hodges looked at the indicator. 'Young madam's bedroom,' he said. 'Kindly proceed at the double, Ada.'

'Help,' said Ada, 'she hasn't gone back to bed, has she?' She went to answer the summons.

'P'raps she's broke a leg,' said Ivy hopefully.

'You been gettin' on all right, Jimmy?' asked cook.

'Fine,' said Jimmy.

'My, you're browner than the family is, choppin' trees up suits you.'

'Poor young feller,' said Ivy.

'Now, Ivy, you've been saying things like that ever since Jimmy started to work here,' said Mrs Redfern. 'Time you looked on the bright side.'

Ada returned.

'What did Miss Sophy want?' asked Mr Hodges.

Ada smiled. 'To ask if Jimmy had arrived.'

'Oh, gawd,' said Ivy.

'What was she doing?' asked Mr Hodges.

'Loadin' a pistol,' said Ada.

'Now, Ada, don't give Jimmy frights like that,' said cook.

'What've I done?' asked Jimmy.

'Yes, you may well ask,' said Ada accusingly.

'It's my fault,' said Ivy. 'Well, there she was, turnin' the kitchen upside-down and me 'aving to get 'er a breakfast. She asked if I knew 'ow you'd been gettin' on, Jimmy. So I told 'er you'd been gettin' on fine, 'specially with the girl next door, accordin' to what Ada said when we got back last evenin'.'

'Next door? What next door?' asked Jimmy. Next door to him was only a dividing brick wall away. There was no real next door here. The houses on either side of The Beeches were the distance of a street away.

'Now then, Jimmy, you did get on well with Clarissa March,' said Ada.

'Oh, that girl,' said Jimmy. On Tuesday afternoon, a girl had emerged from the jungle on the far left of the property. She had a chat to nearby workmen, then made her way up to Jimmy. She was quite nice, even if she talked posh, and was just fourteen. She was interested in what was going on, her name was Clarissa March from Willow Lodge, next to The Beeches. Jimmy had a very friendly chat with her, and she said all boys ought to be doing his kind of work, because it gave them a healthy look instead of pimples. Farmers' sons didn't have pimples, she said. Pimply boys were ugh. Jimmy said if he ever got pimples he'd swop faces with a farmer's son, and Clarissa though that screamingly funny. She turned up again the following afternoon with a bag of apples, which she shared with Jimmy. She didn't mind a bit that he wasn't posh like she was.

'You should've seen the young madam's face,' said Ivy gloomily, with Ada restraining giggles. 'She asked me if I meant Clarissa March, and I said Ada 'ad told me it was. I feel awful that today's goin' to see you carried off to yer funeral, Jimmy. You better 'ave another piece of toast, it might be yer last.'

'I don't see why,' said Jimmy, 'I'm nobody, except me dad and mum's one and only son.'

'Oh, you're the young madam's pet as well,' said Mrs Redfern, giving Ada a plump wink.

'I saw that, Mrs Redfern,' said Jimmy.

'Don't you worry, Jimmy, we'll send a nice wreath,' said Mrs Redfern.

'And our respectful wishes that you'll be 'appy in 'eaven,' said Ada, who found it a lovely lark to tease him. She knew Jimmy would have his own back one way or another. You couldn't tease Percy. He just talked over it, he just didn't recognize it, he just talked and talked, he didn't half like the sound of his own voice. Not that he didn't have some likeable ways, only although he was two years older than Jimmy, he didn't seem as grown up.

'I will make a contribution myself,' announced Mr Hodges in dignified sympathy.

'Oh, yer poor lad, Jimmy,' said Ivy.

'All right, I'll go quietly,' said Jimmy. 'I suppose I'll 'ave to,' he added, 'if I'm dead.'

Ada stifled shrieks, and cook laughed until her tears run.

'You're a one, you are, Jimmy,' she said.

'Well, I'd better go an' do some work while I'm still alive,' he said.

Ada followed him out to the terrace. 'It's awful for you, Jimmy, bein' the young madam's pet and goin' to your doom because of it. Still, it's been really nice knowin' you.'

'Nice knowin' you too, Ada,' said Jimmy, and took something from his jacket pocket. 'Here, this is me deathbed gift to you.' And he put a half-pound bar of Peters milk chocolate into her hand. Ada's eyes opened wide.

'For me, it's for me?' she said.

'You've been a nice kind girl to me,' said Jimmy, ''specially while the fam'ly's been away. Mind, I'm watchin' you, young Ada, and all your sauce, I know when you're bein' larky.'

'Jimmy, thanks ever so much for this,' said Ada.

'Pleasure,' said Jimmy, and went down to his work, in the September sunshine. Patsy and Betsy would be going back to school next week, and Mother would probably still be absent. And on Monday he was going to start work at Mr Gibb's furniture factory in Peckham for a pound a week. He began to whistle.

The landscape gardeners were already at work, and had been since eight o'clock. They'd cleared some huge areas, each of which looked yellow. Little hills of charred bonfires showed silvery grey peppered with black. Groups of beeches, oaks and chestnuts had been left standing, so had a huge willow close to that quagmire of a pond. Farther down, the gardeners had created potential magic by ridding a large mass of high rhododendrons of unwanted saplings and parasitical undergrowth. Jimmy had learned enough from Mr Thorpe to know that that magic would appear in the spring, when the rhododendrons would burst into colour. He felt, not enviously, that when the whole job was finished, Mr and Mrs Gibbs would wake up to something really worth looking at every morning. It would be like living in the country.

He began his usual work of tidying up. That was what he'd been doing every day, tidying up. But Mr Thorpe had said to him, don't you worry, lad, tidying up's got its place in this kind of work, ground like this can't be turned over if it's not been tidied up and tree roots pulled out by a team of horses. All the burning that's been done, that's part of it too, all the ashes will be spread like potash and dug in. It won't be wasted, don't you worry.

Mrs March of Willow Lodge was in her rose garden, brimmed hat shading her face, secateurs in her hand and a trug on her arm. She was snipping dead blooms.

'Oh, hullo, Mrs March.'

Mrs March jumped and turned. 'Oh, it's you, Sophy,' she said, smile a little wary. The daughter of her newest neighbours was already known as a terror. 'How did you get in?'

'I came round the side,' said Sophy, looking healthy from the sea air of Devon and demure in a blue frock worn with a sweet smile. She had a small white cardboard box in her hand.

'Did you enjoy Devon?'

'Oh, jolly famous,' said Sophy. 'Is Clarissa in?'

'She's down in the summerhouse, reading,' said Mrs March. 'She's going out with a friend in half an hour.'

'Oh, jolly good, Mrs March, I'll just go and say hullo to her. I've got a little Devon cake for her. We're back at school next Tuesday, what a life. Aren't your roses lovely?'

'Would you like some for your mother?' asked Mrs March, thinking a neighbourly gesture might perhaps save her husband's greenhouse from accidental destruction by

Sophy. But Sophy was already on her way to the summerhouse. She wasn't there long. She came back, smiling winsomely at Clarissa's mother, who had cut some lovely blooms for her.

'Oh, that's awfully kind of you, Mrs March, Mummy will love them. We don't have anything in our garden, you know. Well, we don't even have a garden, just a half-cleared jungle.'

'You're very welcome to these, Sophy, but mind the thorns on your dress. Did you see Clarissa?'

'Yes, thank you, Mrs March, I gave her the little cake. Goodbye.'

My, she has improved all of a sudden, thought Mrs March.

Clarissa didn't think so. Down in the summerhouse, where she'd been enjoying a gripping novel by Ethel M. Dell, she was trying to clean her face with her hankie. Sophy had plastered it with a wet mud cake. Clarissa dared not complain to her mother. Sophy had threatened to put a frog down her drawers if she did. Clarissa shuddered at the mere thought.

Sophy the Dreadful struck again. This time from behind. Jimmy fell headlong into the foundations of a new bonfire he was building.

'Oh, sorry,' said Sophy, 'I didn't see you.'

Jimmy rolled off the ruined cradle and came to his feet. 'That's all right,' he said, 'I sometimes don't look where I'm goin' myself. I walked into a door once. It didn't half get ratty, it knocked me over. You're back, I see.'

'Excuse me,' said Sophy, a colourful but haughty sprite of the morning. 'Are you the boy who spends all his time talking to girls instead of getting on with your work?'

'No, I'm the other one,' said Jimmy.

'What other one?'

'The one who keeps gettin' tripped up by some potty girl who looks a bit like you,' said Jimmy.

'Oh, that one,' said Sophy.

'Enjoy your 'oliday?' said Jimmy. 'Thanks for sendin' me a card, by the way.'

'I noticed you didn't send me one. Too busy getting off with soppy girls, I suppose, you sickening boy. I've a good mind to push you under a bus.'

'Yes, well, I can't stand about talkin' to peculiar girls,' said Jimmy, 'I've got me wages to earn.'

'I've not come to help you, you know,' said Sophy.

'Hooray,' said Jimmy, 'I've got a chance of goin' home alive.'

'Well, you haven't got any chance of seeing Clarissa March again. She's fallen into a mudhole.'

'Point is, did she fall or was she pushed?' said Jimmy.

'Just let it be a lesson to you, Jimmy Andrews. Still, I might just come and help you this afternoon.'

And she did. She gave him a terrible time, and all because of Clarissa March. Sophy regarded Jimmy as her own private property.

'Dad,' said Betsy that evening, 'ain't our mum ever comin' 'ome again?'

'Well, I'll give 'er a bit more time, pickle,' said Dad, 'then I'll go and fetch her. We can't expect your Aunt Edie to keep fillin' in for her every weekend.'

'I don't mind,' said Betsy.

'It's fun when Aunt Edie's here,' said Patsy.

Jimmy looked at Dad. Dad grimaced. But there it was, his girls didn't think very much of their mum. Nor was he too pleased with her himself. She'd left him with all kinds of problems, including a new one, a hell of a one.

'I might be 'ome from work a bit late tomorrow,' he said, 'so don't wait supper on me.'

'All right, Dad, we'll keep yours 'ot,' said Patsy. She felt for him. So did Jimmy. Patsy, in the event of a parental bust-up, wasn't going to be on anyone's side but her dad's. And she knew that while Jimmy would think poor old Mum, he had too much liking and respect for Dad not to give him support. As for young Betsy, although she missed her mum, it was Dad who gave her cuddles and affection. Her mum's funny ways and strange talk made her feel uncomfortable.

It was Friday evening. Opening the door of the Temple, Father Luke looked at the caller and said, 'What can we do for – 'ere, I know you.'

'Right first time,' said Dad.

'You're not comin' in 'ere,' said Father Luke, and tried to close the door. Dad put his foot in the way. In his brown cap, durable brown jacket and his working corduroys, he looked formidable to Father Luke, who had seen him treat Mother Mary with heathen disrespect.

'Don't play about,' said Dad, 'just fetch my wife down. I don't mind waitin' sixty seconds. In here.' He pushed the door wide open and stepped into the hall. Father Luke's portly figure suffered spasms of uneasiness.

'I 'ope you'll conduct yerself Christian-like in this 'ouse of penitence,' he said. 'The Lord 'as given us 'Is blessin'.'

'Well, the Lord's got His 'eavenly ways, of course,' said Dad, 'and there's no tellin' who He'll bless, but if you don't get up those stairs double-quick and fetch my wife down, I'll give you me own kind of blessin'. Or I'll go up meself.'

'I'll ask the minister,' said Father Luke. After all, the minister was bigger than he was, and a bit bigger than this man, too, who'd come after Mother Mary once before.

'Sod the minister,' said Dad, 'get my wife.'

Father Luke beat a hasty retreat up the stairs. Dad waited a full minute, then made for the staircase, at which point Father Peter appeared, Mother beside him. From the landing they gazed down at Dad.

'What is your wish, sir?' boomed Father Peter.

'I've got no wishes,' said Dad, 'only intentions. Get your things packed, Maud, I'm takin' you home.'

'State who you are, sir,' demanded Father Peter, while Mother stared down at Dad with a puzzled look on her face.

'I'm her husband,' said Dad.

'What impertinence,' said Mother, 'I've never seen you before in all me life.'

'Game's up, Maud,' said Dad, 'so's your time 'ere. You're comin' 'ome. Pack your things.'

'I'll give you pack my things,' said Mother, and disappeared. Dad began to climb the stairs. Father Peter spread his wide shoulders and stood to oppose the intruder.

'Get you gone, sir. Mother Mary has no wish to leave, and has disclaimed you. Depart from this house of God.'

'Now don't make me cross,' said Dad, reaching the landing. 'I don't like gettin' cross, and you won't like it, either.'

'That which a man claims but does not own shall be denied him,' said Father Peter.

'Stone the crows,' said Dad, 'you're all bleedin' barmy.' Mother reappeared. ''Ullo,' said Dad, 'that looks like another umbrella.'

Her new brolly raised, Mother went for him. 'I'll give you comin' 'ere and callin' yourself me 'usband!' she shouted, and down came the umbrella. Dad, fit and strong, dealt as easily with her as he had before. He disarmed her and threw the brolly down the stairs. 'Oh, you disgustin' 'eathen!' shouted Mother.

Other women were on the landing now, staring at the scene. Father Luke watched from a safe distance. 'Oh, 'ow dare you molest me!' Mother shook a fist at Dad.

'Pack your things,' said Dad again, 'an' stop shoutin'.'

But she shouted the more. Dad looked hard at her, seeing the flush on her face, the glitter in her eyes, and the impossible nature of her mood. What good would it do to bundle her out of this place and carry her home? And what would happen when he got her there? What good was she to her family the way she was now? Betsy would see her as a strange and crazy woman, and Patsy had too much spirit to put up with her for very long. Jimmy would be able to handle her to some extent, but was likely after a week or so to recommend taking her back to Bloomsbury. And who'd be able to stop her simply walking out whenever she liked?

Dad sighed. 'I feel sorry for you, Maud,' he said, and went back down the stairs and out of the place.

'Poor blighter,' said Mother Joan, 'I suppose he's some woman's husband who's taken a fancy to you, Mother Mary. Probably met you when you were giving out pamphlets, probably all set to go off his rocker. While some of us have seen the light, unfortunate persons like him only have hallucinations. A cousin of mine had a fatal hallucination several years ago, and went skating on a lake she thought was frozen. Middle of the summer, actually. Sank without trace. Couldn't swim, poor woman. Right, buck up, Mother Mary, it's all over.'

After supper Dad spoke privately again to Aunt Edie, who had arrived for one more weekend. He'd said nothing so far about his visit to Bloomsbury. Now he told Aunt Edie what had happened there.

'I see,' said Aunt Edie, 'so that was why you were late 'ome, you went there from work. Well, I pity Maud for what she's doin' to 'erself, but for what she's doin' to 'er fam'ly I could knock 'er silly head off.'

'The point is, Edie, it's gettin' unfair on you,' said Dad. 'You've got your own life to live, we can't ask you to give up all your weekends on our account. We've got to face up to managin' by ourselves.'

'Yes, and I daresay you could manage to some extent,' said Aunt Edie. 'I daresay Patsy could turn 'erself into a mother figure, but 'ow fair would that be on 'er? Life's 'ard enough as it is without askin' a girl of Patsy's age to take on the job that Maud should be doin'.'

'We'd all muck in,' said Dad, 'we all ought to stand on our own feet and give you a break.' He was at the window of the parlour, looking out at the street, his back to Aunt Edie. She knew why.

'Don't make me spit, Jack Andrews,' she said. 'We've already talked about this, and you know 'ow I feel about you and the fam'ly. In any case, if it comes down to what's right, I'm as good as your children's aunt and I wouldn't be much of a one if I let Patsy do what I know I should be doin'.'

'Edie, you've got to do a bit of livin' for yourself,' said Dad.

'Well, I'm fed up with livin' just for meself. If Maud does go right over the top, like I think she will, I'm goin' to come and look after all of you permanent, as I said before. D'you hear that, Jack?'

'We've got problems, Edie.'

'Well, we'll 'ave to work on them, won't we, love?'

*

'Mrs Hitchins?' called Mother Verity from the passage.

Mrs Hitchins came out of her kitchen and smiled at her quietly-dressed lodger. 'Oh, you're goin' now, Miss Stokes?'

'Yes, I've put away the few things I brought.' Mother Verity had been in her rooms for a while, and from her front window had again seen little Lulu come home from school. 'I must thank you for taking the bed out of the living room.'

'That's all right, me 'usband did that, it's made more space for you, I 'ope.'

'It's all very comfortable, Mrs Hitchins. By the way, I noticed a hall close to the church. Do you know if it can be used for the benefit of the public?'

'Oh, yes, just ask the vicar,' said Mrs Hitchins.

'I will. Mrs Hitchins, are there poor people around here who are in need of clothes and footwear?'

'I don't know when there 'asn't been,' said Mrs Hitchins, 'and the war 'asn't made it no better. I don't know why we bothered to win it.'

'Perhaps I could arrange a distribution to needy families in the hall,' said Mother Verity. 'I do charity work among the poor, you see.'

'Oh, like the Salvation Army,' said Mrs Hitchins brightly.

'Yes, quite like them.'

'You're a kind lady, Miss Stokes.'

'Oh, I'm very ordinary, Mrs Hitchins. Thank you for everything.'

'A pleasure,' said Mrs Hitchins, 'and me 'usband and me'll look forward to you movin' in permanent when you're ready.'

Mother Verity returned to Bloomsbury in time for dinner, over which she was told about the aggressive man who had called in a misguided attempt to claim Mother Mary as his wife.

'I gave 'im something, I can tell you,' said Mother Mary.

'But you are married, you do have a husband, don't you?' said Mother Verity gently.

'My place is now with the Lord,' said Mother Mary, and other little doubts began to assail Mother Verity. She addressed Father Peter, telling him she had decided to help the poor people of Bethnal Green, and that Mother Ruth had promised to assist her.

'I commend you, Mother Verity,' intoned Father Peter from the head of the table. 'I should say we are planning a splendid return to Whitechapel, with perhaps enough garments to clothe the Lord's five thousand.'

'You must spare some for Bethnal Green families,' said Mother Verity firmly, and met the dark enquiring eyes of the minister without a flutter.

'Of course, of course, sister,' he said, 'we must all pursue our work in the way the Lord guides us, and if He has guided you to Bethnal Green, go there, by all means. Clothe the poor and do what you can for those who are hungered, but show them that the way to Christian worthiness is not by bread alone.'

'That's the stuff,' said Mother Joan, tucking in to steak and kidney pie with the relish of an energetic Christian woman who had today forged another cheque to help the cause, this time for a huge consignment of children's boots from Isaac's Warehouse.

On Saturday afternoon, Sophy sat on the terrace steps with Jimmy. They were drinking tea and eating fruit cake. It was the first time today that Mrs Gibbs had allowed her daughter to hob-nob with Jimmy. Much as she liked the boy, she knew it would be unwise to encourage the development of a close friendship. The respective families were poles apart, and in any case Sophy would get bored eventually and Jimmy would suddenly find she had no more interest in him than in a stable boy.

Sophy, denied permission to spend time with Jimmy, became furious in the end, threatening to go up to her room, pull her bed to pieces and chuck it all out of the window. Didn't her mother realize it was Jimmy's last day here?

'Yes, I realize it,' said Mrs Gibbs, 'but if you throw your bed out of the window bit by bit, then you'll go down and pick it all up bit by bit.'

'Doesn't it give you a pain, Mummy, being such a dragon to your only daughter?'

'It gives me more of a pain to know you'd actually do that to your bed,' said Mrs Gibbs, 'but very well, when Ada takes a cup of tea out to Jimmy, you can have a cup with him.'

'It's a relief you've got some good points, Mummy,' said Sophy. 'I expect when Jimmy's working at the factory, you'll let me invite him to Sunday tea once a week.'

Mrs Gibbs did not respond to that. Sophy, however, mentioned it to Jimmy during his tea break.

'I expect you'll come most Sundays,' she said.

'Oh, every Sunday,' said Jimmy, 'in me pony and trap and top hat, and with gold sovereigns flashin' on me watch chain.'

'You didn't tell me your family had a pony and trap,' said Sophy.

'Didn't I? We've all got one each, and Dad drives a carriage and pair as well. Well, a van with shire horses, actually, for a firm of grocery wholesalers.'

'Oh, jolly good,' said Sophy, 'I bet that's a lot more fun

than minding a hole in the road, like some men do. But if your family's hard-up, how'd you all manage to have ponies and traps?'

'That was a joke,' said Jimmy. 'Anyway, I can't come to tea unless your parents invite me.'

'All right,' said Sophy crossly, 'don't come, then.'

'No, all right,' said Jimmy, at which Sophy came to her feet, picked up the tin kitchen tray on which Ada had brought the tea and cake, and smote Jimmy's head with it. The tray clanged and quivered. Jimmy blinked.

'Sophy!' Mrs Gibbs called in shock from an open upstairs window. 'Come up here at once!'

'Oh, blimey,' breathed Sophy. She dropped the tray and looked up at her mother. 'I just accidentally—'

'Come up here! Now!'

Sophy, making a face, went into the house and up to the parental bedroom. There, her mother eyed her in anger.

'Did I do something?' asked Sophy.

'You precocious horror,' said Mrs Gibbs, 'you've just placed one straw too many on the camel's back. It's a boarding-school for you.'

'Boarding-school?' Sophy looked aghast. 'Mummy, you can't, it's all girls and hockey sticks, and it's prison as well.'

'Good,' said Mrs Gibbs.

'Mummy—'

'No arguments,' said Mrs Gibbs. She spoke to her husband later.

'Isn't it a bit late to start her at a boarding-school?' he asked.

'She can have four years at one, from now until she's seventeen,' said Mrs Gibbs. 'It's the only chance we have of civilizing her.'

'She won't like it.'

'She's running wild, Frank. We'll take her down to Sussex tomorrow and see if the headmistress of Hurstfield School will enrol her immediately.'

'I'd rather—'

'Yes, I know, you'd rather keep on spoiling her. She'll end up being burned at the stake. It's our responsibility to save her from that. Take my word for it.'

Mr Gibbs was forced to concur.

'Well, I'll be off now, Mr Gibbs,' said Jimmy, his work finished for the day. Mr Gibbs had been working with him for the last hour, and they had had some man-to-man talk.

'Right, Jimmy.' Mr Gibbs fished around in the back pocket of his trousers and came up with a ten-bob note. 'Here.'

'Thanks, Mr Gibbs, I've got some change.'

'No, it's all yours, Jimmy. You've earned a little extra. Treat yourself. You're all set to start at Peckham on Monday?'

'I'll be there, Mr Gibbs,' said Jimmy. 'Thanks a lot for the extra money, it's been a pleasure doin' this kind of work. I've got an idea you're goin' to have something really worth lookin' at when it's all finished.'

'If it isn't,' smiled Mr Gibbs, 'somebody's going to get the sack. Hop off home, Jimmy.'

Sophy was waiting for him on the terrace and full of the woes of being sent to a boarding-school. There'd only be girls, she said, and they'd all be soppy. Jimmy said cheer up, you'll be able to lick them all into shape, and the teachers as well, probably. Sophy said she didn't think that was very funny, and that he had better write to her or she'd send somebody to throw a bomb at him. She asked for his address. Jimmy demurred. Sophy said she'd kick him off the terrace if he didn't give it to her. He gave it to her to save himself having to go home in an injured state, but said she need only send him a Christmas card.

'Just do as you're told,' said Sophy, 'when I write to you, you write back. All right, you can kiss me farewell now, but I don't want a soppy one.'

Jimmy, looking up at a window, said, 'Hullo, is that you, Mrs Gibbs?' Sophy fled.

Mrs Gibbs came out by way of the conservatory. 'Did I hear you call, Jimmy?' she asked.

'I thought I saw you up at the window, Mrs Gibbs.'

'Well, I'm here now. So, you've finished here and are starting at Peckham on Monday. We'll miss you.'

'And I'll miss you, Mrs Gibbs, all of you. You've all been really kind to me. Mind you, Mr Gibbs said I can come back here as a junior gardener if I don't get on too well at the factory.'

'I think you'll get on very well,' said Mrs Gibbs. 'And thank you, Jimmy, for putting up with Sophy.'

'I hear she's goin' to a boardin'-school,' said Jimmy.

'I hope she doesn't set it on fire,' said Mrs Gibbs, thinking not for the first time how much she liked the boy.

'Well, if she does, I expect she'll take charge of the fire brigade when it arrives,' said Jimmy, 'I expect she'll see they put it out. Thanks for everything, Mrs Gibbs, and goodbye.'

'Goodbye, Jimmy.'

He went into the kitchen next to say goodbye to the staff.

'Best of luck, Jimmy,' said Mrs Redfern who was busy preparing dinner.

'I am pleased to hoffer you my own best wishes, my boy,' said Mr Hodges.

'What a young 'ero,' said Ivy. ''E's still alive, would yer

believe, Mr 'Odges, and 'e's still got both 'is arms and legs.'

'Where's Ada?' asked Jimmy.

'She's busy in the dining room,' said Mr Hodges, 'but we will convey your kind regards to her.'

'Yes, wish her luck,' said Jimmy, who would have liked to say goodbye in person. 'Well, so long, everyone, thanks for all the tea and toast and everything else.'

Going down the drive to the gates, he heard quick footsteps on the gravel behind him. He stopped and turned. Ada came running up, the skirt of her dress whisking.

'Oh, you mean thing, goin' without sayin' goodbye to me,' she said.

'Well, I meant to, but you were busy,' said Jimmy. 'Yes, it's me final farewells, Ada. You've all been corkin', as good as me own fam'ly. Give me best wishes to your dad when you next see 'im.'

'What for?' asked Ada, little white cap looking as perky as ever. 'You don't know my dad.'

'No, but I do know he's got your welfare close to his heart,' said Jimmy, 'you told me so. Well, more or less, like.'

'You're still dotty,' said Ada.

'Look at that up in that tree,' said Jimmy, 'I've never seen anything like that before.'

Ada looked up at the tree. Jimmy kissed her. Ada went quite pink.

'Oh, cheeky,' she said.

'Sorry, Ada, couldn't help meself.'

'I didn't mind, silly. Oh, I've got to get back, but you'll come and see us sometimes, won't you? I mean, whenever you're near enough.'

'I'll do that,' said Jimmy, 'and send you a Christmas

card as well. You're a nice girl, Ada, I wish you all the best. So long.'

'So long, Jimmy.' Ada watched him go, her eyes moist. She wrote to Percy that night, telling him she didn't want to go out with him any more.

CHAPTER NINETEEN

On Monday morning, Jimmy and Dad both had to be at work by eight o'clock, and Aunt Edie, rising early, saw to it that they put a good breakfast inside them before they left. She wished Jimmy luck on his first day at the factory.

Mr Gibbs had two factories, one at Peckham and one near the Old Kent Road. In the latter, reproduction furniture was manufactured. War profiteers of an earthy kind bought it. The larger building at Peckham was really two factories, one for making furniture designed by Mr Gibbs and an assistant, the other for turning out wooden boxes and crates. Mr Gibbs divided his time between the design room, the furniture workshop, the administrative office and the Old Kent Road factory. At Peckham, he had a lady secretary who did all his typing, a girl who wrote out invoices and did the filing, and a book-keeper who looked after the accounts.

He almost always arrived at the same time as his workers, eight in the morning. He was already there when Jimmy appeared at five to eight, and he placed him in the charge of the box factory foreman, Alf Roberts. To Jimmy, the box factory was wood, benches, circular saws and sawdust. There was a market for sawdust.

'Right, Jimmy,' said Alf, 'come along with me.' Jimmy followed him to a bench on which were slats of wood, hammers and other carpenters' tools. There was also a

311

large tin of nails. 'Now, you can make an oggle box, can yer?'

'A what?' said Jimmy.

'Yer don't know what an oggle box is?' said Alf, a balding character of fifty years old.

'Well, I've got to be frank, Mr Roberts, I've never heard of oggle boxes,' said Jimmy. 'What are they?'

'Just wooden boxes with 'oles for the oggles,' said Alf. 'We made a lot of 'em durin' the war. Yer first job is to make one yerself. Two feet wide, three feet long, nine inches deep. Them slats there is nine-inchers. Them boards there is for the tops an' bottoms. Yer'll 'ave to do some sawin'. There's a saw. I'll get you a drawin' to 'elp you along. 'Ere, Dusty, before you start work, bring young Jimmy 'ere an oggle box drawin'.'

'I gotcher, Alf,' said a man. He opened the drawer of a wooden cabinet, rummaged around, drew out a folded sheet of paper and brought it over. ''Ullo, young 'un,' he said, 'bein' apprenticed, are yer? Well, we all 'ave to know 'ow to make oggle boxes.'

'That's a fact,' said Alf, taking the sheet of paper from Dusty Miller and unfolding it. 'The guv'nor's liable anytime to come and ask for someone to knock 'im up an oggle box quick. 'Ere y'ar, can yer foller this drawin'?'

The drawing was a neat pencil sketch of a box perforated by holes along the sides and in the top.

'I did some woodwork at school,' said Jimmy. 'I can follow this all right, Mr Roberts.'

'Well, yer sound a promisin' lad,' said Alf. 'All 'oles an inch in diameter. There's yer 'and drill, with an inch cutter. You can get goin'.'

Work had started. The circular saws were going, cutting through wood like a knife through butter. Sawdust was falling into large deep trays. At one end of the factory, men were assembling slats of cheap wood to put kipper boxes together at astonishing speed.

'Right, Mr Roberts,' said Jimmy. 'Could you tell me what an oggle box is for?'

'Made 'em particular special for the war, Jimmy,' said Alf, 'but I ain't allowed to tell yer what for. The guv'nor might tell yer when you show 'im yer finished one. Leave yer to it, lad. Oh, yer got to put 'oles in the bottom as well as the top.'

'I think I can put one together,' said Jimmy.

He went to work, measuring and sawing and cutting out holes. He wore a pair of overalls that he'd bought out of the money he'd earned at Anerley. Being fairly useful with his hands, he found the work no great problem. At ten o'clock, mugs of tea appeared, and he was given one. The men drank while working.

Mr Gibbs entered the workshop at ten-thirty to speak to Alf. He stopped at the bench Jimmy was using. 'What's that you're doing, Jimmy?' he asked.

'Makin' an oggle box, sir,' said Jimmy, beginning to worry about the time it was taking. Cutting out the holes and chiselling dovetails did take time.

'I see. Very good, Jimmy. Carry on.' He smiled and crossed the floor to speak to the foreman.

Jimmy finished the box at a quarter to twelve. He was quite proud of it, it had dovetailed together very nicely, with the aid of glue. He felt the box might have a livestock use. You could transport rabbits in it or pigeons. Alf came to inspect the results.

'Well, whadder yer know, that's an oggle box all right,' he said, 'yer can be proud of yerself, lad. Let's just 'ave a close look at yer dovetails. Well, not bad, not bad at all. Don't need much of a push to pass that as yer first bit of carpentry. Got all the 'oles in it, 'ave yer?'

'Six in the top, six in the bottom, four in each side and three in each end,' said Jimmy. 'I must say it looks a funny kind of box to me, Mr Roberts.'

'Funny? You better not tell the guv'nor that, me lad. All right, go an' show it to 'im.'

Men glanced as Jimmy carried the box through the workshop.

'Good luck, young 'un.'

'Nice job you made of that, Jimmy.'

'Dunno as I could put a better oggle box together meself.'

It was a puzzle to Jimmy, exactly what it was for. Leaving the workshop, he knocked on the door marked OFFICES.

'Come in,' said a female voice.

He went in. A thin woman sat at one desk, a plump girl at another.

'Hullo,' said the woman, 'are you the new hand, Jimmy Andrews?'

'That's me,' said Jimmy, 'good mornin'. Can I take this in to Mr Gibbs? The foreman asked me to.'

'Well, bless us, look at that,' said the plump girl. 'It's an oggle box.'

'So it is,' said the woman.

'Mr Gibbs'll like that,' said the girl.

'I'm sure,' said the woman. 'Knock on his door and take it in.'

'Thanks,' said Jimmy. He crossed to an inner door and knocked.

'Come in,' called Mr Gibbs, and Jimmy went in. Mr Gibbs, his jacket off, was in waistcoat, shirtsleeves and trousers, a sheaf of papers on his desk.

'Mr Roberts said to bring this to you, Mr Gibbs,' said Jimmy, showing the box that was full of circular holes.

'The oggle box? Stand it on the floor, Jimmy, end up.'

Jimmy did so. Mr Gibbs got up and walked around it, giving it an inspection.

'Is it all right, Mr Gibbs?'

'It's not bad, not bad at all, Jimmy.'

'Excuse me for askin', Mr Gibbs, but what's an oggle box for?'

'For oggles,' said Mr Gibbs. 'This one should be good for several.'

'Excuse me for askin' again, Mr Gibbs, but what's an oggle?'

Mr Gibbs consulted his pocket watch. 'Well, I've a minute or so, Jimmy, and I think I know you well enough to be able to let you into the secret. But keep it under your hat. It's like this.' Mr Gibbs explained. During the war he'd managed to get a contract for ammunition boxes. The product satisfying the War Office, the Admiralty asked him to tender for three hundred oggle boxes, sending a diagram of the design. The tender was accepted, the work secret, the purpose of the boxes secret too. They were delivered to Portsmouth and taken aboard a battleship. The crew asked what they were and were told oggle boxes. What were they for? No-one could say. Their purpose was secret. The officers asked the captain what they were for. The captain said he had no idea, he had only been advised that their purpose would be made known if the German Fleet attacked. Well, the German Fleet did attack, and the battleship was sunk. The captain and his crew took to the boats, and as the ship went down the sea was dotted with oggle boxes. They began to sink. 'And as they sank, Jimmy, their purpose was made known. They all went "Oggle, oggle, oggle."'

'Pardon?' said Jimmy.

'Yes, oggle, oggle, oggle,' said Mr Gibbs gravely.

Jimmy yelled with laughter. 'Mr Gibbs, I've been diddled an' done,' he said.

'It happens to every new hand in the box factory, Jimmy,' said Mr Gibbs, and then he was laughing too.

'What a sell,' said Jimmy.

'Not a bad oggle box, though,' said Mr Gibbs, 'you can take it back now.'

The hooter sounded then for the hour's midday break. Jimmy carried the box back, the plump girl giggling and the thin woman smiling as he passed through their office.

'I'm a mug,' said Jimmy.

The men roared with laughter when he returned.

'The guv'nor passed yer first bit of carpentry, lad?' asked Alf, the foreman.

'Yes, he said it would oggle all right.'

The men roared again. Jimmy grinned. He sat with them in the workshop, and while they ate their sandwiches, he ate those Aunt Edie had made for him. More mugs of tea came up.

After the break, he found what his real job was, carrying the trays of sawdust to an adjoining loading bay and emptying them into a huge crate. There were two crates, one for clean sawdust and the other for sawdust swept up from the floor. And he did the sweeping. The saws were always going, and there was always more sawdust.

'Don't fret, lad,' said Alf, during the afternoon. 'You'll get taught carpentry an' joinery, we'll turn yer into a chippie.'

'Well, I like a job with prospects,' said Jimmy.

'So yer should, Jimmy, so yer should.'

The family sat down to supper that evening. Aunt Edie had been seeing to meals at weekends, and during the week Patsy, with a little help from Betsy, was making a good job of the suppers. The two girls shopped in the East Street market, using money supplied by Dad, and Patsy knew how to spend it to the best advantage. Being on holiday she had taken her time, but she and Betsy would be back at school tomorrow, then they would have to shop after classes were over.

Dad, Patsy and Betsy all wanted to know how Jimmy's first day at Peckham had gone. He told them all about the factory and the sawdust. Dad said shifting sawdust didn't seem much of a job, and Betsy said Jimmy had brought some of it home, in his hair. Dad said well, don't go shaking your head about, Jimmy, or we'll get sawdust all over the floor and the kitchen will look like a pub.

'Yes, we don't want neighbours comin' in askin' for a pint of beer,' said Patsy.

'It's not goin' to be sawdust for ever,' said Jimmy. 'I'm goin' to be taught carpentry and joinery. Dad, d'you know what an oggle box is?'

'Oggle what?' asked Dad.

'Oggle box,' said Jimmy.

'I don't even know what an oggle is,' said Patsy.

'I don't eiver,' said Betsy.

So Jimmy told them the story of the secret wartime oggle boxes, and how they were designed to go oggle, oggle when they sank. Dad roared with laughter. Betsy and Patsy looked at each other.

'Jimmy can't 'elp it, Betsy, he was born daft,' said Patsy.

'What's Dad laughin' at?' asked Betsy.

'Oggle, oggle,' said Dad.

'Is oggles funny, then?' asked Betsy.

'Screamin',' said Patsy.

Joe Gosling was round at Aunt Edie's flat that evening,

making himself comfortable. He hadn't been invited. He'd knocked, and Aunt Edie had said she'd give him five minutes. After fifteen minutes he was still talking about the pearlies and how they were all looking forward to her being his concert partner. He himself, he said, was specially looking forward to something else, to him and her teaming up in a relationship highly recommendable to a widower like him and a lady like her.

'I'm not keepin' you, Joe, am I?' said Aunt Edie.

'Course you ain't, Edie me love,' said Joe, 'my time's your time, yer know.'

'Well, my time's busy this evenin',' said Aunt Edie, 'so hop it.'

'You're a caution, you are, Edie. Always was, always will be. No wonder I got a soft spot for yer. 'Ow about if I come straight out with it an' pop the question?'

'Well, you're a cheerful cuss, Joe, I'll say that much,' said Aunt Edie, 'but don't come straight out with it, just keep droppin' hints.'

'Ah, I got yer, Edie, give yer a bit more time, eh?' said Joe. 'Tell yer what, the pearlies are takin' some kids to Southend for the day Sunday week. We're givin' 'em a taste of the old sea air an' treatin' 'em to some cockles an' mussels. 'Ow would yer like to put yer pearly queen's outfit on again an' come with us? We've got the 'ire of a bus an' driver, an' we'll get the kids singing all the way there an' back. That's where you an' me come in, Edie, leadin' the singsong, eh? Can I put yer name down?'

'Nice of you, Joe, and sounds like a rousin' day out for the kids,' said Aunt Edie, 'but I've got special duties at weekends.'

'Blimey O'Reilly,' said Joe, 'yer cousin Maud's still makin' yer life 'ard for yer?'

'It's not hard for me,' said Aunt Edie, 'it's just me duty.'

'Still, it sounds a bit as if Jack Andrews is takin' advantage of yer good nature, Edie, which I don't favour meself. An' yer neglectin' the pearlies.'

'Nothing to do with you,' said Aunt Edie, rattled for once, 'mind your own business.'

Joe grinned. 'Sorry about me north-an'-south,' he said. 'Listen, was yer thinkin' of puttin' the kettle on?'

'No, I was thinkin' of doin' some ironing,' said Aunt Edie, 'so be a good bloke and hop it.'

'Well, I ain't one to get in yer way, love, yer know that,' said Joe, but it was another fifteen minutes before Aunt Edie was finally able to get rid of him.

It left her thinking again about her life and her need to change it.

The vicar at Bethnal Green was very co-operative. He liked the look of Mother Verity and Mother Ruth, and the sound of the work they were doing. The idea of making a distribution of clothes and footwear to his needier parishioners could not be resisted. He said they could use the church hall on Friday, and that he himself would make a list of the poorest families, and arrange for the relevant mothers to come to the hall at times convenient to them during the day. How would that do?

'Splendidly, vicar,' said Mother Verity. 'We'll bring everything early on Friday morning.'

'Yes, how kind,' said Mother Ruth.

'We mean, if we can, to make regular distributions of the same kind,' said Mother Verity.

Late that evening, after supper and after a long day collecting clothes from the affluent, Mother Magda was groaning, although not from weariness.

'Oh, I don't 'ardly know 'ow to say it, Father,' she

breathed, 'but I still get terrible passionate – oh, lor' – oh—'

'Hush, my child,' murmured Father Peter, 'remember we are fighting Satan together.'

First thing after breakfast at the Temple on Friday morning, Mother Joan drove the horse and van to the church hall at Bethnal Green, and helped Mother Verity and Mother Ruth unload huge piles of clothing and footwear. The vicar was there, and had put up trestle tables in the hall.

From ten o'clock until four, the mothers of families in need came to the hall to collect the most suitable items. They came in ones or two's, at regular intervals, and Mother Verity and Mother Ruth were touched by their gratitude, especially in the matter of children's boots.

'Oh, me boys Johnny an' Charlie'll be able to go to school now, I just ain't 'ad the 'eart to send 'em with nothing on their feet. Bless yer, missus.' That was the kind of thing that was said.

There was very little left by the time things died down at four o'clock. Mother Verity sent Mother Ruth home to the Temple then, saying she herself had a few other things to do. Mother Ruth left. A few moments later, two inquisitive little girls, on their way home from school, looked in.

'Cor, what yer been' doin', missus?' asked one.

'Giving out clothes,' said Mother Verity with a smile.

'Oh,' said the other little girl, 'it's you.'

'Why, hullo, Lulu, imagine seeing you,' said Mother Verity.

'Who's she?' asked the first little girl of Lulu.

'She's a nice lady,' said Lulu, 'she give me a frock once, she knows me Uncle Will.'

'You're living with him now?' said Mother Verity.

'Yes, just round the corner,' said Lulu shyly.

'That's good.' Mother Verity's smile masked her deeper feelings. Here was a child of no more than six or seven who had been sold by her father for half a crown. Was there redemption for such men? Yet perhaps that was unimportant when weighed against the probability that the day Will Fletcher took her away with him was the happiest of the child's life. She looked happy, and she also looked neat and clean. There was no sign that she was suffering neglect, and her eyes were not big with hunger. Mother Verity felt very glad for her, and extraordinarily pleased with Mr Fletcher.

'Me an' Lily's got to go 'ome now,' said Lulu.

'Yes, of course.'

'Goo'bye,' said both little girls and disappeared.

Later, from behind the curtains of her room, Mother Verity saw Will Fletcher arrive at his lodgings. He was home from work, of course. He was carrying his jacket over his arm, and the sleeves of his jersey were rolled up. His cap was on the back of his head, a sign among cockneys, Mother Verity had found, that they were in good spirits. He opened the front door of the house by a pull on the latchcord. He stood on the doorstep for a few moments, and then Lulu appeared. He reached and took her up in his arms, and they laughed at each other. Then he carried her in, closing the door with his right heel.

Mother Verity noted the time. Ten past five. Underwood Road, Bethnal Green, was only a stone's throw from Spitalfields, where he worked. His working day was from eight till five.

In the upstairs back room of the house, Lulu, after some preliminary chatter, said, 'I seen the nice lady today.'

'What nice lady?' asked Will, beginning the preparation of a meal.

Lulu's little smile was knowing. 'The one you kissed,' she said.

'That one? Lulu, now didn't I tell you to forget that? Where'd you see 'er?'

'In the 'all,' said Lulu, 'round the corner.'

'The church hall?'

'When me an' Lily come out of school.'

'Flamin' arrows,' said Will, 'she was in the church hall?'

'She said 'ullo, Uncle Will.'

'Didn't I say so, didn't I tell 'er she was hauntin' me? Gawd 'elp me, Lulu, she'll be on our doorstep next, askin' how me soul's gettin' on. Did you let on where we're livin'?'

'She didn't ask,' said Lulu.

'I'll lay a quid she didn't need to,' said Will, lighting a gas ring and putting thick rashers of bacon into a frying-pan. 'I'll lay a quid she'll get the Lord to guide 'er to our door. Ruddy 'ell, then what?'

'Could we ask 'er to come in and 'ave a cup of tea?' suggested Lulu.

'Give over, sweet'eart, I'm not goin' to be haunted over a cup of tea. I'll let you into a secret. When a lady like 'er knocks at yer door, you don't answer it. Otherwise she'll 'ave us down on our knees sayin' the Lord's prayer. Let's hope it was just a coincidence, her bein' in the church hall. Did she ask about me?'

'No,' said Lulu.

'That's something,' said Will, and ruffled the girl's hair. 'I don't fancy gettin' another lickin', me pet.'

Lulu giggled.

Mother Verity was on her way back to the Temple of Christian Endeavour, very happy about things. At the Temple, Mother Mary was threatening to give Father Luke a taste of her umbrella. He'd bumped into a chair and exclaimed, 'Oh, me bleedin' knee.' Disgusting, she said.

Aunt Edie had arrived at Manor Place to spend another helpful weekend with the family. Over supper, Jimmy told her the story of the oggle boxes. Aunt Edie fell about. She laughed so much that hilarity reigned, although Betsy still couldn't work out what was funny about it, and said so.

'Well, you need to be a sailor to see that it's comic,' said Jimmy.

'You ain't a sailor,' protested Betsy.

'No, but I know one,' said Jimmy.

'I fink me bruvver's goin' potty, Aunt Edie,' said Betsy.

'Goin'? He's gone,' said Patsy, keeping quiet about a boy and girl in her class at school, who'd made rotten remarks about her dad and Aunt Edie.

'Did I ever mention the time when Private Walker of me old battalion went potty?' said Dad. 'The desert heat got at 'im. Well, it nearly cooked blokes sometimes, nearly melted us down to gravy. There he was, poor old Andy Walker, dancin' about in just 'is shirt tails. Up came the sergeant-major.'

'Here we go,' said Aunt Edie.

'Gospel truth,' said Dad, enjoying his supper. '"What's that man doin'?" bawled the sergeant-major. Private Walker was actu'lly doin' the dance of the fairies. "Private Walker, what you up to?" roared the sergeant-major. "You're dressed unbecomin'," he shouted. "Hullo, sergeant-major," said Private Walker, "d'yer like me new frock, and would yer like to 'ave the last waltz with me?"'

Patsy shrieked. Aunt Edie choked on cauliflower. Jimmy grinned, and Betsy's giggles interfered with her mouthful of mashed potato.

'I'm dyin',' gasped Aunt Edie, 'I knew that sergeant-major of yours was goin' to be the death of me, Jack Andrews.'

'Funny you should say that,' said Dad, 'the whole battalion only just got out alive themselves.'

'Patsy, hit your dad for me,' said Aunt Edie.

'Dad's funnier than oggle boxes,' said Betsy.

When Jimmy got home from his Saturday morning's work amid the sawdust, there was a letter for him. It had a Sussex postmark. He opened it, Patsy watching him. It was headed, Hurstfield Boarding-School for Young Ladies, Hurstfield, Sussex.

Dear Blessed Boy,

Look, it's actually happened, I've been sent here by Mummy, isn't it awful what mothers can do to their daughters, I bet your mother's not like that, I bet she wouldn't send you to a boarding-school, specially one full of soppy girls. Some of them talk so posh they sound like plum pie and custard. It was all your fault for letting your head come up and bang against that tray I was holding last Saturday. I've been here since Tuesday, and everything I want to do is against the rules. I notice you haven't written to me, I suppose you'll say you didn't know my address, but Daddy could have given it to you. You'd better write soon or I'll escape from here and saw your legs off.

Your best friend, Sophy.

Jimmy grinned.

'Who's it from?' asked Patsy, keen to know.

'Sophy Gibbs. She's at boardin'-school now.'

'Crikey, fancy her writin' to you,' said Patsy, ''as she got it bad?'

'Got what bad?' asked Jimmy.

'You,' said Patsy.

'I suppose she must have,' said Jimmy, 'she's always tryin' to half-kill me. No, she's just a bit barmy. And she's too posh, anyway, Patsy.'

But he decided he ought to send Sophy an answer, so he did.

Dear Sophy,

I got your letter, your mum told me you were going to a boarding-school, I think she thought that was better than letting you stay at home in case you set fire to the house. I couldn't go to a boarding-school myself as my dad's not rich enough, and I've got to start my career, anyway. I'm working at your dad's factory, I'm a sawdust apprentice. Do you know about oggle boxes?

I expect you'll get to like the school soon, just sit up and pay attention in class and don't get your frocks torn. It was nice meeting you and coming to your house to work, but I suppose I'd better say goodbye to you now. I don't know if you'll have a peaceful life, but I hope you enjoy it.

Yours sincerely, Jimmy.

On Sunday morning, Aunt Edie gave Dad a real talking-to. He went out into the yard after breakfast to clean the kitchen windows, taking an old step-ladder with him to get at the top of the glass panes. Aunt Edie said the step-ladder looked as if it needed to be chopped up into firewood. Dad said it had got a few years left.

'Well, just mind how you go with it,' said Aunt Edie.

Dad said, 'Funny you should say that, I remember—'

'Is this about your old sergeant-major?' asked Aunt Edie.

'Well, as a matter of fact, it does 'appen to be about him. We—'

'We've heard it,' said Aunt Edie, 'just get on with cleanin' the windows, and see that that wonky step-ladder doesn't chop you in 'alf.'

Of course, as soon as Dad reached the third step of the ladder, it collapsed and he fell off. Jimmy reckoned it wouldn't have happened if Aunt Edie hadn't said anything. The noise made everyone rush out into the yard, and there was Dad lying on his back. Aunt Edie visibly paled in shock.

'Oh, Lord above,' she breathed.

'Dad, you hurt?' gasped Patsy.

'You all right, Dad?' asked Jimmy, fearing the worst.

'What 'appened?' asked Dad.

'Oh, crikey,' breathed Betsy, 'can't yer get up, Dad?'

'Stone the crows,' said Dad, 'that perishin' step-ladder, why didn't someone tell me about it?'

'That's not funny, Jack Andrews,' said Aunt Edie. 'You'd better be able to get up or your life won't be worth livin'.'

Dad got up and brushed himself down. 'All over,' he said.

Aunt Edie was so relieved that her sparks began to fly. 'Call yourself clever, I suppose?' she said. 'I told you that step-ladder was only good for firewood, but no, you wouldn't listen, you didn't mind killin' yourself, I suppose, or givin' your girls the fright of their lives.'

Jimmy thought she was all sparks, and that her handsomeness didn't half look proud and fiery. Dad didn't seem to want to know, he wasn't even looking at her. He was gazing at the collapsed step-ladder.

'I don't know a feller can kill 'imself fallin' six inches off a ladder, Edie,' he said.

'Oh, you think that's funny as well, do you?' said Aunt Edie. 'Well, I don't. I should've thought you'd had enough of riskin' your life all those years at the war—'

''Ere, what's goin' on?' The voice came from the other side of the yard wall, from the open back door of the adjacent house. 'Crashin', banging an' wallopin', and now a carry-on.'

'Please, Mr Deakins,' called Betsy, 'Dad fell orf a ladder.'

'What, on a Sunday mornin'?' Mr Deakins couldn't be seen, the brick wall was six feet high, but he could be heard. 'That don't make sense, not on a Sunday mornin'. Is 'e all right, shall I come round?'

'He's all right, thanks,' said Jimmy, and Aunt Edie marched stiffly back into the house.

'No bones broke?' called Mr Deakins.

'Me pride's been injured, that's all, Bill,' said Dad.

'Makes a bloke feel sore, that does, when 'is pride's injured,' said Mr Deakins.

A little later, Patsy said to Jimmy, 'Lor', didn't Aunt Edie give Dad a talkin' to?'

'That's because he gave her the fright of her life as well as us,' said Jimmy, who was beginning to wonder exactly what Aunt Edie's real feelings were towards his dad.

'It turned out a bit of a laugh, really,' said Patsy, 'but not to Aunt Edie.'

'No, not to her,' said Jimmy.

CHAPTER TWENTY

Monday turned out to be the worst day of Dad's life.

When he got back to the depot from his morning round, his foreman asked him to go to the manager's office. The manager, Mr Edwards, was patently unhappy. With him in his office were two uniformed policemen, a sergeant and a constable.

'What's up?' asked Dad.

'It's not good, Jack, and I'm sorry,' said Mr Edwards.

'Are you Mr Andrews of Manor Place, sir?' asked the police sergeant, his expression very sober.

'Yes, I'm Jack Andrews.'

'Is your wife's name Maud, sir?'

'Hold on,' said Dad, 'are you goin' to tell me she's been arrested?' He could visualize that swinging umbrella of hers landing her in trouble with the law.

'I'm afraid it's a little more serious than that,' said the sergeant. 'We found her private address in her handbag, and a neighbour of yours informed us where you worked.'

'What d'you mean, you found 'er private address in 'er handbag?' asked Dad.

'I'm afraid, sir, there's been an accident.'

'To Maud?' Dad's stomach turned over. 'What kind of accident? Where is she?'

'Mr Andrews, I'm sorry, that's a fact I am,' said the sergeant, 'but I have to tell you it was a fatal accident.'

'Fatal?' Dad hardly recognized his own voice.

'I'm afraid your wife's dead, sir.'

'Oh, God 'elp us,' said Dad, and sat down heavily.

'It appears, sir, that she fell from a bedroom window of a house in Bloomsbury, where apparently she resided with some members of a religious sect. Well, as I understand, sir.' The sergeant went on to say that the police had been called to the house by a distracted man that morning. In the large yard at the back of the house was the body of a woman, her neck and back broken. She lay directly below the window of a bedroom she shared with another woman. It would be appreciated if Mr Andrews could accompany them to Bloomsbury and identify the body. Would he be kindly obliging and come now?

Dad was too numbed to do other than nod. All the way to Bloomsbury his mind was trying to accept the unacceptable. Maud dead? Maud, who had been sweet and pretty as a girl, and ardent in no uncertain terms while they were courting? Dead? It wasn't believable. Those had been their best days, their courting ones, with her cousin Edie often around to add to the laughter they enjoyed. It wasn't until after Patsy was born that Maud let religion begin to take its hold on her. And what had it led her to in the end? A kind of craziness, a craziness that looked as if it might have been responsible for her death. He remembered what he had said to the kids when they told him she'd gone off to Bloomsbury weeks ago. *That's mortal, that is.* He'd said it jokingly. He'd felt sick, but he'd had to make a joke of it, he hadn't wanted to upset little Betsy by getting worked up.

He wished now he hadn't said mortal. Had Maud fallen from her bedroom window or had she jumped? Numbly he put the question to the police sergeant.

'We'll talk to you when we get to the house, sir.'

The Temple of Christian Endeavour was a place of

shocked silence, the women in distressed retirement in their rooms, trying to come to terms with tragedy. One had departed in shock, saying she could never come back.

Father Peter, darkly grieving, and Father Luke, agitated, were present. So was a plainclothes detective-sergeant, whose name was Harris. The dead woman lay on a mattress in the Chapel of Penitence. She was covered by a sheet. Sergeant Harris drew it down to expose her face, and Dad looked down at his dead wife. Her eyes were closed, her skin waxy. She was very dead. Dad was tough, physically and mentally, however much his cheerfulness hid this. But moisture pricked his eyes. When all was said and done, Maud had been a good mother, and for four long years of war she had had to be both mother and father to their kids. What if she had lost her way a bit in the end? She didn't deserve to be lying here dead, not when she'd been in the prime of life at thirty-six. God help her. Rest in peace, love.

'Mr Andrews?' Sergeant Harris was gentle. 'This is your wife, sir?'

'Yes.' What else could he say, what else was there to say? And how was he going to tell Betsy and Patsy?

The sheet was drawn over the lifeless face again. A police surgeon came in with two men and a stretcher. Sergeant Harris touched Dad's arm and Dad went with him and the uniformed men to a reception room. Father Peter and Father Luke followed. In the reception room, Mother Joan was waiting. She was pacing about. She was not a woman who could sit still under these kind of circumstances. She pulled up and looked at the man whom Mother Mary had disclaimed.

Her breeziness absent, she said, 'You really are her husband?'

'This is Mr Andrews, yes,' said Sergeant Harris.

'God, I'm sorry,' said Mother Joan, 'what a terrible tragedy for you, Mr Andrews. Shall I explain, sergeant?'

'Are you all right, sir?' asked Sergeant Harris.

'Let her go ahead,' said Dad, his thoughts now on Betsy, Patsy, and Jimmy.

Mother Joan said that when she retired to her bedroom last night, the one she shared with Mother Mary, she found the window open.

'If you'll pardon me, madam,' said Sergeant Harris, 'you'll have to refer to people's legal names.'

'Yes, quite so, quite understood,' said Mother Joan, and went on to say she assumed Mrs Andrews had opened the window earlier to let in some fresh air. The night was dark, she did not look out of the window, it did not occur to her that there was any reason to do so. She closed it and drew the curtains. She had had a long day, and went straight to bed, expecting Mrs Andrews to appear any moment. Mrs Andrews had gone up some time before-hand, to see Father Peter, Mr Wilberforce. Father Peter nodded in silent assent at this point.

Mother Joan said Mrs Andrews had something on her mind, that she wanted to go up and see Mr Wilberforce and ask him to hear her confession.

The three policemen looked wooden-faced at this. Dad came out of his racked world to say, 'Confession?'

'Father Peter – Mr Wilberforce – takes confession,' said Mother Joan.

'That is so, Mr Andrews,' said Father Peter, his grief visibly haunting him. 'It's a responsibility I took on with many self-doubts but with a belief that the Lord would approve.'

Dad, whose own belief was that everyone in this place was a religious crank, gave the dark brooding eagle a straight look. 'What did my wife confess?' he asked.

'Sir, I would not normally break so holy a confidence—'

'I think you can repeat what you told us, Mr Wilberforce,' said Sergeant Harris. 'We've established you're not ordained.'

'I am, nevertheless, a true servant of the Lord,' intoned Father Peter. 'However, because of the circumstances, I will answer Mr Andrews. His wife came up to see me last night and begged me to hear her confession. I did so, I could not refuse her deep wish to unburden herself. She confessed that when Mr Andrews called here a little while ago, asking that she return home, she denied that she was his wife and that she even knew him. It lay heavily on her conscience. I told her I was sure the Lord would pardon her, particularly if she made amends and did as her husband wished by returning home. All members of the League residing here are free to come and go. Mrs Andrews was still very unhappy with herself, very distressed, and it distressed me, too, that she seemed unable to believe the Lord would forgive her. I spent some time trying to reassure her, but when she left to go to her room, she was still an unhappy woman. I am inconsolable at what happened subsequently, and tormented by a feeling that I failed her.'

'No, of course you didn't, Father,' said Mother Joan, 'it was her state of mind, poor woman. Dear God, to think she was lying out there all night. When I woke up this morning, it was obvious her bed hadn't been slept in, and as she didn't appear at breakfast, we all assumed she had gone home last night. Not because we knew of her confession, but because some of us do go home for a while from time to time. But after breakfast our cook, Mrs Murphy, went out to the yard, to the dustbins. She discovered your unfortunate wife, Mr Andrews, lying on the ground below our bedroom window.'

Dad was silent for a few moments. Then he looked at Sergeant Harris and said, 'Suicide?'

'It appears so, sir. There'll be an inquest.'

'If yer'll pardon me,' said Father Luke, a sincerely grieving man, 'might we offer – well, we do 'ave some in cases of shock – might we offer Mr Andrews a drop of brandy?'

'Yes, if that would help a little, Mr Andrews, you are most welcome,' said Father Peter.

'Kind of you,' said Dad, 'but no thanks.' He looked at Sergeant Harris again. 'The funeral?' he said.

'After the inquest, sir,' said Sergeant Harris, and grimaced. He liked the look of this man. The tragedy had hit him hard, that was obvious. Now he was going to be faced with the problem of finding a vicar willing to defy the canon and bury a suicide, if the inquest coroner returned such a verdict, which he undoubtedly would. 'We'll be in touch, Mr Andrews.'

'That's it, then,' said Dad brusquely.

'We all extend our deepest sorrow and sympathy,' said Father Peter, head bowed, 'and we are all greatly troubled by the tragedy, Mr Andrews.'

'Yes. Right. Goodbye.' Dad shook hands with Sergeant Harris and left. He walked with his mind in pieces.

Someone called. 'Mr Andrews?'

He turned. A woman came hurrying up. He looked at her, a lady of gentle countenance, eyes full of sorrow. 'Yes?' he said.

'You don't know me, Mr Andrews,' said Mother Verity, 'I'm Miss Celia Stokes, I reside in that house. I knew your poor wife well, and want to tell you how dreadfully sorry I am.' There was something else she wanted to tell him, but she was not sure she should, or even if it was right to. She only knew that it troubled her. 'She was a good woman, Mr Andrews, and a tireless worker.'

Dad wondered how good was good, and if this gentle-looking woman knew Maud had come to believe religion was more important than her children. 'But what makes a good woman jump from a window?' he asked.

'Who could know she would do that?' said Mother Verity. 'She was a little eccentric, perhaps, but she walked happily with the Lord.'

'Well, you look a nice woman yourself,' said Dad, 'so don't get as happy as she did, or you might end up doin' the same thing. Walkin' like that with the Lord seems a bit fatal.'

'That is true, Mr Andrews, as some of His disciples discovered. But will it help you to know that last evening your wife confided to me her belief that she had done you a grievous wrong?'

'Like sayin' I wasn't her 'usband?'

'Yes, Mr Andrews, like saying that. It really was troubling her.'

A little sigh escaped Dad. 'Well, I like you for tellin' me that,' he said. 'Glad I met you. But I'll get along now, if you don't mind.'

'Goodbye, Mr Andrews.'

'Goodbye, Miss Stokes.'

Mother Verity felt acutely sad for him.

Dad walked all the way back to the depot, trying to gather his thoughts and to decide just what he should tell the kids. At the depot, the manager told him to go home, and to take tomorrow off as well. He would lose no pay.

'I'll see to Patty an' Cake first,' said Dad.

'They've been seen to. Go home, Jack. There's your kids.'

Dad walked some more. Should he go to the school and collect Patsy and Betsy? No, let them spend what was left of the afternoon in blissful ignorance. He went home and made himself some hot strong tea. He thought about Edie. She had to know. He penned her a brief letter and took it to the Camberwell house in which she had a flat, where he handed it to her landlady and so escaped that which he couldn't handle at the moment, having to tell Edie in person.

Then he walked and walked, thinking of Maud and their life together, and of the time when he took a Blighty wound in Mesopotamia and how she had said it was the Lord who helped him to get better. And that reminded him of his subsequent leave at home, and how, when out walking with her, she used her umbrella to make people get out of his way. Who could say that in her own fashion she had not been a good wife, as well as a good mother, until religiousness claimed her? Because of her religiousness they had ended up with not much in common, but she had been his wife for seventeen years and given him three of the best kids a man could have.

He finally returned home at a time when he knew Jimmy would be there, as well as the girls. He began by telling them that their mum would not come home again.

'Never?' said Patsy, and Jimmy looked hard at his dad. There wasn't a sign of his usual cheerfulness.

'I'm afraid not, Patsy,' said Dad.

'Don't she want us any more?' asked Betsy.

'Betsy love,' said Dad, 'I don't reckon we could ever say that about your mum. She did what she 'ad to do, to go an' work for the Lord, but that never meant she didn't want you.'

Jimmy looked harder at his dad. 'Dad, why'd you say it like that?' he asked.

'Well, Jimmy, and you, Patsy, and you, Betsy, we've got to face up to the fact that the Lord's claimed your mum.' That was the kindest way Dad could think of to break the news. 'That's why she won't ever be home again. She's with the Lord.'

They could have made it much harder for him than they did. Betsy cried, of course, and he took her up and cuddled her. She clung sobbing to him. Patsy was very quiet for a few minutes, then went up to her room without saying a word. Jimmy took it stoically, but Dad knew his son was going to ask him questions.

Patsy came down after a while, her eyes red. She kissed her father. 'I won't make no fuss, Dad,' she said, swallowing, 'and it's all right, you still got us, and we've all still got each other.'

'Never mind supper,' said Jimmy, 'I'll make a pot of tea. Betsy can help, can't you, Betsy?'

'I don't want no tea,' whispered Betsy.

'Well, lovey, see how you feel when it's been made,' said Dad.

Betsy had a cup when the teapot was brought to the table. Then Patsy asked if Mum had died of an illness. Dad said yes, it was the kind of illness some people did die of.

Jimmy answered a knock on the front door. It was Aunt Edie, and Aunt Edie was looking stunned. 'Jimmy, is it true?' she asked in a strained voice.

'I don't think that's a very good question, Aunt Edie,' said Jimmy, 'and how did you know?'

'Your dad sent me a note. He told me not to come, but I 'ad to. Can I talk to him in the parlour for a bit? Jimmy, oh, I'm so sorry for all of you, I must speak to your dad.'

Dad had another private conversation with her in the parlour. He was sombre, she was distressed. He told all that he knew from his visit to Bloomsbury and how it pointed to the fact that Maud had committed suicide.

'Because of her conscience?' said Aunt Edie, pale of

face. 'Because she realized what she'd done to you and the fam'ly, and worse, that she realized she'd said to you, in front of everybody there at the time, that you weren't 'er husband, that she didn't even know you? Lord 'elp us, Jack, there'll be an inquest and that'll all come out and be in the papers.'

'I'm goin' to 'ave to let Betsy and Patsy stay away from school for a while,' said Dad.

'Yes, you've got to, or they'll be tormented by all the schoolkids, and kids can be cruel,' said Aunt Edie. 'I'll come and look after them, I'll take me summer 'olidays, which I 'aven't had yet.'

'Kind of you, Edie, but no,' said Dad.

Aunt Edie sat heavily down. 'You don't deserve a blow like this, Jack,' she said, 'you've got to let me come and look after the house and Betsy and Patsy.'

'It won't do, Edie love,' said Dad quietly, 'not a single woman like you. There'd be tongues waggin' all round us, there'd be people sayin' Maud committed suicide because of you and me. I think you can see that.'

'Yes, I can see. I could say I wouldn't care, but I would, because of you.' Aunt Edie drew a sighing breath. 'I've got a weight on me own conscience, and I don't like what it's doin' to me. Just recent, I've wished Maud dead. All these years she's 'ad you, and only ever been half a wife to you. I could 'ave married. I had a lover, Jack, and he wanted to marry me. Just before the war, it was. But I kept sayin' no, I kept tellin' myself there was always a chance Maud might get carried off by influenza, and that would let me in on your life. And this last month I've wished 'er dead. 'Ave I already said that?'

'Don't upset yourself, Edie,' said Dad. 'Most of us 'ave wished someone dead at times.'

'They say some women are saints, Jack. I'm not one of

them. All these weekends I've done me best to take you and your fam'ly over, to make you feel you don't need Maud, that you could 'ave me even if you couldn't marry me. Now I feel like one of them witch doctors that stick pins into dolls made up to look like someone they want to get rid of.'

Dad put his hand on her shoulder. She looked up at him. He dredged up a smile. 'That's a sad song, Edie love, but it don't apply,' he said. 'What 'appened to Maud is nothing to do with you, so don't sing it again. You've been the best thing that's 'appened to this fam'ly all these weekends. We both know, don't we, that if Maud walked in now we could look 'er in the face?'

'I don't know that I could,' said Aunt Edie.

'I'd stand with you on it,' said Dad. He was not a subtle man, but he did have an acquired maturity and he knew something about life and its pitfalls. He knew what made sense and what didn't. He knew his feelings for Edie weren't new, they'd been there for years, waiting to come to life. Maud was gone, Maud who'd been a faithful wife at least, and a good mother, all in all, but he couldn't honestly say he'd been able to stay in love with her. All the same, what would Jimmy and the girls think if they knew what his feelings were for their Aunt Edie when their mother wasn't yet cold?

'You're right, aren't you, Jack?' said Aunt Edie. 'It won't do for me to be here, will it? It wouldn't look good, it wouldn't even look decent.'

'I'll be in touch,' said Dad. 'D'you want to have a few words with Jimmy an' the girls before you go?'

'I couldn't go without seein' them,' said Aunt Edie, and went through to the kitchen, where she comforted Betsy and spoke to Patsy and Jimmy. She did her utmost to be consoling and to let them know they could come and see her whenever they liked. She stayed quite a while, and then left.

After she'd gone, Betsy said, 'Ain't she goin' to come an' stay a bit, Dad?'

'Not just now, Betsy.'

'But she could come round a bit, couldn't she?' Betsy was tearful.

'We'll see, love, we'll see,' said Dad.

'We'll manage, Dad,' said Patsy.

Jimmy sat thinking.

CHAPTER TWENTY-ONE

Alf Roberts, the box factory foreman, placed a sympathetic hand on Jimmy's shoulder. Jimmy had arrived at work on time and given the foreman the news of his mother's death.

'I'm sorry, young 'un, and I mean sorry. We can all put up with a lot, but losin' yer mum like that, well, I know 'ow yer feel. I lost mine before I was twenty and it was like losin' me right arm. Yer needn't 'ave come in, lad – 'old on, I'll 'ave a word with the guv'nor, 'e's in 'is office. 'Old on now.'

'I think I'm better workin', Mr Roberts,' said Jimmy.

'You 'old now,' said Alf, and went to see Mr Gibbs. Mr Gibbs called Jimmy into his office and regarded the boy with great sympathy.

'What can I say, Jimmy, what can anyone say? Would you like to tell me exactly what did happen?'

Jimmy recounted the details given to him by his dad. Mr Gibbs read it as suicide.

'She hadn't been very well lately,' said Jimmy. 'Well, not herself, sir, if you know what I mean.'

'Yes, I know, Jimmy.' Mr Gibbs reflected. There had been a report in the papers about a woman being found dead in Bloomsbury yesterday morning, with an implication that it was a case of suicide. Poor young devil. 'Is there anything I can do? Would it help if you went home?'

'Honest, Mr Gibbs, I'll be better if I'm workin'. Dad's home, lookin' after my sisters.'

'See your point, Jimmy. I think I'd feel the same. But if you want to go off early this afternoon, just let Alf know.'

'Thanks, Mr Gibbs, I've got to say you're a kind boss.'

'Oh, I'm tough as well, Jimmy. Take it easy now.'

Mother Verity was preparing to vacate the Temple of Endeavour and to resign from the League. Father Peter was endeavouring to dissuade her.

'Sister, I'm most distressed—'

'We're all distressed, Mr Wilberforce.'

Father Peter shook his head sadly at not being addressed by his religious name. And it surprised him, the little element of steel that had surfaced in this charming woman. He was not to know that a man called Will Fletcher so exemplified courage and fearlessness for her that he had inspired courage in herself. She had watched him deal with brawny Henry Mullins of Whitechapel, and had known him remove a ragged and hungry child from a drunken father. He was a man who had had nothing except bitterness and contempt for the world as he saw it, and in that bitterness and contempt he had assaulted her lips, not once but several times. Yet he'd been that child's affectionate protector. In her new-found courage, Mother Verity was determined not to let him go out of her life.

Father Peter said, 'I'm distressed by the tragedy, sister, yes, and I'm further distressed that you should be leaving us.'

'I'm sorry,' said Mother Verity, who had found she did not like the minister, 'but I did tell you days ago that I'd be moving to Bethnal Green, to carry on my work there with the help of the vicar.'

'True, true,' said Father Peter, 'but to have you resign from the League is a hard blow. I must endure it, however. I shall miss your presence, your valiance and your serenity. We all will. And at a moment like this, when tragedy has struck, unity is so important. It's a time for standing together and renewing our faith. Alas that one of us should already have abandoned the cause, that her strength of purpose failed her and us.'

'Do you mean poor Mrs Andrews?' asked Mother Verity.

'Mrs Andrews? Mother Mary? An accident, I am sure, an unfortunate fall from her window. No, I meant Mother Magda, who left so soon after we heard the dreadful news from Mrs Murphy.'

'She was in hysterical shock, Mr Wilberforce,' said Mother Verity, who had decided what to do about her troubled mind. 'She found it impossible to stay.'

'Yes, yes. Poor woman.' Father Peter's gaunt features were etched in lines of sorrow. 'I could wish for more time to talk to you, Mother Verity, to pray with you that you might have a change of heart, but I've an urgent mission to attend to and must go out at once. However, it's my earnest hope you'll visit us regularly and join us in prayer.'

'Perhaps,' said Mother Verity, 'but for the moment, goodbye, Mr Wilberforce.'

'God go with you,' said Father Peter, and lifted a hand in blessing.

As soon as she was out of the building, she no longer saw herself as Mother Verity. She went to Bethnal Green, carrying her suitcase, and there her landlady, Mrs Hitchins, was happy to welcome her on a permanent basis. She installed herself in her comfortable lodgings, then went shopping. On her way back, she called on the vicar to let him know she was now one of his parishioners and ready to help in all works of charity. If she had dissociated herself from the League of Repenters, she could not give up her work of helping the poor.

She was in her front room to see little Lulu come home from school, and later she noted the arrival of Will Fletcher. She waited. She must give him time to prepare a meal for himself and Lulu before she went across to him.

'Oh, my God,' said Mrs Gibbs when her husband, home from work, broke the news of the death of Jimmy's mother. 'It's shattering.'

'It has to be when one's mother jumps from a window and kills herself,' said Mr Gibbs with a grimace.

'My poor Jimmy,' said Mrs Gibbs.

'Is that how you feel?'

'I've a soft spot for that boy. What made her do it?'

'I've no idea,' said Mr Gibbs. 'There'll be an inquest, of course.'

'What was she doing up in Bloomsbury?'

'I had a few more words with Jimmy at midday. Apparently, his mother had joined some religious sect. She'd got religion on the brain, it seems.'

'And it made her jump out of a window?' said Mrs Gibbs.

'Who knows?'

'How was Jimmy taking the shock?'

'It's hit him badly, but he was bearing up. I wanted him to go home, but he said he'd be better doing some work.'

'I can believe that,' said Mrs Gibbs.

Miss Celia Stokes braced herself. She had thought about talking to Mother Joan, a forthright and no-nonsense woman, but had decided she would prefer to confide in Will Fletcher instead.

Will, having just finished supper with Lulu, a child full of new life, looked up at the sound of two knocks on the front door. One knock from a caller was for the ground floor residents, two knocks for the upstairs tenants. Lulu scurried down to see who it was. She scampered up again to tell her Uncle Will that it was the nice lady and that she wanted to speak to him.

'Lord, it's her?' said Will. 'She's down there on our doorstep?'

'Shall we give 'er a cup of tea, Uncle Will?'

He looked at the girl, clean of face and clothes. He had a feeling she was going to be his pride and joy. She seemed quite pleased that her nice lady had called. He groaned inwardly himself. That nice lady was unbalancing him. She was also burning his conscience every time he thought about what he had done to her.

'Better if we don't give her tea, Lulu,' he said, 'it'll be fatal lettin' her get even one leg past the front door. I'll go down.'

He went down. There she was, a picture, a ruddy picture, in a blue coat and hat instead of her usual grey garments. Was it even decent to appear at a man's door looking like that? Serve her right if I took hold of her and kissed her silly. Knocking me up when she's looking like that comes close to persecution. And those eyes of hers, they weren't afraid to look straight at Old Nick himself. 'Well, good evenin', Sister Charity,' he said, 'but what's the idea?'

'Idea?' said Celia, making a comparison between him and Mr Wilberforce and finding very much in his favour.

'Trackin' me down and knockin' me up? You'll be draggin' me off to church next.'

'Indeed I won't, Mr Fletcher, I wouldn't even try,' said Celia. 'That must come about through willingness, not

344

persuasion. I merely wished to speak to you, to ask for your help and advice.'

Astonished, Will said, 'Say that again.'

'I've no-one else to turn to. No-one, that is, in whose strength and sureness I have more confidence. I'm really very unsophisticated, Mr Fletcher, while you are a man who has seen much more of real life than I have. I have worries I'd like to talk to you about.'

'To me?' Will wondered if she was all there. 'Now look, lady, you've got to have friends of your own kind who'd be a sight more suitable than me.'

'I have more faith in you, Mr Fletcher. May I come in and talk to you? I've been waiting all day to see you.'

Will shook his head in helpless fashion.

'There's Lulu,' he said.

'No, not in front of the child, please,' said Celia.

'You've really got worries?' said Will.

'Yes, and they trouble me.'

'Well, look, my landlady will take Lulu off me hands for a bit,' he said, 'she's a good sort. Come up, but don't expect a palace.'

Celia expected no such thing. Will had three furnished rooms on the upper floor, one a living room. It was typical of its kind, comfortable and without frills. She noted its tidiness. He was an ex-soldier, of course, and soldiers were taught the value of keeping things in their rightful place.

Lulu smiled shyly at her.

'Hullo,' said Celia, offering a smile of her own.

'Please, 'ave yer come up for a cup of tea?' asked Lulu. 'Only Uncle Will said 'e wasn't goin' to let yer get even one leg past the front door, 'e said—'

'You monkey nut,' said Will, and picked her up. 'I'm

takin' you downstairs for Mrs Burns to look after you for a bit, just while I talk to Sister Charity.'

'Are yer goin' to kiss 'er again?' asked Lulu.

'Didn't I say forget that?'

'I only asked,' said Lulu, allowing herself to be carried downstairs and placed in the care of their obliging landlady for a while.

Will, returning, said, 'I'd feel better if you'd sit down.'

'Thank you, Mr Fletcher,' said Celia, and seated herself. She lost no time then in telling him of the terrible happening in Bloomsbury.

'Don't sound too good,' he said, 'but it was 'ardly your fault. Looks as if she jumped out of 'er window when she was off 'er rocker. Upsettin' for you, I can see that, but what else? I mean, what's botherin' you?'

'I'm not sure it was like that,' said Celia. She went on to say that she'd gone up to her room after dinner that evening and had met one of the other women, Mother Magda, coming out of her own room. Mother Magda said she'd just decided to see Father Peter, he frequently heard confession from her.

'Come again?' said Will.

Yes, he took confession, said Celia. It meant, she said, that when Mother Mary went up to see him herself, Mother Magda was already there, which also meant Mother Magda was the last person to see Mother Mary alive, apart from Father Peter. Celia hadn't mentioned this to the police, she was too stunned, but she'd remembered it just before she spoke to Mother Mary's husband after he left the Temple, and she'd also remembered that Mother Magda became hysterical when the terrible news broke. She packed her things immediately and was shaking like a leaf when she departed. Father Peter tried to calm her and detain her, but she became more hysterical and he had to let her go. Celia said she was in such shock herself that she wasn't herself all day. It made her uncertain about telling Mother Mary's husband that she had just begun to connect Mother Magda's fright and hysteria with the possibility that she knew what had taken place between Father Peter and Mother Mary. And perhaps what took place had had something to do with the latter's dreadful death.

'What's set you thinkin' like this?' asked Will.

'A distrust of Mr Wilberforce, who calls himself Father Peter, and a feeling that Mother Mary would never have committed suicide. She was too devoted to Christian teachings, and would have regarded suicide as a terrible sin.'

'Suicide's a relief to some people,' said Will. 'Point is, lady, what're we talkin' about exactly, that your friend didn't jump, that she was pushed?'

'Oh, Mr Fletcher, that's a terrible suggestion to make.'

'Come on, Sister Charity, that's what's on your mind, I'll wager it is.'

'But it's dreadful.'

'Dreadful? If it's true, it's ruddy murder,' said Will, 'and if it's murder, which of 'em did it, the lady who had 'ysterics or the crazy geezer who calls himself Father Peter? Or did they do it together?'

'Lord have mercy,' breathed Celia, 'how relieved and glad I am that I'm able to turn to you for help, Will.'

He looked startled at her use of his Christian name. 'Now look,' he said, 'you can find that woman easy enough, can't you? What did you call 'er? Mother Magda? I never heard anything barmier, Mother This and Mother That. But her address is in the files at that place in Bloomsbury, I suppose?'

'It should be,' said Celia, 'but it isn't. There's a little

office, used by Mr Wilberforce, in which records are kept. I looked before breakfast this morning. There's nothing in the files concerning Mother Magda.'

'She's gone, and so are her partic'lars, are they?' said Will. 'Fishy. And I don't like the sound of Mr Wilberforce, nor did I think much of 'is preachin'.'

'I know Mother Magda came to us from somewhere in Soho,' said Celia. 'I thought you might know how to find her. I'm afraid that before she joined us, she lived—' Celia was sensitively pink. 'I'm afraid she lived a sorry kind of life.'

'Never heard it called that before,' said Will. 'Still, I'm gettin' you, Sister Charity, you think I know the ladies of Soho, do you?'

'Pardon? Oh, no! No.' Celia's serenity, which had been wavering, deserted her completely. Utterly mortified, she breathed, 'Forgive me, I put that so badly—'

'No hard feelings, I can't afford those kind of ladies, anyway,' said Will drily.

'Please, don't speak of it,' begged Celia.

'What's Mother Magda's real name?'

'Kitty Drake.'

'Well, it so happens I do know one lady in Soho—'

'What lady?' demanded Celia, and was aghast at the way she put the question and her need to ask it.

'An old lady,' said Will. 'She keeps a shop in Dean Street. My old dad once had a stall in Soho market.'

'An old lady, yes, I see.' Celia calmed herself. 'Tell me how you are going to help me.'

'To find Kitty Drake? Here, wait a tick, hold on, whose problem is this? Not mine.'

'We must find Miss Drake,' said Celia with gentle insistence.

'What if he's found 'er first?' asked Will.

'Who?'

'Wilberforce. If he's the one, and if she's a fly in his ointment, she's in trouble. It sounds as if she bolted because she knew she was. If he finds 'er, she might end up gettin' pushed out of a window too, or dumped in the river.'

'Oh, heavens,' said Celia, 'he said this morning that he had some urgent business to attend to.'

'Well, you'll have to hope they've kept their mouths buttoned up in Soho, and that Kitty Drake didn't go back to her old address.'

'How fortunate I am to have your help, Will.'

'Now cut it out,' said Will, 'and stop lookin' at me, you know I can't say no to you. You make every other woman seem – oh, sod it.'

'That isn't like you, Will, to swear,' said Celia, gently reproving.

'Don't you believe it.'

'You're my first real man friend, you know.'

'No, I don't know,' said Will, 'and there's no future in that for me. As it is, you've got me over a barrel. I'm payin' a hard price for a few kisses, but all right, let's say Wilberforce 'ad a good reason for pushin' your friend out of her bedroom window, and that Kitty Drake knows what that reason is. Right, you take Lulu off me landlady's hands and look after her. I'll go to Soho.'

'I'd like to come with you.'

'Well, you're not goin' to, not to Soho. Ladies like you don't go to Soho of an evenin'. Stay here, Sister Charity.'

'My name is Celia.'

'I don't want to know.'

'I'm Miss Celia Stokes.'

'Will you leave off?' Will had never known himself in such a mess. There she was, looking at him, and turning him inside-out. 'Just stay here and look after Lulu, we'll 'ave to take her off my landlady's hands before I go out. I'll go down and get 'er, then I'm off to see old Mama Macaroni in Soho. That's what they call her. Listen, I might be late.'

'I'll put Lulu to bed for you, Will, and wait here for you,' said Celia.

'That's right, be an angel, it's one more way of hauntin' me,' said Will, and went down to his landlady.

For the first time since yesterday morning, Celia smiled. Nothing could bring back poor Mrs Andrews, but something could be done, perhaps, about the dark-souled Mr Wilberforce. And something could also be done, perhaps, through the kindness of Uncle Harold, to ensure Will Fletcher was given every opportunity to better himself.

'I just don't get it,' said Jimmy. The family was subdued, of course, and there were no jokes or giggles. Dad had just put a very forlorn Betsy to bed. 'Why did Mum do it?'

'You keep askin' that,' said Patsy.

'I'm askin' myself,' said Jimmy.

'Well, don't do it out loud,' said Patsy, dreading the thought of her mum's funeral, due to take place after the inquest.

'I'll have to go,' said Jimmy, trying to puzzle out why his mum had committed suicide. 'To the inquest, I mean.'

'If you want, Jimmy,' said Dad, wishing he had Aunt Edie to talk to.

'I couldn't let you go alone, Dad.'

'Jimmy, can't you give it a rest?' asked Patsy.

'Sorry, Patsy.'

Will was not away too long. That was because Mama Macaroni, an old friend to his late father, was able to direct him to a sleek Italian gentleman who, the moment he knew Will had been sent by the matriarch of Soho, came up with the whereabouts of Kitty Drake. However, if it meant that said Kitty Drake would receive damage to her valuable looks, certain lumps of concrete would fall on Mr Fletcher from a great height. Will said he was acting on behalf of a friend of Kitty, who would probably call on her tomorrow. The Italian gentleman said he had friends himself, and they all gave him a difficult time.

'Leave off, Antonio,' said Will. 'I've got responsibilities, I'm a father now and I can't afford to upset the likes of you. Just make sure Kitty Drake don't get damaged by someone else.'

The Italian gentleman, the patron, guardian and protector of the ladies of Soho, said he understood. And he offered Will a job. Will, knowing what kind of job it was, said he hoped there'd be no hard feelings if he declined. The Italian gentleman smiled and saw him out.

When he returned to Bethnal Green, his cross was waiting patiently for him. She climbed on to his shoulders at once by saying she had put Lulu to bed, that he was obviously a very kind father to the girl and that she was so pleased to see him back.

'Would you do me a favour and keep to strict business?' he said. 'Stop bein' pleased and stop lookin' at me as if I'm Father Christmas.'

'I cannot help feeling pleasure at knowing you to be my friend—'

'Shut up,' growled Will, 'I'm a workin'-man, I live in lodgings, and I go to the public baths once a week. I don't take up with ladies, I'm lookin' to take up with a warm-'earted cockney woman hereabouts, one who'll put up with me and the little I can offer 'er, and be a mother to Lulu.'

351

'I shall help you find a suitable woman,' said Celia, who had her own self-surprising ideas about who the woman should be.

'You'll what?'

'I have always thought you a worthy man, Will.'

'Stone me blind,' said Will, 'will you stop standin' me on my head?'

'May I ask if you've found Miss Drake?'

'I've got her address. You can call on 'er tomorrow.'

'By myself?' said Celia in dismay. 'To Soho? To such a dubious place?'

'In the afternoon,' said Will. Soho ladies, whose nights were busy, discouraged morning callers. 'Soho's all right in the afternoons.'

'I shall hate it by myself.'

'Well, hard luck, Sister Charity, I'll be workin'.'

'But if you took the afternoon off?'

'I'd lose an afternoon's pay,' said Will.

'I'll make it up to you,' said Celia.

'Cut it out.'

'Please, I could not manage by myself.'

'Oh, hell,' said Will, 'I'm ruddy licked again.'

When Celia departed, he did not see her cross the street to her own lodgings.

'Oh, not you again, Joe,' said Aunt Edie that evening.

'Can I come in an' put me feet up a bit?' asked Joe with an amiable grin.

'No, you can't.' Aunt Edie was unreceptive, eyes dark with unhappiness. 'I've got a thumpin' headache.'

'Well, that's rotten, Edie old love, but I was thinking—'

'Well, go and think elsewhere,' said Aunt Edie, and closed the door on him.

'This is a bleedin' fine evenin',' muttered Joe to himself

as he went away. He had no idea that a reported suicide in the papers was in any way connected with Edie. Nor did he have any idea that Edie was enduring the unhappiest time of her life.

CHAPTER TWENTY-TWO

Kitty Drake slipped on an imitation silk negligee to answer a knock on the door of her upstairs room in a house in Wardour Street, Soho. She gaped as she saw Mother Verity. With the lady Repenter was a tall man of strong masculine appeal, just the kind Kitty liked as a gentleman client, except she didn't think he was that.

'Oh, me gawd,' she breathed, 'is that a copper you brought with yer, Mother Verity?'

'No, a friend,' said Celia, 'and I'm no longer with the League. Could we talk to you?'

'I could do with that, a talk,' said Kitty. 'I could do with a long talk with someone like you. Come in.'

It was a ton weight on her mind, she said, when her visitors were settled. Yes, she had been with Father Peter that night. She had gone to his private rooms an hour after dinner to receive more instruction about how to overcome sin. He'd given her lots of instructions, except it always made her terrible passionate.

Celia went hot all over as Kitty explained in detail. A grin crept over Will's face. No embarrassment inhibited Kitty. Father Peter, she said, had assured her it was the only way to learn self-denial and sinlessness.

Celia simply could not look at Will, and Will let his face grow straight.

'Something dreadful happened,' said Kitty. It was after she had been on the bed with Father Peter. She was running around his rooms in her underwear, and he was chasing her in a dressing-gown, insisting it was necessary to give her a spanking. He had a strap in his hand. They didn't hear any knock on the door, and they didn't hear it being opened. But they saw Mother Mary enter. Oh, what a terrible shocking scene, said Kitty. Father Peter quickly closed the door and tried to do some explaining. But Mother Mary went for him, calling him a follower of Satan, a disgusting hypocrite and other names as well. Kitty herself ran into the bedroom to put her clothes on. She heard Father Peter trying to calm Mother Mary down. Mother Mary just went on giving him what for, not believing him when he said he had only followed the Lord's way. Kitty came out of the bedroom just when Mother Mary snatched the strap from his hand and struck him with it. Then she said she was going to her room to pray to the Lord, and then she was going down to tell everyone about his disgusting habits. She said she'd come up to confess she'd done her husband a dreadful wrong in saying she didn't know him, that it was heavy on her conscience, but that Father Peter wasn't fit to hear any confession, he ought to be put away and locked up. Then she went to her room and Father Peter followed her, trying to explain how he had suffered in giving such instruction to fallen women. But when he came back, about five minutes later, he said he couldn't do anything with Mother Mary, she was in a strange state of grief about what she had done to her husband.

Kitty didn't want to listen, she wanted to go to her own room and do some praying herself. Father Peter asked her to say nothing about anything, then let her go. She looked into Mother Mary's bedroom on the way, thinking to ask her what she was really going to do. But she wasn't there. The window was open, but she wasn't anywhere around, and Kitty supposed she'd gone down to tell everyone about her and Father Peter. She ran to her own room and hid herself under the sheets, praying as hard as she could. But when Mother Althea came up – Mother Althea shared the room with her – she didn't say a word about Mother Mary. That made Kitty think Mother Mary had kept silent, after all, and she thought the same thing again in the morning, because no-one mentioned it over breakfast. Except Mother Joan said Mother Mary's bed hadn't been slept in. Everyone thought she'd gone home for a bit, she'd done that once or twice before. Mind, Mother Joan said she hadn't taken her umbrella, and some of the ladies laughed at that.

But then Mrs Murphy appeared, screaming blue murder, and saying Mother Mary was out there in the yard, lying dead.

'It was like I was 'it with a thunderbolt,' breathed Kitty, 'it got me all mixed up and frightened, and all I could think of was I'd got to get out of the place.'

'Why?' asked Will.

'Why what?' Kitty lit a cigarette, the match shaking in her fingers. 'What d'yer mean, why?'

'Why did you think you'd got to get out?'

''Ere, look, you seem a nice gentleman,' said Kitty, 'but you got some sense, 'aven't yer? What 'appened to Mother Mary in that place could 'appen to me, couldn't it?'

'Why?' asked Will, making no suggestions in order to let Kitty volunteer everything that was on her mind. The whole thing was nothing to do with him, but he'd have been made of wood if he hadn't been interested right up to his eyebrows. 'Why could it 'ave happened to you?'

'Gawd love yer, mister,' said Kitty, 'you don't think that poor woman fell out of 'er window accidental, do you? Cool as a cucumber, that man was at breakfast, sayin' yes, it was obvious Mother Mary had gone 'ome to see 'er 'usband and make amends. 'Er conscience was a grievous burden to 'er, 'e said. And when Mrs Murphy come in screamin' about Mother Mary bein' out in the yard and lyin' dead, 'e lifted 'is 'ands like 'e was 'orror-struck, but the thunderbolt 'ad 'it me then, and it was me that was 'orror-struck. Well, I mean, 'e'd 'ad five minutes to chuck 'er out of the window, and I went in to see 'er only a minute after 'e'd come back. Mind, I ain't goin' to say so – oh, yer lookin' dreadful pale, Mother Verity.'

'I'm all right, Miss Drake, please continue,' said Celia with an effort.

'Yes, well, I ain't goin' to say nothing, not to no authority, I didn't actu'lly see it 'appen, did I? And I ain't goin' back to Bloomsbury, not with that man sayin' prayers with me and watchin' me. 'E knows I know that Mother Mary caught 'im chasin' me with a strap, and next thing everyone'll get to 'ear that I've fallen out a bedroom window meself. A friend found me this room, I didn't go back to me old address, me room there's been taken, anyway.'

'Didn't you 'ear anything?' asked Will.

'While 'e was with 'er in 'er room?' said Kitty. 'No, I didn't, 'er room was a bit away from 'is own rooms. But I know she was goin' to tell everyone about that old 'ypocrite, only she didn't manage to, did she? Strong as a bull, 'e is, I tell yer. Not like the gentlemen I know. 'E chucked Mother Mary out of 'er window all right.'

'He had to open it first,' said Will.

''Ere, whose side you on?' demanded Kitty, hair loosely wandering about her head and face.

'He might 'ave opened it before he took hold of 'er,' said Will, 'he might 'ave said she needed a bit of fresh air. If he didn't, then even a bull of a man would find it a real job to open a window with a struggling woman in his arms. I'm just makin' a point.'

'There's going to be an inquest, Miss Drake,' said Celia, 'you must tell what you know.'

'Not me,' said Kitty, ''e'll do for me if 'e knows I'm goin' to be there. I ain't partial to bein' turned into a corpse meself, not at my age. One thing, I don't want no more to do with religion. It's shockin' dangerous, religion is. Anyway, there's nothing that can do any good now for Mother Mary, poor woman. You just got to 'ope the cops get suspicious and start askin' questions, only they ain't goin' to ask 'em of me, they'll get me in a corner and gawd knows 'ow I'll come out of it then. No, I ain't goin' to be around for no inquest nor trial. I'm 'appy to say I've got friends in Soho that'll look after me.'

'But why did you tell us all this if you don't want to attend the inquest?' asked Celia.

'Because soon as I saw you at me door, I thought 'ere's just the one I can talk to and get it all off me chest, so's you can tell all them other ladies that Father Peter ain't a gentleman, but a dirty old man. It all come to me when I was runnin' for me life back to Soho, it come to me that Mother Mary was right, that man was an old 'ypocrite. It wasn't confessions 'e was after, it was dirty stories. I'll always remember you with pleasure. Me friend 'ere 'as found me a nice gentleman that lives in the country an' wants me to keep 'ouse for 'im. I'll be gone this time tomorrow. 'Ere, you're not goin' to put the cops on me to get me to the inquest, are yer?'

'But, Miss Drake, Mr Wilberforce should be brought to justice,' said Celia.

'Well, let the cops work it all out,' said Kitty, 'only I don't want them comin' after me. I'd be ever so obliged not to be mentioned, like. It's been a treat knowin' you, and I 'ope this nice gentleman friend of yours appreciates what a nice lady you are, and you've got nice looks too. I 'ope 'e does yer proud now you ain't with that League no more.'

Celia, casting a glance at Will and finding him with a helpless little grin on his face, said, 'Thank you, Miss Drake, but—'

'Come on,' said Will. 'Kitty's done her stuff.'

'Yes, would yer both mind goin' now?' said Kitty. 'I got things to do.'

'Goodbye, then,' said Celia.

'Good luck, don't fall down no drain'oles,' said Kitty, 'drain'oles is for old 'ypocrites.'

Will and Celia descended the stairs and emerged into the street. In a doorway opposite stood a burly man wrapped in a bulky overcoat and wearing a bowler hat. Will knew why he was there. The Italian gentleman had put a guard on the invaluable Kitty Drake, who had been sold at a price to a country gentleman.

Turning, they came face to face with Mr Montgomery Wilberforce. He loomed up, dark and sombre, and Celia lifted her eyes to his. His gaunt features tightened, his eyes glinted. But a smile followed.

'Why, Mother Verity, how splendid to see you.'

Celia steeled herself. 'What are you doing here, Mr Wilberforce?'

'I am on the Lord's work, sister. Here, the sinners are wretched indeed.' Mr Wilberforce sighed, but Celia wondered if he had been in Soho yesterday too, looking for Kitty Drake. 'Is your companion known to me? I feel I've seen him before.'

'We've seen each other,' said Will, 'in Christian Street.'

'Ah.' Montgomery Wilberforce let his dark eyes dwell

searchingly on the man who had molested Mother Verity. 'You have changed your ways, sir?'

'I'm fightin' bein' dragged off to church, but I've got a sinkin' feelin' I'm goin' to lose that one as well,' said Will, studying the man whose towering majesty cloaked a pervert. He was looking for Kitty Drake, of course. There was no-one who would lead him to her. And if he did manage to spot her and follow her, he'd meet with a nasty accident.

'That comment, sir, is beyond my understanding,' said Mr Wilberforce.

'Well, I've been havin' an upside-down inside-out time myself lately,' said Will, and Celia felt what a fine man he was, well able to out-face a creature like Mr Wilberforce.

'Ah, colloquialisms,' said the man of iniquity. 'They are a delight to some, a mystery to others. Mother Verity, am I to hope you'll return to us?'

'My work will be elsewhere,' said Celia, keeping her true feelings to herself. 'Goodbye, Mr Wilberforce, we don't wish to detain you. If I am called to the inquest, I will see you there.'

Mr Wilberforce raised his top hat to her and went sighing on his way, his black cloak fluttering.

'He's lookin' for young Kitty,' said Will.

'Yes, of course.'

'He won't find her. But if he does he'll wish he hadn't. Would you like a cup of tea?'

'Thank you, Will, I'm dying for one.'

'This way, then.'

They ended up in an Italian café with a narrow frontage but lengthy accommodation. The tea came hot and steaming from an urn, but into china cups. It was surprisingly good. They sat at a table that put them apart from other customers.

'What are we going to do?' asked Celia.

'We?'

'I'm so glad to have your strength and experience,' she said.

'Will you stop tryin' to tell me I'm Solomon? Look, Miss Stokes—'

'Please, you mustn't address me so formally, not now our friendship is established.' Celia wondered where all her boldness was coming from.

'You'll drive me to drink before I'm much older,' said Will, unable to work out why a woman he had brutalized insisted he be her friend. 'Listen, there's nothing you can do about Wilberforce. You can speak up at the inquest, if you like, and if I know you, you probably will. What a woman. But you won't be able to quote Kitty Drake. That'll be what's called 'earsay, and they won't allow it. And even if she did turn up 'erself and spoke up, she couldn't make much of a case for the police to prosecute. It would be chucked out at any trial. There's no proof, there's only suspicion, don't you see, Celia?'

'Thank you for calling me Celia.'

'Oh, ruddy hell,' said Will, 'it won't 'appen again, I can't afford for it to, I'll get stuck with something I couldn't keep up with. But are you listening? What I'm tellin' you is that if there's no proof, there's no case. D'you know the dead woman's old man?'

'Old man?'

'Oh, pardon me, I'm sure,' said Will, showing another helpless grin. 'Husband in your upper-class language.'

'I'm not upper class,' said Celia. 'But yes, I met Mr Andrews, the husband.'

'What's 'e like?' asked Will.

'A kind man, a concerned man because his wife left him and their children, and a very sad man because of her death. I liked him very much. How terribly silly we all were to follow such a dreadful fake as Mr Wilberforce.'

'Let it be a lesson to you,' said Will, and climbed to his feet to get two refills from the urn. He brought the cups back. Celia thanked him, she was in need of a second cup. 'A woman like you, a lady, goin' barmy about religion. If you'd been my wife—' He shut his mouth.

'Yes?' said Celia gently.

'I'm goin' barmy myself, talkin' like that.' Will frowned at the surface of his steaming tea. 'Just keep listening. D'you want to make things worse for Andrews? You will do if at the inquest you manage to get everyone thinkin' it was murder, not suicide. If he gets to think it, too, and then finds out the law can't bring a case, how d'you think he'll feel for the rest of 'is life? Leave it, Sister Charity, let 'im settle in his mind for suicide. It strikes me there's one thing the inquest will prove, and that's that his wife was off her ruddy rocker. It might prove that all you ladies were. Look, Andrews could settle for suicide. And there's 'is kids. What's it goin' to do to them if they have to start thinkin' their mother was murdered? If there was proof, no-one would be able to 'elp 'em, poor young devils. I wouldn't, as a kid, want to know my mother was murdered. I'd 'ave a year of nightmares. Let it rest.'

'Let that man get away with it?'

'You're not listening. It's not just that there's no proof, it's the fact that there's a chance she did chuck herself out. Nor would it surprise me, after hearin' from Kitty what went on in that loony bin.'

'I can't believe Mrs Andrews committed suicide, Will.'

'Right,' said Will, and finished his second cup of tea. 'You 'ave it your way. I'm goin' home.'

'No, wait, please,' begged Celia. 'Very well, I agree. I have been listening, really I have. For the sake of Mr

Andrews's peace of mind, and for the sake of his children, I won't go to the police. But I shall tell everyone at the Bloomsbury house how Mr Wilberforce behaved with Kitty Drake. That I must do.'

'I'm not arguin' with that,' said Will. 'Then what?'

'Then I shall settle down in Bethnal Green.'

'You'll what?'

'The vicar has already invited me to help run the Bethnal Green Home for Waifs and Strays.'

'Bethnal Green?' Will's face was a study.

'I have my own lodgings there, opposite yours,' said Celia.

'What?'

'I made up my mind to move from Bloomsbury some time ago. You were right, there was something odd about the League—'

'I didn't say that, I just said some of you were a bit barmy.'

'Perhaps we were in our belief in Mr Wilberforce,' said Celia. 'I decided there was work for me in Bethnal Green, so I took up lodgings there.'

''Oly Moses, I knew it,' said Will. 'I knew you were goin' to haunt me for the rest of me life.'

'No, I'm simply going to interest myself in the welfare of the poor people, and in you and Lulu. I promised myself weeks ago that I'd help you redeem yourself.'

'Do what?' Mentally, Will was all over the place.

'I knew there was a good and worthy man under that show of brutality,' said Celia.

'Jesus Christ,' breathed Will.

'Amen,' said Celia.

'I'm done for, I'm licked all ends up, I'm goin' home to fly a white flag out of my window.'

'Shall we go together?' said Celia, who knew she had

months of patient work to do on a man whose infamous kisses had shocked her and left her breathless and giddy with arousal. He had turned a mouse into a woman.

Outside the café, her hand touched his. Will, a man disbelieving, laughed at himself and a world that was upside-down. He took her hand and they walked up the street together. Celia put behind her the dark shadow of Mr Montgomery Wilberforce.

CHAPTER TWENTY-THREE

The inquest was over. Mr Montgomery Wilberforce had paid admirable tribute to the sterling qualities of Mrs Maud Andrews as a servant of the Lord, and offered a sad description of the unhappy state of her mind on the evening of her death. Because she had denied knowing her husband, she could not be comforted. Asked some pertinent questions by the coroner, he answered them in measured, unfaltering tones and maintained a dignified mien throughout.

Mother Joan and four other lady Repenters were called. They all testified to the fact that Mrs Andrews had been very unhappy that day about disclaiming her husband, that it troubled her conscience so much that she went up to Mr Wilberforce in the evening to confess to him. The coroner asked more pertinent questions, but the ladies could see nothing wrong in Mr Wilberforce hearing confession. They did, however, insist it was difficult for them to believe Mrs Andrews would commit the sin of suicide.

Dad had been called and had spoken of the deceased as a good wife and loving mother who had let religion take too much of a hold on her.

It took the jury a long time to come up with the verdict. They must have been impressed by the testimony of Mother Joan and her sisters, for they returned a verdict of death by misadventure. That, to everyone's relief, particularly the relief of the family, absolved the deceased of the sin of suicide.

Mother Verity – Celia – was not present. She had not been asked to attend, any more than the other ladies had, and she preferred to wait outside the court. Had she attended, she knew she might have asked to give some testimony of her own. Mother Joan, when she emerged, gave her the verdict, and Celia smiled wryly.

'I'm pleased for Mr Andrews,' she said, 'but would like to tell you something about Mr Wilberforce.' And she told Mother Joan that Mother Magda, Kitty Drake, had left the League because Mr Wilberforce was a pervert. She explained, in as modest a way as she could, that the self-appointed minister had had carnal relations with Kitty many times, and in the most hypocritical fashion, in that he had persuaded Kitty to believe it would lead her to redemption.

'Poppycock,' said Mother Joan.

'Pardon?' said Celia. They were standing aside from other people.

'Rubbish,' said Mother Joan.

'No, Miss Drake told me herself.'

'I can believe it,' said Mother Joan. 'All wishful thinking and lurid imagination, my dear. A young woman like that, born to be a creature of the flesh, and given to describing how nice her gentlemen friends were. Nice my foot, I daresay every one of 'em was a randy old goat. Poor dear, she tried her best when she joined us, but of course Father Peter to her was a fine figure of a man far more than a minister of God. Off her head about him, lusted after him. Result, feverish imagination. It happens, you know. Woman fancies a man. Can't have him. So she gets other fancies. Well, fantasies, really.'

'I assure you,' said Celia, 'I believe Miss Drake.'

'Well, you're a believing woman, Celia, a good woman,' said Mother Joan reassuringly. 'You'd give the benefit of the doubt to Judas Iscariot himself, as well as Pontius Pilate. But it's poppycock. Father Peter remains our inspiration and our guide. Damned weak link, Kitty Drake proved, running off like that when he was in great need of unanimous support. Gone back to her randy old goats, I don't doubt.'

'Ah, my dear ladies.' Father Peter himself loomed up. 'How relieved we all are, and how good the Lord has been in inspiring a verdict of misadventure.'

'Goodbye, Mother Joan, goodbye, all,' said Celia, and walked away, leaving the dark-souled Mr Wilberforce to his flock of deluded followers. She had tried, but even Mother Joan was as deluded as the rest. She knew what Will would say when she told him. Well, she had some idea of the kind of words he would use. Let them lie on the bed Old Nick's made for them, they'll chop his ruddy head off when they finally find him out.

Celia smiled to herself. She did not really mind the kind of words he used. Will was a rough diamond, but ten times the man Mr Wilberforce was. Will had no dark secrets, he was as open as a book. She hurried, wanting to get to Bethnal Green in time to meet Lulu from school and to share a pot of tea with her, and give her a slice of cake. Will would come in later, find her there with Lulu and tell her to stop haunting his lodgings.

But he was weakening, and she knew it.

The funeral was over. Mother had been buried in the consecrated ground of Southwark Cemetery.

Dad and his children were picking up the pieces.

Aunt Edie, who had attended the funeral, was waiting. She was not sure what she was waiting for, which meant she was not sure what would turn up. She could do nothing herself. Everything was up to Jack. In desperation, in her need to do something to take her mind off what was close to heartbreak, she participated in a pearly concert. She sang duets with Joe Gosling, she sang solo, she sang with the audience, and she finished by doing a knees-up. Her legs looked corking.

Jimmy received a letter from Sophy. She asked why he hadn't answered her second letter. Didn't he realize what an agonizing time she was having at her boarding-school? She poured threats on his head. The other girls were drips, she said, they were all soppy about boys. There was a boys' boarding-school not far away, and lots of secret meetings went on. So did kissing. Ugh, all that soppy kissing, wrote Sophy, and ordered him to write to her.

Jimmy replied briefly. As her father had obviously not told her about Mother, he said nothing himself. But he did say she was a bit of a soppy kisser herself.

Meanwhile he was giving a lot of thought to Dad, and to Aunt Edie. He and Patsy went to see her one evening. She was so overwhelmed to have them call she actually spilled some tears as she hugged them both. She asked how everyone was.

'Oh, we're bearin' up, Auntie,' said Patsy, 'and the neighbours 'ave been ever so kind.'

'Oh, that's good,' said Aunt Edie. 'Is young Betsy all right?'

'Dad's makin' a fuss of Betsy, Auntie, she likes lots of fuss.'

'And how's your dad?' asked Aunt Edie.

'I think we're goin' to have to do something about Dad,' said Jimmy.

'What d'you mean? 'E's not ill, is he?'

'No, he's fine,' said Jimmy.

'What d'you mean, then, you're goin' to 'ave to do something about 'im?' Aunt Edie seemed agitated.

'Well, we don't exactly know, do we, Patsy?' said Jimmy.

'No, we don't know exactly, Auntie,' said Patsy.

'Well, what's wrong with 'im?' asked Aunt Edie.

'I think it's bein' a widower,' said Jimmy. 'D'you think it's bein' a widower, Patsy?'

'Yes, I think it's bein' a widower, Jimmy,' said Patsy.

'Of course, we can't be sure,' said Jimmy.

'No, we can't be sure, Auntie,' said Patsy, 'we're too young to be sure.'

'I wish I knew what you two were talkin' about,' said Aunt Edie.

'We don't really know ourselves,' said Jimmy.

'It's just feelings,' said Patsy. 'Aunt Edie, when you goin' to come an' see us? Can't you come on Sunday?'

'Well, it's an upset time for the fam'ly,' said Aunt Edie, 'it's best I wait till you've all got over it. I can't come and play the piano and 'ave some laughs with you at the moment. People would think none of us 'ad decent respect. I'd best wait a bit.'

That didn't sound very convincing to Patsy and Jimmy, but they let it go for the moment and spent an hour with their aunt. She made an effort, she became cheerful, and she helped the hour along by telling them she'd performed at another pearly concert. Jimmy asked what numbers she'd sang, and she said oh, the usual old favourites like 'Daisy, Daisy', the kind that kids and their mums and dads were fond of. Jimmy thought her smile a bit forced. She wasn't herself. Of course, she was naturally unhappy about Mum, her cousin, but he felt it was more than that. Making another effort, she suddenly laughed and said she'd finished her turn by doing a knees-up on the stage, with someone playing 'Mother Brown' on the piano.

'Auntie, what a lark,' said Patsy.

Just as suddenly, Aunt Edie made a face. 'I forgot meself,' she said. 'I shouldn't 'ave done it, not a knees-up, it was disrespectful, only a week or so after the funeral. I don't know what got into me. I'd be appreciative if you two wouldn't tell your dad.'

'Well, it wouldn't be very clever to tell 'im,' said Jimmy gravely. 'He wouldn't be too pleased that he'd missed you doin' a knees-up, Aunt Edie, 'specially as he needed a bit of cheerin' up.'

'I think Dad likes ladies' legs,' said Patsy.

'All old soldiers do,' said Jimmy. 'Well, I've heard they do. I think I like them myself.'

'You're not an old soldier,' said Patsy.

'That's the funny thing about it,' said Jimmy. 'I mean, I'm not an old soldier, but I'm pretty sure I like ladies' legs.'

Aunt Edie looked from one to the other of them. They were over their mum's death. It had been some weeks now, and autumn had turned to winter, and there they were, their dad's son and elder daughter, not looking mournful. And they'd come to see her. Her heart warmed to them.

'Loveys, I don't know if we should talk like this,' she said.

'It's all right, Aunt Edie,' said Patsy, 'we've got kind mem'ries of Mum. Dad says we're not to 'ave anything but kind mem'ries of 'er.'

'Yes, she did 'er bit durin' the war, didn't she, lookin' after you all the time your Dad was away,' said Aunt Edie. 'We've all got to remember that.'

'Aunt Edie,' said Jimmy, 'I don't see why you can't

come and spend a Sunday with us. You're our aunt.'

'Yes, we nearly forgot to mention that Dad said the fam'ly would like to see you.' Patsy smiled at her aunt.

'Your dad said that?'

'We wouldn't ask you to play the piano,' said Jimmy.

'Oh, I'll come Sunday week,' said Aunt Edie.

'Oh, good old Auntie,' said Patsy.

When they were on their way back home, Jimmy said, 'Well, you can see how it is, Patsy.'

'I always knew it,' said Patsy.

'Knew what?' asked Jimmy.

'That Dad was favourite with Aunt Edie.'

'That's it, then,' said Jimmy, 'we'll have to move. I'm earnin' regular wages now, so we could afford a bit more rent if we moved to somewhere like Kennington.'

'Like Lorrimore Square, it's nice there,' said Patsy.

'All right, we'll go and do some lookin',' said Jimmy. 'Say Saturday afternoon. We'll see if there's any notices up for houses to rent around there.'

'Who's goin' to speak to Dad?' asked Patsy.

'Well, you bein' a girl, and Dad havin' a soft spot for girls, 'specially you and Betsy, you ought to speak to 'im,' said Jimmy. 'But I'd best do it, as I usually know what I'm talkin' about, and besides I can operate man to man with Dad.'

'Big'ead,' said Patsy.

Jimmy got to the stage where it was his turn to have a private word with Dad.

'You're doin' fine, Dad,' he said, 'and so is Patsy.'

'You're doin' your bit too, me lad.'

'Still, we don't want to go on like this for ever,' said Jimmy. 'Not when it's not necessary.'

'I see,' said Dad. 'No, wait a tick, I don't see.'

'Well, it's not been a very good time for you,' said Jimmy, 'I'm not surprised you can't see straight.'

'About what?' asked Dad, eyeing his son warily.

'About your future.'

'Listen, Jimmy my son, I'm comin' up to forty. I'm livin' me future, I started livin' it when I came of age.'

'Now you're not thinkin' straight,' said Jimmy. 'You've had that future, Dad, it's a back number. I'm talkin' about your new future. You don't want to miss it, and you might do if you don't get started on it.'

'Oh, is that a fact?' said Dad.

'Well, yes, man to man, it is,' said Jimmy. 'When are you goin' round to see Aunt Edie?'

'What?' said Dad.

'Why don't you pop round this evenin'?' suggested Jimmy. 'You two 'ave got to make arrangements to get fixed up some time.'

'Say that again,' said Dad.

'We're not daft, y'know, Patsy and me. Of course, you can't marry Aunt Edie right away, it wouldn't be decent. You'd have to wait a bit, and of course you couldn't settle down here with her, you'd have to move, otherwise the two of you would get all kinds of looks. Your luck must be changin', Dad, because there's a house comin' up to rent in Lorrimore Square in Kennington. Patsy and me 'appened to see the firm that's the landlord of several houses there, and you've got to let them know by the end of the week or you might lose your chance of gettin' the house. It'll be empty the fourth week in November. It's three bob a week more than 'ere, but we can manage that, and Aunt Edie'll go for Lorrimore Square. You could go round and see her now. You've had supper, you've only got to put your hat an' coat on. Tell her Betsy can't wait for her to be her new mum.'

'Well, knock me over,' said Dad. He knew what was happening, he knew he was being told that his son and daughters, far from minding about him and Aunt Edie, were all for it. They'd noticed, they'd noticed how he felt about their aunt during those weekends she'd been here. 'You're comin' it a bit, Jimmy lad, givin' me these kind of orders and doin' certain things behind me back and all. You've grown up more than a bit since you met Mr Gibbs and went to Anerley to work for 'im.'

'Yes, I've got to remind you I'm nearly seventeen,' said Jimmy, 'and I'm doin' some thinkin' on my own account. I fancy 'aving a girl to take out, and I've got one in mind, except I might 'ave to struggle with complications. But never mind that, are you goin' to make a start on this new future of yours?'

'Chip off me old sergeant-major, you are, Jimmy, I'll 'ave to watch you,' said Dad. 'All right, pass me me hat an' coat, no point in waitin' till Aunt Edie comes on Sunday.'

'What?' said Aunt Edie, proud bosom actually fluttering a bit.

'Yes, what d'you think, Edie love?' asked Dad, having said it all, including a move to Lorrimore Square and a possible date in the New Year. 'Am I pushin' you a bit, or takin' you for granted?'

'You want to marry me?' said Aunt Edie. 'You really want that?'

'You're my kind of woman, love,' said Dad, 'you always were.'

Aunt Edie went moist-eyed. 'Then give us a kiss, love, would you?' she said.

Dad gave her the kind of kiss that convinced her once and for all that he wanted her. Weak at the knees, she tumbled backwards on to her sofa. Dad went after her.

His old sergeant-major knew a thing or two about women, even if he had come a cropper with a certain Syrian belly-dancer.

'Women, I'll 'ave you know, come in various kinds, includin' women that's obedient, women that's a handful on account of bein' contrary, and women that's a different kind of handful on account of bein' comely. Any soldier that 'as trouble with obedient women is gormless and should go home to 'is mother. As for women that's contrary – stand up straight, that man there. As for women that's contrary and given to arguin', what you do with them is let 'em give your earholes a rollickin'. Don't answer them back, let 'em get it all off their chests until they're out of breath. Then give 'em a bunch of flowers and knock 'em sideways. Now, women that's a handful on account of bein' comely. Just treat the handfuls with due appreciation and lovin' care. Corporal Andrews will confirm same. Got that, my lads? Right, that's all.'

Aunt Edie being extremely comely, Dad treated her with extravagant appreciation and very loving care. Aunt Edie wondered where all the bliss was coming from.

'Jack, oh, you saucy devil – me dress – me legs—'

'Well, look at that,' said Dad, mourning at an end and a new future beginning. 'I knew it. Edie love, you've got a pair fit for the pearly queen of old London itself.'

Aunt Edie laughed.

Christmas morning was crisp with frost and winter sunshine. Two knocks on the door of number fifteen Underwood Road, Bethnal Green, brought the upstairs tenant down.

Will Fletcher was on the doorstep.

'Good morning, Will,' smiled Celia, 'and a very happy Christmas.'

Will blinked. She was wearing a new costume of silver-grey over a Christmassy red jumper, and her hair shone as if her brush had spent the morning burnishing it. He coughed.

'Yes, merry Christmas, Sister Charity,' he said, and coughed again. 'It's like this.'

'Yes, Will?' said Celia gently, thinking what a handsome man he was.

'What?' said Will, thinking how elegant and out of reach she was.

'What is it you want to say?'

'It's Lulu,' said Will, feeling mesmerized. 'The fact is, as it's Christmas Day, and as she don't know if she's comin' or goin' because of the present of a new frock and doll's house you left for 'er last night, she wants to know if you'd take 'er to church with you.'

'I'd love to, Will, you know that.'

'Further,' said Will, and coughed again. 'Further, Sister Charity—'

'Celia.'

'Oh, hell.'

'I'll forgive that,' said Celia.

'Well, further,' said Will, 'Lulu says would you come and 'ave Christmas dinner with us?'

'Lulu says?' murmured Celia.

'Yes. Our landlady's cookin' our joint as well as her fam'ly's, she's got both ovens goin'.'

'And Lulu would like me to join you?'

Will cleared his throat yet again. He couldn't think why life had to be so contrary. After a long period of unemployment and near starvation, it had suddenly handed him a decent-paid job. Then it had upped and clouted him. People talked about the mysterious ways of God. It wasn't God, it was the aggravating contrariness of

375

life that had landed him with a woman he could never have. Look at her, she could sit for a painter and come out looking like a portrait of a king's lady, and some rich geezer would pay as much as a hundred guineas for it. Was it fair on a man? Or was it punishment for abusing her? Punishment, he thought.

'What?' he said again.

'Really, Will, whatever's the matter with you?' smiled Celia.

'You've got a nerve, askin' a question like that while you're lookin' like that,' said Will. 'I've got more problems than even Bill Sykes should be landed with on a Christmas Day.'

'My poor Will,' said Celia, 'but we were speaking of Lulu inviting me to share dinner with you.'

'All right, I give in,' said Will. 'I'm invitin' you as well.'

'Then I shall come,' said Celia. Actually, she had been invited to have Christmas dinner with Mr and Mrs Hitchins, but had delayed accepting, just in case. There was no telling with a man like Will, no telling whether or not he would leave her outside his life on Christmas Day, however much he was weakening. 'Thank you, Will, for thinking of me. Shall we all go to church together?'

'Oh, no you don't,' said Will, 'you're not landin' that one on me.'

'Very well, just Lulu and I, then. In an hour. And thank you again for thinking of me.'

'Lulu didn't like it that you might be by yourself,' said Will.

'Lulu didn't?'

'Lord forgive you for pushin' me into corners,' said Will. 'Well, all right, we both didn't want you sittin' in your lodgings all alone, not on Christmas Day. Everyone ought to 'ave someone else on Christmas Day.'

'Will, how kind you are.'

'Cut it out,' said Will, grinding his teeth.

'But I shall be very happy to be with you and Lulu,' said Celia, 'and to have her come to church with me.'

'She'll like that,' said Will, 'but don't think you'll get me in a pew.'

'No, of course not, Will.'

An hour later, amid the ringing of the bells, Lulu, Celia and Will were all walking to church together.

She's done for me, thought Will.

He's collapsing, thought Celia.

'Isn't it a lovely Christmas Day, Will dearest?' she smiled, and slipped a gloved hand into his. 'Isn't it simply lovely, Lulu?'

'I likes Christmas,' said Lulu, 'an' we likes you, don't we, Uncle Will?'

'I'm licked all ends up permanent, Lulu lovey,' said Will, and his hand closed tightly around Celia's. Her fingers squeezed.

Lord help me, thought Will, what comes next?

Aunt Edie, laden with presents, arrived very early at the family's new home in Lorrimore Square, Kennington, to be greeted with hugs and kisses from everyone except Jimmy. Jimmy wasn't there.

'Where is he?'

''E's gone out, Auntie,' said Betsy.

''E said 'e's gone on a mission,' said Patsy.

'He'll be back,' said Dad. 'After 'is mission's over.'

'What mission?' asked Aunt Edie.

'To Anerley,' said Patsy.

'Oh, that girl Sophy, that's 'is mission?' smiled Aunt Edie.

'Well, 'e's nearly seventeen, Auntie,' said Patsy, 'and

says he wants a girl to take out, one that 'e likes.'

'That boy.' Aunt Edie laughed. 'Well, Christmas morning's just the right time for a mission, loveys.'

'Yes, 'e's took some mistletoe,' said Betsy.

Jimmy was riding a borrowed bike, and whistling as he pedalled through the handsome roads of Dulwich. He had had one more letter from Sophy, back in early November. He'd answered it. He had spoken to Mr Gibbs at the factory two days ago, about his future. Mr Gibbs, as usual, had responded kindly.

It was not yet ten o'clock when he rang the doorbell of the Gibbs's handsome house in Anerley. Ada, whose duty it was to answer the summons of callers, opened the door and found herself looking at a young man whose solemn expression couldn't be trusted because of his saucy eyes.

'Hullo, Ada, merry Christmas.'

'Jimmy!' Ada's perky little white cap seemed to quiver. 'Jimmy, fancy it bein' you – oh, merry Christmas yourself. What're you doin' here?'

'I'm doin' Christmas collectin' for the deservin',' said Jimmy.

'Deservin' what?' asked Ada.

'Me,' said Jimmy, 'I've got some mistletoe in my pocket.'

'Oh, you've come to collect from the young madam?' said Ada. 'She's 'ome for Christmas, but she's goin' out in a minute, so you'll have to—' She was interrupted by the swift advance of a girl through the hall, a girl in a dark blue winter coat with a fur collar, and a little fur hat on her head. Sophy Gibbs, now fourteen, was so ravishingly dressed up she looked sixteen.

'Ada, I'm – oh, hullo, Jimmy, you're a surprise, Daddy was talking about you at breakfast, and Mummy's pleased about things.'

'That's good,' said Jimmy, 'merry Christmas, Sophy.'

'You too,' said Sophy. 'I can't stop, though, I'm going to see a friend. You can do my room now, Ada. Goodbye, Jimmy.' She sped over the forecourt to the drive.

'Sorry, Jimmy,' said Ada.

'Sorry?'

''Ard luck, I mean. The young madam's got a new friend. His family live on the other side of Anerley, he goes to a boys' boarding-school that's near hers.' Ada wrinkled her nose. 'Are you heart-broke again, Jimmy?'

'Not much,' said Jimmy, who had always felt he was a game to Sophy.

'Never mind, Jimmy, it's Christmas,' said Ada. 'D'you want to come in and see cook and Ivy and Mr 'Odges? We're ever so busy, but madam won't mind you.'

'Well, Mr Gibbs said I could pop in. I asked if I could, just for ten minutes. But first—' Jimmy stepped in, taking his cap off. Ada closed the door to keep the cold out. 'First – well, look here, Ada, if it's not serious with Percy, and seein' I feel serious myself, can I take you out on your next day off?'

Ada's little cap seemed to quiver again. 'Me?' she said.

'You're the nicest girl I know.'

'Me?'

'I knew I'd got complications,' said Jimmy, 'but I thought blow Percy, why should he 'ave all the luck?'

'I 'aven't been out with Percy for ages,' said Ada, 'there's someone I like much better.'

Jimmy looked sternly at her. The spacious hall was empty, but the house was alive with the vibrations of Christmas Day.

'I've lost me Christmas spirit now,' said Jimmy. 'Who is the bloke? Ask 'im if he wants his block knocked off.'

'You'd better ask yourself, then, 'adn't you?' said Ada, eyes dancing.

'Ada?'

'Oh, come on, Jimmy, you silly.'

'Ada, would you be my girl, then?'

'Oh, crikey, you and me, Jimmy? Honest?'

'You and me, Ada, honest.'

'Lovely,' said Ada, and Jimmy produced a little sprig of mistletoe. Ada lifted her face. Jimmy kissed her. Ada did a shy, blushing act, just in case Jimmy thought she was too eager. Her mum had said ages ago that it wasn't wise for a girl to let a boy think she wants to be kissed. Best to make him think you're doing him a special favour. Then you can ask a favour of him, like when you want a new hat. Mind, that's only when you're married, of course.

'I'm comin' back here to work,' said Jimmy, thinking Ada lovely to kiss. 'I spoke to Mr Gibbs about it, I told him factory work's all right, but that I like outdoor work best. He said fine. So in the New Year, I'm startin' here as a junior gardener.'

'Oh, it's goin' to be the best Christmas of me whole life,' said Ada. 'Jimmy, let's go and tell cook and Mr 'Odges and Ivy I'm your girl before I tidy up the young madam's room.'

'All right, Ada,' said Jimmy. 'I think I'm goin' to have new problems, not bein' able to say no to you. Still, I'll grin and bear it.'

'I bet,' said Ada. 'Come on.'

On their way through the hall, Jimmy said, 'Do you and cook and Ivy and Mr Hodges know what an oggle box is?'

'Yes, course we do, Jimmy love. Oggle, oggle, oggle.'

THE END

RISING SUMMER
by Mary Jane Staples

Tim Parkes was three when his parents were killed in a train crash and he went to live with his Aunt May, first in New Cross, and then to Walworth where the living was cheaper. They managed splendidly – and then came the war. Tim Parkes became Gunner Parkes and Aunt May spent most of her nights in the Walworth air raid shelters with Tim keeping an eye on her whenever he was able.

When he got posted to Suffolk he wasn't too pleased – Suffolk was Country, not like London at all. But in fact there were a lot of things about Sheldham that reminded him of home – the Walworth evacuees for a start. Those of them that weren't creating havoc in the Suffolk village were creating havoc in Tim's life. Minnie Beavers – ex-Camberwell – was fifteen, pert, pretty, and wildly in love with Tim. She was determined to inveigle him into marriage the minute she was old enough. Tim was equally determined to escape and choose his own girl.

By the time Tim had gone away to fight the war, and Minnie had joined the WAAF, a great many things had changed in both their lives.

0 552 13845 2

THE LODGER
by Mary Jane Staples

Maggie Wilson was only thirty-three, but life in the teeming streets of Walworth was not that easy in 1908 – not if you were a widow with four young daughters. It was pretty much a hand-to-mouth existence and without the lodger Maggie really wouldn't have managed at all.

Constable Harry Bradshaw thought the Wilsons were a gutsy and brave little family – from the youngest and cheekiest, Daisy, up to the elegant Trary, thirteen-years-old and quite the young lady. But the one who won most of his admiration was Maggie herself, fighting her lonely battle against total poverty.

And his fears for her concerned more than just their lack of money. For a murderer was loose in South London – a rather sinister strangler who obviously knew the local streets and alleys very well indeed. A full scale investigation was put in hand, and Harry was told, in particular, to inquire into any new lodgers who had moved into the district. And there was something very peculiar indeed about Maggie Wilson's lodger.

0 552 13730 8

OUR EMILY
by Mary Jane Staples

Emily had been a quite horrible child. Pushy, rough, and none too clean (for it must have been Emily who passed on her head-lice to the Adams family), she had been the bane of Mrs Adams and her children who lived next door, and especially she had been a trial to Boots, who had avoided her whenever he could.

But Emily grown-up was a different matter. She was still a cockney girl, but now she had a certain elegance, a style. The fighting toughness was still there – and she needed it. For Boots, back from the trenches, was blind, and Emily was to prove the mainstay, the breadwinner, and the love of his life.

Here again is the Adams family from DOWN LAMBETH WAY – Chinese Lady determined more than ever to be respectable, Tommy facing unemployment, and Sammy well on the way to becoming a street market tycoon. And above all here is our Emily.

0 552 13444 9

A SELECTION OF FINE TITLES
AVAILABLE FROM CORGI BOOKS

THE PRICES SHOWN BELOW WERE CORRECT AT THE TIME OF GOING TO PRESS.
HOWEVER TRANSWORLD PUBLISHERS RESERVE THE RIGHT TO SHOW NEW
RETAIL PRICES ON COVERS WHICH MAY DIFFER FROM THOSE PREVIOUSLY
ADVERTISED IN THE TEXT OR ELSEWHERE.

☐	13718 9	LIVERPOOL LOU	*Lyn Andrews*	£3.99
☐	13600 X	THE SISTERS O'DONNELL	*Lyn Andrews*	£3.99
☐	13482 1	THE WHITE EMPRESS	*Lyn Andrews*	£3.99
☐	13260 6	AN EQUAL CHANCE	*Brenda Clarke*	£3.99
☐	13556 9	SISTERS AND LOVERS	*Brenda Clarke*	£3.99
☐	12887 2	SHAKE DOWN THE STARS	*Frances Donnelly*	£3.99
☐	12387 0	COPPER KINGDOM	*Iris Gower*	£3.99
☐	12637 3	PROUD MARY	*Iris Gower*	£3.99
☐	12638 1	SPINNERS WHARF	*Iris Gower*	£3.99
☐	13138 5	MORGAN'S WOMAN	*Iris Gower*	£3.99
☐	13315 9	FIDDLER'S FERRY	*Iris Gower*	£3.99
☐	13316 7	BLACK GOLD	*Iris Gower*	£3.99
☐	13631 X	THE LOVES OF CATRIN	*Iris Gower*	£3.99
☐	13521 6	THE MOSES CHILD	*Audrey Reimann*	£3.99
☐	13670 0	PRAISE FOR THE MORNING	*Audrey Reimann*	£3.99
☐	12607 1	DOCTOR ROSE	*Elvi Rhodes*	£3.50
☐	13185 7	THE GOLDEN GIRLS	*Elvi Rhodes*	£3.99
☐	13481 3	THE HOUSE OF BONNEAU	*Elvi Rhodes*	£3.99
☐	13309 4	MADELEINE	*Elvi Rhodes*	£3.99
☐	12367 6	OPAL	*Elvi Rhodes*	£2.99
☐	12803 1	RUTH APPLEBY	*Elvi Rhodes*	£4.99
☐	13413 9	THE QUIET WAR OF REBECCA SHELDON	*Kathleen Rowntree*	£3.99
☐	13557 7	BRIEF SHINING	*Kathleen Rowntree*	£3.99
☐	12375 7	A SCATTERING OF DAISIES	*Susan Sallis*	£3.99
☐	12579 2	THE DAFFODILS OF NEWENT	*Susan Sallis*	£3.99
☐	12880 5	BLUEBELL WINDOWS	*Susan Sallis*	£3.99
☐	13136 9	RICHMOND HERITAGE/FOUR WEEKS IN VENICE	*Susan Sallis*	£3.99
☐	13136 9	ROSEMARY FOR REMEMBRANCE	*Susan Sallis*	£3.99
☐	13346 9	SUMMER VISITORS	*Susan Sallis*	£3.99
☐	13545 3	BY SUN AND CANDLELIGHT	*Susan Sallis*	£3.99
☐	13299 3	DOWN LAMBETH WAY	*Mary Jane Staples*	£3.99
☐	13573 9	KING OF CAMBERWELL	*Mary Jane Staples*	£3.99
☐	13444 9	OUR EMILY	*Mary Jane Staples*	£3.99
☐	13845 2	RISING SUMMER	*Mary Jane Staples*	£3.99
☐	13635 2	TWO FOR THREE FARTHINGS	*Mary Jane Staples*	£3.99
☐	13730 8	THE LODGER	*Mary Jane Staples*	£3.99